RADIOMAN

RADIOMAN

THE MARTENSEN CHRONICLES
- BOOK II

1883 - 1950

JOHN GERTS

John Streg Publishing

Acknowledgments

Cover art: John Gerts
Contributing Editor: Steve Gerts, Margretta Dumas
Research: Steve Gerts, John Gerts
Archive Collection, Copy Editing: Marda Gerts, Steve Gerts,
Thanks to Terry Gerts, my life mentor.

Thanks to my wife, Margretta, who is my inspiration, love, and life.

Printed in the United States of America
First Printing, 2021
ISBN 978-1-7326034-7-9
John Streg Publishing
Ludington, Michigan 49431

CONTENTS

1

HOMESTEADER

Ants, like most insects, are relatively robust. They can lift three times their body weight and dangle while holding one hundred times their weight.

1883

Shifting from one job to the next, the drifter became known by his name, **Charles Martensen.** No ranches or farms in Cumberland county would hire Charles. Seumas McMaster somehow saw to that, his reach wide and influential. Charles found work after the estate at a sawmill north of Portland. He worked for six months, swinging an axe and floating logs. Then a load of trees came into the mill from the McMaster estate directed by Joseph Conklin, who saw to his dismissal. Charles drifted from lumber camp to lumber camp. Sometimes he lasted four months. At the Kendrake Sawmill, he lasted eight months before McMaster heard he lumbered there.

Charles did not mind the drift. The high pay in the camps allowed him to save money. The axe turned his arms, wrists, and hands to stone. Mindful of the imminent dangers of logging work, not where he pictured himself in the long run.

After five years, Charles had exhausted the opportunities in most of the logging camps in the territory. He found a job as a laborer on a farm just over the border in Massachusetts. The widow Sellars appreciated the quiet man with the strong back who never took his shirt off. The farm was so remote Charles had no fear of

McMaster's reach. He learned more farming techniques from the widow and her two sons in their late teens. The widow had a great crop year and then a rotten, too rainy, too cold second year, and she had to let Charles go.

In 1883, upon turning twenty-four, he had saved enough money for a stake and fare to head west on the train. Since the age of eleven, Charles had reveled in the stories about the transcontinental railroad's completion and the striking of the golden spike. He planned to stop in Chicago, a thousand miles west, for advice from Uncle George, by then a prominent businessman in Chicago. His goal: Nebraska farmland or perhaps California.

Reaching Indiana on the last leg of his train trip, kidneys jostled and bladder full, Charles turned in his seat, looking for directions to the toilet. He became distracted by the eyes and hat of a woman just tall enough to peer over the headrest at Charles. Charles moved over in his seat toward the window. Able now to discreetly glance around, he caught more than a glimpse of the petite woman watching towns rush by out the window.

Charles noted a pleasant profile, a nose just a little long but balanced by a delicate chin and forehead. Her clothes were prim, and her hat was not outrageously ribboned. As if sensing his stare, the woman turned in his direction, garnering further approval. The woman sat straight-backed on the wooden train bench. The rolling and bumping of the train bothered the woman not a whit, further impressing Charles.

After disembarking at Great Central Station, Charles emerged at the new cable car pavilion on Michigan Avenue. He searched for the carriage and driver supplied by his Uncle's company and prearranged by telegraph from South Bend. By chance, he saw the woman from the train, dress blowing in the chilled Chicago wind, rain dripping from the small, clutched parasol. Charles walked up to the woman, set down his satchel, and dug out his dress wool shirt, snapping it in the wind and draping it over the shoulders of the woman.

The woman, startled and purple-lipped, turned to Charles, smelling the shirt on her shoulder. The smell was not unlike the scent of a hug from her father coming in from fieldwork back on the farm. She did not hesitate, slipping her right arm into the shirt sleeve. She did the same with the left arm, Charles helping to overcome the puffed sleeves of her blouse. She fastened the faded brown shirt button at her midriff, paying no heed to the frayed hole in the shirt at her right elbow. Charles, eyes focused on the buttoning, shivered and raised his eyes to her face. Julia, one eyebrow raised, smiled.

"Thanks."

"My name is Charles Martensen."

"Mine is Julia Swart. You were on the train, weren't you?"

Charles's heart fluttered; she had noticed him.

"Yes. Are you waiting for the cable car?"

"Yes, I'm heading to my Cousin's house in Oak Park."

Charles knew little about Chicago, but his Uncle resided in Oak Park. A carriage pulled up, and the driver held up a sign. Intently peering down at the woman at his side, Charles did not notice the sign.

Julia did notice, however, and waved to the driver, placing a hand on Charles' shoulder.

"This is Charles Martensen, driver; he is new to the city."

Charles looked up.

"Yes, sir, we are headed for Oak Park; we'll give the lady a ride and get her out of this wind."

Charles gently took her elbow and helped Julia into the carriage. She handed a card to Charles. The card contained the names and addresses of her aunt and cousin. Charles, in turn, handed the card up to the driver.

The driver, Winslow, chatted with both riders as he snicked the reins occasionally to turn the carriage. Upon arriving at her aunt's home, Charles helped Julia and said goodbye. He watched her turn and walk toward the house, skirts still billowing, her bustle swaying to the measure of her walk. She stopped after twenty feet and turned back to Charles.

"Let me return your shirt."

Charles held up the address card, waving it so she would see his intention.

"I will return for it on a warmer day."

Julia smiled and turned back toward the house. Winslow waited until she had entered before turning his horse and trotting off.

Julia smiled and turned back toward the house. Winslow waited until she had entered before turning his horse and trotting off.

As the carriage approached the home of George Edward Martensen, Charles pulled at his mustache. The home and carriage house seemed grand. George had left Portland, Maine, before the birth of Charles. His father, however, had extolled his uncle's Chicago prominence when Charles began expressing his desire to head west. Charles helped Winslow back the carriage into the carriage house, broke hay from a bale, and led the horse to its stall. Winslow led Charles into the house and showed him to the guest room upstairs, indicating dinner would be ready soon. Charles washed up, buttoned his collar, and used the brush on the dresser to remove trip dust from his pants and shoes before venturing downstairs. He examined the marking on the brush and found the Martensen, Lumbard & Co. Stamp on the handle.

In the parlor, Charles met Mary, 21, Kate, 18, and Walter, 12, as well as Mrs. Martensen and his Uncle George. Over dinner, Charles updated the group with the family members' activities, whereabouts, and dispositions back east in Portland and Boston. Charles learned of Walter's schooling and sports endeavors, Mary's and Kate's embroidering circle, and the layout of the rooms in the house. After dinner, the family and Charles repaired to the parlor to become further acquainted.

In the morning, Walter knocked on the guest room door, waking Charles from a deep sleep and a vague dream of a purple-lipped girl. They ate breakfast together. Uncle George finished his coffee, and he and Charles met Winslow in the carriage house for the ten-minute trip to the plant on the corner of N. Hoyne Avenue and W. Grand Avenue, a brand-new three-story building. The building itself impressed Charles. George left Charles to examine the company's showroom samples of over fifty different brush styles while he went to his office to check his calendar. Charles picked up and tried out brushes for house painting, grooming horses and humans, brooms, and custom designs.

George returned with a cleared calendar and led Charles to the factory floor. George pointed out the lathes, drill presses, and metal brakes spaced neatly in a machine checkerboard layout across the eighty-foot square concrete space. A maze of belts and gears overhead reached up to the fifteen-foot-high ceiling, all interconnected to drive shafts on the west wall. The noise deafened, but the men working the machines seemed at ease and expert at their tasks, waving or nodding at Uncle George as he stopped at a few stations. Two dozen men and women in white aprons sat at tables, hand-inserting bristles into varnished wooden brushes. The tables comprised a large section of the floor. Proud of his modern plant, Uncle George explained that if rewarded, hard-working men were contented, making for a profitable company. George also noted that Charles didn't shy away from the noise and the action, was interested in each step of the process, and asked questions that indicated a familiarity with manufacturing.

Next, George and Charles toured the offices. George explained the paper flow through the various departments, from engineering to order processing. Accounting offices were one floor up, both receivables and payables. He met Mr. Lumbard, Uncle George's secretary, and two inside salesmen on the next floor. Other New York, Boston, St. Louis, New Orleans, and Houston offices housed outside sales and warehouse facilities.

In Uncle George's office, Charles sat in a comfortable armchair facing a five-foot-long oak desk while George sat in the swivel chair behind the desk. George produced a well-used notebook from a drawer, thumbing to a dog-eared page showing a chart of sales versus time and a red marking pencil line showing a steady increase, especially in the last ten years.

"Charles, I'll give it to you straight. There is an opportunity here. My brother tells me in a letter, somewhere on this desk, that you are a worker who has never been in trouble at the bar or on the street, and like my brothers, grandfather, and great-grandfather, you have the guts to strike out on your own."

"Uncle George, my hard work has garnered me a stake I intend to put into land out west. I see what you have done here, what Uncle Lemuel has done with the clothing store in Boston, and what my father has accomplished. Where I'm different, maybe, is my liking for the outdoors, the space to stretch my arms out wide. I guess that's my dream."

"Where is that dream taking you, Charles?" asked Uncle George.

"Maybe as far as that Overland Route Railroad can take me," replied Charles.

"California, eh?"

"Maybe. I need to stretch and see."

"Charles, that sounds fine and much like my tune years ago. Chicago was barren as a baby's bottom when I got here. The 'west' began here. I saw potential. I don't mind telling you that potential is still only 10 to 20% realized. Chicago has places to go, and men of adventure like yourself are working to keep that momentum going."

"I saw it too, Uncle George; from the train station to Oak Park, everything is building up; busy."

"Charles, it's been only ten years since O'Leary's fire roared through this town. You can't see half of what we've done. Brick streets that won't burn. This factory; is brick. Zoning laws for house spacing. Why this city is just starting to roll. We've rebuilt as my good brother did after the Portland fire in 1866, only better and bigger."

"I understand that. But with the railroad, wouldn't anywhere west of the Mississippi have that potential?"

"Alright, Charles, I see you have your mindset. Here's my problem. I'm 55 years old. Walter is 12. He'll be set if he takes to the business, but that's a few years off. Maybe he'll be like you and look to take off for Alaska. Who knows? It is a family trait to make our own way, usually a new way. But I have an opportunity for you right here, starting in our shipping department."

"I don't know, Uncle George, I have been working five years on this stake and-"

"Charles, hold it, I won't pry, but you won't believe how fast that stake will evaporate when you begin building that dream. I don't say forget your plan. Hold off. Commit to giving me five years, and build your stake even higher. Your father has always been a good brother to me. I'll ensure you won't regret postponing your next move a little longer."

Charles sat, thinking, weighing all he had heard against temporarily abandoning his dreams and building his nest egg. At twenty-four years old, it came down to one consideration. A consideration crept into the back of his mind. It formed during the factory tour and while meeting all the workers and discussing with the president of one of the ten original Chicago manufacturing companies. The one that mattered was the purple lips and midriff buttoning of a girl from the train.

1893

The two boys stood for inspection before their mother on the third step of the stairs. Lemuel, eight, stood a couple of inches taller and two years older than his brother holding the baluster. Both boys are dressed in knee pants over dark stockings. Their vests and jackets sport gold braids and buttons. Lemuel pulled his cap on tight, but the other boy held his hat in his hand as he scratched behind his ear. The boy thought the suit was awfully itchy but wanted no trouble, attempting to stand still. Two towheads.

Julia picked up the Chicago Daily News from the end table and thumbed to page three, and the National Weather Bureau report for the day. The day should be fair with a good breeze; no rain is predicted. Charles had determined that today, Tuesday, would be the least busy day at the Exposition. The line for the Ferris Wheel would be the shortest if they arrived at the fair before nine o'clock, just as it opened to the public.

Charles clambered down the stairs from the bedroom, tugging his tie straight, brushing by the boys.

"Let's go. Let's go."

Julia pulled and straightened the jackets of both boys, glancing at Charles as he rushed out the front door.

"We're ready."

Julia grabbed her parasol from the peg in the hall. The family shuffled down the front steps of the porch, hustling the few blocks to the corner of Milwaukee and Fullerton. They stood at the cable car stop, waiting. Charles checked his suit jacket pocket for nickels.

Two minutes later, the streetcar stopped before them, and they boarded. Charles slotted four of his nickels. The horse-drawn streetcar stopped every three blocks to pick up more commuters on the four-mile Milwaukee street route. After forty-five minutes, the family transferred to the Milwaukee St. cable car, always incredible to Charles for lack of horse.

Another transfer, and they headed due east toward the lake. The final transfer in the heart of Chicago put them on the train that would take them south of downtown to the terminal at the World Columbian Exposition.

Charles looked away from the crush of people building up at the transfer points. With over a million people in Cook County and beyond, Chicago could not be more incongruous with the wide-open spaces of the horse ranch he dreamed of in his younger past. In Chicago, one had to glimpse a view of the sun between the ten and twelve-story skyscrapers dotting the loop.

Charles had nodded when he had read in the Daily News last year that the city council had set a limit of one-hundred-fifty feet for any building in the city limits. Chicago kept growing up and up and up. The stench of horse shit permeated the downtown. People crowded into every available corner, and more were pouring in. Cheap soft, readily available coal sooted the city, clothes, and lungs. The slaughterhouses, the manufacturing plants, including the brush factory where Charles worked, and the retail shops and businesses in the loop continued to do well. Now a twenty-year distant memory, the great fire had hardly dented Chicago's destiny as the rail mecca of the Midwest.

Charles and Julia benefitted from the growth of Chicago as well. Charles headed the shipping department, fourth on the organizational chart under his uncle, the company's president. Four years ago, Charles had saved enough to buy their home on Fullerton Street with fifty percent down. He only had four more years of loan repayment to his uncle to be free and clear. Charles had earned his position in the company. Uncle George recognized his hard work and efficiency innovations in the shipping department. Compared to felling trees in the dead of a Maine winter, shuffling papers and meeting shipping deadlines seemed inconsequential; yet the raises and responsibilities kept coming.

Charles often reflected on his history and next steps in the quiet squeak of his front porch rocking chair. His dream had not withered. Charles' house equity grew with the city's expansion, and he would soon have the capital to build his Western vision. The prairies seemed safer now, more appropriate for a young family.

Much of the American 'west' had been grabbed and settled, to Charles's dismay. Land prices kept rising. This month, Kansas farmland topped thirty-six dollars per acre. The longer Charles waited and saved his dream, also further away. In the meantime, Charles would tell Lemuel and the boy sitting around him on the porch steps stories of the west. He planned to do the same with the rest of the children he and Julia would produce.

Charles viewed Chicago as a stepping stone. He had found and courted Julia, the petite aristocratic farm girl from Indiana. He had temporarily committed to his uncle's vision of the brush company goals, and the shipping department allowed him to bide his time while preparing for his dreams. George's son Walter grew progressed in the company along with Charles. Soon Walter would surpass Charles in stature within the company. Charles did not envy Walter. Brushes were not his dream.

The boy jumped up from his seat as the train slowed.

"There it is, Daddy. There's the big wheel you told us about!"

Charles nodded. Lemuel stood up, squeezing next to the boy to see the Ferris wheel in the distance out the window to the west. The Midway stretched beyond the giant wheel. Rides and attractions lined the esplanade. The grass looked deep, dark green, manicured, and edged in multi-colored pansies. The fountains began squirting water as workers rolled out canvas awnings and positioned and spruced their displays.

Julia stared, fascinated by the white buildings in view out the train windows to the east, just as excited as the boys. Uncle George's brush company exhibited in the Manufacturers and Liberal Arts Building. Charles worked at the exhibit every third week, talking to potential customers and distributors. The exposition opened markets for Martensen, Lombard & Co. Inc. in Alabama, Missouri, Utah, and Japan. Charles knew every inch of the fair, and Julia couldn't wait to see the Women's Building exhibits.

Imagine! An entire building devoted to women. Designed by a woman architect, the building contained arts and crafts traditionally oriented to women. Julia had read of a conference hosted at the Woman's Building attended by two hundred thousand. Julia smiled at the surroundings, pacing forward straight-backed, considering the clawed and scratched progress women accomplished in Chicago.

Julia had not told Charles yet about her pregnancy. Next month if all goes well. Charles would be pleased. Julia shared most of Charles's dreams. She knew full well the work involved on a farm or ranch. She had handled her chores on the farm of her youth proudly. Julia knew how important children were to the operation of the family farm. Many hands.

Yes, like Charles, she missed the wide-open spaces a farm provided. The sense of connectedness to the soil, animals, and plantings. The smells of wagons full of corn, the bales of hay. The wheat, waving and hypnotizing.

Like Chicago, the World's Columbian Exposition provided opportunities that a farm could not. No fool Julia, she would learn in this White City.

Chicago provided modern schools, including high schools for her boys. Charles had time to take the boys to baseball games. His day no longer involved eleven or twelve hours of grind as when he worked with horses, but rather eight to nine hours with the occasional deadline. Charles rarely worked Saturdays.

The stores in Chicago lacked for nothing, essential or luxury. The city pulsated, alive with industrial progress, noisy, exciting, and closing in and building up.

The boys tugged Charles along toward the Ferris Wheel. The boys had no trouble finding the way since the Chicago wheel could be seen from anywhere on the six-hundred-acre site and the two-hundred buildings of the exposition. Charles looked back at Julia, stunning in her finery, twirling her parasol. She looked radiant today.

"Alright, you two, straighten up. Wait for your mother. This place will be crowded in another hour, so stick close. Understand? Lemuel? Boy, are you listening?"

"Ok, Daddy."

"Yes!"

The line waiting for a ride on the wheel looked over a thousand people. No matter. Lemuel counted thirty-six passenger cars attached around the circumference, and Charles told the boys each car held forty chairs. Julia white-knuckled her parasol.

"Are you sure this is safe, Charles? Maybe I should stay down with the boy while you take Lemuel."

"I'm going too, Mommy. I'm not scared at all. Daddy?"

"Sure, son, we're all going. Julia, you can't miss this. Chance of a lifetime."

The family advanced to the front of the line. Six platforms for loading six cars at once accommodated the crowds efficiently. It was a good thing because all but Charles became more nervous as they waited for the next empty car to drop in front of them. In fact, entire families decided against chancing the giant wheel once they looked straight up two-hundred-fifty feet to the car at the top of the wheel. That wheel towered one-hundred feet above the skyscrapers visible in the distant downtown Chicago loop.

Charles and Julia found two adjacent chairs, and the boy sat on Charles's lap. Lemuel stood at one of the windows in front of the chairs. Windows lined the front and back of the forty-foot-long passenger car. They started up with a jerk. The windows had screens in front for safety, but Lemuel kept backing up and ended up on Julia's lap, looking down as the car rose. The boy slid down off Charles's lap and stepped to the window. Determined, he looked first out at the buildings in the distance and then down gradually at the ground far below. Thrilling. Standing close behind him with a hand on the boy's shoulder, Charles looked down. Lemuel and Julia remained seated.

At the top of the wheel, the passenger car jerked to a stop, swaying. More cars exchanged passengers down below at the platforms. The people beneath, the size of ants, scurrying on and off their passenger cars. Then the great wheel revolved two slow complete revolutions as the family searched in the direction of home, looking for landmarks. Too soon, the ride finished, and they stepped onto a platform. Julia wobbled for a step. Charles caught her at the elbow to steady her.

Beyond the Ferris wheel, queues formed at several sweet-smelling booths. Charles treated the family to two popcorn bags re-baked with a caramel coating. Julia tucked her gloves into the waistband of her skirt.

"This is delicious, Charles. Boys, slow down. Lemuel, let your brother have a handful."

Sticky hands were rinsed in the next fountain, overseen by swans nipping at a crying little girl and her frantic mother on the opposite end of the pool. The Midway kept the family occupied until the middle of the afternoon. Anxious to move on to the pavilions on the other side of the train tracks, Julia relented each time the boys found a new fascination. At one point, Charles crossed with the family to the opposite side of the promenade. Julia wondered for a moment until she saw the so-called *Little Egypt* dancer on the stage of the *Street in Cairo* exhibit across the esplanade. Her women's circle had much to say about this blatant midriff display, but out of the corner of her eye, Julia found the dancer intriguing. Charles continued to herd the boys, attempting to look nonchalant.

The family, hungry for lunch, crossed over to the White City from the Midway midafternoon and stopped at a food pavilion. The menu at the front of the cafeteria line suggested: hamburgers – 10 cents, potato – 5 cents, and an apple – 5 cents. Charles stood in line while the boys and Julia found a seat at one of the dozens of tables. Charles returned with the hamburger, a split bun with a grilled patty of ground pork and ham, and a potato and an apple. Each family member took a bite from the sandwich. With a grin, Charles returned to the line and bought a hamburger for each of them. They shared a potato and an apple.

Julia ruled the tour after lunch. The family spent an hour at the Woman's Building and sauntered through some foreign country pavilions. The Japan Building gave the boys a taste of culture, clothing, and architecture, seemingly strange and fascinating. Women in geisha costumes and white makeup bowed and handed out souvenir tiny paper cranes.

They found the mammoth cheese block made in Canada, an incredible engineering feat to ship the twenty-thousand-pound round block to the fair. They sampled cheese from the same plant, but the boys spit it into the nearby trash bin.

Charles directed the family to the life-size reproductions of Christopher Columbus's three ships, the Nina, Pinta, and Santa Maria.

"In 1492, Boys, Christopher Columbus first discovered America, four-hundred years ago. Came over from Spain across the ocean. Only Indians here before that. He started the whole thing. These little ships made it to this country by Columbus' sheer guts, determination, and luck. Can you imagine? Your great-grandfather did the same thing three hundred years later. A ship's captain he was, just like Columbus. You can do anything you apply your mind and sweat to. Remember that, boys; mind and sweat."

"Did your great-grandfather know Columbus, Daddy?"

"No, but it says here that Columbus landed south of Florida, in the Bahamas. Granddad sailed to the Bahamas and Puerto Rico, as well, on many trips."

Lemuel thought the ships looked just the right size for adventure.

"Wow, could I be an explorer, Daddy? Like Columbus?"

Julia put her hand on Lemuel's shoulder.

"You and your brother have been explorers all day, Lemuel, and we'll come back so you two can explore some more. We have not seen the moving sidewalk or the exhibit your father helped build for his company in the Manufactures and Liberal Arts Building, the Machinery Building, or the rest of the Agriculture Building. We'll have to come back, Charles. It's getting so late."

"No question about it, my dear. Much to learn here. Much to learn."

As the family walked toward the train terminus, the electric lights of the White City switched on, illuminating the entire fair. The boys blinked to adjust. An audible communal gasp among the fair visitors, followed by applause, echoed across the Grand Basin. Julia found a bench seat to gather the family and stare at the fountain, far out in the middle of the reflecting pool, stream water in the lights. A vast, gilded statue of the Republic, lit up and magnificent, reached up to the heavens.

Charles carried the boy from the corner of Fullerton and Milwaukee, his head nestled in his neck, asleep. Lemuel could hardly keep his eyes open. The whole family crashed into bed.

Julia visited the exposition twice with five members of her sewing circle unaccompanied by Charles and the boys: breaking Victorian mores. The next time the entire family visited the fair, they went straight to the moving sidewalk. They went around and around the pier to the casino and back. Julia and Charles sat while the boys walked ahead as the floor moved, hurrying around to where their parents sat, admonishing them not to run. Then the boys took turns walking and running alongside the moving walkway while the other stood and waved.

The family moved to the Agricultural Building, where they found ostriches and a map of the United States made entirely of pickles. They saw two Liberty Bell models--one in wheat, oats, and rye, and one made of oranges.

One corner of the Machinery Building held the Fair's power plant, with 43 steam engines and 127 dynamos providing electricity for the Fair. The boys yelled at the top of their lungs to overcome the whir of the dynamos, to no avail. Julia held her ears shut until they left the area.

In the Manufacturers and Liberal Arts Building, Charles greeted many associates at the company's booth, and the boys nearly bowled over Cousin Walter. He tossed both of the boys high in the air. He gave Lemuel and the boy licorice sticks, and Julia politely asked for one.

The next booth displayed furniture from the palace of the King of Bavaria, and further down, the family viewed exhibits of the manuscript of Lincoln's Inaugural Address and Mozart's Spinet. The building housed eclectic exhibits, combining goods for sale with items of historical and artistic interest.

In the third week in October, Charles came to the White City one last time. He organized the crew from the factory that would dismantle their booth and return the displayed goods to the warehouse. The boys tagged along. Four booths down the aisle and a row over a load of Lake Michigan Sand had been dumped in a giant sandbox to occupy the children. Charles suggested the boys could supervise the tykes with buckets and shovels.

"I'll be back at the company booth for a while, but if you need me, come and get me. Otherwise, don't leave the area. Don't leave the sandbox. I'll be as quick as possible, and then we'll see what the line is like for the Ferris Wheel. Got it?"

"Yes, Daddy."

Fifteen minutes after Charles left, a man in a brown derby and plaid suit ran up to Lemuel.

"Your father has been hurt, Lemuel. He asked me to take you and the boy to the first aid booth in the next building."

The boys followed the man out of the Manufactures and Liberal Arts Building to a copse of trees near the beach of Lake Michigan. Another man joined the first, kneeled before Lemuel, and grabbed him solidly by each shoulder. Lemuel felt his skin start to itch as the man got the attention of the boy's eye.

"You're going to be a good boy, now ain't ya, Lemuel, and you'll see your daddy real soon."

Lemuel surprised the man with his swift kick to the man's knee.

"Run, get Daddy."

The boy tore away from Plaid-Suit, eluding him in a stream of people exiting the Manufactures Building. Then he became confused. Which door had they come through? He stopped and turned around, choking back the bile rising from his stomach. He turned around again and again, wiping tears from his eyes. He could see the tops of the trees where the man held Lemuel. He would have to backtrack to Lemuel and gather his bearing from that point; without being noticed by the men holding Lemuel.

As the boy approached the copse, the man rubbing his knee took Plaid-Suit by the arm.

"Forget about the kid. We got the other one. Getting let go from the brush factory has turned into your lucky day. That and seeing the kids at the sandbox. We won't be working in no factory from now on. Now we just got to get him out of here."

"But if the kid finds his father?"

"Chances are zero in this crowd. Go get one of them carts people rent to carry their fair stuff to their cars. Be quick, but don't call attention."

The boy turned in near panic. Daddy? He had to find Daddy. He had to be brave like the Texas Rangers and fast on the draw. As his breathing deepened, he saw the Ferris Wheel in the distance and headed that way on the run. Once he got to the center of the esplanade, he turned and found the front entrance to the Manufacturers and Liberal Arts Building. From the front gate, he remembered the way to his father's booth and pulled up out of breath when he saw Charles.

"Daddy, Daddy, they've got Lemuel. They're trying to take Lemuel away in one of those wagons."

"Where, son, at the sandbox?"

"No, not there."

The boy tugged at Charles' sleeve and started running to the sandbox, Charles following. At the sandbox, the boy turned down the aisle and ran as fast as he could along the same route the man had led them ten minutes ago. Charles and the boy burst through the exit doors, and after a couple of more turns, the boy pointed to the copse. Charles could see a man and a boy in the shadow of the trees. Now he took the lead at a furious run.

Charles burst into the center of the clearing. Upon seeing Lemuel, Charles rushed the man holding him, surprising him with an axe-like hammer blow to the man's jaw. The boy heard the bone crack as the man went down and out. Charles hugged Lemuel and the boy.

Plaid Suit abandoned his cart at the opening in the trees.

"Hey, there, mister. Let me gather up my brother there, and we'll go."

"Your brother! He won't be moving for a while. Say I remember you from the shop. You couldn't be trusted for a day's work. Now I'd say you both have botched whatever you planned out here. Leave your brother and get!"

"Seems to me you're the only one who can recognize us, mister. Gots to take care of that."

Plaid Suit retrieved a bowie knife from the sheath beneath his suit jacket. He began to move to the right and back left, looking for the best opportunity to lunge at Charles.

"Lemuel, give me your jacket. Now. Boy, get behind me. Lemuel, you run for the police."

Lemuel took off. The boy crouched behind his father and peered out at the snarling man from behind his father's knee. Charles wrapped Lemuel's jacket around his left arm without looking at Plaid Suit. He moved to his right, toeing a thick fallen branch, probably rotten, but bent to retrieve it.

Plaid Suit lunged. Charles grabbed the stick, fended off an overhand thrust of the bowie knife with his protected left arm, hearing the cloth tear and feeling a sting below the elbow, and crashed the stick across the head of the attacker. Sure enough, it broke into shards of wood dust, not hurting the man. But the cloud of dust affected the man's eyes, and Charles pressed forward. While pushing his attacker with his left arm, the man's knife still buried in the jacket, Charles created an opening for a driving blow to Plaid Suit's stomach. The man doubled up. Charles followed with two hammer blows to the man's head. Plaid Suit fell backward, tripping on a root, shaking his head to clear his vision, and dropping the knife.

Charles kicked the knife clear and advanced again, but a whistle, insistent and nearby, caused him to back away, hands at the ready.

Two policemen led by Lemuel, billy clubs in hand, entered the clearing, attempting to assess the situation. Charles explained.

"These men tried to kidnap my boys, officer. The young one came and found me and led me back here. I defended my sons, officer."

The taller policeman looked first at the stupefied sitting man and then turned to the other man, out cold, with his jaw askew, before looking up at Charles.

"I'd say you defended the boys rather good, mister. This boy said something about a knife being involved?"

"Yes, sir. He got me a scratch. The knife is over by that bush."

Charles had unwrapped the jacket from his arm, glanced at the wound, and held it against the injury. The bleeding wasn't bad.

"Still, I'd say you were mighty lucky, mister. Been in some scrapes before, I'd guess."

"I spent five years in the Maine lumber camps before coming to Chicago, officer."

"Say no more, fella. Log jumpers are a rough bunch, I know. We'll take it from here. The first aid station is back near the promenade. Can you make it there, or do you need help? My partner will go with you and take a statement. I have heard of only one other case like this from a few years ago. These two won't be seeing the light of day ever again."

"Thank you, officer. Let me give you one of my business cards. My uncle and I would appreciate keeping this out of the newspapers. We don't want to give anyone else the same idea as crazy as that seems."

Charles shook the officer's hand, and the officer, in turn, leaned over and shook each of the boy's hands.

"You boy's held up real good through this. Brave as they come, I'd say. Quite a father too."

With his arm bandaged, Charles pulled at the tear in his suit coat to make it unobtrusive. Julia saw nothing amiss when the boys and Charles entered the parlor where she sat, knitting. Charles had instructed the boys not to show excitement when they arrived and to let Charles relate the day's events to Julia.

Both boys appeared chagrined that Charles left out all but the barest facts, giving credit to the two policemen that Lemuel had brought to the scene for their rescue. But silently, secretly, they were bursting inside, and Lemuel threw an arm around his brother as they headed up the stairs to bed, inseparable.

That night, in their bedroom's privacy, Julia saw the bandage. She knew her husband well; she had heard the story of his scars and his struggles out east.

"Now you tell me what really happened, Charles Martensen."

SCOUT
1893

Daniel traveled from Portland, Maine, to Chicago in May of 1893 to visit his younger brother, George, and his son Charles' family and to see the World's Columbia Exposition. A vibrant seventy-five-year-old at the time, he reveled in the sixty-five-thousand exhibits at the fair and took a turn on the giant Ferris Wheel. Charles' family gathered around the fireplace in Charles' home, learning of Daniel's exploits during the Mexican-American war. Daniel had never broached the subject whilst Charles grew up back in Portland. That evening, Charles's sons, eight-year-old Lemuel and Lemuel's six-year-old brother, heard about Daniel's horse Sandy and Daniel's friends, Lorenzo, and Slim, for the first time.

Daniel stayed in Chicago, alternating between Charles' house, George's house, and Walter's house, his nephew's. During the summer of 1894, while staying for three weeks at George's home in Oak Park, Daniel met a young architect, Frank Lloyd Wright. The architect dropped in, carrying a roll of sketches under his arm to show George and Walter. Mr. Wright, twenty-seven at the time but known as one of the most sought-after architects in Chicago, helped clear the dining room table. He unrolled the sketches of two cottages set into a backdrop of trees and a slope to the water. Walter pointed to the site plan.

"Look here, Uncle Daniel, this shows the plot of land Father, and I purchased in Whitehall, Michigan, on the water. We intend to build a couple of summer cottages."

Daniel and Mr. Wright leaned over the drawing.

"As you can see on the site plan and the perspective sketch, the cottages will span the spring, flowing down the ravine-like bridges. You will be entranced by the sights and sounds of the gurgling brook while sitting on your decks.

George hoped his brother could appreciate the drawings.

"What do you think, Daniel? Will you join me in my retirement on the shores of White Lake and Lake Michigan, listening to the restful sounds of the birds and a flowing stream?

Wright made sure Martensen's expectations remained realistic.

"I have several projects to start and complete before your Whitehall cottages. It will be at least three years before we can begin."

Walter, younger by four years than Mr. Wright, could not wait to show the plans to Mary Robeson, the girl he intended to marry. Daniel, always impressed with the accomplishments of his younger brother and nephew, viewed the strange low, linear lines of the roofs and decks suspiciously. The buildings seem to melt into the trees and foliage of the hill rather than standing tall and proud as a proclamation of George's success.

In the spring of 1895, Daniel began having trouble with incontinence. George's doctor determined that Daniel had prostate cancer. Daniel passed in October; his body was shipped back to Portland to be buried in the family plot. Officials lowered his coffin to rest next to his wife Cordelia, who had passed fifteen years prior. A longstanding member of the Portland community, many Portlanders, friends, and family attended his memorial. The Odd Fellows Lodge members in Portland provided flowers and refreshments and spoke of Daniel's good works at the funeral.

HOMESTEADER
1903

The boy squeezed, shoved, and separated Samuel and Leroy to give himself room on the bench to sit before his eighteen-year-old brother. The ballfield, if you could call it that, in Humbolt Park on the west side of Chicago, had been put in five years earlier as baseball became increasingly popular. A home plate and pitcher's rubber sixty feet out in a tree clearing marked the ballfield. Baseball is played so often here that ruts for the first and third baselines made the diamond clear. Lemuel, captain and coach of the Fullerton Fury, addressed his team this Saturday morning, 1903, as the boys willed the dew on the grass to dry before their nine-thirty starting time.

"Alright, fellas, this is the first fancy ballfield we'll play on today. We've got a game in Douglas Park at two o'clock and a third game in Garfield Park at four o'clock. We'll start Josie pitchin this game and Leroy at Douglas Park. I'll pitch the last game against the Bulldogs. They're by far the hardest team to beat."

Lemuel paced up and down the bench to make his point.

"It took me a month to put this series together. The Bulldog's captain Jimmie Smite, wouldn't even talk to me when I told him we played in the field behind the school. The Bulldogs won't even take the field this afternoon if we don't win these first two games."

The boy began stomping his feet in the dirt, joined by the rest of the team. They were all fired up. Lemuel waved them to be quiet.

"Their clean-up batter is eighteen, and I doubt he can spell his name, but if he gets a hold of a pitch, Harold will be running all the way to the Lake to get it. First, the other team just showed up, so let's warm up on the side here. They're the home team batting last for this game."

Everyone jumped off the bench, excited to loosen up and get the game started. The boy took Lemuel aside for a moment.

"How's your arm today, Lem? Playing shortstop for two games, one right after another, won't do your pitching any good with the Bulldogs."

"You know I have been resting it for a week. It's fine. Don't worry about my arm. Besides, we must beat the Eagles here and the Garfield Ghosts to play the Bulldogs. Go hit some fly balls over on the side. We'll need you to connect whenever you come to the plate today, brother."

"I'll do my best, Lemuel."

But would his best be good enough to aid Lemuel, the baseball hero of the neighborhood? Lemuel, known for pitching all over the west side, could play shortstop or third base better than anyone within twenty blocks of their home. Maybe, just maybe, the Chicago Colts would take him on in a few more years. The Colts, or Cubs, as the brothers liked to call them now, were talked about everywhere in town. The sport of baseball was a source of tremendous pride for all who lived in Chicago.

The boy revered Lemuel as a hero as well. Now sixteen, the boy knew he would never be as good as his older brother. Lemuel had been good at baseball as young as twelve, and the boy only ten. Two years later, when the boy turned twelve, he struck out every time he batted. Every time. Lemuel had been so patient with him. Lemuel always picked his brother to be on his team, even though they both knew he would strike out whenever he picked up a bat.

Worse, the boy could not catch a fly ball to save his neck either. The ball arced high in the sky, and he would run too far back, and the ball would drop to the ground in front of him. Or he would misjudge the other way, running forward, and the ball would fall behind him. For two years, the ground balls went right through his legs most of the time. He tried. He tried and failed, and Lemuel still picked him for his team.

Then, one day, sometime after his fourteenth birthday, Lemuel's regular catcher could not make the game, and Lemuel came up to his brother and asked him to catch. The boy did his best, and as it turned out, he did well. Something about seeing the ball coming straight at him appeared to be easier for the boy. The actual test came on game day in the third inning when the boy on first tried to steal second base. The boy saw the runner out of the corner of his eye, and with Lemuel's fast pitch caught, the boy stood and threw to second as hard as he could, right at the bag, a perfect throw. The second baseman tagged the runner out. Lemuel came running up to him, slapping him on the back.

"What a throw, brother; how do you like playing catcher."

"Great!

"Yes, great. The outfield is so dull in comparison. As a catcher, I'm in on every pitch, every play." The boy improved rapidly. Even when the batter hit a high foul ball, the boy could scramble, watch it go straight up, run underneath it, and catch it for the out.

Baseball became more than a time to be with his friends and his brother, his baseball hero. It became something he could be good at as well. Lemuel, the pitcher, the boy, the catcher.

The boy's hitting took longer to improve. There came a day when their team's leadoff batter hit a single and held on first base. Lemuel made the sign for the boy to bunt.

After striking out repeatedly, the boy, willing to try anything, squared around after the pitch to bunt the ball. While facing the pitcher, the ball screamed toward him. Now in the catcher's position, he had no trouble seeing the ball come at him. Instead of catching the ball, the boy gently tapped the ball to the ground in front of him. The boy's one natural talent, speed, allowed him to beat the throw to first. For the first time, he stood on first base in a game. Thrilling.

For the rest of that year, the boy bunted on every turn at the plate, sometimes ignoring Lemuel's sign to hit away and placing a bunt down either the third or first base line. Rarely did the ball roll foul. Nine times out of ten, the boy beat the throw to first.

At the end of his fourteenth summer, the boy, more confident and loose at the plate, began to connect with the ball in full swing. His swing leveled out. He began to achieve infield hits and powered the ball beyond the right fielder for a triple.

At sixteen, the boy no longer bunted unless called for with a sign from Lemuel. The boys were a team within a team, and most of the time, their team won the game. Lemuel had developed a wicked curve ball that would have fooled even his brother if he had not expected it. Lemuel's knuckleball and spitball were equally effective, but the boy called for fastball after fastball in a tight game. This usually intimidated batters, which is an impressive strategy to watch.

Both boys had paper routes that kept them stocked with baseballs and bats. The boy had also invested in a catcher's mask and a pillow-style mitt. Once a week, they rode their Schwinn safety bicycles to West Side Park and sat in the cheap right field bleachers to watch their Cubs play and try to pick up hitting, pitching, and strategy. Baseball became their world and Lemuel's future.

This afternoon, the boy began hitting fly balls to his team's outfielders, determined to stay focused on defeating the Eagles.

Something his father had said two nights ago, while Lemuel delivered papers, gnawed at him enough that he missed hitting two toss-ups in a row. Father was ready to move the family to the prairie and begin farming. The boys knew the day would come sooner or later. His father and mother spoke of it often as he and Lemuel grew. These days the whole family would gather around Charles on the front porch and listen to his preparations for moving to the *wide-open spaces of his dream ranch*. Except for the two eldest brothers, the other siblings were too young to comprehend their father's rocking chair aspirations. The boy's family consisted of his sister, Edith, nine years old; his little brother John, five; baby brother Paul, two, bouncing on his father's knee; and Julia, his mother holding baby George.

But two nights ago, Father had shown the boy his ledger sheet, noting the articles he had purchased for their eventual move. This included two horses being boarded at Uncle George's stable, a wagon, and large and small farming equipment. His father's dream appeared more and more to be moving toward reality. The boy wondered how Lemuel would take this new direction in their lives.

The younger brother loved baseball, but he knew a career as a major league player would never happen.

The boy would not mention any of this to Lemuel today.

The Fullerton Fury won the game against the Eagles seven to three. The boy had contributed four hits out of five at-bats and caught two foul balls for outs, one of which he had run down halfway to first base. One base runner stole second on him, but he threw out the same runner trying for third. Lemuel went five for five with one triple. He had thrown out numerous batters as a shortstop trying to make it to first base. As a coach, he congratulated the team members and praised Josie's pitching. Those with bikes gave handlebar rides to those that did not as they traveled down to Douglas Park for the game against the Base Racers, a respected team among the neighborhoods of Chicago. The boy pulled two sandwiches Mother had prepared from his bike basket and handed one to Lemuel. They ate in silence, resting against a tree trunk near the ballfield. They inspected the ballfield, walking the bases and checking out the outfield for obstacles or ruts. The ballfield had been newly developed; the first and third base lines were exceptionally smooth. The pitcher's rubber staked down on a slight mound. Lemuel brought the team together as the Base Racers took the field to warm up.

"Fellas, don't think this game will be easy like the last game. We'll need everyone to stay sharp. No errors. Keep your head in the game. Think before each pitch about what you will do with the ball if it comes to you. Be ready."

Lemuel made sure each boy on the team nodded in agreement.

"By the coin toss, we're the home team for this one, so we bat last. When you're at the plate, wait for your pitch. Leroy, you're our pitcher. The longer you can throw straight and hard, the more rested I'll be for the Bulldogs game. But we must win this one to play that one. Ok, let's race rings around these so-called Racers."

The game stayed close, tied at six going into the sixth inning. Lemuel and the boy had crossed the plate twice each, with Josie and Harold also contributing. With two outs in the bottom of the sixth, Lemuel cracked a corker down the left baseline. The left fielder had no chance of backing up fast enough, and with the ball rolling away, Lemuel slashed across home plate. Josie hit a double in the seventh, and the game ended after the ninth, eight to six for the Fury.

Two games in a row took a toll on the team. Exhausted, they mounted bikes for the ride back north to Garfield Park. As they arrived, the Bulldogs on the field whipped the ball to first base as their coach hammered it to each infielder. They looked crisp and not in the least tired. The Fury dropped their bikes and sprawled under some trees to rest. The brothers dug out their remaining sandwiches and ate them in silence. Even more intimidating, the ballfield at Garfield Park sported bleachers along the first and third base lines. To the team's surprise, enthusiastic spectators filled the bleachers behind the Bulldogs' bench. Behind the Fury bench, the bleachers held a handful of hopeful watchers. Steadily the bleacher behind their team became well-populated. Some of the Ghosts and Racers players had come to watch the game. The boy could not tell if they came in support of the Fury or to see them hopelessly trounced by the Bulldogs.

Lemuel waited a while and then ordered the team out for warmups. By a toss, the Fury would be the home team for this game, even though the Bulldogs considered the ball diamond their home. Just before the start of the game, Lemuel called the team together around the pitcher's rubber.

"I don't know how many of you know about these guys, but I have scouted them some. The sloth over there is the one we want to back up on. I've seen him hit it way over the heads of left fielders, so be aware and back way up. If we keep the ball in front of us, we should be able to prevent a home run."

Josie raised a timid hand.

"What about their pitcher, Lemuel. What does he throw?"

"Never mind what he throws. Get the feel on the first pitch and keep the ball in play until he gives you something you like."

The boy, the catcher's mask in his lap, slapped Josie on the back.

"Like the last game, Josie, you stand there and hit the ball. Lemuel, let's get to it."

"Wait," said Lemuel. "The other thing is they play dirty. You hear me? I have seen it. They'll hassle the shit out of us. I know it's hard, but don't let them under your skin. Please ignore it. Play our game our way, error-free. Hit the ball through the gaps."

The Fullerton Fury returned to their positions for the start of the game. The brothers waited a moment until the others had left the mound.

"Lemuel, I feel good about this game; what do you say?"

"Brother, we'll do it just like we've been doing it all season. I'll pitch, and you catch. We'll out-hit these bastards and ride out of here with respect. You know it. I know it. Now let's educate these assholes."

The game appeared to be a pitcher's duel from the start. Two strikeouts and a ground ball to second for the third out brought the Fury up to bat. Three up and three down. Lemuel struck out two more in the second after their huge batter skidded a ball between the first and second basemen. A fly ball caught by Josie in left field retired the side.

The boy walked casually to home plate, batting in the fourth position. Even if the other team did not know the boy's reputation, they could guess that as a cleanup batter, he should be taken seriously. He bounced his bat against the corner of the plate and made ready. The first pitch curved, sinking away from him for a ball. The pitcher threw a heater for his second pitch. The catcher took his glove off and blew on his hand, a strike down the middle.

"Jesus, that pitch burned you, boy. Didn't see it comin, did ya? You won't believe what's comin next, either? You guys are, what, the Fullerton Fury? More like the Fullerton Fuckups. You'll never hit my guy."

The boy had been catching fast pitches for two years. The next heater came in a little low and just as fast. The boy swung low but level. He met the ball square on and never even felt the ball against the bat. The ball tore over the second baseman's reach and bounced between the center and right fielder rolling away. The boy reached second for a stand-up double. Respect.

The Bulldogs pitcher bore down on the following three Fury batters to retire the side. Four more scoreless innings were posted in chalk on the scoreboard to the right of first base. Lemuel walked the leadoff batter for the Bulldogs in the seventh, which brought up the sloth. All the Fury fielders backed up as instructed, with the left fielder backing up even more. The boy signaled for a curve, and the big batter swung and missed by a mile. The boy called for another curveball which resulted in a second strike. To be safe, the boy signaled for a spitball low from Lemuel. Lemuel shook his head in disagreement. He had not thrown many spitballs in this game and did not want to take a chance on it. Lemuel also shook off the boy's low curveball sign. That left the fastball, which the boy signaled. He wanted it inside below the sloth's knees, urging the correct target with his catcher's mitt.

But the ball drifted dead over the plate, and somehow the sloth anticipated the pitch and slammed the ball, swinging late and sending it to right field instead of left, over Harold's head. The sloth, comparatively slow as a base runner, began to round third when Harold chased the ball down and threw to the relay at first. Manny turned and fired it at the boy standing over the plate. The boy caught the ball and turned toward third base just as Sloth-Boy slammed him, sending him flying backward and popping the ball loose. Lemuel and James rushed to the boy's side, whose vision blurred as the field spun.

The boy sat up, shaking stars out of his eyes.

"Sorry, fellas!"

"My fault, brother," Lemuel offered a hand to help the boy up, "I should have listened to your signal. A freight train hit you. He didn't bother to slide. His arms were crossed, shoulder high, and he went for your head. Can you get up?

The boy rose, wobbled a step, and sent his teammates back to their positions. The Bulldogs bench celebrated wildly, congratulating the sloth and yelling profanities at the boy and the rest of the Fury.

"Fullerton, Fuckups! Fullerton Fuckups! Fullerton Fuckups!"

The chant unsettled the boy's teammates after the play at home, towing dirt nervously in the infield and standing with a hand on a hip in the outfield. It cost them. The Bulldogs scored two more runs in the inning before Lemuel settled and struck out two batters, and a third hit a fly ball out to Josie.

Dejected, the Fullerton Fury players were lost in their thoughts as they gathered on the bench. Lemuel looked at his team from left to right.

"Yeah, so they showed their true colors that inning. We can still get back in this game in the next two innings. We've got great batters going out there. Everyone is capable, and I know you can do it. Josie, get up there and start us off. Gather round. Put your hands in. Ready?"

"One! Two! Three! Fury!"

Josie watched two fastballs go by for strikes and then fouled off a curve ball and a spitball to stay alive. The next fastball Josie got a hold of and sent it past the outstretched glove of the second baseman. Manny, up next, laid down a perfect bunt on the third base line and beat the throw to first, although the entire Bulldog bench exploded, surrounding the first base umpire, calling for an out.

The next Fury batter flied out. Harold, up next, watched two called balls, then hit a blooper that landed in fair territory behind the third baseman.

Bases loaded. Lemuel approached the Fury batter in the on-deck circle.

"Brother, it's up to you again. There is one out. Kick ass out there."

Lemuel jabbed his brother playfully in the shoulder, and for some reason, they both started laughing. The brothers, best friends, a team within a team, shared the moment like they had shared so many moments growing up, just the two.

Before stepping to bat, the boy made eye contact with his base runners. They looked back, nodded to the boy, and then looked to

Lemuel for any signals he might offer. Lemuel just kept his arms crossed, leaning back on the bench.

The first pitch fastball came at him like a dream come true, and the boy slammed into it, pulling it up over the third baseman, staying fair. The boy took off at top speed. The first base coach swung his arms wildly, urging him to take second. The boy knew it would be tight and panicked when he saw the Bulldogs' second baseman had kicked second base three feet toward right field. He began his practiced slide toward the new position and caught a tree stump sticking up with his right leg shin bone.

The crowd could not hear the bone crack over the din of the moment, but the boy thought it sounded like a branch breaking off slowly in a thunderstorm. The boy's slide turned into a tumble, his left leg tangled, and he rolled into the second baseman; his broken right leg hitting the fielder's shin at the thigh with another thud. He lay in agony as the second baseman kicked him aside and held up the ball. The boy looked down at the bone sticking out of his shin like the jagged peak of Mount Everest covered in red snow and fainted.

Lemuel reached his brother first, protecting him from the rest of the two teams pushing and fighting near second base. The bleachers emptied, and everyone crowded the boy. The fighting and noise subsided as concern for the boy overtook the hysteria of the game.

Lemuel eyed the captain of the Bulldogs.

"We concede the game. Now get these people back. Josie, run over to the conservatory and call the nearest hospital. If the conservatory has no phone, keep going to the police station or hail a policeman. The blood isn't pouring out but hurry."

"Which hospital? I don't know which hospital you mean. Who should I call?"

"Harold, you go with Josie. Children's Memorial, Mercy General, I don't care. I think the Children's Memorial is closest. Get it done."

Lemuel looked up and spied a man in the crowd in a white shirt and a cardigan sweater.

"Could I use your shirt on his leg, sir?"

The man stripped off his sweater and shirt and handed the latter to Lemuel, who gently lifted the leg to get the rolled-up shirt underneath and tied it across the break. He tied the sleeves together to create a tourniquet just above the knee. The boy had not moved; he was still out.

The crowd had dwindled at the pleading of Lemuel as Harold returned with news that the groundskeeper at the conservatory had used the brand-new telephone to reach the emergency service of Children's Memorial. An ambulance would be arriving soon, fifteen minutes out at the most.

Josie now returned, trailing Harold. Lemuel sent them both off on their bikes. Josie returned to the conservatory to call the Brush factory where the boy's father worked. Harold went to the boy's home to inform their mother to meet them at the hospital.

The boy began to come around, turning his head this way and that as Lemuel sought to keep him calm. Minutes later, a siren announced the oncoming ambulance, still blocks away. The boy's teammates could flag the ambulance down and direct them to where the boy lay; the horses were dressed in a white foam lather. The two medics bent over the boy, and a gurney was laid beside him for transport. One nurse untied the tourniquet and retied it, noting the bleeding soaking the borrowed shirt covering the shin. The medic held the boy's left leg in a static position while the other doctor directed Lemuel and two other men to lift the boy onto the gurney and carry him to the back of the ambulance, sliding him inside. Lemuel hopped into the ambulance and assisted the medic in keeping the leg still. The driver gathered the reins and set off for the hospital. Lemuel said nothing to his teammates, focusing on the boy and the jostling ambulance. The horses galloped back to the hospital, the ambulance siren wailing.

The boy lay on a cot in the living room of the Fullerton house six weeks after the slide. Daylight had not broken yet, but the boy couldn't sleep. His leg itched, and his forehead dripped sweat from ignoring the urge. He stuck the two-foot wire down into the cast (which extended from his ankle to his hip) and poked as far as it would go. Wrong spot. He did not care. The boy kept poking, creating pain in a different part of his leg to take his mind off the itch he could not reach.

Sunlight filtered into the living room at the dawn of another day of struggling to get to the bathroom. The boy had to leave the door open for his extended appendage as he tried to shit without soiling the cast. Last evening one crutch had knocked off the drinking glass from the sink. It shattered on the tile floor while he tried maneuvering in the tangle of cast and crutches in the small space. Father had helped sweep the shards out of the way while the boy struggled off the toilet and back to his makeshift living room bed.

He struggled to return to the cot this morning, sick of it. All of it. The doctors said it would be four more weeks in the cast, then another six weeks on crutches, then four additional months before he may or may not be able to run again. The boy only heard the *'not run again.'* He would be useless if he could never run again in baseball or any sport. His leg itched all the time. The compound fracture five inches below the knee had been complicated with a second break five inches above the knee when he hit that fucking second baseman. He dreamed of hunting the bastard down and beating him to death with his bat for kicking second base out of baseline alignment where that stump protruded in the grass. He could scarcely think of anything beyond his inability to scratch and the need to murder that Bulldog fielder. He picked up yet another one of the books Lemuel had piled from the library, found his place, and lost himself on the page.

Father called out from the dining room table that evening at dinner time.

"Come on to dinner, son."

"I'll just eat it here, Dad, if you don't mind."

Charles came roaring into the living room.

"I damn well do mind. Your mother has been waiting on you hand and foot long enough. Now stand up and come to the table like everyone else."

"Alright! It's just hard to sit at the table. No room for my leg."

"I don't care about hard. I know it's hard. Don't you think it's hard on us? Lemuel does two routes every afternoon until you can pick it up again. Now stop your whining and carrying on and act your age."

"What can I do with this leg? What am I going to do?"

"You will pick yourself up and eat dinner with the rest of us. Now!"

The boy waited impatiently in the doctor's examination room. His leg itched more than ever in anticipation of the removal of the cast. As a distraction, he scratched his left leg like crazy and read the poster on the wall warning about tuberculosis. The door opened, and the doctor walked in with a nurse. He picked up what looked like a keyhole saw and began sawing down the length of the cast along the outside perimeter. The doctor made several cuts across the cast perpendicular to the first lengthwise cut for the next hour. The boy felt the blade cut his skin once but never flinched. He just wanted the doctor to finish taking the damn thing off.

The doctor picked up pincher pliers with sharpened claws for the last step and began breaking the cast into pieces. Down to the gauze now, the boy gripped the table till he thought it would break. He wanted to shove the doctor aside, rip the gauze away, and scratch his leg. The doctor kept talking and reassuring the boy as he worked.

The gauze gone, the boy looked down at his scaly, emaciated leg and then back up to the ceiling while the nurse bathed the leg repeatedly, removing loose scales and bandaging the small cut made by the saw. The doctor returned, examined the leg, and instructed the boy to use his crutches to stand up and apply weight to his leg. The boy felt pain at the breaks as he stood. The Doctor said he must use the crutches for the next six weeks as his leg healed further. After the next appointment, and not before, he might be rid of the crutches, although some pain would remain.

Limping home from school in January 1904, the pain in the boy's leg sweat-soaked his shirt. His snail's progress frustrated and embarrassed him as the rest of the class passed him. Turning onto Fullerton, it still took him two minutes to reach the stairs to his porch. Light snow covered the steps. If he slipped, his fragile leg might break again. In the house, he plunked down on the settee in the living room, opened his math book, and began his homework. In an hour and a half, with all his tasks completed, he nodded off. His father, clunking up the porch stairs, startled him awake. Father strode past into the kitchen, and the boy heard the bustle and gaiety of the little one's greetings. Julia called his name and asked for help setting the table for dinner. The boy took his time standing up and poking around in the dining room, limping around the table and setting the silverware.

Lemuel arrived just before dinnertime. John and Paul ran up to Lemuel as he kneeled before the settee and wrestled with the boys. He stood and tossed them high until his mother cautioned him about the chandelier in the living room.

Later, after dinner, Lemuel went to a church youth meeting. The boy's sister and brothers were in bed, and the boy sat reading his latest book. Mother finished the dishes in the kitchen while Father dried them. The boy heard a low murmur coming from the kitchen. After a few minutes, Father walked by and took hold of the handle to the front door.

"I want to show you something outside, son. Come along, will you?"

The boy gingerly stood and followed his father out to the porch.

"What is it, Dad?"

Father pointed at the thermometer.

"Twenty-eight degrees out tonight, son. Cold enough for you?"

"Yeah, Dad, it's freezing out here! Let's go back inside."

"In a minute, son, I'm making a point. You're tired of hearing me go on about living on a farm. Arms outstretched with no walls or buildings blocking your way. Looking right and left, front and behind, seeing nothing but prairie and trees until the earth curves out of sight. The utter quiet except for the sizzle of wheat swishing in the wind; birds whistling by. The smell, or rather the lack of it, in the air that's so clear you'll rub your eyes. Sky, not through the opening between buildings, but everywhere, the way sky should be."

The boy, nodding, wrapped his arms over his chest to keep out the cold.

"Right," said Charles, "I have not said how much toil and trouble life will be up there. Twenty-eight degrees? We'll see negative twenty–eight-degree temperatures. So cold your ungloved hand or finger could snap after three exposed minutes. Work, hard work; we'll see that too.

"I figure we need to be up there ready to go by the middle of May. The spring thaw takes longer where we're going, and we must be prepared for it. We'll need every bit of daylight all summer to build a suitable cabin for Mother and the kids, a place to keep out the winter and the cold. With sweat and grit, we'll finish the house and be back here for the first winter. The whole family will join us next spring to help plow and plant. Our goal will be thirty acres of wheat, alfalfa, and corn.

"Cold enough? Think about it being fifty degrees colder."

"Dad, my leg. You don't need me limping around, useless when all that work needs doing. Lemuel can do it. I know that. I'd be in the way."

"I'm saying you wouldn't be in the way, son. I'll need you both. The plan has always been the three of us. Mother and I decided to postpone when you broke your leg, but it's now or never. I know I won't have Lemuel much longer, or you, for that matter; got your own lives to determine. I need you now, son."

"I don't think my leg is up to it, Dad? I can barely walk!"

Father looked down, pressing his lips hard, silent, while the boy shivered. Then father nodded, a decision made. He looked up and leaned in with almost a whisper.

"Listen, I knew a girl once about your age. The horse she rode sideswiped the barn and crushed her leg; I'd say about as bad as your breaks.

"From that day forward, that leg defined her. She pulled into herself, pitied herself, and believed everyone else pitied her too. She told me no one saw her. They only saw her limp. A beautiful girl. Gorgeous! Strawberry blond hair. She had freckles down to her shoulders. I could not describe her adequately if I tried. The most obnoxious person I have ever known, I'm telling you.

"I don't care if you limp or struggle to walk. I need you, son. Look at your shoulders, built up from eight months on those crutches. You'll be a help because you're my son. Limp and work, that is what I'm asking. I'll just bet that you'll just be thinking, work, work, work because that's how hard it will be; for all of us.

"You can be tall and limp or small and limp like that girl. Start by taking back your paper route, no matter how long it takes you to finish each day. Your opportunity, your adventure; our adventure starts in May."

"Dad, can we go inside now? I don't want to freeze to death before we head west."

Lemuel hitched up the horses to the buckboard wagon in the pre-dawn of a day in the last week of May 1904. Charles oversaw the process. Lemuel's brother also watched. He would unhitch the horses after the wagon and horses were loaded into the railroad box car. The boys had practiced these tasks several times in the last month. Charles supervised as if the two horses were his favorite members of the family. He saw Lemuel from the corner of his eye as he spoke softly to Bessie and Beau, the two Irish Draught horses. Charles had been acquainting Bessie, a dapple grey, and Beau, a rare and beautiful Palomino, with his voice commands for the past year in his spare time while the boys played baseball. Both horses had been five years trained before purchase. He scratched Bessie and Beau each in turn behind the ears as Lemuel bridled them. The boys were amazed at the horse skills Father demonstrated and taught them in preparation for their trip. They were still as green as could be but eager to learn. Even Lemuel, torn from the baseball he loved, pranced proudly around the stable, sorting supplies and carefully packing every square inch of the wagon with the supplies and equipment the three of them settled on taking.

Lemuel's brother could hardly contain his excitement. He could not wait to go; he had been dreaming of closing the box car door and hanging on as the train jolted out of the city for weeks.

The boy limped hurriedly, hefting one of the saddles into the rear corner of the buckboard. His leg would be sore tonight, but he hardly felt the pain these days. Until Josie took over his paper route two weeks ago, the boy had walked it, delivering the papers rain or shine by himself. The canvas bag went thirty pounds total, and the boy put the strap over his right shoulder, draping the pack against his left knee to relieve some of the weight of his bad right leg. He could finish the route in an hour and fifteen minutes now, whereas it took the boy two and a half painful hours of sweat those first weeks of his return to the route. Of course, his brother Lemuel could finish his own paper route in eighteen minutes on his bike, but the boy's progress on his own had given him the confidence to tackle this trip north with Lemuel and his father.

"Dad, everything is packed, just like we practiced."

"Good work, boys; looks like we're ready."

A buggy rounded the stable corner with Cousin Walter driving. George and Edith, John and Paul crowding the back seat, Julia jumped down to hug the trio one last time. The older boys hugged their mother, and the boy could not help but cry.

"Thank you, Mother, for putting up with me."

Julia whispered, "You're the levelheaded one, son. You hear me? You bring these two devils back safe and sound?"

"I'll do my best, Mother."

"You always do, son, you always do."

As the family exhausted farewell hugs and words dwindled into silence, Charles turned away from Julia and anxiously examined the wagon. Everything was packed tight and tied down. One small section of the wagon contained the trio's personals and blankets for the nights on the train ahead. Julia told the rest of the family to stay put and followed Charles to the other side of the wagon.

She turned Charles away from his examination of the wagon and embraced her husband, pushing against him with a tight hug. She then took his face in her hands. Julia looked up to Charles, and her last kiss for the man she loved and respected ended in Charles's choked statement of love. Still holding Charles' face, Julia locked his eyes with hers, the equal partner in their endeavors.

"Now, Charles Martensen, we both know you're going to work too hard and too long up there, and I want to remind you to set a sustainable pace. I want you back here come the middle of winter, no later. Now you promise me that."

"I promise you, Mother, we'll be back before you know it."

"You know, I will not hold my breath on that exaggeration. Take care of the boys. I love you."

"I love you, Julia. I'll come to get you!"

Walter Martensen looked up at the three as they squeezed onto the buckboard bench.

"Wish I could go with you."

"I know, Walt, but you'll have your hands full here taking over the shipping department and marketing."

The horses took off in a shuffle to a walk, the little boys wailing behind them. The three travelers did not look back. Charles waved his hand without turning around.

Charles paid for a flatbed wagon and an open-air stock car at the train terminal for the horses and three passengers. They sat in the rail terminal while the station master sent a messenger out to the train crew with car serial numbers and loading directives. A switchman approached with directions to the rail car loading area. Charles drove the horses and wagon out into the yard to the designated flat car. A ramp hooked to the end of the flatcar allowed the horses to pull the wagon to the car's front end. The train crew and the boys blocked the wheels and roped the wagon to turnbuckles, tightening each to secure the wagon.

The horses were unhitched and individually led back down the ramp. The station engine backed a slatted stock car up to the flatbed car. The flatbed coupling engaged with a thudding jolt. The station engine decoupled from the stock car and left the two railcars alone on the spur.

Three hours later, another engine with perhaps twenty boxcars slowly rolled back onto the spur, coupled with the stock and flatbed cars. The train spent another two hours maneuvering to additional tracks and picking up more flatbed and stock cars. Quitting time arrived at the yard, and miles of the rail became quiet except for the watchmen patrolling each hour on the hour. Charles and the boys bedded in the stockcar.

At nine-thirty the following day, the brakeman stopped by the stock car with a pitcher of coffee for the train's three passengers. He indicated the Burlington freight train would leave the station in an hour. The trip to St. Paul, Minnesota, would take the rest of the day. He indicated that if they were lucky, their cars would be transferred to the Northern Pacific line tomorrow and be on their way to Winnipeg. After that, Charles' cars may sit in the Winnipeg yard for up to three days until the Canadian Northern Railroad picks up the flatbed and stock car for the final leg to Saskatoon.

The boys closed the stock car door that morning at ten-forty-five as the train moved forward. The horses needed to settle through the numerous stops to Minneapolis until they became accustomed to traveling by train. The next day the traveler's freight cars sat at the terminal for only two hours before being connected to a Northern Pacific Railroad engine, and they were off again for the two-day trip to Winnipeg.

Their luck ran out In Winnipeg, and they waited four days before the Canadian Northern Railroad line coupled with their cars. Charles and the boys spent the morning practicing their newly acquired horse skills. In the afternoons, Charles spread out his topographical map of the section of Saskatchewan where their homesteads were located, near Cut Knife. Due to Charles' lumberjack days in the foothills west of Portland, Maine, he could find his way in the wilderness. The prairie would need those same skills. With the prairie being so incredibly flat, few landmarks would mark their bearings. The boys were sent off in different directions and asked to meet at the diagonal point of a square half mile, the size of one 160-acre quarter section defining a Canadian homestead. Counting paces in a steady gait, the boys accomplished this task and ended up within waving distance of each other. They successfully made a compass beeline back to Charles. The boys carried a ditty bag identical to Charles's.

Each bag held a spoon, compass, territorial map, matchbox, saltbox, emergency ration (packed in a tin and consisting of smoked beef and bacon, a packet of tea, bouillon capsules, and hardtack), punkie dope (insect repellent), fisherman's knife, nails, tacks, needle and thread, candle stump, razor and piece of a strop, looking glass (mirror), toothbrush and tooth powder, and fishing supplies. A porcelain cup detachable from a ring on the strap. The most essential item, the compass, would provide a sense of direction in the vast prairie. The combined homesteads of Charles and the boys amounted to 480 acres.

On the fifth day, the wait to continue their trip ended. The five-hundred-mile trip to Saskatoon, Saskatchewan, lasted five days due to all the stops, rail car drop-offs, and pickups.

Charles and his sons stepped out of the stock car onto the train station platform in the small town of Saskatoon on a cloudless day, the twelfth of June. They were anxious to unload the wagon from the flatcar and find a hotel room for the night before setting out for their claim in the morning. The blacksmith near the station provided a corral, feed, and water for the horses. The blacksmith led them to a small house on the next block with a 'Hotel' sign attached to two porch posts. Charles knocked on the screen door.

Be right there.

We're looking for a room for the night.

Come in, Come In.

A grey-haired elderly lady with beard stubble came to the door and looked the trio over, addressing Charles.

"Five dollars for the night in advance will get you supper, a room, and breakfast, Saskatoon style. From out of town? From the States, I'd bet. Come in, come in. Rest your bones in the parlor if you wish. How about some tea. Name's Sylvia Winslow."

"That would be delightful, ma'am. Yes, we're from Chicago. Headed to find our homestead near Cut Knife. My name is Charles Martensen, and these are my sons."

"How about that. Hope you make it. Lot of 'em don't and head back."

"We've been studying on it for several years. I'd give us good odds."

"No offense. I like to give newcomers a heads-up. That's all."

Over tea, the boys listened carefully to this woman of the northland, trying to catch speech patterns foreign to their ear. Mrs. Winslow said she knew right off they were Chicagoans. After tea, the travelers put their personals in the allotted bedroom and explored the town. First stop, the saloon up the street. Charles ordered three beers, and they all carried their mugs over to a table.

"Almost there now, boys. We should be in Battleford tomorrow evening and on to Cut Knife the next day by noon. It will be map and compass work to find our corner marker. I want to spend a few days exploring. Get the lay of the land. We'll look for available water, trees, and tillable land. I'm not anticipating too much clearing; rocks, maybe. Hang on, I'm going for another beer."

The boys looked at each other, sensing an opportunity. Lemuel spoke up.

"Dad, we want to explore the town a little more. Can we meet you back in the room?"

"Sure, go ahead. Mrs. Winslow said dinner would be called at six-thirty. Be on time."

The two boys took off down the street, deserted for the most part. They smelled various dinner dishes through the open windows scattered about the town and a restaurant they passed.

That explained the deserted streets. Not much to see in such a small town. A general store and a hardware store; another saloon at the end of the road. The boys headed back to their room via a second street behind the stores on Main Street. Signs pointing toward the small settlements of Riversdale and Nutana tempted the boys' curiosity, but hunger won out as they continued back to the hotel.

They came across a connecting alley and a girl challenging three older boys barring her way out of the lane. The brothers leaned against a rail to watch. The boy in the middle pushed on the girl, who stumbled back two steps, regained her balance, and stood tall in front of the taunting of the middle lad. Lemuel straightened and scuffed his shoe in the dirt.

"Say there, we're new to this territory. What kind of game involves pushing girls around? Never heard of such a thing."

The tallest boy elbowed the dark-haired boy.

"My friends and I like to have a little fun with Nikki here, is all. Don't pay us no mind."

"If the young lady wishes to continue with us, we'll give **you** no, never mind."

The third pimpled boy in the plaid shirt stepped before the girl.

"Say, you might want to run along without her. We don't take to strangers interfering with our business. It could get dangerous for you. Where are you two from? Never seen you in town before."

"That's right. My brother and I are from Chicago, USA. We're on our way to the Cut Knife region. We like to have as much fun as the next fella, but this doesn't look like a game she wants to play."

The dark-haired boy looked reluctant, less anxious than his friends to scrap.

"Billy, these two are Chicago Irish, I bet. I heard about them. Mean street fighters. Maybe we should let the girl go with them."

The brothers laughed.

"That's funny," the boy said, "Cause we're not Irish. You're right about 'em, though. I'll tell ya that Irish fellas are good and mean in a fight. We've been in a couple of scrapes with the like, huh, Lemuel.

"True enough, little brother."

The tall boy would not let it go.

"There are three of us, though, and that limp don't seem to help your brother."

Lemuel approached the girl pusher. His brother grabbed his left arm and held him back, stepping around to face Lemuel in between Lemuel and Girl Pusher.

"Maybe he's right, Lemuel," The boy began to turn toward Girl Pusher, "With this bum leg of mine, I probably,,," dropping his hand from Lemuel's arm, he made a tight fist, his thumb curled tightly against his palm as Charles had taught the boys. Combining the momentum of his turn with the whip of his throwing arm, he tagged the boy on the left side of his jaw, sending him back and down. The girl deftly stepped back and out of the way as Girl Pusher sprawled in the dirt, dazed.

"Now it's two for two, Lemuel. Shall we see if they have a bit of the Irish in 'em?"

Lemuel smiled at his younger brother and toed the boy on the ground. "You two pick up your friend and move along. That's right, get going."

Lemuel turned to the girl.

"Which way are you heading, miss?

The three boys regained their bravado when the two groups were a block apart.

"Injun lovers," Billy yelled at the brothers, "Your father must have fucked a squaw. You wait, you motherfuckers. You're done for."

Lemuel turned back a step toward the other boys, but the girl took his arm and pulled him back.

The two brothers looked at the girl with renewed interest. She wore a skirt down to her ankles that covered brown scuffed work boots. Her long sleeve blouse puffed at the shoulders, the collar embroidered with tiny colorful beads. Her long hair, smooth, like silk, and midnight black, scattered over her shoulders. The girl's face had been hidden from the boys in the shadow of the building in the alley. Now they saw the color of her skin, a deep sunburn, but it did not look sore or seem to hurt the girl. It looked as natural as the sun and the sky on the frontier. Her walk defined her. She was not the prettiest girl the boy had seen, but she walked tall with her chin straight, proud.

"What' s your name? Are you an Indian?"

Lemuel grimaced.

"I apologize for my brother; we've never met an Indian before." The girl stared right back at Lemuel, chin up.

"That's OK. Lemuel, right? My father would say you and your brother have deep honor. My name is Nichina Starblanket. My friends call me Nikki. I am a Sweetgrass Cree. My family lives in Nutana. My father sets type for the newspaper there. I ran an errand for him, then Billy, Joe, and that other boy I never met before stopped me."

"Yes, I'm sorry if I sounded rude," The boy said, "Will those boys bother you again tomorrow?"

"No, but I must live with their ignorance."

Nichina reached into her left sleeve and produced a small, thin-bladed knife.

"I'm not too worried that they'll bother me again. I could tell the story of the two non-Irish from Chicago that showed them as fools. My father's boss will speak to their fathers. Ignorance is not so tolerated here in Saskatoon these days.

"This bridge will take me home. It's only a couple of blocks now. I appreciate your friendship. Someday I will visit you in Cut Knife."

The boy shook Nichina's hand.

"I'm pleased we met you, Miss Starblanket."

Lemuel also shook the girl's hand and did not soon let go.

"Yes, incredibly pleased to have met you, Nichina. Good evening."

"Goodbye," said Nichina, waving, "and good luck in Cut Knife."

Over dinner, Father asked if they saw anything interesting on their walk. Lemuel explained.

"We met an Indian girl, Dad, Nichina Starblanket. How do you like that name?"

Mrs. Winslow became distraught.

"Did she cause trouble? They rarely come off their reservation. The Sweetgrass Cree reservation is over by Battleford."

Lemuel straightened out Mrs. Winslow.

"Her father works at the newspaper, so I guess she doesn't live on the reservation."

Lemuel caught his brother's eye, and they dropped the conversation from the dinner table. Lemuel filled Father in after they retired to their room.

"Little brother decked the biggest one. The three of them decided to stop teasing the girl."

Charles looked at the boy, inwardly proud. The boy thought of Nichina's proud stance when confronting the boys.

"I bet she could hold her own if pressed to the limit, Dad. Why did Mrs. Winslow assume Nikki made trouble?"

"Son, it's only been twenty years since the Battle of Cut Knife. Leftover bad feelings on both sides, I am sure. Eight soldiers and five or six Indians died in the skirmish, but there would have been many more deaths if Chief Poundmaker had not let the soldiers retreat.

"But Nikki thought many people were getting over the uprising."

Charles thought for a minute before answering.

"Nichina said she lives with ignorance. It sounds like Mrs. Winslow is another example.

"Let us get to bed. I want the wagon hitched and out of the stables at dawn."

On the way to Battleford, the boys hopped down from the buckboard, fanned out, and hunted for wheel ruts, attempting to follow the two-track. Charles pushed on in the twilight that evening, and the wagon rolled up to the little red brick building of the Land Registry Office long after the office closed. The travelers pitched their tent behind the small red brick building and tied the horses to a tree, allowing them room to roam and graze. Then they bedded down themselves without supper.

Charles met with the officer working the desk at the LRO. He brought his maps and documents defining the quarter sections they sought. An inked stamp on the one-quarter section gave Charles' name as a homesteader, and the brothers' names appeared on their own quarter sections. Four hundred and eighty acres in total. The gentleman indicated on the map the location of the survey monument in Cut Knife. He helped Charles draw a crude map with directions from the Cut Knife monument to the township and range defining the family's homestead tracts.

Battleford offered a saloon that served breakfast. Charles and the boys ordered twelve-ounce steaks and four eggs each. Father told the boys breakfast might be the last meal provided by others for a long time. They set off due west by compass to find Cut Knife.

They spotted the Cut Knife settlement among the rolling hills and aspens on the horizon by eleven o'clock. There were only four buildings grouped together. To greet them, a shiny topped bald man wearing an apron scooted out of the building, 'Cut Knife General Store.'

"How do folks, welcome. My name's Henry Trumbull. If you need supplies, I got 'em, or I'll get 'em."

"Pleased to meet you, Henry; my name is Charles Martensen. I'm sure my boys and I are starting off well-stocked, but soon we will be back to restock. Looking for your survey marker, Mr. Trumbull. Can you steer us?"

"You can spit on it over there, Mr. Martensen."

"Then we're anxious to find our way, and thank you for your hospitality."

"Welcome, again, you're the third homesteader this spring. I believe you have beaten the rush."

"That's the plan, Mr. Trumbull, that's the plan."

Charles dug into his ditty bag for his compass and directed his boys to dig out the rope line measure from the wagon. They grouped around the monument, each with a compass in hand. Lemuel walked due south until the four hundred forty feet long rope stretched taut between the brothers. Mr. Trumbull watched as Charles drove the wagon to meet Lemuel, and his brother caught up, winding the line. Then the boy walked past Lemuel the entire length of the rope, observing his compass. The brothers hopscotched south in this way twelve rope lengths or one mile. The boys drove a five-foot stake into the ground and then searched in widening circles from the stake center point, hoping to locate the Dominion Land Survey marker in the tall prairie grass. After fifteen minutes of searching, Lemuel spotted an iron survey marker. The boys climbed up and sat on either side of Charles on the buckboard. The younger boy uncorked the water bottle, took a healthy swig, and passed the bottle to Charles, who took a drink and passed the bottle to Lemuel. Charles clasped each boy with a hand on their shoulder and pulled the three of them close. They had found a stake. Their simple surveying system worked.

The three partners stood in the buckboard and briefly surveyed the land. Cut Knife in the hills behind them, the land flattening out in the distance ahead of them, areas of trees and lower rises to the west. Charles had spotted deer on a distant hill while they traveled, and now Lemuel spied a fox slithering through the grass fifty yards left of the wagon. Prairie chickens were numerous. The boys thought they might kick one as they walked the prairie. The boys hopped down, and Charles indicated they would continue for another mile due south, hopefully finding the next survey marker another mile away.

At six-thirty, the younger brother found the second-mile stake. The three set up camp near a group of trees. Charles went off with his Winchester 1900. The boys heard three shots while gathering firewood, clearing the prairie grass, and digging the fire pit. Charles returned with three prairie chickens that needed cleaning. They spitted the fowl over the coals of the fire. Potatoes were boiled; dinner was served. A small pond provided the water for their pot and the cleanup.

The prairie offered everything needed within easy reach. The temperature at night dropped into the forties, but the sun warmed into the sixties by noon each day. Charles brought out three of his precious cigars that night to smoke up the tent and drive away the mosquitos until they could fall asleep.

The stars on this cloudless night were unimaginable to Charles' city-slicker sons. A sliver moon hugged the horizon, and Charles spent an hour pointing out constellations, passing on their great grandfather's north star navigational lessons.

After breaking camp, the three explorers gathered at the iron marker they had hunted down yesterday. They turned east by the compass and began measuring out four hundred forty feet right through the group of aspens and poplars near their camp. Luckily, Lemuel could walk around the pond to the opposite side and stretch the line tight, but Charles was not satisfied with the accuracy of the line. Charles scrounged the axe out of the wagon and handed it to the boy. The boy cut a path through the small forest so nothing interfered with the measuring rope. The boy returned to the iron survey marker and checked his compass. He signaled Lemuel in the distance to move left until the boy's compass read due east. Charles, satisfied, waved the boy to gather the line and proceed as they had the day before.

The group located the mile marker running east within five minutes and another mile marker forty-five minutes later. Three trails had to be cut through tree groves as they headed east for the third mile: adding an hour to the dwindling day. The next problem involved a hill that the measuring line must overcome. Lemuel judged his east direction and tightened the line on the far side of the rise out of sight of his brother. All three conceded the inaccuracy of the measurement. Charles solved the problem by pinching the line at the top of the hill and letting the boy direct him right and left until he resolved to the east. Then Charles turned toward his eldest son and repeated the process, referring Lemuel right or left to true up the line. The signs at the fourth, fifth, and sixth-mile markers only took fifteen minutes each to locate.

Charles gathered the boys around the survey map.

"Boys, we're now standing at the southwest corner of Lemuel's quarter section. Our three-quarter sections meet one-half mile north and another half mile east of this marker. Then we'll be at the center of our homesteads. We'll add that fourth quarter section either through homesteading or purchase sometime soon; if the farm produces as I expect."

Excitement could hardly be contained between the three explorers. Charles took a moment to calm the boys down.

"To fulfill the requirements of the Canadian homestead act, we need to build homes, one on each of the one-hundred-sixty-acre quarter sections we've been allotted. In addition, we must farm at least ten acres on each quarter section within three years, or we lose the rights to the homesteads."

"We won't lose… Ten acres, you say, father?" The boy began to question his own enthusiasm." Charles nodded.

"Now it makes sense to me to build our structures close to the center of the three parcels. That way, we'll all be close enough to lend a hand, help in an emergency, or be neighborly. What do you think of that idea?"

The younger boy agreed but wondered about Lemuel and his dream to play professional baseball. At least for the moment, Lemuel agreed with the strategy.

"Of course," Charles said, "We need to see what the land offers us at that juncture. We should be fine if it's anything like the lay of the land we've seen so far. Let's go see."

Charles cautioned the boys to be accurate with their compass readings as they walked off six lengths with the measuring line. They, of course, found no survey marker when they reached the half-mile corner, so Charles drove a permanent stake deep into the ground. Then he affixed a wooden sign to the stake, which he had prepared back in Chicago, that said:

Homesteads of Charles Martensen

And Sons
Welcome, Friend!

The three homesteaders continued toward the northern mile marker of the boy's quarter section. They met the creek again and were obliged to cut a trail through another group of trees. Beyond, the stream emptied into a lake too significant to be spanned by their measuring line. They unwound twine from their stores in the wagon, attached sealed glass bottles to the measuring line and fishing bobbins to the attached cord, and floated the extended contraption across to the other side of the lake. When it hung up on weeds at the side of the lake, the boy stripped down and swam the twine off the obstruction so that Charles and Lemuel could pull it tight and push a stake in the bank on the far side of the lake.

Now they turned the horses east again. The boys carefully measured six-line lengths to an unassuming point where they staked the division between the boys' and Charles's quarter sections. They found the northeast corner Dominion Land monument stake at still another half mile east. Charles placed another stake a half mile south before turning west for a half mile, reaching the center of their homesteads, where Charles drove another permanent stake. They set up camp near the stake and opted for beans and jerky for dinner. The brothers found a running creek heading northwest in a ravine bordered by prairie grass on one side and scrub bushes on the other stretching to the horizon.

On the morrow, Charles and the boys postponed their property exploration. Instead, they continued their survey of all the corners of the homesteads, placing demarcation stakes with signs attached. The group headed due south again for one-half miles across short prairie grass, pounding a stake and sign at the southeast corner of Lemuel's quarter section before heading west. They continued with their survey and, at the half-mile point, searched and found the section stake where they had begun their property survey the day before.

Charles took a northeast compass reading, and the three meandered back to their base camp, noting some of the features of the land on one of their maps. For the next three days, each explorer (compasses and maps in hand) wandered their individual parcels, recording creeks, lowlands, and significant hills and tree groupings. On the evening of the third day, the boys pleaded for another two days of exploration. Charles agreed.

At noon the next day, the boy sat down among clover, resting his back against a tree overlooking the lake on the northernmost border of his quarter section. Turning to an empty page in his journal, he sketched the lake on the map. Many of his friends and adults in his Chicago neighborhood had expressed either concern or incredulity over his family's homesteading ambitions. Some had called him crazy to even think of leaving the city. To a person, they knew all about the prairie they had never seen. Flat. Flat and boring. Cold. It's Cold all the time. He would be lonely. He would freeze. Where would he find a girlfriend? Where would he play baseball? How would he live without electricity? A final question always ended the conversation: "What about your leg?"

As he had heard the doubts and questions, it had only strengthened his resolve to put his leg back into shape and support his 'crazy' family. All those comments and questions seemed so trivial to the boy now. Over two thousand five hundred miles away from those naysayers in Chicago. He felt alive and warm, chewing on jerky, at peace. Today small, billowed clouds drifted east. The blue of the sky between the puffs appeared delicate. Everything looked soft. Little red berry dots sprinkled among the vast acres of yellow and blue wildflowers blanketed the rolling hills surrounding the boy. They had proven that you could not walk two miles without running into a small lake or stream. Groves of aspen, poplar, and pine trees broke up the landscape, running up rises and down into the valleys. There were no jagged mountains or grand canyons, or giant oak trees. Instead, the boy had found a gentleness of small undulating hills. There were places to escape the sun and, presumably, the wind in the winter. He would get to know his land and could not wait to shape it. On this day, the boy felt solid and proper. He rose and headed back to tell his father how right he was.

Charles, a mile away, imagined wildflowers turning into wheat fields. He estimated that eighty percent of his acreage could be turned into wheat or oats at just fifty cents per bushel and fifty bushels an acre, amounting to at least two thousand five hundred dollars a turn. The boys' farms would be productive as well. Of course, that might be years or decades in the future. He thought back to the long walk out of Portland to the McMaster horse ranch and how free he felt to escape the city in the valley on the bay. This day, this view seemed the same. The day, the summer, and the years ahead were his to make.

After scouting for the day, Lemuel decided he would not let his father down. Firstborn children rarely do. His quarter section had a satisfying mix of hills and tillable fields. The law stated that three years occupied made it his legally owned land. He could do that much for his father. When he turned twenty-two, the Cubs' tryout age, he would ensure his quarter section was prosperous and in top shape. He must lay out a diamond and a pitching mound for practice. There would be no time for that this summer, but his brother would help and keep him in shape next year. When he and the land were ready, he would deed it to John or Paul, who could pay him yearly installments until he made it in baseball. His father had dreams. His brother just wanted a place in the world. In this silent land, Lemuel heard the crowd yelling at the crack of a bat against a hard ball. On the horizon, he saw the runner he would throw out at first, the first flip of the ball in a thrilling triple play; the shut-out sullenness of the other team when he pitched the distance. Baseball was in his future, so hard work stretched before him without bitterness. As his father often said, "Work is work."

Standing over the campfire that night, the two brothers and Charles reviewed their day and shared their maps.

"We've seen the beauty and charm of the land, and surely more discoveries may be made."

The brothers nodded in agreement. Charles, looking up, saw no stars.

"I think we've seen enough to start making the important decisions about building locations and then getting to work on them. It does not seem possible that it is already July. Four months of decent weather left, I reckon. What do you think? Got any ideas?"

"I have a site in mind to show you tomorrow, Dad."

"Yep, me too, and I saw where little brother staked, and I'd be real close by."

Charles smiled.

"Good! If the rain holds off, we should be digging by tomorrow afternoon."

The rain did not hold off. Horizontal rain mashed the tent, and gusting winds flapped the canvas most of the night. The boy lay waiting for the whole camp to blow away and imagined being out in the lightning, gathering tins, clothes, and horses lost in the storm. The storm had passed when he awoke in the morning, but the camp did need repairing, and things laid out to dry. Charles, believing the prevailing winds in Saskatchewan blew down from the northwest mountains in Alberta, thanked the storm for reinforcing his perception.

Clouds moved west to east nine days out of ten. In the afternoon, all three homesteaders gathered at the site where the boy had roughly staked. The trio moved the site east off the rise, down the gentle slope, protected in the lee of the hill. That put the building site closer to the stakes Lemuel had driven in the hollow of a slight valley. Charles walked from Lemuel's stakes to a triangulated spot on the opposite side of the center stake. He ended on the next hill, two hundred yards from the boy's home site. Then he backed off the rise within the protection of the slope where his younger son had stood.

"Before we go hog wild with squaring foundations, we've got an even more important decision. The location of the well."

The boy wanted to build buildings, something substantial to look at, not just a hole in the ground. He broke in on his father's explanation.

"Do we have time to put in a well this year, Father? Won't that take a month of Sundays? After all, the creek is just south, and a left-field throw to home away."

"It may take that long! Probably will! But the possibility of not finding groundwater near our center stake would mean we would have to move all three sites and start over. I say we try digging three holes in this valley if that's what it takes to find well water and move the whole camp if we don't."

Lemuel drove a stake to mark the well dig near the center homestead stake, even lower in the valley than where Lemuel had staked out his foundation and approximately half the distance down the valley to the creek. They would need lots of rocks, and the gravelly north bank of the lake the boy had sketched on his map would provide them. They hitched the horses to the wagon and steered toward the lake a half mile away. Charles kicked in the gravel and soon pulled an adequate rock for their purpose. By dinner time, they had piled twenty-two rocks into the wagon. They headed back to camp, Charles describing the operation on the way.

"Now, when we start digging, we'll thin out the grove of small poplars by the lake and use them to vertically reinforce the sides of the well. The hole will be square, and we'll support the sides with additional horizontal trunks. That will get us down twelve feet. If we must, we will repeat the process for another twelve feet. If we do not find water by then, we must start over, pull all the wood up, fill the hole, and pick another spot.

When we find water, we must go deeper to prevent draw down by the pump from exhausting what's available."

"What are the rocks for if we're reinforcing with the trees?" the boy asked."

"Ah, that's where it gets tricky. The tree trunks are temporary. Once we've gone deep enough, we will start at the bottom and line the whole well with rocks cemented into the walls. We must keep the water in the well bailed out to allow the cement to become set. Then we keep going up the walls with rock till we reach the surface, and then three or four feet further for the wellhead.

So, we must decide how large to make the hole. The bigger, the better for digging. If it is five feet square, maybe two of us can dig shoulder to shoulder, so we must find more rocks to line it. What we saw today may make only one foot of casing for the well.

Let us hope we find water before we reach China." Charles chuckled. The brothers did not laugh.

Digging commenced. Charles shovel cut a circle six feet in diameter. The prairie grass proved to be challenging. The one-foot-deep grassroots were woven together like the shredded wheat the boys had tried at Chicago's World Columbian Exposition. Cutting through the mat proved difficult. The prairie grass would be equally challenging for the homesteader's new plow, specially equipped with a curved steel blade to cut through the stringy roots of the sod. The boys could hear the roots tear as they tried to bury their shovels.

The circle was cleared of sod, and all three men began digging earnestly. Their shovels met dark brown dirt for the first three feet of the dig. By early afternoon, a five-foot-deep pit had been created, and pitching the soil to the surface became more and more difficult. Climbing out of the hole became problematic. The horses and wagon were brought near the well. The dirt from the pit was shoveled in for disposal by the lake. They collected more rocks. While at the lake, Charles demonstrated safe techniques for swinging an axe and felling the trees needed for the temporary well casing. The four-inch diameter poplars grew eighteen to twenty feet tall and arrow straight; perfect. The group found three or four six-inch diameter trees Charles planned to use as a tripod for bucketing dirt from the well.

The diggers spent the second-day building and anchoring the tripod of poplars over the well at an acute offset angle. A block and tackle assembly attached at the tripod's apex could lower the empty dirt holder down along the side of the well. Lemuel emptied an oak box that held groceries and lined it with canvas, turning it into the dirt holder. When pulled back up, the box could be grabbed by the man standing at the edge of the well, dumping the container filled with dirt into the wagon to be hauled away. Charles and the boy chose a couple of the poplars to form rails for a ladder. Rungs were sawn and attached, and the ladder was lowered into the pit. While two men continued to dig and fill the dirt bucket, the third man worked at the surface, emptying the dirt bucket and trimming the caisson poplars. By the end of the day, the crew achieved a depth of eight feet.

That evening in the light of the campfire, Charles worked on a sketch, a poplar framework that would allow the crew to reinforce the sides of the well as they dug deeper, preventing cave-ins. The circular pit would be outfitted with a square frame consisting of four corner posts, five feet apart, and cross pieces tied to both sides of the posts in a square so that the thinner poplars could be slipped between the frameworks. As the dig deepened, the vertical poplar trunks could be shifted downward.

After breakfast, the following morning, another trip to the lake provided more rocks and poplar trees for the vertical corners of the framework. Rocks loaded, trees felled and trimmed, the three returned to the wellhead and buried the four corner posts vertically in the bottom of the dig. Then they connected the columns with the horizontal trunk pieces in a square on the inside radius of the posts. More horizontal pieces were attached to the outside radius of the posts forming a slot. The inside/outside square braces were repeated at the top and middle of the vertical corner posts to hold the smaller diameter, eighteen to twenty-foot-long trimmed poplar trunks. These vertical pieces initially stood above the eight-foot-deep pit by more than ten feet. The vertical trunks on one side of the square framework were trimmed flush with the ground surface, allowing the dirt box to raise and lower into the pit without interference. Another day went by.

Digging recommenced the following day. Charles and Lemuel dug, and the boy hauled up the dirt box and dumped it in the wagon. Intermittently, the boy shifted the vertical poplar trunks as the workers at the bottom of the pit dug the base deeper. The dirt moistened two more feet down, and water puddled at the diggers' feet after an additional foot of digging. The crew had reached the groundwater aquifer, eleven feet below the surface. Charles and Lemuel spooned out two more feet of wet earth and climbed out of the well for a late lunch.

Upon their return to the dig, they found about one foot of standing water covering the bottom of the well. They lowered, dipped, and hauled a clean water bucket back up. The water was cool and refreshing. Wonderful! Lemuel broke out in song with a parody of *The Farmer in the Dell*, changing the word 'Dell' to 'well.' The boy stamped his foot and clapped as Lem and Charles locked elbows and jigged in a circle, all three singing the verse repeatedly. The three calmed, sat down at the hole's edge, legs dangling, and laid back, looking up at a cloudless sky. Charles allowed that the water in the hole signaled good luck for their venture. They would continue the dig until they could go no further from hitting rocks. The brothers had conferred over lunch, and both started down the ladder, leaving Charles stationed at the surface, dumping sludge into the wagon.

"You two have got to be careful down there. Thirteen feet down. Not an easy scramble up if things go south."

"We'll watch it, Dad," Lemuel said.

"OK. It should not be a problem yet, but there may come a time when fresh air may not reach you. Let me know if either of you gets lightheaded. Let me know the minute you hit rock strata or, for that matter, any change in the ground composition."

"We will, Dad; let's go, Lem!

Charles sent the pail down when the boys reached the bottom, knee-deep in water, their boots sinking into the mud. He rapidly pulled up the bucket, dumped the water, and dropped the bucket down again. It took thirty bucket trips to the surface to empty the water from the bottom of the pit. Charles sent the dirt holder down, and the boys dug in the wet soil, filling it only two-thirds full of dirt and mud so as not to be too heavy for the block and tackle man at the top. By evening three and one half more feet of heavy, wet dirt had been excavated. The exhausted boys climbed out of the hole, now nearly seventeen feet deep.

In the morning, all three got dressed in the wet clothes of the day before, still soaked and freezing from the nightly temperature drop. They had brought only one change of clothes each on the trip from Chicago, and those were now to be saved for trips to Cut Knife, Battleford, or Saskatoon for supplies.

The boys danced around the coffee fire warming up. The boy, shivering, queried Charles.

"What's next, Dad. The tops of the wall poplars are even with the surface. The ladder will be below the surface if we keep going."

"Yeah, Dad and the water is six feet deep down there this morning," Lemuel added.

Charles scratched at his beard, at a bit of a loss.

"We keep going until we hit the rock. The deeper we go, the more assurance we'll have that the well won't dry up or draw down too fast for our needs when we start pumping water for the crops. Any suggestions on where to start?"

Lemuel ticked off what needed to be done.

"We must bail water, we have to somehow reinforce the sides of the pit, and we must have a taller ladder."

The boy had been thinking through some possibilities.

"How about we build a second framework inside the first; cut more four-inch poplars and slot them down as we've done so far."

"Yes, little brother," Lemuel said, "We could attach our ladder to one of our first framework corner posts and then use a second ladder to reach the first."

"Good thinking," Charles agreed, "Mother passed a few smarts down to you two. We'll need to pump water out from now on. We'll work on attaching our pitcher pump to a post at the surface. Then we'll join sections of a two-inch steel pipe to the pump and the filter section at the bottom. At the bottom, we'll have to slip our smaller diameter pipe, filter attachment inside the larger tube, and clamp the two together watertight. We'll have to continually remove the tape from the connection, shift the inner pipe into standing water, re-tape, and clamp. The surface man can pump the well dry, dump the sludge we bring up, climb down the second ladder and push down the framework poplar trunks.

The diggers finished the second framework two days later, positioning the additional poplar trunks. They built a second ladder and attached the first ladder to a framework corner post. They readied the pitcher pump, connecting it to a pole at the surface and extending the steel pipe and filter to reach inches above the bottom of the dig. The crew now began to go deeper.

They did not talk much, concentrating on the exhausting, physical work. Every foot down hard fought. Progress slow. The dirt was wet and heavy. Not much room for two to work. The second framework could not be squared as simply as the first, so the vertical four-inch poplars converged as they pushed the posts further down. If the boys rested for five minutes, the top man had to pump out a foot of water. They also had to stop to slide the inner pump pipe further out of its sleeve to draw out the water, so they could work.

In two more days, the crew had dug down another six feet. Each morning, it took two hours to pump the water out of the well and extend the pump pipes. On the third morning, the brothers acknowledged that two people could no longer dig in the three-and-a-half-foot space at the bottom of the well. Each man took a two-hour digging shift before rotating to the dirt container job at the surface. The third man rode horseback to the lake to sort and pile more rocks. After lunch, the rock finder traded positions with one of the diggers. Three more days for another six feet. Total depth: twenty-nine feet.

The digging never got more manageable, but each foot down meant less sludge to dig out. The wall reinforcement poplars were converging as they were being pushed down, making the bottom of the well smaller in diameter.

While Charles was digging during his shift the next day, the dirt turned to coarse gravel, and soon his shovel hit rocks more often than gravel. Charles believed they had hit the strata that might extend to the lake and gravel pit where they gathered stones.

Both boys joined their father at the surface of the well. Charles suggested they were done digging. The brothers looked at each other, laid back in the prairie grass, closed their eyes, and stared heavenward in relief. Charles did not let them rest long.

"I know you are tired, boys. We all are. Exhausted, right? But we have done it, dug that hole thirty-two feet deep, and we found plenty of water."

The boy wanted to celebrate, but Charles would not have that yet.

"Until we build and finish the rock caisson from the bottom up, anything could screw up that hole. Heavy rain, poplars breaking, filter clogging; I don't know what."

The boy sighed, "I don't know, Dad, it seems every day has been more demanding and wetter, and we're spitting more dirt. I guess I must be getting used to it. Each day has brought a new challenge and more complex work, and we've accomplished it."

Lemuel rubbed his dirty hands on a semi-clean area of his pants, "Me too, Dad. The way these clothes are rotting away, we may be working barefoot in our underwear but the hell with it. Let's get started."

Even at the late hour, they removed the bottom two sections of the pipe, including the temporarily taped sleeve, and brought the parts to the surface. Lemuel and the boy sent standard pipe lengths down, and Charles coupled them more permanently to reach about two feet above the bottom of the well. He also attached a much shorter sleeve pipe for the last two feet and then buried the filter at the bottom of the sleeve in the gravel.

During the dinner routine, with a fire to dry their tattered clothes, Charles told of the man he had witnessed being sawed to death at 'Lumber Camp 11.' He ended the story with another admonishment to be careful and *'mind sharp'* in everything they attempted.

Charles punctuated the night's celebration by handing cigars to the boys. The three men perched on makeshift poplar chairs around the campfire, sending smoke puffs curling upward in the windless night. So far from home, the boy imagined pictures overlaying the night sky; memories of his old street, bed, little brother's finger continually up his nose, and mother's hand on the back of his neck, pulling him down for a kiss on his forehead. The sweetness of a rum-soaked cigar, a new experience, a grown-up piece of a new life, brought settling contentment.

After beans and coffee, all three spent the morning at the lake piling the wagon high with rocks found and set aside during the digging. The crew pulled and chewed jerky for lunch as they unloaded the wagon back at the well, adding to the rock piles. They took turns pumping the accumulated water out of the well.

Now they were ready to build the stone well caisson. The boy, positioned at the surface, continually pumped water out of the well to maintain a dry area at the bottom of the well. His brother manned the dirt container, now half full of rocks which he sent to Charles, working at the bottom of the well. Lemuel also mixed the special Portland cement and sent it down in the pail. Charles covered the bottom of the well over the gravel with a layer of rocks smearing Portland cement in all the crevices. The goal was not to make a waterproof membrane at the bottom of the well but rather to have a solid structural base. Not all the gaps were sealed, allowing water to move through the rocks and relieving any possible pressure buildup. Charles laid a second layer of stone and cement. Next, he ringed the base, beginning the wall up the side of the well. With the ring completed, Lemuel descended to the bottom of the initial poplar framework and pulled up on the vertical poplar trunks a few inches above the first rock ring. Then he lowered the dirt container filled with gravel from the lakeshore. Charles packed it in the space behind the rock ring.

As dusk approached, darkness set in at the bottom of the well. Charles had built up five feet of the rock wall. He climbed up to the surface.

"Now it begins, boys. We must keep that caisson dry enough for the cement to cure. That means we must man the pump twenty-four hours a day for at least seven days. We have about fourteen feet before we are above the groundwater table. I'd say two more long days. So, we'll have to keep pumping for at least nine days."

"I'll take the first shift, Father," Lemuel volunteered, "Four-hour shifts?"

"In the middle of the night, you'd never make three hours without dropping off. No, we'll go two hours at a time. Your brother will bring you a dinner plate, Lem."

"We can do it, Dad," the boy said. "I'll take the second shift."

"The other thing I'm worried about is running out of cement before we're beyond the top of the water table. That will slow us down if one of us must get more supplies.

By mid-afternoon the next day, Charles realized the Portland cement would run out before they finished. Weep holes and unfilled cracks between some rocks would keep the water pressure from building up. That Pressure could crumble even the most substantial wall. The gravel behind the wall prevented ninety percent of the sand and dirt from entering the well, acting as a natural filter.

But there it was. Either Lemuel or the boy must travel to Mr. Trumbull's store in Cut Knife for Portland Cement. The boy pulled the short straw and took off with the wagon. Charles told him to buy whatever Trumbull had in stock. Taking a compass reading compared with his map, he plotted a beeline course to Cut Knife. Two hours later, the boy spotted Cut Knife to his left and turned Bessie, Beau, and the buckboard.

When Charles used up the cement in his pail and the rocks he lowered down, he climbed out of the well, mixed some cement, filled the dirt container with stones, and repeated the routine. All the while, Lemuel continued with the pump. So far, no water had pooled at the bottom of the well, although the wall remained moist, the best they could expect. Then the two switched tasks, and Lemuel built rock rings while Charles kept at the pump. The expected time for the boy's return came and went, but the two kept going until dusk.

Mr. Trumbull tried to accommodate, even though he had no Portland Cement. He expected to run to Battleford to replenish his store in about five days. Trumbull's son would return from Edmonton in that time frame to man the store in Mr. Trumbull's absence.

Not good enough. The boy did not hesitate. After the horses were fed and brushed down, he left for Battleford. Again, he used a compass reading to point a straight line to Battleford. He had no time and not much light to look for wagon tracks that marked the trail to the town. In two and one-half hours, dusk turned to night, but a glow to the east meant Battleford straight ahead.

The streets were dead quiet when the boy pulled into town; the squeak of his axle was all he heard. The general store was closed. Tempe's Hardware store was closed. In fact, the only hubbub emanated from the Happy Dollar Saloon, so the boy headed there. A few men at the bar directed the boy to the Grain and Silo warehouse on the edge of town, which opens at 7:00am.

The boy drove his rig to the courtyard next to the silo. He tied and fed the horses, unhitching them from the buckboard. Then he crawled into the back of the wagon, wadded his shirt into a pillow, and pulled over a blanket, falling asleep in minutes.

The horses, hungry for oats, braying, woke the boy, the sun already up. He thought it must be close to nine o'clock in the morning when he walked into the Grain and Silo office to inquire about Portland Cement. With great relief, the clerk led the boy to a corner of the warehouse and several pallets of stacked Portland Cement bags. Father had asked for at least seven sacks, so the boy bought fourteen bags and heaved them into the wagon.

He hustled out of town. With the help of his compass, the boy targeted a direct route to the well and the homestead. Twice he had to bypass larger lakes, circling around, taking another compass reading on the opposite shore. The boy continued, nervous, tired, knowing that if he miscalculated his direction over the thirty miles back to Charles and Lemuel, he would miss the mark and be hopelessly lost. After four hours, he scanned the horizon from left to right, hoping to spot a familiar landmark on their quarter sections.

After another hour of travel, the boy's stomach began to knot, and he contemplated turning back, waiting for night and the glow of Battleford to retrace his route and find his way.

Finally, off a little to the left, he spotted his lake. He could see Poplar stumps and the brightness of the gravel shores. He turned sharply north and giddy-upped when he gained the beach to get to the well fast.

When the boy arrived, Charles sat in a chair he had pulled over to the well while Lemuel worked the handle of the pitcher pump. The rock masons had run out of cement just after one o'clock. The boy began unloading the cement with two more hours of daylight remaining. Charles descended into the well. As the boy lowered the mortar pail, then the dirt container of rocks, he saw that the caisson wall stretched sixteen feet from the bottom of the well. Amazing. The second framework and the second set of poplar trunks had all been removed. Where the rock caisson ended, two short poplar trunks braced into the sides of the well provided a platform for building rock layers. Lemuel mortared two feet of rock rings. The boy hung a lantern low in the well as Lemuel continued laying rock.

At eight-thirty, the top of the caisson wall reached nine feet below the ground surface, possibly a foot above the groundwater seeping into the well. The trio needed to keep water out of the well until the mortar was set, seven days. Two-hour shifts at the pump were therefore continued. After two hours, the worker manning the pump slept four hours until needed for his second nightly two-hour shift at the pump and then four more hours of sleep.

During daylight, the pumping continued in the same two-hours-on, four-hours-off routine. Two men busily laid out the foundations for each cabin when not pumping. Thus, five days went by, and the men, almost bursting with coffee and with bloodshot eyes, began to call the pump *'the devil.'*

The boy would shake Lemuel awake.

"It's your turn to go to the devil."

"Oh, hell," Lemuel would reply.

On the sixth morning, Charles suggested they shorten the steel pipe to its final position, twenty feet from the surface. All three workers assisted in wrenching the pipeline apart at the first joint. Being sure not to let go of the pipe, the three men hauled the rest of it up and out of the well. Next came the careful extraction of all the poplar trunk side wall bracing. Then they pulled the original Poplar framework up and out. Charles readied two twelve-foot pipe sections with the screen/filter at one end. Charles planned to build a two-foot-high platform at the surface of the well. The caisson would continue three feet above the platform to prevent contamination of the well from above. The pitcher pump would be remounted on the cover of the well. The filter would end up eleven feet from the bottom and ten feet below the top of the groundwater table, with plenty of room for drawdown. The brothers went to bed and slept after supper, hoping to get eight hours.

Charles awoke in the middle of the night, carried a lantern over to the well, and lowered it. The well continued filling up with water. Charles predicted it would still fill by the time they woke for breakfast. He returned to bed and went to sleep.

In the morning, Lemuel brewed coffee, and all three sipped from their mugs around the well. Water had risen to about four feet below the top of the rock wall caisson. Only nine more feet of rock caisson needed to be set. By eleven o'clock, three more feet of rock wall had been built. Rocks could now be handed down from the surface, and the men on the surface could shovel dirt and gravel into the cavity behind the stones, speeding the process. Charles slathered mortar thickly between the rocks and layers of each course. The caisson wall no longer needed to be porous. Charles wished the walls to be as strong as the rocks could make them. During the last two feet to the surface, the gravel and dirt could be tamped from above; compacted to prevent future settling.

When the rock caisson reached the surface, Charles drew a circle around the well to outline the platform. Both Lemuel and Charles worked at laying the rest of the rock. The boy kept the rocks coming and mixed mortar when necessary. At six-thirty, the three masons completed the rock wall caisson. Thirty-five feet in total height. Three feet at the bottom, four feet in diameter at the top, and extending three and one-half feet above the ground.

The caisson showed no evidence of the engineering marvels incorporated into its creation. A coarse stone and mortar open-ended cylinder had been integrated with the caisson, ending two feet from the top. The steel pipe would pass through the stone cylinder, and the pump mounted to the top. Charles traced the circumference of the well all the way around with his hand.

"It's beautiful, don't you think, boys? I can't tell you what a feeling I have standing here next to this well and my two oldest sons. I have not told you enough but thank you."

"Shucks, Dad," the boy said, "It doesn't seem like much now! Now that it's done."

Lemuel clapped his brother's back.

"I see what you mean, brother, but I could wait a lifetime to do it again."

Charles rubbed his chin. "I'd like to build a sturdy open-air enclosure over the well. We can use the framework corner posts again and bury them in a seven-foot square. We'll use the smaller poplar trunks to create the roof."

In two days, the structure was complete. Lemuel chinked the poplar roof with Portland cement mortar. The platform formed around the well-caisson using stone and mortar incorporated a step around all the sides. Until the pump mount cured, the boys bucketed water out for drinking. The pump pipe would be lowered in seven days, and the pitcher pump would be attached. A satisfied Charles declared the well complete except for the pump attachment.

"Boys, I don't know about you two, but I could use a steak with eggs, breakfast, and a beer. Let's change out of these rags and head for Battleford. Hell, why stop there. We can push tomorrow to Saskatoon and stay at Mrs. Winslow's hotel for a couple of days."

Lemuel began to take off his shirt.

"Dad, now I'm thinking about that hot water bath she offers. I'm itchy all over."

The boy laughed.

"No kidding, Lem, you have a smelly stink about you. You could stand to jump in the creek more often."

"Great idea, my boy; let's wash up in the creek before getting dressed. When we hit the town, I want us to look clean and tall to tell about the first well dug in Cut Knife country."

The three men doffed their rags and set them on fire. One man after another picked his way barefoot down to the creek and jumped in, splashing himself clean. They all returned to the camp and air-dried while gingerly sitting naked on the poplar chairs. The boys could not wait any longer. They dressed and swept out the wagon and hitched the horses. In the meantime, Charles wrote out a list of groceries and supplies. Lemuel and the boy asked to look over the list. They did not add anything but smiled at each other when Lemuel pointed to the fifth item on the list: more cigars.

They pulled into the blacksmith's corral in Battleford just before five o'clock. The one downtown hotel, a bunkhouse, contained four bunk beds. A blanket hung across one end of the room, and behind the veil, one bunkbed for woman travelers.

The three moved on to the saloon where they had dined when they had first traveled through Battleford, heading west to Cut Knife. They ate a forgettable stew dinner. Salt and warm beer salvaged the meal. The bartender offered a pack of cards, and the three men played rummy and ordered another beer. After Lemuel won three games, they strolled back to the bunkhouse for the night.

The boys were up at dawn. After a morning brushing, the boy retrieved the wagon, hitching up Bessie and Beau, offering each hay and an oat bag. Father, awake and dressed, came over and settled with the blacksmith. Charles and the boy met Lemuel at the saloon for one of those steak and egg breakfasts Charles had promised. The companions were on the road for the twelve-hour trip to Saskatoon by seven-thirty.

For the first two hours, the three rode in silence. Lemuel crawled into the wagon and somehow fell asleep. Lem rolled around in the wagon bed as a wagon wheel bumped over rocks in the road. The boy kept Charles company and took over the reins for the second hour.

When Lemuel woke up, he took the reins for the next two hours. Halfway to Saskatoon, they stopped at a stream to rest and feed the horses and to eat lunch, sandwiches they had purchased at the saloon in Battleford. After a short lay down under a tree, Charles climbed onto the buckboard. The boys chose to walk for a while. The boys rode in the wagon two hours later, and Charles walked.

For the last four hours of the trip, Lemuel and Charles sat on the buckboard bench while the boy knelt in the wagon just behind them. The three travelers each took turns dredging up a childhood story for the amusement of the other two. A song would come to mind between accounts, and the three would sing and repeat the verses until they could no longer stand the repetition. Charles decided he and Julia had blessed the boys with fine singing voices. The sky dome swallowed their voices and laughter. At around seven o'clock, the boy pulled the reins and told Bessie and Beau, "Whoa." Mrs. Winslow sat in her rocking hair on her porch.

"Say, aren't you the family that arrived by train in June? Looking for a room again, right?"

"That's right, Mrs. Winslow. Three nights stay, including tonight, if you have room. We've been going hard at it since you saw us last. We're here for supplies and a break. The boys and I just finished putting a thirty-foot-deep well in the center of our homesteads."

"Step down, boys, and let me look at you. Lemuel, right? Hey, your brother here has shot past you in height this summer, I'd say."

The boys stoked the stove that heated boiler water for bathing. Charles went first, then Lemuel, and finally, the boy. Lemuel's short straw claimed the second bed, so the boy settled on the floor. All three were out in a minute after extinguishing the lantern.

Mrs. Winslow's breakfast included porridge, sausage, scallop potatoes, and cinnamon sweet cake. Charles read The Saskatoon Phoenix from the front page to back, and Mrs. Winslow filled in with some town gossip and world happenings as she hurried between the kitchen and the dining room carrying replenishments. Apparently, incidents in Russia were making politicians nervous, including President Roosevelt. Albert Einstein had written a science paper that no one understood. The boys gravitated to the description Charles read about the Philadelphia A's beating the Boston Red Sox four to two in a twenty-inning game. Lemuel waited for Charles to hand him the paper, so he could reread the whole article. When passed the newspaper, Lemuel noted a small paragraph in the lower right corner. In oversize type, an exhibition baseball game between the Edmonton Legislatures and a volunteer Saskatoon team was scheduled for the next day at two o'clock, weather permitting. Anyone interested in playing should arrive at the field at one o'clock and sign in with Coach Alex Meeks. Lemuel leaned over toward the boy and stabbed the notice. The brothers exchanged glances but did not say anything at the table.

After breakfast, Mrs. Winslow directed the three men to Glock's Haberdashery down the block. The store stocked suits, ties, pants, and dress shoes. Luckily, the store included a section for dungarees and Hudson Bay woolen shirts, coats, and knit wool caps. Long johns, boots, and calf-skin gloves were also available. The homesteaders picked out, tried on, and set aside their choices in a pile on the front counter. The prices were outrageous, but Charles handed over the money. They were a long way from Marshal Field's.

The three spent the rest of the day shopping Charles's list. Charles jotted down prices and attempted to find competitive stores and the best quality. By three o'clock, he sat down with the boys and reviewed the list again. They planned out what the wagon could hold; measured that against their ability to store and protect the supplies at the homestead. Charles crossed off only a couple of items and totaled the prices. Thankfully, the budget still afforded the cigars they had found at the general store.

By five thirty, all items had been purchased, loaded, and tarped in the wagon. That evening, Mrs. Winslow's dinner table held a Blue Willow pot of beef stew and potatoes. When Charles and the brothers sat down for dinner, another gentleman entered from the staircase, and Mrs. Winslow introduced him as Mr. Wickham, a John Deere gang plow salesman. Steam rose from the loaf of fresh bread brought forth by Mrs. Winslow. Mr. Wickham asked to say grace, and the dinner began. Mrs. Winslow spooned portions of the stew, and the diners thought the food delicious. Lemuel compared it to the mulligan stew they had choked down in Battleford. The apple butter on the warm bread was delectable. A small crystal glass of port at each place setting spurred a toast by Charles to the chef and housekeeper, Mrs. Winslow. Charles and Mr. Wickham talked farming shop; Mr. Wickham ruefully acknowledged that the prairie grass plow Charles had purchased in Chicago compared with a similar John Deere model. After dinner, the men excused themselves, and the four walked to the saloon for a beer and cards.

Mr. Wickham suggested Euchre and partnered with Lemuel. Charles and the boy sat across to form the other team. By nine o'clock and two beers each later, Charles, yawning, suggested retiring. The boy agreed; it was his night to sleep on the bed.

Charles went down alone to breakfast in the morning while the brothers begged off. They slept in until ten o'clock, opting for a sandwich and beer at the saloon at noon. The brothers located Charles and Mr. Wickham in the hardware store, discussing corn-planting attachments with the proprietor. Lemuel interrupted the discussion.

"Dad, we'd like to try and find the baseball game I saw advertised in the paper yesterday. It's an exhibition game, and the newspaper indicated the Saskatoon team accepted volunteer players."

"Alright, son. Tread lightly, Lem. You and your brother are strangers here. You shouldn't be disappointed if the bench sees much of your playing time." The boy promised.

"We know, Dad, but it'll be great to see a ball and bat for a change instead of a shovel or a pitchfork."

The proprietor sized up the boys.

"I think they've chalked an area in the field behind Lemke's Saloon on Macdonald Street. Mr. Lemke is sponsoring the game and keeping the crowd supplied with beer. The game is supposed to start at two o'clock."

"Mr. Wickham and I have a couple of stores to visit, but I'll be over later to see if you are lucky enough to play. Remember the last time you wandered the streets of Saskatoon. Stay out of trouble."

"We promise Dad," Famous last words.

The bell above the door of the hardware store dinged as they left,

The brothers arrived at the ball field shortly before one. The bases were indeed chalked. The pitcher's mound looked to Lemuel as the correct distance from home plate and mounded to regulation height. Otherwise, the field left everything to be desired. The prairie had been mowed to nubbins. A fence row had yellow ribbons tied to it in both Left-field and Right-fields so that the outfielders would not kill themselves running into them. The fences met at ninety degrees in the Center field. Both borders were far from home plate, maybe a little shorter distance than the boy remembered as regulation.

The Edmonton Legislatures were uniformed in all-white woolens. The Saskatoon players wore everything from cowboy boots and Stetsons to sweaters and knee pants. The brothers had opted for their worn-out boots, Levi's, and new wool shirts. They stood out, noticeably similar in looks, brothers. They mingled on the outskirts of the group surrounding Mr. Meeks, a take-charge man in his fifties sporting a gray handlebar. So far, eleven men of various ages were shaking hands with Mr. Meeks. He wrote each of their names on his roster. He knew everyone personally except for the brothers.

"Men, thanks for coming out today. The Edmonton team plays these exhibition games to sharpen up for the league series next month. I know I sure enjoy being a part of their success. It's not about us winning. It's about giving them a good respectable game. So, keep your chin up and try your best, regardless of the score. I see we have some players I've never seen before."

As all eyes turned to the brothers. The boy saw Girl Pusher for the first time, looking sour.

"Watch out for those two, Mr. Meeks. That guy is from Chicago, and the other one is 'Trouble.'"

"What about it, you two. What's your story?"

Lemuel: took a step forward.

"We're new to Canada, that's for sure. Working a homestead over near Cut Knife. In town for supplies. All we want to do today is play baseball."

"I'll watch you warm up and maybe put you in in a later inning."

"That would be great, Mr. Meeks," the boy said.

"Can either of you two pitch? Joe, here, can go about three innings before his arm bothers him too much.?"

"Lemuel pitches. I catch."

"We'll see."

Taking the right side of the field, the Saskatoon players tossed the ball around a phantom infield, and Mr. Meeks hit fly balls to outfielders. Lem threw easy pitches to the boy to loosen his arm. They scouted the Legislature's warm-up, impressed with their ability to snap the ball around the bases in double and triple play practice. The brothers also glanced at the rag-tag group of Saskatoon players. Just not much skill there. Joe, the pitcher, warmed up next to Lemuel, and after fifteen minutes, Lemuel decided to test his arm. It had been a long time between games. He signaled his brother and smoked one into the boy's borrowed glove with an audible smack heard above the din in the infield. The Legislator's turned their heads in the boy's direction as he tossed the ball back to Lemuel.

The Saskatoon players were allowed a few minutes of field warm-up and batting practice, and each player took five swings before passing the bat. Joe lobbed strikes that were easy to hit but not much help for facing a real fastball from the Legislators. Lemuel and the boy clobbered their five lobs, and Coach Meeks made a note. Just before two o'clock, Coach called out the roster, and the brothers were bench warmers as expected.

The game began with the Edmonton team scoring three runs before two of their players flied out in a row to left field. Two more runners crossed home plate before the second baseman picked up a grounder and flipped the ball to first for the third out.

The lead-off for Saskatoon, the home team, came up to bat. After the first two batters for Saskatoon struck out, Lemuel pointed at the catcher.

"Are you seeing what I'm seeing?"

"I think so. The pitcher throws almost every pitch low and over the outside corner of the plate. He's not all that fast. He's wild with the curve ball."

"Yeah, and every third pitch he tries is also low but coming straight across the plate."

"Yeah, but our guys either haven't caught on or just can't hit."

"Coach hasn't figured it out yet either. Oh, well, it's fun to watch a semi-pro team up close like this. I don't know. The Fullerton Fury could give them a run for their money."

Three up and three down for the Saskatoon team.

The second inning played out like the first inning. Four more runs for the Legislators and three strikeouts for the Saskatoon players. In the third inning, Joe struck out an Edmonton batter, but he rubbed his elbow after every pitch. Somehow, Saskatoon retired the Edmonton side without giving up another run. Saskatoon had a baserunner off a walk in the bottom of the third inning. This excited the local observers of the game, slapping backs, clinking beer mugs, and shouting "at a boy." For the first time in the history of the Saskatoon/Edmonton games, Saskatoon had a baserunner. Then two batters struck out, and a third hit a pop fly to the first baseman.

Next inning, the first Edmonton batter singled, and the next two batters walked on Joe's wild pitches. With bases loaded, Joe looked over to the sideline rubbing his elbow. Mr. Meeks called time and walked to the mound. Both Joe and Coach shook their heads, Joe earnestly rubbing his elbow. Coach Meeks looked up and down the bench. He walked halfway back.

"Ok, Chicago, here's your chance. You're pitching. I hope you have five innings in you."

Lemuel jumped up and began jogging to the mound. Then he stopped and turned back to Coach Meeks.

"Coach, this is a tight spot. If your catcher lets any of my pitches by him, you'll see at least two more runs come in."

"So, what can we do, put your brother in to catch?"

"I can guarantee he can handle my pitches, sir. He's been catching me for three years."

"Alright, he's in."

Coach Meeks walked back to the Saskatoon bench.

"Hey, Trouble, you're in as catcher. Billy let him borrow a pillow glove. I suppose you know, Trouble, if you let anything by, it's another run scored."

"I'll do my best, sir."

The umpire allowed the brothers to warm up with ten pitches. He said, "Play ball," and the Edmonton batter approached the plate. Testing Lemuel, the batter let the first pitch whistle by; a fastball by Lemuel, a smoking-fast burner. The batter backed away, signaled for time, leaned over, dusted his hands, and looked over at his coach, who shrugged. The batter stepped back to the plate.

The boy called for the curve, a pitch Lemuel had not thrown since the summer of the broken leg. No other Fullerton Fury catcher could snag Lemuel's curve ball in the boy's absence. Lemuel had been restricted to fastballs and change-ups. He smiled and nodded to his brother as if to say, *'Here it comes.'*

A perfect curve came in, sweeping low and outside. The batter swung and missed. Strike two. Lemuel threw to the inside corner for a ball, keeping the batter guessing. Then he came back with his heat. Strike three.

The boy threw the ball to the third baseman, who sent it round-robin to the rest of the infield.

Two more Edmonton batters fared no better. The entire field sat stunned, quiet as the brothers walked to the bench. Mr. Meeks, also silent, grinned with a raised eyebrow, twirling the right wing of his handlebar.

The first Saskatoon batter struck out while Trouble practiced swinging on deck. Time to step to the plate. He had not played all last summer but catching for Lemuel had felt good, and the feel of the bat and the strength in his rock-lifting forearms and his crutch-swinging shoulders helped the butterflies in his stomach. As he looked over at the bench, his smile signaled Lemuel that things would work out fine.

The first pitch crossed the plate on the outside corner, low, just as the boy and Lemuel predicted. The second pitch would be a curve; the boy looked it over and did not swing. A ball. Sure enough, the third pitch dropped low but centered over the plate, the boy connecting with snapping wrists, following through with a broad, level swing. The ball headed straight for center field, with the center fielder giving chase. The line drive kept climbing and dropped ten feet beyond the corner where the left and right field fences met.

The boy jogged the bases, trying desperately to minimize his hitch steps. The crowd poured onto the field as he rounded third, swinging beer mugs wildly, jumping up and down, screaming. The boy continued his jog to the Saskatoon bench and sat down next to Lemuel, who winked at him and squeezed his knee. Nine to one.

Lemuel continued to rule the mound, striking out all three batters in the top of the fifth. Lemuel pulled a hit between the first and second base in the bottom of the inning, but the rest of the Saskatoon batters could not bring him home.

In the sixth inning, Lemuel struck out the first two batters again, but their cleanup batter crushed a ground ball between the shortstop and third baseman for a single. Lemuel turned to the second baseman, indicating the youngster to be ready for the steal. He turned on the windup and threw to first, keeping the runner pinned to the bag. On the next pitch, the runner took off for second base. Lemuel hurled his fastball right by the swinging batter, and the boy stood from his kneel and threw down to the second baseman. He put the ball right down in front of second base with the precision of a Lemuel strike. The Saskatoon second baseman was ready for the catch and the tag-out. The runner bore down, breathing hard from the sprint, enough to distract the second baseman. He glanced at the runner, and the ball hit the side of his glove and squirted beyond second base as the spectators groaned, the runner safe.

Lemuel came over to the second baseman. The sixteen-year-old looked about to cry.

"I'm sorry, Chicago. I should have gotten this guy out. That throw by your brother came at me much faster than I'm used to."

"A damn good throw. Shake it off. We'll get the next one."

"You bet we will. I'll catch the next one for sure."

The next batter popped a foul ball high and behind the plate. The boy, flipping his mask off and running backward, never lost sight of the ball, even in the bright sun, and made the play for the third out.

The boy batted third with two outs in the bottom of the sixth. The pitcher threw outside pitches, and the boy walked to first. The next batter hit into a force at second for out number three, and the Saskatoon team took to the field again. The boy, who found his stride, signaled every pitch in Lem's arsenal to retire the side with three more strikeouts.

The game continued, reduced to a pitcher's duel, and neither team scored. In the bottom of the ninth, a Saskatoon player hit a stand-up double that sent the crowd roaring. The boy approached the plate. With the game handily won, the Legislator's coach signed the pitcher to throw to the boy. Looking over at the bench, coach Meeks indicated bunt, an intelligent strategy to move the runner to third. The boy looked over at Lemuel, not due to be up unless three more Saskatoon players made hits. Lemuel shrugged.

The boy laid down one of his perfect 'bunts of old' along the third baseline. He took off running with a surge of adrenalin, pounding the ground with both old boots, flying past first base, safe. The boy thought beating the throw, his leg carrying him adequately, was almost better than his line drives over the fence. The game ended with two Saskatoon players left on base, nine to one.

The Saskatoon team lined up, standing in front of their bench, and the Edmonton Legislators approached in a moving line to shake the hand of each of the Saskatoon players. The coach of the

Legislatures and the team manager was the last in line. They congratulated Mr. Meeks on a game well played and asked him if they could speak to the brothers. Mr. Meeks encouraged them, so the manager turned to Lemuel.

"That was a hell of a pitching exhibition, Chicago. You have a hell of a spitball. Don't see how your brother could catch 'em. From where I sat, you called all the right pitches at the right time, boy."

The boy squeezed his brother's right arm.

"I had a lot of trouble when I started catching. Lemuel and I practiced every summer day back home."

"What's your story, Lemuel? Who have you played for?"

"We're from the west side of Chicago, sir. I put together a team called the Fullerton Fury in our neighborhood. We're homesteading with our dad over near Cut Knife."

"Fury, Fury, huh, that rings a bell, son. One of our league scouts went down there to watch a city park series and still talks about the two brothers who practically beat a team alone. One of them got busted up sliding into second."

The manager looked down at the boy's leg.

"I guess my running is still not as smooth as I want."

"Hey, you were fast enough; I hardly noticed it. You'll be walking the bases often with the way you can hit the ball.

"My scout took the shirt off his back to help that day."

"A scout?" Lemuel asked.

"Yes, Lemuel. Small world, right? As I recall, you impressed 'ole Clarence with how you handled the crowd, the other team, and your brother's leg as much as your pitching.

"We'll be moving on, but I hope you'll give us consideration when you are of age. You, too, 'Trouble,' you two are a hell of a combination punch.

"Thank you, sir, you have made my day. We both had fun today. Felt a little like back home."

"You make this place your home, son. Canada is a fine place to call home."

"Sounds wonderful when you say it that way, mister."

The Saskatoon players and Mr. Meeks had heard a little of the conversation, and now they gathered around the brothers. Most spectators had left the field and headed for Lemke's saloon. Charles and Mr. Wickham approached. Mr. Wickham shook Lemuel's hand.

"Great game, fellas. Lemuel, you were equal to that pro pitcher on the other team."

"Thanks, Mr. Wickham. Did you get here to see little brother hit it over the fence?"

Charles put an arm around the boy.

"We did, son. Saw that run to first base, too."

Mr. Meeks raised his voice to get the teams' attention.

"Hey, everyone. You can join me at Lemke's for a beer at the house. Nine to one. Hell, a win for me. I'm proud of you, boys. I can't wait for next year."

A great day for the brothers; even 'Girl Pusher' vied for their attention, eager to move past the incident with Nichina. Lemuel and the boy ignored him as much as possible. The three drank one beer at the bar, and then the brothers left with Mr. Wickham for the hotel and a last home-cooked meal by Mrs. Winslow. Charles settled with her before the three went up to bed. They also said their goodbyes to Mr. Wickham, indicating they would be up way before dawn to try to make it to Cut Knife in one long day.

While passing through the hotel's front door, the well-diggers grabbed a pile of sandwiches and six jerky sticks that Mrs. Winslow had left on a nearby table. They walked to the corral, hitched Bessie and Beau to the buckboard by lantern light, and left town. The clomp of their horses' hooves was the only sound echoing off the storefronts. Fifteen long, slow hours later, the three crawled into their homestead tent. They stripped to their underwear and flopped onto their bedrolls, lined up like three sardines in a can. They were soon asleep as the rain began to spatter the canvas.

Waves of rain showered the prairie grass outside the opening in the tent. The brothers did not stir until eleven, and Charles let the day pass in respite. The rain continued until late that night. The next day as the sun dried out the tent, the equipment, and all the supplies brought back from Saskatoon, work commenced mounting the pitcher pump to the stone base. Lemuel and the boy lowered each section of the pump pipe into the well, threading the ends and wrenching each section to the next. The brothers attached the pump pipe assembly to the pump, primed the pump, and brought forth the first sweet water from the finished well. Charles fashioned a heavy iron screen, attaching it to the circumference of the well so that dropped buckets or small children would be safe from falling in.

The confab over lunch mapped out the next project; the first cabin. Charles had brought a sod plow from Chicago and flat shovels for stripping sod bricks. He had also brought felling axes, wedges, chip axes, saws, and planers. Any acreage they plowed to pry up sod bricks would be ready for tilling and planting cash crops next spring. Charles had experience building log cabins in the Maine lumber camps. Traveling back on a direct route from Battleford, the boy had pointed out the forest he had skirted during his own trip back to Battleford with the Portland cement, four miles from their building layouts. There were plenty of right-sized logs available there. The sod bricks would be steps away from the building sites.

The group examined the calendar. Now the third week in July, they considered how long the first cabin would take to build, one or two months? Sod or Log? It would take about the same amount of time either way. They had the manpower and horsepower to set the higher logs on the wall and the roof beams. Charles had investigated sod structures enough to know they were good at insulating from the cold winters. The sod bricks might turn to mud in the spring and slither away. Logs were more permanent.

Charles hoped they could complete the three required homestead structures with hustle and grit before returning to Chicago for the winter.

It came down to Charles' needing the feeling of permanence log structures would provide. As in the decision to build a trustworthy well, Charles did not want quick; he wanted solid. The boys approved. It was beyond their comprehension that their mother might have to live in a mud house. Charles emphasized that the log cabins would be converted to granaries or stables as soon as the lumber and framing material became available by train to a depot nearer the homestead, and the cost became feasible.

Everything Charles did had been preceded by years of planning, saving, procuring, and keeping his dream alive. He had heard of homesteaders believing that free land assured success. He had spoken to some experienced farmers who gave up, turned back, and abandoned their stakes. There were so many factors to consider. The weather, drought, the winters, the loneliness. He missed Julia with an incomparable ache. Every decision he measured against a need to return to her soon and a requirement to provide a future she would admire with a smile. Charles resolved to show Julia progress worthy of her sacrifice in sharing his dream.

The next day Charles and his sons broke camp. The axes, saws, block and tackle, food stores, tent, bedrolls, and horse tack were packed into the wagon, and the three set off for the forest. The forest contained the typical aspen and poplar trees indigenous to the area, including cedar and jack pine. Cedar would resist the moisture and not rot where it contacted the ground. The group found many six-inch trees and some eight-inch trees stretching up as high as twenty feet. For three weeks, the three men felled trees and stripped branches off. With the help of Bessie or Beau, they dragged the tree trunks to the edge of the forest, ready for transport. The boy built a travois with connections for the horses' harness for both horses. The boys hauled the sixty-four logs back to the building sites for another week. All this was done without accident or incident under Charles's lumbering tutelage, bringing back memories of Charles' days of lumberjacking when he was Lemuel's age.

Charles staked out the cabin on the corner of his quarter section about fifty feet up the rise from the well. The log cabin would not be built at the top but on the hill's east side. The door would face south to catch as much sun as possible when open on warmer winter days. The mound would protect the cabin somewhat from the strong winter winds out of the northwest. The three men broke through the sod and leveled a sixteen-by-twenty-foot base for the house. The twenty-foot west side of the cabin would be backed into the hill three feet. They dug a hole five feet down at one corner. Flat rocks and gravel were tamped, and an upright log was buried and plumbed; the base was well below the frost level to prevent upheaval. They repeated the procedure at the other three corners of the cabin. The cabin builders excavated six inches and leveled the rectangle formed by the corner posts. Then they dug a six-foot by eight-foot rectangle seven feet down, lining the large grave with small diameter cedar trunks driven vertically into the ground around the hole's perimeter. The vertical logs were braced with horizontal poplar branches halfway up the hole. This area would form the root cellar for the family, accessible with a ladder and a trap door on the floor. Then Lemuel and the boy filled the cellar floor and the base of the cabin area with three inches of gravel from the lake. They planned a rough, poplar floor for the interior.

Charles laid out a rock hearth on the northwest corner. Using his caisson wall-building skills, Lemuel began masonry work on the fireplace.

Meanwhile, Charles notched each vertical post at ground level to receive the bottom logs of the cabin. Charles and the boy placed a bottom eight-inch diameter cedar log on the sawhorses, and Charles used the chip axe to flatten one side of the cedar log. He chopped a notch into the ends beyond where they would tie into the vertical posts. These notches would form the fitted connection to the second row of logs. The boy worked at chipping a second log under the watchful observance of Charles. When the first four logs were notched and flattened, Charles and the boy hefted them into place and adjusted the notches until the logs were locked into the vertical posts and each other. Within three days, Lemuel had finished the hearth with ash dump and begun on the firebox. Charles and the boy had flattened, notched, and stacked six logs around the cabin. A doorway had been sawn on the south side and temporarily reinforced.

The night temperature hovered around the forty-degree mark on the first of September. The days were still warm, but Charles feared October would see the end of pleasant weather. He decided to stop construction on his home and start the other two structures. They needed all three in place to satisfy the homestead requirements. Charles wanted to get all three foundations placed before the ground froze. The walls and the roofs could be finished in cold weather.

They moved camp back to the forest. Charles began to push the workday from ten to twelve hours per day. The lumbermen reserved the axe work for daylight hours. In the dwindling light, logs were dragged to the forest edges. The brothers, adept and axe strong, could now fell and trim three trees each per day in keeping with Charles' furious pace. In two weeks, they had one hundred twenty-eight logs ready for hauling back to the homestead. The horses, their most precious resource, worked as hard as the men. The three moved the base camp back to the homestead in ten days.

The schedule called for the foundation of Lemuel's cabin to be tackled next, similarly to the first cabin. The days were getting shorter, the men exhausted, and the nights downright cold. Over coffee before sunrise, Charles asked for suggestions from the brothers that might speed up the construction of the cabins.

"I'm afraid we don't have enough days to finish the work here before the snow flies. I made a promise to your mother to be home before Christmas."

Tired as he appeared, the boy thought of his mother and tried to encourage Charles.

"But, Dad, we're so close. We've come so far. If the family stays in your cabin next year, our cabins can get by without fireplaces."

"That's true, son. Come to think about it, one root cellar should hold enough for us for a great while. That cuts out a lot of digging."

"My thought," offered Lemuel, "is to make the next two cabins smaller, say twelve feet by twelve. It's not like we brothers have wives to worry about. As you say, twelve by twelve should be plenty if these cabins are replaced with frame houses or used for storage."

Now that the boy had begun thinking about his mother, he remembered the rest of the family.

"Hey, Dad, do you think little Paul will remember us after being gone all summer? I miss John as well. I've grown some. Will they recognize us?"

"I'm more worried about George, "Charles said, "He had trouble breathing when we left. He'll be scared to death of us."

"I bet he's OK, Dad. Overall, we're healthier than many families of my friends back in Chicago.

"Boy, won't Mom be surprised with this place, the well, the land. I think our hills and copses are more beautiful than Grampa Swart's farm in Indiana."

Charles whispered. "She'll love it, alright. She's a farm girl at heart." *She has just got to love it!*

All three went about the work that morning in a state of reverie. Sure, they were all proud of the homestead and their progress. But the family, the whole family, would make the place a home.

That night Charles began to light a lantern and hang it on one of the corner posts of his cabin in case a wandering neighbor or new homesteader might need an overnight stay.

By the third week in October, the foundations of the two remaining cabins had been scraped of sod and dug out twelve by twelve. Gravel had been leveled three inches deep on the interiors. Logs had been chipped and locked three feet high in both cabins. Progress on the houses sped along as each man worked on their building routines. Then it began raining.

For every two sunny days, there were three rainy days. Chip axes were slipping instead of biting, inviting dangerous accidents. The logs were slippery when wet, and by midday in the rain, the workers needed a fire to warm their bones and prevent hyperthermia. Exhaustion came faster in the rain shower. They stopped considering cigars at night; sleep became much more critical. The three went to bed tired and woke up bleary-eyed and sore. Charles kept pushing.

The crew focused on the first cabin. All three men worked on building up the walls. They went higher by a foot and one-half above a typical seven-foot ceiling height to accommodate a loft for beds. Charles debated a shed roof versus center pitched. A shed roof would give them more head height for the loft on one side of the cabin, but the tall part of the roof would directly face the wind and form a valley in conjunction with the hill, which would load up with snow. He decided on a mid-peaked roof design.

All three workers set the basic framework of the roof in place with the help of Bessie and Beau and the block and tackle. They laid down leftover poplar trunks from the construction of the well, one right next to another, forming tightly spaced rafters. Over the rafters, Charles tacked down and overlapped tar paper purchased on their Saskatoon trip. They had no shingles, so Charles put down a second layer of two-inch diameter poplar tree trunks to cover the tar paper, spaced six to eight inches apart. These poplars secured at the peak and at the eave along the exact alignment of the rafters did not penetrate the tar paper rows. The gables of the cabin were filled in with two-inch vertical poplar trunks similar to the roof. Charles insisted on keeping the overlay poplars in neat vertical lines.

Snow fell every day but did not accumulate. The temperature hovered at freezing during the day and dropped into the twenties on clear nights. Christmas was two weeks away, and Charles still would not stop. Lemuel built a small fire on the front edge of the hearth, warming up the stones and mortar for laying up the chimney for the fireplace while his brother and Charles turned their attention to Lemuel's cabin, continuing with the walls. In a few days, Lemuel completed the fireplace and chimney: the mortar set.

Charles installed the two small, glass-paned windows packed in paper confetti from Chicago. Julia had demanded and packed curtains for the windows as well. Charles chuckled while the curtains were hung. Curtains out here in the prairie, miles from any possible neighbors. However, all three men appreciated this little touch of Mother.

A tarp draped across the doorway; completed one cabin except for the floor and a permanent exterior door. The boy packed the tent away. He moved the bedding and their possessions into the cabin. The campfire became the cooking fire inside, built and lit in the new fireplace during the day for warmth and clothes drying. The men felt no need to continue the fire at night. Cozy wool blankets on cold nights helped them sleep.

Work rushed forward to finish the other two cabins. The week before Christmas, the poplar roof rafters were placed on Lemuel's house, and the last cabin's walls were completed by Christmas Eve. The trio would not make it home by Christmas, so they decided to finish the roofs on the brothers' cabins. That way, they, too, could be buttoned down, varmint resistant. The crew had papered one-half of Lemuel's roof and overlaid poplar tie-downs on New Year's Eve by the end of the day. The boy built a bonfire pyre at their old campsite to celebrate, lighting it as night approached. Charles passed out cigars and produced a bottle of Yukon Jack, pouring a healthy shot into three coffee mugs.

Perhaps exhaustion, the light-headed euphoria of a long draw on a good cigar, or the sweet honey byte of the liquor; whatever, the red glow heat of the fire coals warmed more than the hands of the three pioneers, at peace inside and out. The Northern Lights, bright waves of shifting colors, flashed across the vastness of the dark sky and kept the boy staring upward. He shut out the earthly horizon, the cabins, and even his brother and father standing at his shoulder. Spiritual and sublime, in the God-awful cold, each breath a steaming overlay against the glorious lights.

The three were about to turn in when a young voice hailed them out in the dark beyond the bonfire, asking permission to approach. Charles had lit the lantern every night for just this possibility, welcoming the traveler to the warmth of the fire. The boys nearly dropped their mugs when they recognized Nichina approaching by the firelight, followed by a tall man, a woman, and a young boy. Lemuel, his brother, and Nichina exchanged 'Hellos' and introductions. Nichina's mother, father, and brother, traveling late, had misjudged the snow depth heading north. They were on their way to the Sweetgrass Reservation, which Charles knew to be due north of the homestead. Charles went off with Mr. Starblanket to help feed the horse and unhitch their travois. Mrs. Starblanket requested permission to set up their camp nearby, and Lemuel suggested the family bed down for the night under the tar-papered half of his cabin. When the two fathers returned, they agreed with Lemuel's suggestion, and the Starblanket family left the bonfire to arrange their night's accommodations. The young boy, named Chogan, sniffled and coughed, reluctant when sent to bed.

In response to the dime novel stereotypes he read about in his youth, Charles discreetly put the Yukon Jack away. When the family returned to the fire, minus the youngster, Charles had a pot of tea ready to offer his first house guests. Mr. and Mrs. Starblanket were led by Charles on a tour of the cabins and the well. Nichina and Lemuel followed.

Mr. Starblanket had taken leave from the newspaper where he worked in Saskatoon to visit his relatives at the reservation. They would arrive at the reservation on the morrow, so they would only be intruding the one night. Charles assured them they could stay if they needed to wait for better weather but that he and the boys would be up early for work. He explained his desperation to return to his family before the snows made travel unrealistic. Goodnights were exchanged, and Charles and Mr. and Mrs. Starblanket retired. The brothers and Nichina stayed by the fire. Nichina and Lemuel sat side by side, and the boy sat a short distance apart, choosing to be more upwind of the smoke. Nichina thanked the brothers again for being so welcoming to her family.

"Some would refuse even the warmth of the bonfire to an Indian family crossing their land."

The boy shrugged.

"That's not us. Our great-grandfather captained a ship that sailed to many countries and experienced many cultures. Dad says a Martensen looks evenly in the eyes of anyone and everyone, not down or up at them, a family trait. Dad has been hoping a neighbor or anyone would stop in one day.

Lemuel stuffed his hands in his jeans pockets. Nervous.

"Did you see how excited he was? Do you come this way often? You are welcome anytime, Nichina."

"Not often, Lemuel, because of father's job, but at least three or four times a year.

"Lemuel, you can call me Nikki. All my friends do."

"You can call me Lem as my little brother does, but I will call you Nichina if you do not mind. It is such a beautiful name! Nichina Starblanket. It fits a pretty girl."

The boy groaned audibly, thinking, *"What is happening here?"* He decided to switch subjects.

"How did you find us, Nikki? It seems like a long shot; one of the only people we know in Saskatoon crossing our path again!"

Nichina turned around to warm her backside with the fire.

"You're one of the first homesteaders in the Cut Knife RM 439. The newspaper reports on the growing population in the area. They have a map in the office with a brass tack in your homestead's general location. It did not take much to talk my dad into heading this way after the story of the ballgame made the paper. My father wanted to meet your father and thank you for stepping in last summer when those boys were teasing me."

"Heck, that explains it. So, what's going on in Saskatoon, Nichina? What do the town folk do in the winter to pass the time?"

"Checkers indoors, and ice skating outdoors. That is what they do. Because of that baseball game with the Edmonton Legislators, you two are legends now. Everyone still talks about 'Chicago' and 'Trouble,' the baseball Yanks. The home run, the pitching. I wish I had watched you pitch, Lem. I knew it had to be you two when I heard about it."

"You'll get another chance next year, Nichina. I'll be ready, and with a little luck and this guy's big bat, we might win that game."

"That would be something alright," Nichina replied.

The banter between Lemuel and Nichina never ended, and the boy's thoughts drifted into working on the roof in the morning. Nichina, not wanting to overstay her welcome, rose to leave. She said goodnight and turned away from the flames while the boy dusted his behind and checked the fire. When he looked up, he saw Lemuel grasp the girl's wrist as she turned to go, holding her back.

"Good night Nichina Starblanket!"

Lemuel gently held the girl's wrist and moved to her, kissing her cheek, surprising Nichina momentarily, and smiling the next. With a hand on each of Lemuel's shoulders, she elevated on tiptoes, pulled Lem down a bit, and kissed him lips to lips.

The boy looked away, toeing the coals of the fire.

The Starblanket family packed and reattached their travois to their horse in the morning, ready to leave. At the same time, the homesteaders readied breakfast for everyone, beans, coffee, and jerky. Mrs. Starblanket brought tortillas to the cabin fire, which were terrific, with the beans wrapped inside. Lemuel asked Mr. Starblanket if he could visit the reservation sometime next year to learn more about growing hay, one of the reservation's best-producing money crops. Both families exchanged Goodbyes along with many thanks. Within half an hour, work on the other half of Lemuel's roof somehow made the previous night's visit seem like a dream.

Nine days later, Lemuel dragged himself out of bed with shortness of breath and a soreness in his limbs unmatched by the general aches of hard work. From then on, Charles worried more each day. Six nights later, Charles heard a restless Lemuel moaning feverishly. At first, during the day, Lemuel had picked himself up and continued work. The morning after that sleepless night, he just could not.

Charles insisted that Lemuel stay in bed and rest. Once outside the cabin, Charles walked over to assess the remaining work on the last cabin's roof. His younger son had begun to grab poplar trunks, leaning them against the cabin wall for hauling up onto the peak. Charles interrupted the boy's task.

"That's it, boy. We'll have to leave off your roof until the spring. We should have left a month ago. You and I will spend today packing the rest of our supplies and equipment into the root cellar or tarped inside the cabin. I want to be ready to leave for Battleford in the morning if Lemuel can travel."

"That's ok, Dad. I can wait to build my cabin. I think we did a hell of a job getting this far."

"That's right, son, one hell of a job."

It took a day and a half to pack up, tie everything down, and load the bedrolls and emergency food supplies into the wagon. The boy disposed of all other foodstuffs far away from the cabins. Charles hitched up the horses, and the three set off for Battleford; Charles glancing back once over his shoulder. They headed north on a white, blinding, snowy day, hoping to pick up the trail between Cut Knife and Battleford. The sun at noon on that day only made it high enough in the sky to view the cabin as they started off. Lemuel laid down in the back of the wagon, and the boy, sitting next to Charles, continually wiped the wet face of his compass to keep them moving in the right direction. Luckily, they crossed recent wagon tracks heading east and southeast. A glimmer of sun on the horizon pierced the snow clouds as they pulled up to the blacksmith's coral. The boy cared for the horses and wagon while Charles aided Lemuel, hobbling to the bunkhouse.

The boy trudged through the snow to the saloon and returned with a soup pot for supper. The next day the temperature dropped into the teens, but the snow ceased, and the sparkle covering the buildings and fields was mesmerizing. The air was dry, and the temperature tolerable with the sun on the boy's back as he returned to the saloon to bring back breakfast for Lemuel.

While the brothers kept to themselves in the bunkhouse, Charles met with Mr. Barker, the blacksmith. The ninety-mile trip south to Saskatoon could not be undertaken by wagon at the time due to a storm that had built up snow on the road too deep for travel. Mr. Barker recommended his brother, Sturgis, who sometimes carried passengers by sleigh to Saskatoon during the winter.

Thinking that Mr. Sturgis Barker may be his only hope for reaching his wife in Chicago, Charles negotiated to board the horses for the winter with the blacksmith. He also rented a corner of Mr. Barker's barn for wagon storage until his return in the spring. Charles stopped off at the bunkhouse to check on the brothers and then walked on to the other side of town and found the address of Sturgis Barker.

Sturgis Barker would be willing to make the two-day trip to Saskatoon for the price of three passengers. He would not risk the journey in twenty-five degrees below zero centigrade temperatures.

For the next two days, Charles trekked to Sturgis Barker's house to see if Sturgis would venture south. He returned to the bunkhouse for checkers and cards with his sons. Lemuel seemed to respond to the warmth of the bunkhouse bed, playing his cards from under his covers. That night a warm front blew into the territory. Sturgis Barker tromped into the bunkhouse at five-thirty in the morning of the next day, stomping off snow and announcing his readiness to travel.

Charles and the boys were ready fifteen minutes later, and the bundled-up group climbed into the sleigh's enclosed coach. Mr. Barker snapped the reins, the horses wheezed steam, and the sleigh lurched forward.

Mr. Barker found his way on the well-defined road even with the snow blanket. The sleigh ride was smooth and whisper quiet. The day was long and cold. Short but frequent stops were made for exercise to ensure circulation and decrease the chances of frostbite. Charles piled blankets on Lemuel, still struggling with his cold/flu/fever. As the night sky overtook the sleigh, the four gathered in front of the sleigh, hopping from foot to foot. Mr. Barker wanted to continue to Saskatoon rather than stop to make camp. Charles and the boys were just as anxious as Sturgis to push on.

Hours after dark, the lights of the town appeared on the horizon, and within another hour, Charles knocked on Mrs. Winslow's boarding hotel front door. Lanterns were lit upstairs and down, and Mrs. Winslow opened the front door and welcomed the group in from the cold. While Charles signed and paid for the night's layover for himself, the brothers, and Mr. Barker, the boy and Sturgis went to the stables with the horses and sleigh.

Mrs. Winslow, always appreciating company, brought out cake and coffee for the travelers, insisting on hearing about the progress on the homestead. Lemuel went to bed; the younger brother would be on the floor again. The three remaining travelers listened to Mrs. Winslow's news and gossip about the town folk. Then she snapped her fingers, went over to the stack of newspapers by the fireplace, and picked an issue for Charles to read to the others.

The article gave credence to previous reports of the railroad expansion north of Saskatoon. Apparently, within the year, the Canadian Northern Railroad would be laying track north to Battleford and then beyond, past Cut Knife, reaching Edmonton, Alberta. Charles grabbed his son's hand with his right hand and pulled Mrs. Winslow up from her chair with his left hand. The three made a circle around the ottoman in the living room, and Charles danced a heel-and-toe jig with the three of them, first to the right, then back to the left.

"Mrs. Winslow, this is the greatest news you could offer. We just spent two and one-half days in travel time getting here. With the railroad passing outside our door, we will surely see profits. I'll be smiling at home to my Julia with this news. Good night Mrs. Winslow."

Mr. Barker cleared his throat. Charles had not forgotten him.

"And here is your bonus, Mr. Barker, for helping us take one day off from our trip home. Thank you again. Come on, son, let us go up and tell Lem."

In the morning, Charles made his way in blinding snow over to the train station and by seven-thirty had sent a telegram to Julia:

Julia Martensen

> 8350 Fullerton Chicago Illinois
> Boarding the CNoR today -(STOP)- Home in three days
> -(STOP)- Lemuel sick but recovering -(STOP)- Love -
> (STOP)- Charles -(STOP)-

The station master helped work out the train schedule and route. Charles had an hour to collect the boys and board the train.

The brothers were in high spirits as the train pulled out of the Saskatoon station. The snowfall was so heavy that the window offered nothing but white. The train stops for the first three hours of the trip displayed nothing but sepia ghost towns. The train pushed on eastward and outran the storm. By late evening, with a transfer in Winnipeg, the three men were on the way to Emerson, Manitoba, near the Canadian/USA border. Emerson offered a bunkhouse a short block from the train station, but Charles and the boys decided to wait the night out on a bench in the station with their satchels. Two other groups of passengers found similar accommodations on seats in various corners of the station. Lemuel's constant cough intruded on everyone's sleep.

The Great Northern Train to St. Paul pulled to the station at 8:00am. By nine o'clock, the conductor repeated "All Aboard" down the line of passenger cars, and the train steamed away; Lemuel seated in front of Charles and his brother.

With stops and a two-hour layover in St. Paul, the train did not start the last leg of the trip until eleven o'clock that night. Lemuel had a restless night of coughing again, finally falling off to a heavy-breathing sleep long after midnight. Charles woke his sons to view the sunrise and the familiar skyline of Chicago, pulling into Grand Central Station at eight fifteen in the morning.

A half-hour out from the station, Charles allowed himself to miss his wife, Julia, for the first time since leaving Chicago. He tried to think of her smell. Charles remembered her delicate, straight-back posture sitting across the aisle on that first train from Indiana so many years ago. The hat he had admired and, thank God, her fantastic bosom. He longed for her now, allowed himself to long for her. Nine months of pushing forward, working on his and Julia's dreams of returning to a farm.

Stepping off the train, passing through the station, and finding the State Street cable car stop, familiar territory to Charles. Only it did not seem familiar anymore. He breathed city air and smelled the city. Almost an ugly choking air. Horseshit plopped randomly on the brick street. Looking up, he remembered the narrow patches of the sky viewed between the buildings. He could not tell what kind of weather the day would bring.

The boy sensed his father's urgency and nervousness. He wanted to sleep in his bed: bounce his brothers on his knee and hug his sister. He wondered what stern words his mother would have for Charles for staying away so much longer than promised.

Lemuel's legs were sore. His chest hurt, and he concentrated on returning to a warm bed and his mother's gentle care. A mother is essential during times of illness. Julia would help him get well. She would know what medicine to offer. Lemuel would get better as soon as Mother could hold his hand and place a cool washcloth on his forehead.

The three men had climbed the first step of the porch when the front door swung wide open, and the rest of the family rushed forward to greet them. Charles herded everyone back into the house, carrying Paul and patting John on the head. Now almost two and a half, George peeked out from behind Julia's skirt. Edith, eleven, would not let go of her father, arms around his waist. Julia and Charles waited patiently while the children captured their father's attention.

Julia's concern over Lemuel's appearance displaced all other thoughts of news or affection, and she ordered everyone into the parlor and marched Lemuel up to bed. She did not return for over half an hour. Upstairs, Julia reassured Lemuel, comforted his distress, assessing his condition. She masked her concern when she returned downstairs to share the traveler's stories. When Julia settled in her rocker in the parlor, Charles quieted the family.

"Son, why don't you describe our survey of the homestead quarter sections, and then I'll relate our progress on the cabins.

The boy needed no further inducement. He proudly launched into a description of the lake, poplar stand, and gravel embankment on his quarter section, providing many of the materials used in the buildings and well. He described the vastness of the sky, the rolling plains, and the wonder of the Northern Lights. He became so excited he forgot to leave out the times the three had enjoyed cigars around the campfire. Edith asked about the bathroom, bathtub, and windows and mirrors installed in the cabin. The boy briefly explained the latrine, bathing in the cold creek, and the absence of mirrors. He added descriptions of the torturous mosquitos, and the sub, subzero temperatures and ended with the loneliness of missing his brothers and sister. It was, he concluded, all and all, still a fantastic experience.

"And, oh yes, Lemuel and I met an Indian girl named Nichina Starblanket, a member of the Sweetgrass Cree nation.

John's eyes widened.

"Did she wear scalps on her belt? Was she red?"

"She looked sunburnt, John, except she wasn't. She did have a knife in a holster that she hid up her sleeve. She is brave and proud, and I think Lemuel likes her." The boy glanced at Mother, but she did not react.

The boy continued, "We met her family on their way to the reservation. They dressed like us, pretty much, and we sat around the campfire and enjoyed the stars. Mr. Starblanket pointed out the Indian names of the constellations, and Dad offered great grandpa's names for them."

The boy thought a moment, then turned to John.

"Nichina had a brother about your age John. Next spring, maybe we'll take a trip over to the reservation of Saskatoon, so you can meet him."

The rest of the afternoon, Charles and the boy reminisced about the trip's adventures as, one by one, the children became more interested in their usual daily activities. In the end, Edith and Julia stayed attentive as Charles described the features of the cabins. Charles, Julia and the boy discussed the plans for their return to Saskatchewan in the spring. There would be sod stripping, wheat, corn planting, work on the boy's cabin roof, and more permanent outhouse facilities.

Charles finished with the news about the Canadian Northern Railroad expansion plans he had read about in Saskatoon. The train tracks would surely pass along their north property line. Loading their cash crops for transport to the great lakes shipping dock in Port Arthur would be simplified.

That night in the privacy of their bedroom, the house quiet except for Lemuel's persistent cough, Charles took Julia in his arms and somewhat awkwardly hugged and kissed her urgently. He feared they had ignored their passions for too long and would be unable to reconnect in Charles' urgency. If anything even more urgent than Charles, Julia stripped off her nightgown, standing before him and tugging at his nightshirt.

Charles caressed Julia's arms as he hesitated for a minute to stamp her again into his memory. Julia, at forty-four, having to care for four children and single-handedly take care of the house, yard, and garden on her own for eight months, appeared in exciting shape. Charles, at forty-six, back to lumberman form, lean and tanned, walked over to his wife. He closed with Julia, covered her breast with his hand, and backed her to the bed. In comfort, they kissed as if they had never been apart. The urgent excitement of new lovers heightened their unfamiliarity, and, in a while, they lay side by side, smiling at each other; the husband, her husband again, and the wife, his wife.

For the next few days, Lemuel continued to improve. His fever subsided, and he coughed less frequently. The following Tuesday, Lemuel woke up again coughing up mucous. By that evening, his fever had returned, and Julia sent for the doctor. Doctor Crandel's examination took half an hour. He marched down the stairs for a conference with Julia and Charles in the parlor. The boy would not hear of dismissal from the room. The doctor set his medical bag down, sitting opposite the three on the settee.

"Julia, your son has developed pneumonia. He has always been a strong boy, and I have no doubt he will recover from this episode. Fluid in his left, yet the right lung sounds like he has fought off the disease on that side. His fever is reading one hundred and two. We must call for an ambulance and take him into the city. I would think he may be there under observation for the next week. At his age, recovery could be a week or two away."

Julia's face drained white, and Charles rubbed his clenched left fist knuckles with his right hand. They agreed.

The ambulance arrived and took Lemuel away.

Julia went with the ambulance and would stay at Lemuel's bedside for the night, all day tomorrow, and the next night as well, at which time his younger brother would watch for two nights, and then, if necessary, Charles would take over.

When the boy turned up at Lemuel's bedside at Children's Memorial, Lemuel lay visible beneath a cloudy tent surrounding and covering his bed. The nurse said it helped Lemuel breathe and kept fresh air blowing inside the tent. The boy pulled up a chair and waited for Lemuel to wake up.

When Lemuel woke, he smiled and thanked his brother for coming.

"Good to see you, little brother. Mother annoyed me with her wrinkled brow. How about some gin rummy?"

The boy played his cards, lost in concern, just like Mother, but he vowed not to let Lemuel know or talk about it. He could tell from the weakness in Lemuel's voice that he suffered. Lemuel would exhaust himself from coughing after each card played through the fold in the tent. Sometimes he would drop off to sleep mid-play. When he stirred again, he would not believe he had been asleep. After an hour and a half of card play, reaching through the tent fold caused Lemuel's chest to tighten, extending his coughing. The boy told Lemuel he had tired of cards and wished to read for a while. Lemuel just smiled and nodded.

That evening after the nurse brought a tray of food for Lemuel, the boy went down to the corner coffee shop for a hamburger. When he returned to Lemuel's floor, he stopped at the nurse's station for a report on Lemuel's condition. The nurse looked up at the boy with quiet concern.

"His temperature is now at one hundred and five. The doctor just examined him. Your parents have advised us that you will receive medical information about your brother. You do realize that his pneumonia has worsened in both lungs. The doctor is concerned about Lemuel's lack of improvement. In the morning, we will hope to see progress."

Lemuel still slept when the boy sat down at his bedside. This seemed a positive sign to the boy; the coughing had stopped, although his breathing sounded like a gargle.

Then, at nine o'clock, Lemuel stirred again.

"Hey, brother, are you sure you don't want to go home? That chair is way too small for your frame."

"Naw, I'm Ok; I just dozed off a little. I'll be fine. You sound better, Lem. How do you feel?"

"I do feel better. Been thinking about the last time I stayed in the hospital, sitting in a chair. Boy, that leg of yours looked bad. Never thought you'd catch for me again."

"Believe me, I thought the same thing, Lem. I can hardly remember how those first steps hurt like hell. Running? Not a chance, I thought. Now we must get you out of this damn place, so you can try out with the Edmonton Legislators."

"You're thinking too small again, brother. The Cubs, that's who's going to,,, I'll be whippin' your butt when we play Montreal's team. You'll play for Edmonton, sure."

"Ah, go back to sleep. The sooner you get better, the sooner I'll leave this chair."

Lem rested, coughed, calmed, stuck his arm out of the tent, and took the boy's hand.

"I have been thinking. Remind me to tell Dad tomorrow how much last summer helped my baseball. Winning is about working through pain and fatigue. He taught us that, in spades, little brother. Good to see Mother again. She's a gem."

Lemuel nodded off again, and the boy fell asleep as well.

The boy woke up sweating and went out of the ward to visit the bathroom, noticing the time on the clock high on the wall in the hall; two thirty. He returned and sat down again. *"You're right again, Lem,"* the boy thought. His frame did not fit in the chair; he was uncomfortable. The chair arms were sticking into his side. As he adjusted in the chair, the boy became aware of a change in the room. For a minute, he could not put his finger on what might be the difference. Then he knew. The gurgling sound of Lemuel's breathing had stopped.

Finally, the boy thought, an improvement. But then he decided the room seemed too quiet. Half a minute went by as the boy listened intently to the tent. He could hear the whirring of the small fan at the base of the bed. The boy listened for another minute. Again, nothing but the sound of the fan.

The boy reached through the tent and shook Lemuel. Then he shook him harder. Then the boy panicked, running out of the ward to the nurse's desk.

"Please come and check on my brother. He seems,,, quiet. Passed out, maybe, from the fever."

The nurse pressed a button on her desk. Ten seconds later, two other nurses appeared. The three nurses and the boy ran to the side of the bed. The head nurse reached through the tent fold, taking the patient's pulse. The second nurse positioned his stethoscope through the tent fold on the other side of the bed and then threw back the tent. The nurses swarmed Lemuel, and one wrapped Lemuel's chest and pumped his arms, trying to resuscitate their patient. The boy kept backing away from the bed, afraid to watch.

A white-robed, white-haired doctor entered the hospital room in another two minutes and used his stethoscope on Lemuel. The doctor turned to the boy.

"I'm sorry, Lemuel has passed."

The boy walked out of the room past the nurse's station and climbed the stairs to the next floor. The hospital consisted of hallways and rooms, hallways and rooms. Some of the doors were open. As he walked by, the boy heard breathing, snoring, moaning, or nothing. He walked each hallway. When it seemed apparent to the nurse at each floor's nursing station that the boy just wandered around on that floor, he would climb the stairs to the next floor and repeat the hallway walk.

He figured the nurses downstairs had called his parents and that they would be arriving soon.

Tired of walking, tired of everything, the boy returned to Lemuel's floor, asking the head nurse if he should or could do anything.

The nurse produced a form she had filled out titled **'Time of Death.'** Lemuel's full name and particulars, address, age, and so forth appeared on the form. The time: three ten, on the twenty-seventh of February 1905. The boy knew that to be the wrong time, but what did it matter. At the bottom of the form, a line next to his name needed his signature as a witness.

The boy took up the pen and signed:

Harry Raymond Martensen

In the next slot, where the form asked about his relationship with the deceased, he wrote 'Brother.'

Harry turned from the nurse's station and focused on the doorway down the hall. He walked casually into Lemuel's hospital room and closed the door. He stood at the side of Lemuel's bed. The tent had been removed. Lemuel's head and shoulders protruded from the tightly tucked, smoothed, clean sheets and a single blanket on the perfectly made-up bed. Harry smoothed the blanket over and over. He thought he should say something. Goodbye, maybe. Or hello! Instead, he stood there for as long as he could. Minutes went by. His older brother did not move. Harry shook Lemuel gently by the shoulder. Nothing. Harry spoke casually, brother to brother.

"Goodbye, brother." Harry said, "You were the best. You're the best."

Harry walked out of the room, down the hall, and downstairs to the lobby. Off the foyer, an inner courtyard accorded access to the outside. Cold rain drizzled outside, but the boy sat on a bench under an eave as rain sprinkled the sidewalk.

Everyone else in Chicago shivered. Not Harry. As if the sweep of Canadian cold could not reach him. Wet, yes, but not frozen.

"How did this work," he thought.

Lemuel had the arm, the ambition, and the ability to strategize and lead. Lemuel had a future; Harry had always been sure of it. The Edmonton manager said as much.

Lemuel had protected him always. Backed him in fights. Took over his route.

"Lem worked both routes for months while his leg...."

"I had the bum leg; he deserved...." The boy tried not to think. *"How did this work?"*

In the end, the cold and wet began to prick Harry's hands.

"How did this work?"

Harry stood up, shoving both hands in his pockets, now the oldest son, turning to head inside to meet his parents.

1907

Reprint from The Nebraska Advertiser:

September 20, 1907 - Nemaha City, Nebraska

WHAT DID FATHER AND HARRY ACCOMPLISH?

An Illinois Man Writes Regarding His Success in Western Canada. Change in Homestead Regulations Makes Entry Easily Accomplished.

"Nothing succeeds like success" is an old and true saying having many applications in Western Canada. The following letter is an illustration. The writer, Mr. Martensen, left Chicago a short time ago. His success may be gained by anyone having pluck and energy by locating on the free homestead lands in Western Canada. A change has recently been made in the Canadian Land Regulations concerning homesteads, which makes it possible for any family member to enter for any other member of the family entitled to a homestead. The only fee required is $10 for each entry.

A man may apply before the local agent for his father, brothers, or sons. A sister, daughter, or mother is also entitled to make an entry.

Read what Mr. Martensen has to say:
Battleford, Sask., Aug. 4, 1907.

Dear Sir:

Thinking a letter from Northwest settlers might interest you, I write a few lines to let you know we are progressing finely and well pleased with our new home.

I wonder about the many hardworking, industrious men East with families struggling for a living, laying up nothing for old age. There are thousands of acres of land here yet to be plowed and cultivated, capable of raising sixty to eighty bushels of oats and thirty to forty bushels of wheat, and it seems a pity the two cannot be brought together. But I will repeat, this country is only for the industrious and thrifty; also, I might add it requires some capital to start.

A man should have at least a team of three good horses; better to have mares to have some Colts coming along each year. It is best to bring them with him, as good workhorses are high. He should be able to purchase a plow, disc and drag, harrow, drill, binder mower, and bay rake. Of course, several taking up claims or buying land near together can divide purchasing the above machinery and exchange work. This plan will work well for a few years or until crops warrant everyone purchasing a complete outfit.

We have 480 acres of good farmland in the famous Cut Knife District. Every foot can be plowed. Last year our oats ran sixty bushels per acre. I sold them for 50 cents per bushel on the place.

The indications for a good crop this year, though we were late seeding due to the late spring. Last winter was the coldest known in this country by the oldest settlers (some who have been here thirty-five years), but with a comfortable house and plenty of firewood, which we hauled four miles, we passed the winter quite pleasantly. The air is clear and dry. On some days I came from work, the thermometer registered forty degrees below zero. Though we never kept the fire at night, nothing froze in our cellar.

Our stock and chickens wintered fine. I have a yearling heifer who would be prized in any "fat stock show." She has never had a drop of milk since turning four months old and has never had a mouthful of grain. A gentleman who saw her remarked, "He bet that heifer had eaten her head off with grain," but would hardly believe she had never had any grain.

This country is excellent for growing various vegetables, and we enjoy our garden. The flavor of the green peas is terrific. Last season, Mrs. M. canned many of them, and we have enjoyed them up to the fresh crop.

I am sorry I did not have time this past season to attend to transplanting trees; I will keep the land I had prepared worked up for next season's planting. I received several small trees (ash and maple) from the Government Experimental Farm at Indian Head. I put them around the garden's edge, and they are fine. I also received many other seeds, oats, wheat, potatoes, and rhubarb roots, which were acceptable.

It is useless to bother with garden flowers, as wild ones grow in profusion. We are located near a fine creek, which is soft and delicate for bathing and washing. We have a well of water near the house, 32 feet deep, and

21 feet of water all the time, though it is harder than the creek water.

Land that could be bought for five dollars per acre three years ago is now worth $14 per acre and advancing yearly!

All kinds of improvements are going on. Steam plows and large threshing outfits are already in. Roads are being graded, and bridges are being built across rivers and creeks. Last year I took my family and a wagon across the Saskatchewan River in a rowboat. I swam my team across, and now the contract has been made for a $200,000 bridge at that place.

The C. N. R. have run their final survey from Battleford to Calgary, running west about one mile north of us. The C. P. R. has run a study that runs northwest and passes about 500 feet from the northeast corner of our farm. The country will soon be covered with a network of railroads, and it will keep them busy hauling grain output. It is encouraging to the settlers.

Two years ago, Harry, my son, and I, as you know, unloaded our car at Saskatoon and drove 130 miles to our claim. Last fall, we had only eighteen miles to haul our wheat to the railroad, and, as you see, the prospects are we will have a railroad at our door and a town nearby. This district can support a good town.

Harry arrived home at 12 pm last night after going fourteen miles to the blacksmith shop to get the plowshares beat out. The shop was so full of work at 8 pm when Harry left for our home that there were still parties in line for welding. We will need stores nearer and good mechanics.

We are all enjoying the best health, which is a great blessing. When we left Chicago over a year ago, my youngest son's (4 years of age) health had been so poor since birth I almost despaired of raising him. He is a hearty, healthy little fellow now. The pure fresh air has done him worlds of good.

So, to sum up: Why should we not be glad we made the break? A good farm, stock increasing, health, and independent life. What more can we expect?

Did we have to try? You can bet we did, and hustle, too. Should you pass this way with your shotgun this fall, we should be pleased to let you shoot prairie chickens off our grain stocks.

Respectfully yours,

Chas. M. Martensen and family

June 6, 1916: Charles Martin Martensen, 57, dismounted Grindle to move a newly found boulder over to the edge of the field. Watching from his mount, John noted his father's struggle, the rock apparently larger below ground than they had assumed. About to dismount, John heard Charles grunt and saw him lift the boulder to his waist. Just as he turned to waddle off the field with his burden, his horse kicked up with both hind legs, landing a neck-cracking blow to the nape of John's father's head. Charles dropped the rock, diving headfirst into the freshly turned earth, a blood fountain forming over the back of his shirt. John swung down, swatting Grindle's rump, sending him off.

With a handkerchief and his left hand, John clamped over the wound and turned Charles over, trying to decide if he could get them both on the horse to find a doctor. Or perhaps he should leave Charles and ride for help. Or maybe ride back to the cabin for Julia, Charles's wife.

Within two minutes, Charles stopped breathing, turning a deadly shade of blue; gone. John stood and ran in panic, stopped, bent over, heaving. Maddened by the quiet. He turned back and saw no movement, stillness. Impossible stillness. John turned, still bent over, dizziness hitting again, his forehead cold even in the sun.

Then John straightened, slowing his breath, and returned to his father. Kneeling, he put one hand on Charles's shoulder. He softly stroked the man's speckled right wrist and vein-bulged right hand, memorizing this last alone time with the best man he would ever know.

Julia, the matriarch of the Martensen family in Saskatchewan, never remarried.

2

Queen ants have one of the most extended lifespans of any known insect – up to 30 years.

1917

National Service

PUBLIC NOTICE is now given under the authority of the "War Measures Act, 1914" that during the first week in January 1917, an inventory will be made by the Post Office Authorities of every male between the ages of sixteen and sixty-five residing in Canada.

National Service Cards and addressed envelopes for their return to Ottawa have been placed in the hands of all Postmasters for distribution amongst all persons required to fill such cards. Every male person of the prescribed ages must fill in and return a card enclosed in an envelope within ten days of receipt.

Any person who fails to receive a card and envelope may obtain the same upon application to the nearest Postmaster.

R. B. BENNETT
Director General
Ottawa, 15th December 1916
GOD SAVE THE KING
NATIONAL SERVICE WEEK: 1st to 7th, JANUARY

The boy froze, listening for Mother's call over the scratches of fluttering wheat heads. Indistinguishable in the golden field, his sun-bleached hair slapping both cheeks in the wind, barely taller than the stalks, the boy heard Mother call a second time. Glancing up at Saskatchewan's bluest August sky covering the homestead fields of oats east and north, wheat west, and corn and garden south, the boy sighted the towering windmill, his guidepost, and emerged from the field like a ghost.

Mother carried pots from the well to the rough plank table in front of the cabin. Today, Flossie Mae was charged with dinner.

"Wash all the potatoes well and hurry so your sister can start peeling. Then run and pick six ears of corn and shuck 'em over by the compost. Then go get six more. Set the table for seven; everyone is coming over."

The boy dunked a potato from the pile into the pot, scrubbing caked dirt with a small brush and cleaning each potato before handing it to Dorothy. He would be four in four months at the end of December. Only a year and a half older, Dorothy handled a knife and skinned each potato, plopping it in a pot of water. The first time the boy washed potatoes, Dorothy whined to Mother when she found an unclean spot.

The substantial meal of the day needed to be on the table at 4:30 pm, the designated time that all the men would come in from the fields for the afternoon break. The boy finished his dinner chores on time and tried to look inconspicuous to avoid further assignments.

Uncle John arrived first, tearing up the drive on the buckboard, dust flying. His young wife Edith was sitting beside him, one hand cupping baby Marjorie resting on top of her pregnant stomach, the other tight on the arm rail.

Uncle George, the youngest at fifteen, except for the boy and Dorothy, came around the barn, stopping at the pump to wash up. His face lined with dirt and sweat, and his gloves mud-caked, he waved to the boy, smiling, proud to be a working farm hand.

Father arrived on the back of Beau, one of his workhorses, careful not to tangle his legs or boots in the straps as he slid down. The boy ran to him and jumped, Father, catching him in solid and callused hands. Father threw the boy high in one continuous arc, grabbed him underneath the arms, swung him between his legs, and then up again for another toss. The two of them continued to the washing trough.

Granny appeared in the cabin doorway, fifty-seven years strong, unbattered by prairie life. She moved forward daily, encouraging her boys to get their fields threshed and their garden's yield harvested. Grandchildren better have chores to tire them for bed. She glanced beyond the barn to the top of the rise where the sun showered a flower garden she weeded daily in remembrance of Charles, buried not far away in Rockhaven Cemetery. Then she set off for her spot at the table.

Raymond, now head of the family, sat at the table end while Flossie Mae, plunking the second tray of chicken down, sat on the bench to his right and brother John and Edith to his left. Then George and Dorothy were next to Edith. The boy sat beside Flossie Mae, his mother, leaving space for Uncle Paul. Across from Father, Granny took her position in the chair she had occupied since arriving at the claim, her jaw twitching into a snarl.

"Harry, where is Paul?"

"Working the back oats field at your place. Call me Raymond, Mother, less confusion with the boy."

"He will miss supper if he is not here on time."

"Paul is eighteen, mother. He needs a little space."

"Charles would have given him space with his belt."

The table grew quiet.

Everyone at the table turned when Paul appeared at the cornfield's edge, walking his horse. He tied up Spar at the trough, setting down a two-foot by one-foot board against the windmill, and shuffled to the table. The boy squeezed over further off the edge of the bench giving his favorite uncle room to swing his legs across. Paul put an arm around the boy's waist and slid him back onto the seat with a tickle.

Julia stared hard at her son as he filled his plate and buttered a piece of bread. Paul only saw the food on the table. Reaching for a potato, Paul grabbed a too-hot piece of corn and slid chicken from the platter onto his plate. The boy hoped Granny would not start in on Paul.

Returning to family conversation, Father reviewed with Uncle John, Uncle Paul, and Uncle George the field progress for the day and the plan for the evening work stretch. Paul had the most to finish for the day and noted he would be late. Irked, Granny clanged her fork hard on the table, but Father ignored the noise from the other end and expressed satisfaction to his brothers with the day's progress. Looking up at the sky to the west, Raymond searched the horizon for weather clues.

"Somethin's movin in, fellas. My leg is singing soprano today. Better try to get as much done today as we can."

"I can't hear anything, Daddy," the boy said.

"Son, I'm the only one who can feel it. Just reminds me my leg's still there, is all. The weather will change, so get to your hoeing."

The boy twisted his pierced mouth, looking down at his plate, sorry he had called attention, remembering the three rows of hoeing in the garden he oversaw.

No one in Cut Knife, Gallivan, Rockhaven, or New Battleford could recall Raymond's uneven gait. Years of plowing, planting, and harvesting had strengthened and straightened his walk and stance.

Raymond was stockier than his brothers and the oldest at thirty-one, although his face looked rounder and softer. Dark blue eyes. Flossie Mae would say the most handsome. Neighbors knew him as a hard worker and a fair gentleman. He assumed the head of the household role when Charles died, not by decree or bluster but in cooperation with his equally-minded brothers. They avoided fights and even squabbles because so much work needed to be accomplished. They all relished the family's progress and reassured each other during the setbacks. Risky business; farming. Sure, they had hard work, a hard life, homesteading, and they had to hustle, but at the end of every day, each brother's stronger muscles and the reflection of another good day on earth rewarded their efforts.

John, though, had his doubts. His farm seemed to struggle the most. Two years ago, seven weeks after the spring planting, torrential rain flooded his fields and ruined his season, his farm lower lying than the others. Water runoff from surrounding farms inevitably ended in his section. John worked with little effect every extra hour on diversionary dams and settlement ponds. The brothers had absorbed the total loss of John's fields and moved on. Last year an early killing frost had settled in the lowlands of John's acreage and taken over half his crops, but the brothers treated the separate quarter-section farms as a co-op. One for all and all that.

After dinner, Paul headed over to the windmill tucking the board he retrieved under his arm, and started off for the oats field, leading Spar. The boy tagged along. The boy tugged at Paul's arm along the path.

"Can I see your board, Uncle Paul?"

"Sure."

Paul stopped and held the board out for the boy to see. The boy recognized a panorama of the oats field with a deer munching wantonly on the down-right side of the board. The chalk and charcoal drawing portrayed a deer ready to leap off the board. The muscles of the deer's shoulders and hips and the position of the legs suggested the deer would be prepared for instant flight. The oats were detailed at the front of the picture and smoothly merged with the horizon in the distance. On the left side of the board, the boy identified the beginnings of a fox.

"Gee, Uncle Paul. Can I have it when you're done? Maybe we could put it on the wall near my loft bed."

"How about I make another board for you, and you can draw your own picture?"

"Ah, I couldn't do it as good as this."

"With practice, you could. When I finish the fox over in this corner, I'll wash the board and use it again."

"Why, Uncle Paul? Why don't you keep it? It's perfect."

"I keep practicing. Someday maybe! You better get back. Didn't I hear Raymond say you had to hoe?"

The boy did not want to hear such talk. He turned and returned where they had come, looking for Dorothy. The boy hoped Dorothy would play hopscotch with him behind the barn. He would tell Daddy he had been so busy he forgot about the hoeing.

Paul continued to Julia's oats field. The stump at the edge of the area in the shade of a grove of trees proved inviting. The artist sat down and chalked in the fox on his board. He told himself that the fox would be taking shape in fifteen minutes, and he would get to the task in the field.

A half-hour later, Paul held the board up and looked first at the fox on the left, then the deer on the right. Then back at the fox. No, the scale of the fox felt out of scale. He looked again at the deer, reasonably good, one of his better drawings. Ten minutes later, Paul had erased the fox entirely from his board, another advantage of working in chalk. An hour later, satisfied with the scale and position of the new fox hiding deep in the oats field, Paul drew some additional plantings over the fox. He now appeared stealthy and hidden from the deer. Satisfied, he leaned the board against the stump and set to work in the oats field. The dark of night spread over the horizon. There was nothing for it. Paul kept working until he finished, exhausted. Then he stumbled over to the stump, picked up his board, and headed for the farmhouse.

During their third game behind the barn, Granny caught Dorothy and the boy as she headed to her flower garden. She inquired about the vegetable garden hoeing both children were charged with twice daily. The boy had three rows to hoe in the morning: and three in the afternoon. Dorothy's assignment consisted of four rows in the morning and four in the afternoon.

Julia would swat the boy when necessary. Today, the necessity arose when the boy tried to tell Granny he had forgotten. Four swift underhand roundhouse swings later, the boy's behind stinging and his eyes watering for telling stories, both children ran off to gather hoes.

Funny thing about chores; when they are half done, they do not seem hard to finish. Of course, the boy used to hoe only two rows morning and afternoon, and now that he could handle three rows, he feared the jump to four.

Julia continued to her garden and her own sprucing of the small plot. She picked a bouquet that would match the curtains in her house. Satisfied, Julia returned to her home and rocker, picked up her knitting, and stitched fifteen more rows on the boy's Christmas sweater in the lantern light before heading to bed. She cherished her quiet time alone in the frame house Charles and the boys had completed in 1910. George and Paul would keep her company overnight in their beds in the loft. Granny never worried about her youngest son and his comings and goings. Responsible as Harry Raymond, George had been four when Charles brought the family north. Granny remembered the times of George's labored breathing back in Chicago when the summer wind died. The low clouds above their bungalow on Fullerton were thick with 'smog,' a word Julia had read in the Chicago Daily News coined that year in London. Paul, though, bedeviled her. Julia prodded Paul, calling him out for his wandering in mind, spirit, and location. She worried, scolded, and cajoled Paul. The more she pushed, the more he pressed back, wandering further afield.

George, always first done with his chores, brought a pail of water from the well to the bathwater boiler on the stove. As soon as the water warmed, he dumped it in the tub on Raymond and Flossie Mae's porch and stepped in, scrubbing dirt from fingernails around his ankles, wrists, and neck. The galvanized tub had just enough length for George to stretch his legs. Julia sometimes teased that cleaning up fast before the water turned cold and your butt froze matched the work of getting dirty in the first place. George liked a clean feeling before bed and rarely missed his every other day bath. In the summer, setting the tub on the porch made it easy to pull the plug and drain the bath water into the grass.

Raymond rode by on his way to the stable. Beau would be fed and rubbed down, the last of Raymond's chores for the evening.

Since Beau had been working the corn field with Raymond all day, Beau's stall would not need attention until morning.

Raymond liked to bathe in the mornings. He would watch the stars fade to sunrise while the bath water turned cold. The crispness of a new day always put Raymond right and in charge of his world; the occasional desperation of a previous day was forgotten. At night he bucketed water at the well into a wash basin and scrubbed up.

Stepping onto the porch on his way into the house, Raymond tipped his hat to his brother George.

"Good work today, George. I checked out the north forty. Good progress."

George raised a hand from the tub and signaled thanks. Without breaking a step, Raymond continued into the house. He called for Flossie Mae as he closed the door. No sense in waking the kids. Flossie came out of the kitchen carrying a cup of tea with a biscuit perched on the saucer.

"The children are asleep, Raymond. Tomorrow, maybe during a break, you can read to them. You have not finished Swiss Family Robinson, have you?"

Raymond sat down at the table.

"Close, but we have a few chapters to go. The book is falling apart. I hope we have all the final pages. Read that book to Paul and George when they were young."

"Speaking of George, you have got to speak to Julia about George's studies. We'll all have to put more into the education budget to make that work. George has his eye on the University of Saskatchewan."

Raymond stood and encircled Flossie Mae's waist from behind.

"I guess so, darlin, but remember, I came up here and homesteaded at his age. No one talked of college! Charles expected help, and I gave it. Gosh darn, he is the best we've got around here. I can't afford to lose him."

She shrugged Raymond away, and he sat back down to his tea.

"He's still got to finish high school over in Moose Jaw. He might change his mind. He's good at farming."

Flossie Mae sat down at the table close to her husband and jabbed a finger into the table.

"He's not changing my mind, Harry Raymond Martensen. This is a different time. The towns and cities are coming up. He'll take his own pick of his future. I'll ensure that Dorothy and the boy have the same opportunities."

"Alright, alright, I'm too tired to argue. I'll speak to Mother sometime tomorrow, and if she agrees, we'll all meet and discuss the education budget."

"I'll hold you to it. Mother will agree; I'll see to it. My children are going to have that same opportunity someday. They'll turn on the lights with a wall switch instead of a match. They'll run water in the kitchen and have heat in every room. They'll have…."

"They'll have the same good life we have. They'll appreciate what they have because they work hard for it."

Raymond carried his dishes into the kitchen, returned, opened a small door in the cupboard above his desk, removed the cigar box, extracted one cigar, replaced the box, and closed the cupboard door. He walked out onto the porch without another word. George had left for Mother's house and bed. Raymond lit that cigar and leaned back on the porch railing, looking to the west to see if clouds were covering the stars near the horizon. Six long draws later, he felt at peace with the world.

Inside, Flossie Mae rested her hands on the sink, watching soap bubbles swirl for a moment, not so sure. Not sure at all that her children would appreciate this life. Committed to her husband but still a Buffington at heart; *would she ever fit in up here?*

Flossie Mae met her husband when he applied for a grain shipping permit in Chicago in 1908.

Raymond, struck dumb by her beauty, sat across from her at her desk in the new Chicago Federal Building at the corner of Dearborn and Jackson. Her hair was curled and cut short, and Flossie had a soft mouth, chin, and jaw. She possessed piercing, challenging eyes. A serious-minded, beautiful girl.

For her part, Flossie looked back at a man with broad shoulders and a massive chest. Clearly, a hardworking man but a little lost with the complicated shipping permits. He looked like a doer, not a paper pusher. His hands were rough but gentle in a handshake. He clearly respected women. His eyes hinted a sadness, perhaps from some hurt in his past. His smile was broad, wholesome, and optimistic. Somehow discovering they were both twenty-one then, he asked her for coffee in the cafe on the ground floor after she finished work.

Raymond courted Flossie Mae the entire winter of '08 to '09. He stayed at his second Cousin Walter's house while he made supply purchases and arranged rail shipment for the next year up to Cut Knife. Perhaps half looking for a companion simultaneously, the limitless skies of Saskatchewan begged to be shared.

Flossie Mae, a working girl, a "woman adrift" as she would be called by some in those years, conducted due diligence on the persistent Canadian farmer. Wary of the life she would lead at the top of the world, Raymond promised his dream would someday provide the amenities she expected. She had sense enough to refuse his hand in marriage that first winter but was smart enough to accept his engagement ring. If a year's separation could sustain their ardor, then two smart people could imagine a future together in the loneliness of the great Saskatchewan plains.

Still, the amenities were slow to come on the homestead. Flossie Mae had two beautiful children with her steadfast husband. Dorothy had been born in Cut Knife, with midwife help from her mother-in-law. The boy came just two years later in the winter of 1913, and Flossie insisted on a Chicago birth and hospital.

There were days when Flossie Mae would walk to the far edge of one of the fields and scream. No one ever heard her because the farm was too vast. The chores were never-ending. The work was oppressive. Her mind yearned for exercise, and her schooling in Chicago went unappreciated, lost to the stars. Raymond is a husband of worth, a gem, and always will be. He never screamed, never lost his way. Always showed his love for her; in most ways, she felt lucky to share her life with such a man as Raymond.

Paul shuffled into view and waved to Raymond before stopping at the stone well caisson to wash up. He paused again before Raymond, noting his day's stopping point in the oats field. Raymond offered a cigar.

"You know where they are!"

"Thanks, Ray, be right back."

Paul went into the house, said hello to Flossie Mae, retrieved one of Raymond's cigars, and returned to the porch, slurping and wetting the cigar. Raymond had moved from the rail to the porch swing next to the bathtub, shifting south to provide more room for the two men to sit on the swing. Raymond handed his cigar to Paul, who used it to light up. Silence prevailed for a while, except for the slow, gentle creak of the swing as Paul worked up his cigar ash. Relaxed and quiet, Raymond wished to continue his reverie, looking out above the barn at the stars. Paul, never one to worry what the morrow would bring, the contemplative silence on the swing satisfied both brothers.

Raymond, twelve years older than Paul, could not explain his kinship for this brother. Perhaps Paul, the dreamer, whose sweat and work-a-day farm contributions never seemed to cloud the wanderlust in his head, reminded him of Lemuel throwing pitches to Raymond in practice. While Lemuel threw, he gave a running commentary of each pitch as if he were the Cubs pitcher scheduled to start the game that day. Lemuel had dreams of a future beyond the homestead. So too, has Paul.

Raymond, a respected community leader in Gallivan and Rockford, hoped for a good crop year, a positive rather than a negative one. He wanted his son and daughter to know the stars and the constellations as he did. He tried to push ahead for Flossie Mae's sake. The church still met at his house until the committee began construction in town. He had helped with the school and the first grain silos near the railroad. Raymond reluctantly led his family and friends. He stepped up; the only way he knew, as always, was garnering respect. Raymond leaned forward, feet stopping the swing.

"Still miss Dad, do ya?" Raymond asked, aching for Lemuel.

"Yup, a year ago; hard to believe, even now."

"Still thinking of Paris. For drawing?"

"Someday, maybe. Don't know about getting mixed up in the war, though. Mom sure wouldn't take too kindly to that."

"You do what you got to do. I'll never curse you for it, Paul."

"I know, Ray, but thanks for sayin' it. I'm off to bed.

After Raymond had fed, watered, and milked the cow; he brought water in for the bathwater boiler and heated it on the stove.

The August temperature had not dropped five degrees during the night. Yet, the water in the porch bathtub invigorated him. Still dark out, Flossie Mae stepped naked in the tub. Raymond poured hot water into the tub, and his wife stirred with her foot.

Raymond loved the morning bath routine. As beautiful as the day he offered her coffee in Chicago, Raymond still stared when given a chance. She put a hand on his arm to stop pouring. Raymond smiled and kissed her shoulder before she dropped into the tub. Minutes later, he held the towel for her to step into, wrapping her tight with a hug.

As he settled into the tub for his bath, the sun peeked over the horizon in the east, shining a splash of orange/red on a thin line of clouds on the western horizon. The air hung heavy in the heat.

During breakfast, George knocked and entered with Paul. Flossie Mae cracked six more eggs into the frying pan while Paul poured coffee, refilling Flossie's and Raymond's cups. Raymond cut strips from the steak in the center of the table and plated them, ready for the eggs over easy Flossie shoveled out of the skillet. The boy sleepily laddered down backward from the loft. Raymond marched him back up the ladder to get dressed if he wanted breakfast.

The men knew that the day would continue yesterday's tasks and not much needed saying over breakfast. Dorothy and the boy, ready for the day, descended the ladder and waited a turn at the small table. Raymond looked them both over.

"Your shirt's buttoned wrong, son. Come here and get straightened out."

"Ah, Daddy, I can do it."

"Come here."

Both fumbled with the buttons, their hands getting tangled in each other.

"You kids stay close today, you hear me? Your mother may need help with the shutters."

Flossie Mae set a plate with more eggs on the table.

"Still think we're in for it, Raymond?"

"Who knows, maybe, probably."

Breakfast over, the men gathered once more on the porch before heading to their respective crop stands in three directions. Just then, John drove up in the family Model T Tourer. John left the car idling while jumping out to consult with the three men on the porch.

"Mornin fellas, does anyone have any time this morning to give me a hand draining off the settlement pond on my place. I'm afraid it might overflow in the next downpour."

Raymond stepped off the porch and climbed into the Ford, glancing at the sky in the west.

"Let's go."

Paul and George waved at the car, kicking dust and heading for John's place. They both started for the barn to muck the stalls and feed and water the horses. Today, George would finish with the in-row cultivator he had left in the field the night before. Paul would work the oats field planted three weeks earlier with the blind cultivator. Perhaps he would be done with his lot after supper.

The boy came tearing out of the house, the screen door slamming, and ran after Paul. Dorothy also emerged from the house and headed toward the well. At six, her chores included feeding and watering the chickens, geese, and pigs.

The boy caught up to Paul. "Uncle Paul, can I ride with you to the field?"

Paul knew a stall tactic when he heard one. "Sure, after you finish hoeing three rows in the garden."

"Oh, alright. That won't take long."

The boy tackled his weeding of the first row with quick, substantial cuts with the point of his hoe. His chopping resembled a shuffle as he ran out of energy looking down the second row. He took a short break to break sticks against the apple tree to see how far the pieces would fly, expending a lot more energy than hoeing entailed. Next, he threw smaller sticks at a robin flitting around in the upper branches of the apple tree. The boy figured the robin had a nest nearby. Maybe he would find a nest with some of those little blue eggs. Perhaps they were about to hatch.

He did not find the nest. His sister, Dorothy, approached, hoe in hand, and the boy returned to the cornrow where he had left off. Dorothy finished her four rows methodically and left the boy to complete his third row. The boy, deciding he needed another break, dropped the hoe. Climbing the apple tree, the boy could not quite reach the closest apple and had to climb down, clumsily climb back up, stick in hand, to bat the low-hanging apple out of the tree. Retrieving the little green apple on the ground, the boy wondered if it would squash if he threw it hard enough against the barn. The apple dented the barn boards, undamaged. After three tries, the boy worried that someone might hear the thuds. He returned to the garden. In fifteen minutes, he had finished his third row. He took off for the oats field to ride the cultivator with Paul.

The temperature had climbed into the eighties by eleven thirty, but the breeze had picked up and cooled the sweat off the men working the fields. Raymond and John attempted to remove the third board from the sluice, water pouring through the wedged opening, emptying another five inches from John's sediment pond. While waiting, Raymond swept the western sky with an outstretched arm from north to south, pointing out the lightning flashes too far away for the sound of the storm to reach them; the thunderclouds speeding toward them. Twenty minutes later, the two men had no problem hearing the thunder. The wind whipped the aspens in the copse west of John's wheat field, the storm, still several miles away, moving fast.

"Looks like our piece of the 'Land of the Living Skies' may be hit square on, John. Gonna be a doozy. I better see to my place."

"Sure, Ray, thanks. I pray to God it turns south."

"Need help buttoning up here, John?"

"No, I'll take care of it. I better check on Edith and the baby. Take the car."

Rain began to shower the homesteads. Raymond jumped into the Tourer. He spent two frustrating minutes starting the damn thing and coaxing it to a smooth idle. Halfway home, only half a mile from the sluice gate, the howling wind and spattering rain suddenly stopped. The day was absolutely still again. Startled, Raymond stopped the car, letting it idle, while he jumped out to look at the weather to the west, sure he would see a funnel cloud or two bearing down.

George made it to Julia's house just before the rain started. Under her direction, he returned and closed all the west and north shutters. George returned to the barn and secured the animals and door. He stepped onto the porch again then he, too, noted the rapid drop in the wind.

Paul believed he and the boy had plenty of time to make it to the boy's home, judging by the thunder delay after lightning strikes in the west. A mile, at least, maybe two miles away. He tied Spar undercover in the field shed and wrapped a blinder across the horse's eyes. He could not chance Spar rearing or bolting with the two of them on his back. The boy did not want to look scared in the face of the thunder. Nevertheless, the boy took Paul's hand, holding on for dear life as they tracked back toward the barn.

Dorothy and Flossie Mae had taken care of the shutters and the barn doors. Flossie Mae had located all the loose items in the yard and brought them into the house. With the wind billowing her skirt, she had managed, with Dorothy's help, to pull the tub into the parlor. Flossie Mae had securely tied the porch swing back to the house so it no longer clattered in the wind. Storm-ready now, she could devote her full attention to worrying about Raymond and the boy. Flossie Mae had seen the boy run after Paul, so they were most likely together. She knew Paul would be the last person to look up and recognize the danger in the sky. She also knew that Paul would gather up the boy and head home, safe as both might be expected.

When John closed his barn door, he heard a plop/splash behind him. He turned in time to see hailstones he could swear were the size of baseballs splash in the sediment ponds, raising geysers three feet tall, like a swimming hole bombarded by boys' cannonballs. The infrequent hailstones crashed down hard on the ground and fragmented like bombs. The roof on the barn and the house took a pounding, and the clothes drying rack in the front yard splintered. John could only imagine what the hail could be doing to his wheat stands.

Raymond heard a rip and bang and turned to the car to see an ice baseball had torn through the Tonneau cover, landing on the driver's seat. A second hailstone hit next to his left foot. Raymond turned in all directions, looking for shelter. A copse of Aspens seemed perilously far away to the west; hailstones pummeled the path across the field. A third ice baseball shattered in the dirt three feet from the left front tire, and another hit the car's hood, producing a sizeable dent. Raymond reacted, crawling under the car into the mud the rain had created to wait out the hailstorm.

When the first hailstone fell near Paul, he could not believe the size of the thing. The boy dropped his grip on Paul's hand to run over and examine the oddity while a second and third hailstone shattered near the boy. Paul grabbed the boy under his right arm and swung around wildly, figuring out the nearest cover. He spotted Lemuel's original log cabin, now a storage shed, two hundred feet away. Paul ran full speed, the boy bouncing with teeth chattering in rhythm to Paul's pace. His luck ran out twenty feet from the cabin door when a tennis ball-sized hailstone hit the back of his thigh, bowling him over. The boy went skidding in the grass. Paul scrambled up, roughly pulling the boy and hobbling to the door and inside. Paul's thigh hurt like hell, but the bone seemed unbroken. The boy had scraped his chin, and he rubbed his forehead. They heard squirrels or mice within the quiet of the thick logs. Through the door, they waited for the storm to pass. Two more minutes and the hail stopped. The lightning and thunder, far from over, seemed closer than ever. Paul decided to stay put.

When the hail stopped, Raymond jumped into the car, which had sputtered and died while he hid underneath. He struggled to start it once again. Every second now meant the possibility of a lightning strike. Shaking his head and attempting to stay calm, the engine cranked, whined, and finally started. Balls of ice made the road bumpy. Flossie Mae heard the car drive into the yard. Raymond idled in front of the barn, leaped out to open the barn door, and jumped back in to drive the car inside. He ran to the house, finding Flossie Mae and Dorothy, but no son. Rather than panic his wife further, Raymond inquired about his brothers, Paul and George. Flossie Mae shrugged her shoulders. Raymond went back out to the porch, examining the sky. Out of the corners of his vision, three lightning strikes in quick succession smoked the dirt on either side of the barn. No sign of Paul or the boy. The rain and lightning dropped off in a few minutes, and Raymond looked to the west, hopeful for a brighter sky. A swatch of blue was headed his way, but behind that, Raymond saw a second storm, a mountainous panorama of towering thunderclouds. He prayed Paul, and the boy would not be fooled by the calm and remain undercover. As the bright patch moved overhead, the temperature soared again, and only minutes later, the wind began to build.

In the calm after the lightning subsided, John hurried out to his largest wheat stand to assess the consequences of the hail. He discovered the damage, as expected, but John believed it minimal, so as the wind picked up, he wandered toward a second stand.

Suddenly the wind increased three-fold. John turned toward the barn as the gale pushed him into a run. Then, hail again, driving horizontally in a violent wind. Pea-size snow-stones danced, slid, and pummeled anything in their way. Instantly covering the ground in John's path, some of it the size of marbles, slippery at each step, slowing John's rush for cover. Like shotgun-shot pellets, the wind drove the hail against John's back and legs. The back of

John's neck, where his hat did not reach, and his cheek facing the wind were scratched and bleeding. John pitched to the ground. He yanked his hat down to his ears and placed his gloved hands behind his head to protect his face, burying his nose in the hail ground cover. The wind tore his shirt from his belted pants, and the hail pummeled his back. Within less than a minute, white ice an inch deep covered John.

The hail stopped.

The storm blew on by. As John looked up, the lightning and clouds shifted south; to the north and east, the day appeared clear and ready for a rainbow.

Paul and the boy approached the house while Raymond leaned against one of the porch posts. The boy took off running, yelling to his father, holding a melting baseball hailstone. His story ran down as he arrived at the porch looking up at his father. Raymond relaxed, unreadable. The boy became quiet.

"We'll see what your mother has to say. I recall asking you to stay close to the house this morning."

"Daddy, I got all my hoeing done before I rode on the culvenanor with Paul."

"Go see your mother."

The boy went inside.

"Thanks for seeing to the boy, Paul."

"He's a boy with no fear, Ray, and loves this farm."

Raymond shrugged, "Maybe his undoing, but thanks again. How about we mount up and see to the fields. I'll saddle up, Beau."

"I left Spar at the field shed."

"Good thought," Ray agreed. "he's still skittish in a storm. Meet you at number two wheat stand."

Raymond's and Julia's fields sustained minor damage from the two storms. Perhaps a two to five percent loss in some stands from the first storm; is acceptable and allowed for in a Saskatchewan farmer's planning. Raymond and Paul found pea size hail melting around the edge of one of Julia's oats fields, but the storm had bent south, and the crops were generally OK. George rode up to join them. They decided to ride over to John's farm.

John sat, head bowed, on a boulder near his largest wheat field as Raymond, George, and Paul approached. Looking out over the area, the men surmised a total loss. The stalks left standing were cut below the head as if a scythe had swung down the row. The young spikes were sprinkled everywhere. The wind flattened anything not still standing as if Jack-In-The-Beanstalk's vindictive giant had stomped all over the field.

John stood, his shirt ripped like the field, blood drying on his cheek, down his neck, and into the collar. Tiny hailstones were melting into rivulets headed to John's sediment ponds. A blistering sun now hung high in an all-blue Saskatchewan dome. The brothers tied up their horses and sat down on the boulders they had all helped move out of this field to its edge. No one said a word.

After fifteen minutes of silence, Raymond stood, brushed off, leaned over, rubbed John's back briefly, then mounted and rode off. Paul and George made the same silent gesture.

When the three brothers were out of sight, John stood and paced back and forth in a ten-foot circuit. Taking off his torn shirt and using it to wipe away the dried blood, John turned toward the barn.

Julia walked over to Raymond's house in early fall and invited herself to breakfast with the men and Flossie Mae. She set a folded newspaper, the Saskatoon Phoenix, September 12, 1917, on the corner of the table. Flossie Mae waited for the men to leave before pouring another cup of tea for Julia, ready to discuss next year's education budget. The two women had already agreed on the necessity of providing funds for George to attend college. They had met previously to write letters to several institutions inquiring into entry requirements, tuition, housing, and textbook costs. Now they worked on reviewing the responses from the Battleford Collegiate Institution, the Saskatoon Normal School, The University of Saskatchewan, and the University of Manitoba in Winnipeg.

Even though Julia's blood and sweat had continuously been poured into farming, she recognized the changing world of the twentieth century. In an hour, both had agreed on a new education budget.

Then Julia spread the newspaper on the table and referred to the quarter-page bulletin on the front page. The headline read:

Military Service Act, 1917
Explanatory Announcement by the
Minister of Justice

Julia waited for Flossie Mae to read the lengthy article. Then she pointed to what she had determined were the two most important paragraphs.

> It is the intention of the government to immediately exercise the power which the act confers to call out men for military service to provide reinforcements for the Canadian forces.

> And

> The first call was limited to men between twenty and thirty-four, unmarried or widowers without children, on July 6, 1917.

Flossie Mae shook her head, asking Julia, "Does this mean Paul? How old is Paul?"

"He just turned eighteen last month."

"Thank Goodness! He's still too young."

"Yes, Thank God! There have been fewer volunteers this past year. That is why Prime Minister Borden pushed this conscription law through Parliament. Paul will get it in his head to go. You tell Raymond not to tell Paul about this draft business."

"Certainly. The war has got to end. The Western Front has killed so many on both sides. Neither side can go on much longer."

Stories of the carnage and horrors of mustard gas at the Western Front had penetrated the souls and minds of mothers and men alike for over a year. The stalemate made for reluctant volunteers.

Julia left the house to tend her flower garden beyond the barn. Flossie Mae prepared to take the wash down to the creek. As she carried the clothes basket, she decided to tell Raymond about the newspaper article as soon as possible. She hated the thought of adding another worry to her husband's shoulders.

Raymond had delayed the family meeting until early October to give the family time to recover from the August storm, harvest most crops, and begin preparations for the winter. George had returned to Moose Jaw for high school, and Dorothy left every day for Stringer School on the bus.

Julia, Raymond, Flossie Mae, Paul, John, and Edith attended the meeting sitting in chairs set out in the parlor, with the boy busy eating cake at the table. Raymond began with the state of the farm, attempting to put a positive spin on the family's accomplishments and looking ahead to the following year.

"Since the August storm, we've done well. The loss of John's fields was a major setback, but the rest of the co-op had a banner year. So, we have a net profit, albeit not as much as we all would have hoped. Surely not as bad as three years ago when our farms took a hit from all the rain for a co-op loss."

Raymond always tried to illustrate the balance inherent in a farming business.

"Don't forget," he continued, "We still have about twenty percent of the fields to harvest. The bushel price of wheat has been inching up this month. We siloed some of last year's harvest. We're going to be fine starting off next year."

Julia applauded by loudly patting her thigh. The rest offered no objections or comments; Raymond continued with new business.

"I have only two items on the agenda. A consensus on how much to silo versus sell this year and a discussion on the education budget."

Julia rose and shooed Raymond to his chair.

"Flossie Mae and I have researched college tuition and books and such. George has expressed his desire to attend college. He would be the first in this family to go to college. We believe it is worth our sacrifice to make certain that happens. Based on our investigation, we should increase the education budget to two hundred fifty dollars annually."

To fill the silence, Flossie Mae backed up Julia.

"I realize the education budget will be a significant percentage of the overall budget if the two hundred fifty-dollar amount is approved. There will be funds for the rest of the children, Edith's and Paul's, and for Dorothy and the boy."

The proposition met with unanimous approval. The silage proposal received consent as well. Sensing the meeting winding down, Flossie Mae rose to fetch the cake and tea. John called after her.

"Flossie Mae, I have an item of importance I'd like to discuss for a moment. Can you hold off the refreshments a bit?"

"Certainly, John, go right ahead."

Raymond suddenly detected a stillness in the room. No rustling.

"I'll tell you," John said. "We've another baby coming along in a couple of months. You have all been so supportive. Edith and I have talked and planned and looked at all our options. I have been speaking with our sister Edith-Cordelia and her husband, Chris Scoular, about buying us out. I have been writing to establishments in Edmonton, and my prospects for a job are excellent. With the railroad stretching that far, the town is booming. I believe this would be the best for my family."

Raymond, an ache forming in his chest, tried to think of his best approach to this new circumstance while John continued.

"Now I know most of my crop failures have had nothing to do with me, but I'm ready for a steady wage to watch my family grow instead of wheat."

Raymond found his voice, even as he searched for a good answer.

"John, I don't know what to say. I know these last few years have been tough on you but haven't we clarified that we're in this together? A couple of good years at the scale of growing acreage we control would set us all up for good. We will have a string of good years to put us right."

Straight-backed and composed as ever, Julia looked at each of her sons with narrowed, ice eyes.

"That's right, Raymond; Charles never downplayed the hard times. I've seen downtimes before, back in Indiana. You, boys, are good farmers. You as well, John. The land is a legacy you cannot beat in the long run. It will happen, believe me. You boys jumped in front of the rest of the homesteaders in the Cut Knife region. The learning, the mistakes, why, making a profit will get to be routine."

John did not back down.

"Mother, Edith, and I must try a different direction. Raymond here was born to farm. George was as well. I bet when he comes home from college, you'll get twice the yield out of half the acreage we're working. Paul works hard while buying Father's farm and still finds a way to ease his mind with his artworks. Besides, Edith Cordelia is as much a part of our family as I am. You will see that Chris is eager to build the farm.

Flossie Mae, an independent, nearly as strong a force as Julia, nodded at Edith and turned to John.

"John, I, for one, believe that it may be the right decision for you and Edith. Whatever your future holds, Raymond and I wish you the best. Never forget there will always be a place for you here, awaiting your return. Isn't that right, Raymond?"

"Oh, of course, Flossie Mae. I'll miss the hell out of you, John, that's all. Edith and baby Marjorie as well. Edmonton seems far away, but we will still be neighbors with the train."

Raymond took two steps toward John. John sighed in relief.

"I'll finish the harvest and winter preparations and help Chris and Edith as much as they need. We hope to be packed and ready for Edmonton by Christmas."

"Then let us celebrate," Flossie Mae said, "Tea and cake, anyone?"

Raymond did not celebrate. The problems he would have to keep the co-op going without John weighed heavily. Cut out for farming or not, Raymond depended on the family and John, who always did his best. Chris Scoular may or may not work out. When might George be gone for good? Paul? A wild card, dependable if he continued buying the farm from Julia, but who knows where he would be if the war ended tomorrow? He may also be called up for the Canadian Expeditionary Force anytime. Determined not to wear his distress, Raymond shook John's and Edith's 'no hard feelings' hand and clapped John on the back. When all the guests left and Dorothy returned from school, Raymond sat down with his children on his lap and read two chapters of Swiss Family Robinson, requiring and absorbing his children's closeness.

Then he left the house and strolled toward the barn; time to milk the cow and get at the rest of the evening's chores.

The final threshing crews left the brothers' farms the second week in December during the first deep snowstorm of 1917. Raymond knew that the brothers had surpassed their own endurance limits, working twelve-hour days right up to the day the storm hit. Everyone pitched in to help John and Edith migrate to Edmonton. Their house had been stripped bare of their possessions. Everything they owned was tarped in the corner of the barn, ready for train station transport. John had combed through the pile twice, moving non-essential furniture and trunks to a second pile for Edith-Cordelia to use or dispose of as she saw fit. The bedroom furniture would be dismantled when the new baby arrived, and train tickets were purchased.

On the evening of December 14th, Edith began having real labor pains. The sun that day had beat back the snow on the roads. Raymond drove the Ford nine miles to Cut Knife to call Doctor Tempe of North Battleford from Mr. Trumbull's General Store telephone. He laid down seventy-five cents on the counter to cover the call. After multiple attempts at nine o'clock in the evening, Raymond finally reached the operator to place the call.

"Raymond Martensen here, Dr. Tempe. I'm calling for John and Edith Martensen over here in Rockhaven. Edith has a baby coming tonight. Think you can make it?"

"When did her pains start, and how close are they?"

"I left the farm half an hour ago. According to John, Edith grabbed hold of him every ten minutes."

"This is her second baby. Marjorie, her first, arrived a year ago, as I recall, after a twenty-hour struggle. I do believe."

"That sounds about right, Doctor. I know with my wife, Flossie Mae, she spent fifteen hours in labor for our daughter, Dorothy, but only five hours in labor with my son."

It seems like they tend to come along faster after that first baby. It is only about thirty miles to your farms from here, but you never know in winter with the road. I would not count on my help for another hour. You can return and tell them I'm on my way. If I don't make it in time, your mother, Julia, and your wife will be in charge. Get them over to Edith."

"Paul is driving both over in the buckboard. I stopped in to fetch them before heading to Cut Knife. Thanks, Doctor Tempe; see you when you get to the farm."

"Good luck. I'll be there."

Raymond returned to John's farm, finding John and Paul playing thirty-one at the table. Raymond stepped past the table and knocked on the bedroom door just as Edith cried out, so he waited to enter until the wailing subsided. Upon entering the bedroom, Julia let go of Edith's bedside arm and approached Raymond. Paul and John stood in the doorway. Raymond leaned in close to Julia.

"The Doctor said he could be here in an hour."

"That will be cutting it close. Edith's contractions are three minutes apart now. The baby is beginning to crown already."

"The Doctor said it would be up to you and Flossie Mae."

"Yes, I've helped plenty of times, but,,,"

Edith began to howl again, gripping Flossie Mae's hand like a vice.

Flossie Mae looked up at Julia, "Nothing for it."

"Raymond, keep John and Paul out of here. Flossie Mae and I have all the towels from our two houses. We sterilized the scissors and knife and tore a sheet into bandages. God, I hope we won't need them. Put a kettle of water on the stove to boil and keep bringing pitchers in and replacing the water in the basin."

"I can do that," Raymond said, leaving the room, "Holler for anything else you need."

"Make like the Doc will be here any minute to John."

Julia returned to Edith, taking Edith's right hand in hers and gripping Edith's right arm with Julia's other hand. Edith, quasi-sitting against the headboard with four pillows stuffed around and behind her, kept her eyes closed, waiting for the next contraction.

Raymond left the room, put a water kettle on the stove, and stoked the firebox. Then he returned to the table.

"Mother said it may be a while. Doc Tempe is on his way, John."

"Thank goodness. The last contractions were strong and close together. Maybe I'll peek in and see if I'm needed."

"No, Mother's in charge now, and she wants you out here. Deal me in. Penny, a point?"

In the next fifteen minutes, John threw two cards to the widow that he should have remembered would fill Raymond's hand. Paul gripped the leg of the table nearest him to keep from screaming himself during each contraction. Finally, a tremendous wail and grunting from the bedroom, and the men threw down their cards and gathered at the bedroom door; Raymond barring John from opening the door. Still, another fifteen minutes passed with more grunts and wails before they heard a tiny wailing baby.

"It's a boy, Edith," Julia called out, "John, you hear me? It's a beautiful baby boy."

"Can I come in, Mother? How's Edith?"

"Not yet. We have some tidying to do. Edith is doing fine. Tired maybe, but smiling."

A few minutes later, Doctor Tempe arrived with his black satchel and snuck into the bedroom, pushing the men back. The men could hear the Doctor congratulating Edith, Julia, and Flossie Mae on an excellent job.

The women allowed John into the bedroom, and Flossie Mae and the Doctor emerged. Doctor Tempe sat down at the table and filled out a birth certificate for: Jack Frederick Martensen, born on December 15, 1917. Raymond paid the Doctor twenty-five dollars and handed him a cigar before he left on the trip home to North Battleford. John opened the bedroom door. Sitting up in bed holding baby Jack, Edith invited all of the family to see her son. Miraculously, baby Marjorie slept through the ordeal in her loft crib.

Raymond stood behind Flossie Mae, encircling her in his arms, staring at the little seven pounds six. The baby scent and softness of the little one and the women in the room contrasted with the rough hands, disheveled farm shirts, and the unlit cigars John handed out to Raymond and Paul. Amid everything that had occurred in the last two years, the death of Father and the farm management, Raymond and Flossie Mae had let the growth of their own family slip out of their minds. The couple spent their spare time on their responsibilities at church and the school building project in Gallivan. Baby Jack reminded Raymond to look to his future family, the sons and daughters inheriting the legacy of the homestead, his life's work. He bent down and discreetly nibbled Flossie Mae's ear.

John and Edith, each holding a baby, were seen off at the train stop in Cut Knife on January 5, 1918. They had been ready for ten days, but Julia enticed them to stay for her grandson's birthday and Christmas and New Year's celebrations.

Of course, the boy had looked forward to Christmas as he assisted John and Edith in packing their belongings. Edith kept pulling out what the boy had clumsily wrapped and transferring it to a trunk labeled for the correct purpose. Finally, the boy asked to play with his toys in the same room as the two babies to watch over them (stay out of the adults' way.)

The boy knew it would be his birthday five days before Christmas. He concentrated instead on what Santa Claus might bring? He and Paul had ventured the five miles on horseback to the aspen forest, where the boy picked out a small jack pine for cutting. Unfortunately, the boy's first pick would not have fit in any of the living rooms on the farm. With Paul's assistance, the boy's second, smaller choice prevailed, and they hauled it back to the farm.

To keep the Christmas story prominent in the minds of the Methodist family, a birthday cake dessert with five candles (one to grow on) and no presents followed a dinner at Julia's home. The boy proudly blew out all the candles in one breath; (four attempts.)

Santa Claus did bring the best present ever for the boy. He unwrapped a Sears, Roebuck & Co. model train with a circular track. The boy spent time every day until the New Year and beyond, pushing the train around the track.

The family and many members from the family's Methodist church congregation had participated in the Gallivan New Year's traditional potluck on the Sweetgrass reservation. Every attendant from the community contributed a dish to pass. In addition, each member brought a pie as a gift. Nichina Starblanket Cawdell and the rest of her family and relatives also prepared traditional food.

Raymond and Nichina's friendship had grown over the years. Her firstborn, Matisoon, and Dorothy played together on Raymond's visits. On church/reservation get-togethers, Raymond's son wandered the reservation with Paul and his friend from the reservation, Echa.

Paul stopped by the Post Office on a supplies trip to the Cut Knife General Store in late January to check for mail. Posters encouraging enlistment were tacked up on the front door, near the Postmaster's window, and near the mail drop.

Paul handed out the letters he retrieved at the post office at the family dinner that evening. One for Flossie Mae from her father, Chester Buffington of Chicago. The other letter came from John for Julia. Flossie Mae read the letter aloud for the benefit of everyone at the table. In the letter, John described his challenging new job as a mechanic for the Canadian Northern Railroad. Baby

Jack kept his parents awake most of the night, but Marjorie now toddled around while holding onto the furniture. Edith described the church they were attending as friendly and the minister as a firebrand. Paul waited for the delight from the mail to calm down before speaking up.

"The United States declared war on Austria and Hungary last month. The US will send over a million soldiers to Europe and the front by next summer. The call-up of the conscription soldiers in Canada begins this month to start training."

Julia set her fork down and clasped her hands before her plate.

"Bound to happen. I do not know if it is a good or bad thing. More men will die; I know that much. So many have died already."

Raymond, anxious over the direction of the conversation, said, "I heard at our men's fellowship meetings that most conscripted men from the homesteads are applying for exemptions, and they're being granted."

"Raymond," Flossie Mae added, "Since Paul is legally the man of Julia's farm here, he would be eligible for exemption. Would he not?"

"Nothing is certain, but I believe there would be a good possibility for an exemption. This month's conscription call-up applies to men at least twenty years of age. Paul will be nineteen in August, so conscription will not come into play unless the war continues for another year and a half or longer."

Paul waited until the family continued eating the baked chicken and corn dinner.

"I guess none of that is the point. There's talk in the states of calling up men eighteen years old next summer. Canada will follow suit; you can bet on it.

"I'm trying to say that both my countries are at war. A deadly war, I know. I understand that. Father and Julia, Lemuel, Raymond, John; we've all fought the land and the weather up here to make a home for ourselves, and if it hadn't been for Canada, our country, and the homestead act, we wouldn't have anything. It's time I paid our dues."

Raymond listened to Paul, elbows on the table, both hands rubbing his forehead. John has gone, Paul going. Another blow to the conglomerate. Let alone the arguing that he knew would erupt between Julia and Paul. Flossie Mae would be mixing it up as well. *Hell, and damnation!* Raymond looked up, placing his hands on the edge of the table.

"Here is the truth of it! We all do what we got to do. That's the strength of this family. Look... My brother died. Our Father died. I do not understand it... No, I do not... Paul may die over there, and I could not comprehend that either. I remember being Paul's age when I came here and learning how hard life and the land can be. Not a day goes by that I don't think about Lemuel and what he would be doing now if he had the chance."

Julia and Flossie Mae set their forks down again, glancing at each other, but Raymond, the family's patriarch, forcefully assumed the stern voice of his father, Charles.

"Mother, I expect you and Flossie Mae will go on about the need to talk Paul down or bar him from going, but he makes a solid point. So, I will bundle up, grab a cigar, stand out in the quiet cold, and smoke."

Raymond stood, grabbed a cigar from his desk cupboard, went to the coat hooks near the front door, pulled on his wool coat and hat, and slipped out the door. The rest of the family remained seated, stunned, and no longer interested in the meal. Julia looked at Paul, her mouth shut hard enough to wrinkle her chin, her eyes clouded wet, then she pushed back from the table, sitting straight in her chair, silent.

Flossie Mae began shuffling dishes.

"Paul, would you mind fetching more water for the boiler?"

"Not a bit, Flossie Mae. Not a bit!"

The boy stood between Julia and Raymond on the North Battleford station platform, holding Raymond's pant leg and waving goodbye to his Uncle Paul. He had waved goodbye to John, Edith, and the two babies only a month earlier. They had been gone a long time. Now it seemed Paul would be gone a long time as well. War. The boy had no idea. Most of the posters Paul had pointed out had shown a boy dressed all in brown, a long gun always prominent in the picture. Quite different than overalls and the red and black checkered wool shirt Paul wore around the farm.

Granny cried. The boy looked up at Raymond, sobbing.

Raymond drove the three of them home, watching the road ahead for icy patches, his thoughts drifting into his plans for the coming season. He and Julia had discussed hiring a farm hand to replace Paul. Both agreed that the man would be temporarily hired for the season. Paul would return to the farm after his year of service unless the war dragged on even longer. Paul would return; fingers crossed.

The boy lay with his head in Julia's lap and his feet across Raymond's. The boy, four now, would be four and a half in the summer. He would be assigned four rows to hoe morning and afternoon while Dorothy would be upped to six. That would take care of most of the family garden, the sweet corn a different matter. The boy could start to help Dorothy with the chickens this year. Flossie Mae would teach Dorothy how to make the bread.

Raymond and Flossie Mae decided to wait one more year before adding another child to the family. Family planning had to be a balancing act. In thinking of the future, reliable family member farm hands were essential, but in John and Paul's absence this year, Flossie Mae suggested she could take up some of the slack. Raymond agreed. The farm operation needed to adjust to the change.

Paul dogged the corner of his book page, staring at the white countryside out the coach windows. Too excited to sleep or read, he studied each of the nine people in the coach with him. A man on the left side three benches up. Two families were crowded together in front of Paul. The single man looked about his age, perhaps a few years older. Possible conscripts. Maybe they knew how to play thirty-one? Regina remained six hours away, with stops. He wondered how hard it would be to make friends. For now, Paul decided to keep to himself. He would be a volunteer among many conscripts. The draft so new to Canada, how would conscripts react to being pulled from their lives back home? Paul decided to return to reading his book.

Raymond sorted through the papers on the lower shelf of his cupboard and found the flyer on the Fordson. On top of the brochure lay a letter from the provincial government office in Regina. Raymond bundled up, folded the flyer and letter into his inside coat pocket, and told Flossie Mae he needed to see Chris and Edith-Cordelia.

On the porch at John's former home, he asked Chris to accompany him to Julia's house for a meeting. Edith-Cordelia was welcomed to attend but declined. Chris and Raymond walked over to Julia's house, and the three sat at the table. Raymond placed the flyer in front of Julia.

"This is the first tractor we could maybe swing, Mother. It costs just seven hundred and fifty dollars. Ford runs them off an assembly line like the Model "T." Just last year, a tractor would have cost us over two thousand dollars."

"That's still a hell of a lot of money, Son. Paul is gone. Should we not rein in expenses and tighten our belts as best we can?"

"Just the opposite, Mother. I received this letter from Regina last week. The Henry Ford & Sons Ford Motor Company provides the first one thousand Fordson "F" tractors off the line to Canada and another thousand to England to help increase food production for the war effort. The Germans would love to starve the Brits into submission. With a tractor, we could do our part to prevent that. We were one of the first homesteaders in the area, and that has always given us a bit of a leg up. I also want to be the first to learn about this tractor business.

"The government is offering a one-hundred-dollar subsidy on these tractors. I want to split the cost between our three operations.

That is just $217.00 for each farm. I would sell one of the horses to buffer the cost. I should be able to get around $100.00 up here."

Raymond paused to let Julia and Chris cogitate a moment.

"We'd need a much larger kerosene tank, but I have checked with Standard Oil. They now have a bulk storage facility in North Battleford and a tank wagon to convey fuel to the Hardware store in Cut Knife and the surrounding area. They will stop here on the way to Cut Knife to supply the farm."

Chris seemed to appreciate the idea but tried to stay objective.

"Edie and I will support you, Raymond, but who will run it. I am not one for engines and such."

"I'll have to learn it, I guess. The sales rep will spend the first day with me reviewing the operation of the tractor. Then we must adapt some of our equipment to attach to the tractor. That will mean some trips to one of the blacksmiths in North Battleford. They say one of these tractors can pull the same load as four horses. Faster too."

"Son," Julia said, "I guess it's like everything else we do here. We will pray for the best."

Paul's butt (what little he had) drove him nuts from sitting on the wooden bench outside the recruiter's office. He guessed he had been sitting for well over two hours. He had now made it to the end of the seats. Five others had slid to this spot on the bench before being called into the office.

He had arrived in Saskatoon after midnight, too late to hope to find a room in a hotel for just a few short hours of sleep. Luckily, the vestibule of the recruitment center remained unlocked and warm enough to provide a comfortable lying down. He had slipped out for breakfast early, returning to begin the sign-up process.

He had taken the CEF's first rule to heart: *"Hurry up and wait!"* Paul had filled out an application and then waited in line to hand it in. Next, he waited three hours before being herded into a gymnasium with about twenty conscripts. A sergeant asked him to strip down to his skivvies. White coats measured and poked him at various stations, and his eyesight was checked and noted.

Dressed again, Paul stood in line for forty-five minutes before entering another room with four desks. Soldiers at each desk took the hand-written paperwork and formalized it on a type-written form. Finally, Paul, holding the type-written attestation, made it to the room with the bench lineup.

When he entered the inner office, the officer stood and shook Paul's hand across the desk, motioning him to sit down and looking over the attestation form.

"I suppose you have discovered you're much younger than the men coming through today. I see here you are eighteen. Most of the conscripts are at least twenty-one. Many of them are older than that. You are also the shortest guy who walked in here this month. What makes you think you can cut it as a soldier?"

"Sir," Paul answered, "I've been helping my mother run her homestead farm for over a year since my father died. My brothers and I have been working the land near Cut Knife since we arrived in 1907. I would put up my sweat against any other man you have measured today.

"No offense meant, son. But if you are going to waste your time, it's better to find out now instead of later. I will tell you this. You're not working with stubborn land here. I guarantee you will be working with some stubborn men in your company. You will depend on them, and they will depend on you. Last chance to head out of here."

"No offense taken, sir. I have heard it before. I wasn't drafted; I'm enlisting. I've thought on it."

"Alright, sign the Attestation Paper. You are now a member of the First Depot Battalion Saskatchewan, Regina. See the Quartermaster on the first floor for your uniforms. They will assign you to a barracks and bed. You'll be rousted early in the morning for the parade drill. Congratulations!"

Raymond spent the next three weeks planning his farm's crops, coordinating his ideas with Chris Scoular's. Chris and Edith-Cordelia, excited about expanding their holdings due to John's acreage, were tempering their expectations because of the distance between their two parcels.

Chris would be very busy this first year. He bowed to Raymond's advice in these early planning stages. They worked out planting schedules as well as the stand locations.

Raymond inventoried his seed stock and repaired his farm tools while waiting for the tractor to be delivered. He bought a larger fuel tank from the bulk storage facility. He installed the tank on a steel framework, which was easy to fill by the fuel wagon; easy to draw down when filling the tractor tank.

The tractor arrived near the end of March. A six-horse wagon pulled up to Raymond's barn. The two delivery men were joined by Raymond and Chris to help roll the great machine off of the trailer: Edith-Cordelia steering. There the tractor sat, waiting for McDermott, the Ford Sales Representative, to make the rounds and train Raymond on its operation. Raymond read both the operation manual and the maintenance manual repeatedly. Charles, Raymond's father, had added the windmill and the pump to the stone caisson well serving the farms. At the time, it was the most sophisticated equipment on the homestead. John historically wore the title of master mechanic in the family, but regretfully, he worked on trains in Edmonton. Raymond read about the vaporizer needle, but what purpose did it serve? Why were there different notches on the governor controls? Wait, wait! Patience!

Raymond posted signs in the general store, the hardware store, the Post Offices in Cut Knife, and the Battlefords. The flyers outlined the duties of the seasonal farm hand Raymond needed to replace Paul. Interviews would be conducted on Sunday afternoon after church, March 24th. Raymond had posted his note next to several other similar notifications. He banked on the reputation of the family name in the Cut Knife territory as fair, hardworking homesteaders to draw some worthy candidates.

Fifteen gathered around the windmill on that Sunday in two groups. Raymond recognized several men in one of the groups; local, Cut Knife, Gallivan, or Rockhaven acquaintances. The other group of men seemed to know each other as well. They were from the North Battleford, Battleford area. A lone man stood apart from both groups nearer the barn.

Raymond interviewed each man from the Battlefords and all men in the more familiar Cut Knife group. Three candidates stood out in Raymond's mind due to their experience and maturity. Glancing up, Raymond spotted the lone wolf standing near the barn and called him over.

An older man. Raymond guessed maybe mid-forties. He was tall and broader in the shoulders than Raymond, and his face was rugged with creases. Maybe fifty. Unlike the other men who stamped around in the cold, this man stood still as if he lived outside. Raymond looked into steady eyes.

"You're from the reservation. Sweetgrass nation?"

"Yes, I am."

"You grow mostly alfalfa over there, don't you?"

"We do, but I have hired out over the years. Corn, wheat. I see you do oats here as well. I have experience in those crops."

"Why hire out at this time?"

"You posted a good wage. I want to pay off my daughter's medical expenses by the end of the summer."

"What about transportation?"

"It's a twelve-mile walk from the reservation. That's not a problem for me."

"We start early in the summer, five-thirty."

"I would be here."

"What's your name?"

"Joseph Longbow or Joseph Cawdell. I answer to either."

"Cawdell? Nichina Starblanket?"

"She's a niece by marriage. I could get a letter from her."

"I wouldn't worry about you being called up for service. You have as much or more experience as these other fellas. I could do room and board and twenty a month if you stay at the farm."

"If you are serious, Mr. Martensen, I am for it."

"One last thing. You see that tractor over there? Any fear of driving that thing?"

"Just the opposite, sir. I have always been called on to tinker over at the Res. A tractor represents forward thinking, I would say. Maybe the reservation could use one. It would be an opportunity to learn it."

"Alright, Joseph, we're first names around here. Mine is Raymond. Your first task will be to clean out Lemuel's cabin for a bunkhouse. You are welcome to stay during the week. See you on Wednesday."

The master drill sergeant called Paul and the remaining servicemen to stand to attention in the expanding Saskatchewan battalion. One hundred twenty-five men filled the field behind the recruitment center in ten rows, with twelve or more men standing at one arm's length apart, ready for drill. Five to ten more men joined the ranks daily, mostly conscripts without exemptions. Many of them are reluctant due to being forced to serve. All of them were inept at basic parade drill directions. With so many new men daily, it seemed impossible for the regiment to ever *march sharp*. Paul's company would be assigned at least one new man daily. The new man, always clueless for at least a week, prevented the company from ever getting a perfect score on the company drill.

New skills learned included making a bed so tight a quarter bounced an inch high when dropped. Paul washed and ironed his wool breeches every other day. Same with the uniform tunic, ironing out the wrinkled sleeves and collar. He could wrap and tie his wool putties to stay up neatly above his calves all day. Paul routinely spit-shined his ammunition boots before lights out. On rainy days he could wear his waterproof Larrigans. When the sun came out, he would wax and buff those.

Four and a half weeks after Paul's arrival on base, his company entered the barracks to find three new conscripts lying on their newly assigned cots. Two men swung their legs over and sat up to shake hands with the rest of the fellas, introducing themselves and hearing the names of the others in the company. The third man, a near giant, continued lying in his bunk. Someone asked his name.

"Carlton Cartinelli," he replied, "You all can call me Carl."

At supper, Carl looked for room at the table where Paul's squad gathered.

"Shove over, Shorty; give a man some room."

Paul, irked, let it pass.

"Sure, Carl, welcome aboard."

But it did not end there. Evenings were spent dusting and sweeping out the barracks. The showers and toilets were scrubbed down, and fixtures polished. The new men were given a pass for a day to get acquainted with the routines. Most of the men spent another hour sprucing their uniforms. Paul began polishing his ammunition boots. Carl, prone on his bunk, four beds down and on the opposite side of the aisle from Paul, swung up to a sitting position and picked up one of his newly issued boots.

"Hey, Paul, right? How about showing me how you get that shine on your boots. Mine look like the dog shit on them."

"Give me one, and I'll start it for you, Carl. You will get there in about a week of buffing. You want to shine 'em up as fast as you can, though. The whole company gets extra duty if anyone's boots do not reflect the Sarge's ugly mug."

Carl threw one of his boots over to Paul, who spent ten minutes cleaning it, holding the boot up occasionally for Carl to learn the technique. After cleaning, he began the first polish. Then he took the boot over to Carl's cot.

"There you go, Carl, that's a start. Any questions?"

"Just one," Carl replied, checking to make sure the rest of the barracks paid attention, "How about you get started on the other boot, Shorty. You don't want to let the company down. You got a real skill in boot licking, I'd guess."

"Not a chance, Carl. Your boots, your job."

Carl stood up and grabbed Paul's collar as he turned away. Paul wrenched away, turned, and backed up a step. He took a boxer's stance, right fist at his chin, ready to lead with a left jab, just like Charles had taught all the boys. He had sparred plenty with Raymond, John, and George.

"Oh, it's that way, eh, Shorty? You got to be kidd..."

Paul jabbed the man's chin twice and then right-crossed, thrusting with his shoulder and swinging his right hip into the punch as well, his fist landing on the left side of the soldier's head between his eye and his ear, sitting Carl back down on his cot.

Carl stood back up, shaking the stars from his eyes, swinging wildly. The big man, who had a five-inch reach advantage over Paul, connected with a powerful blow, glancing off Paul's left clenched fist, catching Paul above his left jaw below his left cheekbone. Paul staggered right, dropping his hands. He knew he had to keep his hands up to protect against the next man-mountain blow from Carl, but shaking his head did not help, and his hands would not come up.

Five fellas jumped Carl, pinning his arms down and encircling his chest. Three men caught Paul before he staggered to the floor, straightening him upright. Paul's head cleared, and he shrugged the men away.

"Come on, ass hole. You call me Paul or private or soldier or sir. But never call me Shorty again. I'm ready; let's go again."

The men draped all over Carl let him go. Carl looked at Paul, his vision clearing, the meanness subsiding. He headed for the door, closing it after he left. Paul and Carl were called before Lieutenant Shrader. He sternly informed them that the brig awaited them if the Sergeant heard them mixing it up again. They were required to shake on the promise of no further trouble.

Weeks were spent on spit polishing the barracks, the grounds, and the men's personals. Overall, Paul thought the marching drills looked no better than when he had first arrived in camp. One morning the sergeant gave the company ninety minutes after reveille to pack and board the train to Montreal. Two mornings later, the battalion, still disorganized, boarded three passenger ships; Paul being assigned to the *Missanabie*. At sea, Sergeant Miller informed the company they were heading for England in convoy with three other passenger ships and a battleship.

They were finally heading to the war on March 24th of 1918, and Paul had not handled a gun or any artillery. He could about-face, turn left and right with the best of them. He could stop a double-time march on a single-step dime. As far as the war on the western front went, Sarge told the squad they must "Hurry up and wait."

Mr. Colin McDermott arrived for the Fordson tractor training on April 2, 1918. Raymond, Joseph, and a somewhat reluctant Chris stood near the tractor, ready for instruction. Raymond insisted Chris participate as a backup operator/driver. The boy sat on the corner of the washing trough thirty feet away, fascinated by the enormous gray machine. The boy thought his dad had a train right in the backyard. He had asked Father several times if he could drive it. Raymond had told his son he would be welcome to try when he could hoe the entire garden without Dorothy's help. The boy had glanced over at his three rows and frowned. The boy climbed into the tractor seat when all the men were elsewhere. He tried to turn the steering wheel, even though he had been repeatedly reminded to stay far away from the tractor.

Colin, the Ford Sales Rep out of Wisconsin, first checked the oil levels, gasoline, and kerosene tanks. He also looked in the radiator and assured himself the air filter contained no water. Mr. McDermott, stocky, of medium height, never doffed the fedora perched on his balding sand-colored hair. He wore suit pants and a solid blue shirt with the sleeves rolled up, ready for farm work. Raymond had filled or emptied everything correctly. Colin turned to his three students.

"Yah eh, you did good getting it ready to go, Mr. Martensen. We'll go over maintenance a little later, but first, I like to start with a few safety precautions. This here piece of equipment weighs nearly three thousand pounds. You want to be aware of it always. These oversized wheels stabilize it, but that don't mean it can't tip. You want to ensure you are going straight up or down a hill, not angled on the side of an incline. You try that, and this thing will roll; chances are right on top of you, squashing a leg, arm, or chest like a pancake."

Mr. McDermott pointed to the boy standing by the windmill.

"You boy, you stay away when it's running. Understand?"

The boy nodded, still in awe. The Sales Rep sounded severe; the machine must be dangerous.

"As I say, when the tractor runs, the driver best stay in the seat. Another man can hook up the plow, cultivator, or whatever, but the operator should stay seated when the tractor is running. Everyone understands, eh? Yah, you got that, OK."

The instructor spent ten minutes starting the tractor. Raymond took the seat while Colin pulled out the choke, fiddled with the vaporizer needle, turned the crank in the front below the radiator four times, pushed the choke in a way, adjusted the ignition level, moved the governor control to the tenth-notch, then cranked hard once and the engine started. Colin directed Raymond to push the choke in while he closed the vaporizer needle several times. Mr. McDermott pointed to a switch on the right of the steering column.

"Now, ensure the engine is warmed before switching to the kerosene position on the sediment bulb tap. We will give it another couple of minutes."

Raymond had followed the procedure well. He had studied the manual enough to know the names of each of the parts that Colin had adjusted, but it sure looked like he had a magic touch as he feathered each of the controls. Colin turned off the engine.

"I don't want it to get warm yet. Now we'll give each of you a shot at startin' the tractor. Who's first."

Raymond wanted to try, but then he had another thought.

"How about it, Joseph? Are you up for this?"

Joseph did not hesitate, "Alright."

Joseph seemed almost ahead of the instructions as Colin McDermott talked him through the steps. Raymond could not believe he had memorized the levers and gauges so quickly. Plus, he seemed to have the same feathery touch as McDermott. The engine started on the first crank.

Raymond did not have the same luck when he took his turn. He started the procedure over three times before receiving the welcome chug chugging from the engine, and it took four stiff cranks.

The chugging smoothed out once the tractor had been switched over to kerosene. The engine still overpowered any conversation short of a shout. The boy would have covered his ears, except the men did not seem to mind the noise, so he decided he shouldn't. Mr. McDermott climbed up and squeezed onto the seat with Raymond. Colin put the tractor in gear, and the lurch when Raymond let the clutch out threw Raymond's head back with a snap.

The boy got excited as the wheels churned the dirt and moved into the field. After about one hundred feet, the tractor stopped, and Mr. McDermott stepped down, leaving Raymond in the driver's seat. When Raymond reached the first forty-acre marker, he turned the tractor, driving out of sight and earshot of the group waiting at the windmill.

Ten minutes later, Raymond brought the tractor back for Joseph to try. Joseph took the same route that Raymond had and returned fast. He had opened her up to full speed. Chris tried to drive the tractor next. The clutch got the better of him, and the tractor stalled. The warm engine started up again. Chris got the feel of the transmission this time, and the tractor lurched a couple of times and took off, almost at a crawl. Raymond had to admit that the tractor would not be Chris's forte. Joseph, however, had no issues with the loud machine, which pleased Raymond. In fact, he seemed to already be at home on the heavy equipment, a natural. The speed at which Joseph returned with the tractor started Raymond calculating when he might expect a field to be plowed.

Lost in thought, the boy swung his legs against the washing trough. *Maybe he could hoe the whole garden this year. He better practice turning the steering wheel.*

For the next five hours, Mr. McDermott reviewed the maintenance procedures, including possible problems that might need addressing, such as mud accumulating in the water tank and cold weather starting.

Paul walked down the gangplank of the *Missanabie*, stepping on English soil for the first time on April 3, 1918, at 0600 hours, at the Port of London, on the Thames. The convoy had avoided German submarines while crossing the Atlantic, making it through the English Channel without incident.

Paul's company formed up third in the battalion. An hour later, with the ship empty of soldiers, the Sarge called the company to attention, and they began marching. Paul had no idea where they were marching or how long it would take to reach their destination. He noted a British army truck taking off before the battalion to clear the way for the marching troops. The regiment marched in step for four hours and then sat at ease in the middle of the road until called to attention for another four-hour march. Paul thanked the stars for his light personal pack.

After two more four-hour marches, the battalion entered Camp Bramshott southwest of London. Two hours were spent waiting for barracks and bed assignments. Paul's legs were throbbing, and his back felt like someone stabbed him with a bayonet as he crawled into bed at 0312 hours in the morning.

After 0530 hours, reveille, and breakfast, the battalion ran through marching drills overseen by a cadre of British officers. Company by company, stepped out of the battalion formation to be processed into the camp. At 1400 hours, with the completion of Paul's paperwork, he had officially been *"Taken on Strength"* of the 15th Canadian Reserve Battalion.

The next day the quartermaster issued Paul a Lee-Enfield (SMLE) Mark III rifle: with no ammunition. Marching drills for his company were resumed with two differences. First, everything had to be accomplished with his rifle in hand. Secondly, a British drill sergeant, Sergeant Miller, worked over the company mercilessly for six hours until they performed a complicated parade routine flawlessly six times in a row. If the company screwed up the fourth iteration of the exercise, the count started over. Sergeant Miller recorded the names of all the soldiers that screwed up the drill more than twice. Those soldiers reported for extra drills the next morning instead of breakfast. Four days later, the battalion again passed by the same cadre of British officers. The drill sergeants varied the routines to catch the soldiers off guard. Paul's company passed review and marched to the field house for rifle assembly instruction.

Raymond and Joseph spent the month of April getting acquainted with the peculiarities of the new Fordson tractor. Some days even Joseph had difficulties starting the engine. Raymond would get frustrated, especially when it took an hour between them. Joseph remained perpetually patient. Raymond called it "*the damn thing.*" Of course, when it would get warmed up and Joseph took off into the field, Raymond and Flossie were amazed at what "*the damn thing*" could accomplish.

Joseph typically brewed tea and cooked oatmeal on the fireplace as breakfast for himself in the bunkhouse (Lemuel's original cabin.) He would fill the fuel tanks, check the oil and water tanks and fire up the tractor, warming the engine until five-thirty. Then he would start plowing the field Raymond assigned the previous evening. When a lot had been turned, Joseph dropped the plow and attached the broadcast seeder for wheat planting. Joseph worked the tractor until eleven thirty, when Raymond took over. Raymond worked the tractor until four or five-thirty in the afternoon. After dinner in the afternoon, Raymond spent time recording the day's weather and progress in his books and discussing with Joseph and Chris the next day's plan.

Raymond and Chris arose even earlier than Joseph to feed the horses. Alfalfa hay, a pail of oats, and maybe a few cobs of corn were necessary to energize the horses for the long day ahead. The men milked the cows on their farms and slopped their hogs. Dorothy fed the chickens, geese, and ducks all summer. Every third day Raymond and Flossie bathed. The children were called to sit at the table for a hearty breakfast. By the end of April, the farms were in full swing with plowing and planting.

Record rainfall that April made the soldiers miserable at Camp Bramshott. The officers were delighted that the muddy training grounds simulated the harsh conditions the boys would endure under fire. Crawling under and over barbed wire, scrambling out of bunkers, rifle in hand, advancing in straight and zig-zag patterns under fire. These exercises were a daily routine. Paul could now dismantle and assemble his rifle blindfolded. The uniforms would need washing at the end of the long days, and boots would have to be polished for the early morning parade march.

News of the war reached the troops at Camp Bramshott via the London Times and other newspapers. The officers generally told the battalion the barest minimum about the battles on the western front. Paul knew the Germans were pushing an offensive this spring, but they were bogged down in the Battle of the Lys. The same held true of the Battle of Hazebrouck and Messines.

The Allies were holding fast during this latest offensive by the Axis powers in the spring of 1918. The Americans would be arriving soon in massive numbers with incredible firepower. If the Germans broke through, the British army might be defeated, and France might be forced to seek armistice terms. But if the British held and the Americans joined them, the resulting pushback could be a route, and the Germans would have to admit defeat.

The soldiers at Camp Bramshott wondered when they would deploy to the front. The only reasonable explanation seemed to be the battalion's reserve status. The seasoned divisions with experienced soldiers were fighting well, and the Generals might have felt that green troops might be more a hindrance than a help. "*Hurry up and Wait;*" is still the name of the game at Camp Bramshott. In the meantime, Paul's company began to jell as a unit.

Sergeant Miller had his eye on both Allen Price and Paul Martensen as squad leaders. Allen appeared older than most men and could give stern reminders of the work to be accomplished without '*commanding.*' The company's members constantly asked Paul's help, though the youngest, as he was more knowledgeable and proficient than the rest. He led by example, resulting in an exemplary skill level within the company. Both men had the respect of the rest of the company.

Even Carl got along with Paul. To the astonishment of the battalion, the two were now inseparable. Carl needed Paul's brains and skills to avoid being at the bottom of the company and getting assigned extra duty or practice drills. Paul let bygones be bygones. If a routine required the strength of three men, Paul encouraged Carl to step up, and the company benefitted. Carl had slowly gained good graces with all the men.

Thus, when issued the company's first three-day pass at the end of April, Carl asked to tag along with Paul, James, and Raul for a night or two in London to see the sights.

The four soldiers started early on Saturday morning, catching a bus outside the Camp gates into the heart of London. Paul suggested a motor bus tour of the city to get their bearings. Everyone agreed. Crowds everywhere, people hurrying out of the way of the bus. More people, horses, taxis, motor cars, and buses than Paul had seen since leaving Chicago twelve years previous. The four servicemen sat in the open upper deck and listened intently to the megaphoned tour guide describe the sights.

Big Ben, a conspicuous landmark, was the tour's first stop. The bus halted for fifteen minutes so the tourists could hear the bell at ten hundred hours. Next came the dome of St. Paul's Cathedral, the third largest in the world. Raul could not help cracking a joke for the upper deck patrons to hear.

"This here soldier is Paul of Saskatoon, Canada. Obviously, the church is named after this brave lad. As you can see, the Dome is modeled from his big head. Stand up, Paul, and show off the likeness."

Paul obligingly stood, doffed his uniform dress cap, and took a bow. Carl also stood towering over Paul, mussing his hair while the upper deck tourists joined in the laughs.

The bus continued past Trafalgar Square and Westminster Abbey, crossing the London Tower Bridge before returning to the tour bus ticket booth. The four soldiers split up for the afternoon to pursue their interests, agreeing to meet at Gordon's Wine Bar at eighteen hundred hours. Paul could not be swayed from spending most of the afternoon at the National Gallery of Art. James accompanied Paul, but Carl and Raul headed for the Bromley Football Club ground on Hayes Lane, although football remained suspended during the war. Carl and Raul would also bus up to the Lord's Cricket Ground in St John's Wood, London, if they had time. Exhibition games between American and Canadian army baseball games were sometimes played at the massive stadium with twenty-two thousand cricket patrons.

For his part, Paul missed his sketch pad and charcoals. Although the National Gallery did not compare to the Louvre in Paris, Paul wanted to wander the exhibits, pleased to take advantage of the opportunity. James and Paul spent the rest of the afternoon browsing the gallery. Raphael's Mondo Crucifixion and Renoir's Umbrellas were highlights for Paul. The impressionists intrigued him. Paul's charcoal sketches seemed to mirror these great paintings' blurred areas. Working on the farm and drawing in his spare time, Paul chose areas of his drawings to concentrate on detail. Backgrounds and landscaped areas were left to quick suggestions.

James people-watched, especially the young ladies. James found many women in the quiet of the Gallery approachable for a quick question. He figured no question could be too dumb for chatting up the debutantes.

After the Gallery walk, Paul dragged James twenty blocks to Oxford Street's huge Selfridges & Co store. On the way, they purchased falafels for an afternoon snack from a street vendor. Paul bought three drawing pads, a box of pastels, and charcoal at Selfridge's. The store itself fascinated the two soldiers. They spent the rest of their free time roaming the store's merchandise displays, reading rooms, and restaurants. The flora on the roof terrace flourished like the tall corn in August on the farm, lush and refreshing. The deck offered a vast and breathtaking view of London. James found the strolling women shoppers as eager to chat as the patrons in the National Gallery.

Then the two walked back the way they came past the National Gallery and on down to the Thames and the Victoria Embankment to meet Carl and Raul at Gordon's Wine Bar for dinner. After two glasses of wine, Paul spotted their friends searching the bar, hailing them over to their table. Raul and Carl recounted the afternoon's adventures over an excellent dinner. A plaque on the wall opposite their booth caught Raul's eye. Apparently, Rudyard Kipling had once been a tenant in the building.

The four soldiers postponed the desert until after Paul's planned entertainment for the evening. They walked three blocks to the theater, where Paul presented the tickets he had purchased on the way to dinner. The long-running musical comedy "The Boy" played at the Adelphi Theater, one of the most popular attractions in London. There were many servicemen on leave in the audience. Paul, James, and Raul laughed till stitches would have hurt. Paul explained the ruse to Carl during the intermission. The divorcee fudged her and her boy's age by four years to remarry well. The society ladies were attracted to the boy thinking he was eighteen when he had just turned fourteen. The older ladies could not get enough of the precocious young 'man.'

After the theater, the four soldiers enjoyed pints at the pub near the hotel until 01:00 in the morning. Paul left his three companions and crawled up to bed: his stomach rumbling.

The following day both James and Paul felt ill enough to cut their site seeing short and return by bus to the base. The two checked into the Woodcote Park Convalescent Hospital in Epsom on May 1st with extreme diarrhea. Five days later, they were released back to duty.

Paul never ate another falafel.

Raymond and Julia each received a letter from Paul in late May.

May 4, 1918

Mother,

I have been too busy training to write until now. Camp XXXXXXXXX is ten times harder than our Regina training. As a result, our battalion is better prepared for the fight ahead. Soldiering is vastly different than farming in every way except one. Hard work prevails in both. You may know more about the war's progress than I do.

XXXXXXXXXXXXXXXX,
XXXXXXXXXXXXXXXXXXXXXXXXXXXXXXXXXX
XXXXXXXXXXXXXXXXXXXXXXXXXX;
XXXXXXXXXXXXXXXXXXXXXXXXXXXXXXXXXX
XX.

The returning injured say our brave lads are holding the Germans off. I have no reason to believe our battalion is shipping out any time soon, so I am more than safe.

I received your latest letter a week ago and appreciated the news about the farm and the family. This world of war is so different than the quiet of the plow. I will welcome my return to more consistent summer sun and the ability to hear crickets and tree frogs instead of XXXXXXXXXXX.

Your loving son,

Paul

May 4, 1918

Raymond,

I didn't want to alarm Mother. I am sitting in my hospital bed to write this letter, recovering from a difficult time with dysentery and diarrhea these last five days. I believe some rancid grease I consumed on my first leave to XXXXXX is the culprit.

Your last letter about the XXXXXXX tractor made this soldier more than a little homesick. It sounds like Joseph Cawdell more than makes up for my absence. I remember seeing him on the Reservation. Big man.

I have seen a bit of the world now, and I'm anxious, as you know, to see more. Please assess the farm's success in my absence at the season's end. If "hurry up and wait" for discharge ever turns into "let's get this done," and I'm still able, I hope to see more of the world before returning. I'll be discharged from the hospital tomorrow.

Sincerely,

Brother Paul.

Raymond, Chris, Joseph, and George (returned from school) settled into the season's planting tasks. The wheat seed broadcast on the three farms was completed, and the oats sowing progressed on Julia's acreage. In the afternoons, Raymond pulled the tractor up to the manure pile, and George took up a shovel or pitchfork to pick up the manure and throw it in the spreader. When the spreader filled up, Raymond drove out into the field, threw the spreader in gear, and it spewed the ground-up manure over the crop rows.

In June, the corn planting commenced. Raymond reviewed the co-op's progress daily, pleased that all the crops were on schedule, due in no small part to the tireless tractor. Everyone still kept plenty busy. Dorothy and the boy were picking up more of the hoeing in the garden. Julia's flower garden flourished, and more trees were delivered by the Provincial Agriculture Agency. Julia and the children planted all the six-inch firs, which would form windbreaks along the western borders of some of the critical crop stands.

The boy nagged Raymond to measure his height weekly, marking a new line on the kitchen door frame. Typically, no change could be measured since the last mark. Raymond fudged the ruler back to the same spot, even when a bit of change occurred. He figured he would make a new mark at the end of the summer, so the boy would think he had grown overnight. Raymond cautioned Dorothy to go along with his trick. Dorothy had grown almost three-quarters of an inch by the end of June.

The boy missed his Uncle Paul. Granny encouraged the boy to write a letter to Paul. He drew a picture that looked much like the tractor, and Granny put it in the post, cautioning the boy that Paul may not receive the letter for three weeks or a month. The boy asked Granny every other day if Paul had written him back.

Even Flossie Mae appeared optimistic for a good year. She hoped the telephone lines would reach the farm by August. Perhaps her isolation from the world would ease if Flossie Mae could occasionally speak to a friend. Her chores had not increased as much as she feared in Paul's absence. Dorothy enjoyed helping with the bread; the boy had not gotten into trouble this summer. Fingers crossed for a good harvest and sustained good behavior by the boy.

Paul continued his training. He could hit an apple at fifty yards with his Lee-Enfield. In the second week in June, Paul began training on the Lewis machine gun. Light enough to be carried by one soldier, it could deliver one hundred rounds per magazine.

The company kept in tip-top shape, increasingly becoming frustrated with the battalion's lack of involvement in the war. The same question haunted every soldier's mind: *"When?"* Paul suggested to Sergeant Miller that a morning three-mile run might work some of the tension out of the company. That turned into three miles in the morning and three miles before bed. It helped.

News of the June Battle of Belleau Wood reached Camp Bramshott. Deemed vitally important, the base's commanding officer related the report to the entire battalion on a late June morning muster. Apparently, the U.S. Marines had shown Fritz they were in for a brand-new war by digging shallow trenches instead of retreating to deep ditches in the rear. They had picked off the unsuspecting German companies coming through the forest. The fact that the Americans had joined the war gave a definite psychological boost to the entire camp.

In the third week of June, a Canadian injured returning from the French front spent a few days at Camp Bramshott. They were awaiting beds in the hospital or passage on ships returning to Montreal. Paul went through the cafeteria line at dinner and spotted a seat at one of the long tables. As he sat down, the soldier sipping soup across from him looked up. He had a huge black patch over his left eye that Paul had not noticed until he sat down.

"Sorry, I didn't mean to stare. Back from France?"

The man put his soup spoon down on the table, pulled a faded handkerchief out of a pocket, and coughed hard, trying to catch his breath.

"Name's Patrick Timmerman. Sorry about that. Yeah, I'm heading home. I'm used to the stares. At least I can pick up a spoon and walk the cafeteria lines. Some days my headache gets to me, and sometimes I cannot remember my mother's name. All in all, I'll take what I got."

"My Name's Paul Martensen. I have been here since April, waiting to be called to the front.

"Well, be careful what you wish for," Timmerman scowled, "There's nothin' about this war that you'll want to run to."

"I guess I can agree with that," Paul countered, "Just wanted to let you know I'll go when the time comes."

"I believe you, Paul. We do what we have got to do, right? Just to be sure, keep your head down. I have known a lot of buddies that never walked off the field. I have seen blown-off arms and legs."

Patrick coughed again.

"Anything I can get you?" Paul asked.

"I'm fine. You might fetch some more soup for Rueben at the end of the table. He lost both eyes."

Paul looked up and noted the shaking man with both eyes bandaged.

"Certainly."

Three days later, Paul began coughing aggressively. On June 27th, Paul was admitted to the hospital, complaining of shortness of breath and an unrelenting cough.

The Military Convalescent Hospital Woodcote Park, Epsom Hospital.

Medical Case Sheet: Paul A. Martensen
Bramshott
27/6/18
Complaint
Pain in Rt chest, 3 days duration. Cough/shortness of breath.
Family History
One brother died at the age of 20
The rest of the family neg inclined to chest trouble
Personal Past History
Born Chicago, 19 yrs. of age, had Diphtheria and Scarlet Fever when a child, otherwise healthy, good recovery from both, denies Venereal disease, farmer, enlisted Feb 1918, arrived in England April. In Hosp in May, 8 days,

with dysentery and diarrhea, otherwise on parade every day since coming to England.
Present Illness
Three days before admission, with chills, loss of appetite, and vomiting. Epistaxis, pain starting in RT chest, worst on exertion or coughing, symptoms running much the same until admitted.

Physical Exam
His face was not flushed, tongue coated, no odor to his breath; his thyroid and tonsils looked good, soldier well nourished. Lungs Ref 28, Rusty sputum, limited expansion throughout. The whole base of the rt lung is very painful, and the expiration of the left lung is apparently transparent.
Heart sounds regular, well heard, good pulse quality, rate 104
Abdomen - no rigidity, distention, or tenderness
Temp 103 Diagnosis Pneumonia.

Paul's temperature hovered around one hundred-three to one hundred-four degrees for the first six days in the hospital. Exhausted from coughing, he kept his eyes shut, concentrating on shallow, slow breaths, trying to sleep. Paul felt better after the first week. His temperature was only slightly elevated, and the chills subsided.

Early in July, Julia read aloud the letter she received from Paul to her grandson:

June 10, 1918

How is my favorite nephew? I received your picture of the tractor. Nice drawing. I showed everyone in the barracks. They voted to post the image on the barracks door so that anyone outside for training would see the tractor. The tractor has become our symbol and mascot since we cannot have pets in the barracks.

I have been learning more shooting skills. I will be a great hunter when I get home. We will have to go prairie chicken hunting after the war.

I miss you and the rest of the family. Are you excited to attend school this fall and learn your ABCs? I have been working on some drawings too.

I better get back to training. Thanks again for the picture. It is special.

Love,

Paul,

P.S. Say "Hello" to the chickens for me.

The men were busy with weed management for all the crops. When not sitting atop the tractor, Raymond cleaned the bins of leftover old grain from the previous year. He inspected for insects and sanitized the floors. The farm geared up for the wheat harvest. Luckily, the inevitable hailstorm missed the family farms entirely. Flossie Mae welcomed all the rain that fell in July.

Paul relapsed in the hospital on July 10th, sending his temperature soaring back to one hundred three with chills and night sweats, coughing, and loss of appetite. His condition remained close to critical; every day, his temperature stayed consistently over one hundred and one.

Nurse Trudy spent three nights during those weeks at his bedside. If Paul woke up wanting water, she supported his head, holding the glass. Paul knew from the coughing sounds in the rest of the ward that many soldiers were just as sick. He believed Nurse Trudy rotated each night among the men most. One night he tried to stay awake, staring at her, understanding that he must still be alive if he saw her sitting there fidgeting. Her legs in white stockings were not shapely. Her shoes were also white but scuffed. Everything else about Nurse Trudy remained foggy.

Medical Case Sheet: Paul A. Martensen
19 July 1918
Soldier still having daily chills, high temp, exploratory needle at a lower angle of RT scapula. No fluid was found dullness at Rt. Vent.

Raymond received the telegram on July twenty third:

22-83756

TTY - 2736458
Private Paul Augustine Martensen was hospitalized with Pneumonia on June 27. Still fighting and in good care.
Sergeant K. J. Miller
Camp Bramshott, England
MGMCOMP 06:35 GMT

Raymond's hands thudded to the table, telegram fluttering before him. Lemuel, all over again. This cannot be. For months, the family had worried about bullets, bombs, bayonets, or gas. Raymond closed his eyes. In the gray, he saw Lemuel struggling to breathe under tight, starched sheets and his plastic cocoon. Smiling up at him before leaving him forever.

Raymond pictured Paul in the same condition. What is it about this pneumonia beast? He visualized a specter standing over Paul's bed draped with a ribbon embroidered from shoulder to waist with letters spelling "PNEUMONIA." He wanted to swing his old wood bat at the disease sending the ghost over the fence in the center field.

Eyes opening, Raymond stood to find Flossie Mae and then headed to Julia's house.

Two weeks of fretful worry passed before the inevitable work of the harvest pushed the fate of Paul to the back of Raymond's worry list. He and Joseph had one week, working far into the night on the tractor with the binder attached, to cut the wheat stalks and gather them into bundles. George and Chris followed along, aligning the bales in windrows to dry.

Near the middle of August, the regional co-op steam thresher came thundering onto the farm and spent a day setting up inside the barn.

The two-man steam engine crew arrived at six a.m. the next day to get the engine fired up. A head of steam is necessary for the whistle to blow. When the dew began to come off the grass, the engine crew blew the whistle to alert Chris, Edith-Cordelia, Julia, and George to meet at the barn; to begin the threshing operation.

The neatly shocked rows of wheat and oats were ready to be loaded. Joseph drove the tractor pulling the farm's most extended wagon along the rows of shocks to be loaded. The bundles were stacked on the wagon as high as Raymond and George could reach with a fork. Then Joseph returned to the threshing barn.

Julia, Flossie Mae, Edith-Cordelia, and Chris helped pitch the bundles heads-first into the separator. It had to be done right. Throwing too fast or slow did not allow the thresher to work correctly. The machine is designed to operate the best under the proper load.

At noon, the steam engine whistle blew, signifying lunch. Flossie Mae and Dorothy had prepared fresh squeezed lemonade, plenty of water, sandwiches, and cake. The threshing crew and the steam engine men, Jeb and Bill, gathered at the plank table to enjoy the food. The boy scrambled to be first in line, picking over the sandwiches, finding his favorite amidst a slap on the hand from Granny Julia.

The danger became a distinct possibility during the threshing operation. The women wore men's coveralls and tied back their hair tightly for fear of the whirling belts and pulleys of the thresher. Jeb kept a watchful eye on the gauges of the steam engine, preventing a disastrous explosion.

The horses would bolt if spooked by the noise of the thresher. Flossie Mae kept an eye on her son and daughter, telling them to stay out of the way of the tractor and threshing crews. Julia reminded them to get after their hoeing.

In three weeks, the wheat grain bins were full.

Medical Case Sheet: Paul A. Martensen
    28 August 1918
    Improving daily lungs clearing

Paul sat in the chair next to his hospital bed, reading a letter from Raymond:

July 22, 1918

Brother Paul,

We have been praying and pulling for you since we received Sergeant Miller's telegram. We sure appreciated his thoughtfulness. When you are recovered, please thank him.

I can only trust that you are now improving every day. The willpower we possess and the steadfast and knowledgeable doctors and nurses at your hospital will see you through.

You are getting better, I'm sure of it.

Write back soon and tell us about your date with your nurse.

Thinking of you and all my brothers and sister.

Raymond

At that moment, the creaky reading cart rolled up to Paul's bed, pushed by the day orderly. Paul wiped his eyes dry, brushing his cheeks with his sleeve. The orderly showed a couple of books to Paul.

"Up for reading something, Private? We've got your Tale of Two Cities by Dickens, a Sherlock Holmes collection, and A Boy's Life by Robert Frost? See anything interesting?"

"Is that the Times from yesterday?" Paul asked, "I'll take that, OK?"

"Sure, here you go."

Paul, drawn to the headline, scanned the article:

The battle of Amiens kicked off the Allied offensive.

Philip Gibbs on the Battle of Amiens, 27 August 1918
In July, Rupprecht's army was the chief threat against us----

----It is now the enemy who is on the defensive, dreading the hammer blows that fall upon him day after day, and the initiative of attack is so entirely in our hands that we can strike him at many different places.

Since August 8th, we must have taken 50,000 prisoners and upwards of 500 guns, and the tale is not yet told because our men are going on----

----The change has been more in the minds of men than in the taking of territory. On our side, the army seems to be buoyed with the enormous hope of getting on with this business. They are fighting for a quick victory and peace, so they may get back to everyday life, clean this surge from the map of Europe, and restore the world to sane purposes.

.... Those German soldiers and their officers have been changed men since March 21st when they launched their offensive. They no longer have a dim hope of victory on this Western front. All they hope for now is to defend themselves long enough to gain peace by negotiation.

On August 26th, the arrival of the Canadians surprised the Germans immensely. The last heard of them was outside of Roye after their glorious advance on the left of the French, and the enemy least expected to find them right in the north beyond Arras----

By morning they held the spur. This body of Canadians had taken over 820 prisoners yesterday. They added another 150, with many machine guns, most captured in the valley below the ridge. All told, the Canadians and Scots attacking with them had taken about 1,800 prisoners----

This advance gives a sense of the enormous movement behind the British lines, and there is not a man who is not stirred by the motion of it. They feel that they are indeed getting on with the war. It is like a vast tide of life moving very slowly but firmly.

Paul let the newspaper fall to his lap. How about that, the Canadians. The sooner he recovered, the sooner he could help.

The days were long and hard, but the farm's harvest that year was abundant, and the gathering was accomplished in record time with the new tractor. The women were excused for the last two weeks of oats threshing to start harvesting the vegetable garden. They canned the tomatoes and pickles and pulled the potatoes and squash to store in the root cellar. The men completed the threshing of the wheat and oats on all three farms. After a good night's rest, the steam thresher rolled out on September 16th, heading to the next co-op member on the threshing route.

Dorothy returned to school in Gallivan. The boy came home every day from Kindergarten excited, listening for the sound of the tractor, searching the farms until he found the field where Father worked. The boy waved the tractor to a stop. Raymond stepped down for a few minutes to listen to the boy update him on which letter in the alphabet he had learned that day.

George attended the Battleford Collegiate School. Raymond tended to pick up George's workload, but Joseph also took on extra duties in George's absence. Joseph never shirked these additional responsibilities or complained about his workload to Raymond. He went about his tasks silently, with an occasional grunt when called on for heavy lifting.

Medical Case Sheet: Paul A. Martensen

5 September 1918

Both lungs are apparently clear, with no blood in the sputum; the general condition is much improved. The patient is released to Epsom Convalescent Base.

Recovering from pneumonia is a long and slow process. Paul had spent three months in the hospital. On September ninth, Paul read about the sinking of the *Missanabie*, the ship he had sailed to England aboard; forty-five men lost. On the 30th, he transferred on strength from the Fifteenth Reserve Battalion to the Second Canadian Convalescent Depot at Bramshott.

He started with floor exercises in the gymnasium, just three series of five repetitions of sit-ups, pushups, and jumping jacks. In the second week of his recovery, Paul increased his repetitions to ten in five sets. In the third week, Paul added a half-mile jog and increased his repetitions to twenty push-ups, twenty sit-ups, twenty squats, and ten pull-ups.

On October 1st, Raymond posted a note in Trumbell's General Store. He needed three laborers for three weeks to pick corn. Room and board plus five cents a bushel. At eight o'clock, interviews will be conducted at the town hall meeting room on October 2nd.

Next to Raymond's notice, another recent posting garnered his attention:

To Prevent **Influenza!**
Do not take any person's breath.
Keep the mouth and teeth clean.
Avoid those that cough and sneeze.
Don't visit poorly ventilated places.

Keep warm, and get fresh air and sunshine.
Don't use shared drinking cups, towels, etc...
Cover your mouth when you cough and sneeze.
Avoid Worry, Fear, and Fatigue.
Stay at home if you have a cold.
Walk to your work or office.
In sick rooms, wear a gauze mask.

Surprisingly, Raymond found only three applicants gathered at the town hall the next day. All three were experienced pickers, and Raymond hired them all.

"We start tomorrow. Bring a bed roll for your bunk. I want to be out in the field by eight o'clock. I'm glad the three of you are available. I figured many more pickers would be looking for work at this time of year."

"Word is Mr. Martensen," Andrew Morse explained, "you got an Indian workin' out there."

"That's true enough, Joseph Cawdell, Sweetgrass Cree. You have a problem with that?"

"No sir, I don't. I just heard that some think you are bypassing town folks,,, your neighbors, for cheap Indian workers. Some don't want to work with Indians neither."

Raymond had heard such talk over the years since meeting Nichina Starblanket. He never let the talk slide, nor did his anger show.

"I don't know where that's coming from," he said, "I pay Joseph standard wages just like I would with any worker. As far as that goes, I'm as close to the Sweetgrass Reservation as I am to Cut Knife. See you, fellas, tomorrow."

The next day when the crew arrived, Raymond ensured Joseph's presence. Raymond judged each interaction. The men chose a hook, peg, or finger stall for shucking and were sent to the first corn stand. Joseph drove the tractor out with the wagon rigged with a bang board on one side to deflect the ears of corn thrown into the wagon. The shucker never looked at the wagon. Andrew, the best picker, shucked seventy bushels that day. The other two crew members were nearly as good at sixty-five and sixty-three bushels.

The three laborers bunked in with Joseph. On Saturday night, the three asked Raymond for permission to head to town. They had prearranged for a friend to pick them up and return them to the farm when their poker game finished. Raymond, unconcerned with drunkenness or hangovers due to the national prohibition, wished the crew a good time. Raymond learned the next day that the card players had ended their poker game early, joining a dance at the town hall before returning to the farm.

Julia brought home a letter for Raymond from Paul on the twelfth of October.

September 28, 1918

Dear Brother,

I appreciate your uplifting letter of faith in my recovery. Letters from home are like that. They keep you going.

I'm in rehabilitation now. I'm trying to be patient. I'm up to about fifteen pushups a set now. Still, a long way to go.

There are rumors now around camp that we may be shipped over soon. Can't say more, but you've read about the efforts of the Canadian soldiers on the front. I hope to rejoin my regiment soon.

Stay safe and healthy. An illness like I had makes you appreciate the good days, that's for sure.

Say 'hello' to your boy. Tell him I have two sketchbooks full of drawings for him to hang by his bed.

Sincerely,

Paul

That evening Raymond read the letter to his son and daughter sitting on his lap. The boy coughed a bit, and Father wiped his runny nose. Flossie Mae came over and felt her son's warm forehead; too warm.

"The boy had better stay in bed tomorrow," she commanded, "I'm hearing there's a nasty flu going around."

Raymond thought for a minute, rubbing his chin.

"Are you sure? Fresh air may do him some good."

The boy began to squirm.

"Can't I even go out on the porch, Mommy?"

"Not tomorrow, probably," Flossie Mae remained firm, "we'll see in the morning."

By morning the boy was coughing uncontrollably, and school was out of the question. Flossie Mae heard that the school was closed due to the flu on a trip to Gallivan that day. Flossie Mae picked up a newspaper. Tension began crawling up the back of her neck as she read accounts of the so-called "**Spanish Flu**" sweeping west across Canada. Something about returning soldiers bringing the disease from Europe. Flossie Mae thought of Paul and his close call. She hurried home to nurse her youngest.

Flossie Mae fretted to Julia. Both worried over the youngest member of the family. Julia asked Raymond to drive her to North Battleford, where she collected as many national newspapers as possible. She found astonishing articles in the Vancouver newspapers.

Spanish Influenza

By order of the Port Coquitlam Board of Health, acting under powers conferred by the Provincial Board of Health, it has been decided to close all Schools, Churches, Theaters, and Lodge meetings, and until further notice, all Public Meetings will be forbidden.

All persons owning or harboring dogs are hereby ordered to keep the same tied up or under control on their premises. <u>Any dog found running at large is liable to be destroyed.</u>

Citizens of Port Coquitlam

In the face of the terrible epidemic sweeping the country from one end to the other, I ask you to observe all necessary precautions. In particular, forbid your children from frequenting the depot and its vicinity, as the trains bring germs from infected districts. Keep them warm and their feet dry. Congregating should be avoided. Smother your sneezes and cough; their handkerchief should be held before the mouth. Spitting on the sidewalks and street is a public offense and will be punished accordingly. By attention to the above regulations and keeping the body in as good a state of health as possible, a great deal of the danger from influenza may be avoided.

Allen W. Keith, Mayor

Julia suggested to Raymond that they drive over to Cut Knife. Parking on Irvine Ave., Julia queried several friends she saw on the street. She learned of multiple cases of the flu right there in Cut Knife. Slim Jenkins, a lad of twenty-four, had died that morning supposedly from this flu sickness before the doctor had arrived from New Battleford.

Julia and Raymond drove home relatively quietly, both worried for the boy. At the farm, Raymond took off to finish his evening chores. Julia found Flossie Mae at the boy's bedside and reiterated her day's investigations. The boy's temperature now stood at one hundred two.

The boy coughed up blood two days later, and his temperature remained at one hundred two. Raymond drove to the nearest phone and called for help, but the doctor could not say when he would arrive. The doctor depended on Julia to give the boy plenty of liquids and keep his forehead cool.

Joseph approached the farmhouse and told Raymond that Andrew and the other pickers were too sick to go into the field. They had suggested to Joseph that they must have caught something at the dance the week before. Joseph told Raymond he needed to visit the reservation to check on his family.

Raymond realized the time had arrived for the farm to temporarily shut down operations. He cut back on all the farm work beyond feeding, watering the stock, and milking the cows. Raymond poured over the newspapers Julia had bought, trying to understand how he might help the community through this "Spanish Flu."

Raymond lost track of time the following day just trying to keep up with the care of the animals, check on the boy, and help Julia and Chris with their chores.

At breakfast on October 18th, Flossie Mae prepared a tray of oatmeal, toast, and coffee for the corn pickers over in Lemuel's bunkhouse. She heard muffled coughs as she approached. She struggled to unlatch the door while holding the tray, managing to get a toe around the base of the door, and kicking it open.

"I brought some breakfast for you, fellas. I'll put it here on the table. Anything else I can get you? You best stay in bed until we get a handle on this flu. I will bring over some soup for lunch. How's that?"

The man in the farthest bed lifted a shaking hand to acknowledge Flossie Mae's breakfast tray but began coughing and let his hand drop back to the bed, unwilling to waste breath talking. Flossie Mae looked over at Andrew lying in bed, mouth open.

She approached the bed, touching the man's arm, shaking him awake, bile rising in her throat. He was dead and stiff; his mouth never moved. Flossie Mae walked over to the second man, who also looked very still in the dim sunlight coming through the one window in the cabin. He was dead and stiff as well.

Flossie Mae turned and ran from the bunkhouse, heading first toward Julia's house before stopping and turning to the dinner bell by the porch, ringing it so that anyone and everyone could interpret it as an emergency. Both Raymond and Julia came running. Edith-Cordelia and Chris joined them, out of breath, hurrying from their farm. Flossie Mae, shaking, gave the group the news.

"They're dead, Raymond; two of the pickers are dead. I think the third picker is just as sick."

"That cannot be Flossie Mae; they were fine four days ago. Joseph left three days ago when they took sick. They cannot be dead."

"They are. Believe me. Now, what are we going to do?"

"Alright, you say one man is still alive? We will have to bring him to the hospital in New Battleford. I'll get the car."

Flossie Mae, hysterical, near shock, cried out.

"Oh Raymond, I'm so worried. Our boy is so sick. We have got to get him to the hospital as well."

Julia began massaging Flossie Mae's hand and wrapped her arm around the woman's shoulder, calming her hysterics.

"The boy's been sick for at least five days now, right?" Julia asked, "He seems to be holding steady, and his cough is better today. We can give him care as well or better than the hospital. That sick man is more than I want to handle, so Raymond, get him over to the hospital."

"What about the dead men?" Raymond asked."

"Inquire at the hospital what we should do. Pick up any literature or advice they are giving."

Raymond thought it best.

"Alright, Chris, give me a hand with the sick man getting him in the car."

Raymond and Chris loaded the sick, listless man into the passenger seat of the Model T. Leaving Chris at the farm, Raymond took off for New Battleford, driving as fast as the old Ford would go, gripping the wheel tightly with both hands. He was angry, furious, banging the wheel with a fist. He did not know who he was angry at or why he was mad. Sometimes anger hides frustration. Sometimes anger masks a deep fear. Anger gets one through.

Raymond found the hospital lobby and emergency room crowded with coughing, ill people, primarily men. Young men. When he finally reached the counter, the receptionist told him no more beds were available.

"We are bringing in more beds as fast as possible, but it will be a few hours. You say the sick man is waiting in the car outside? I suggest you take him back to Cut Knife or the school in Gallivan. There are nurses now in both locations setting up makeshift hospitals."

Raymond returned to the car and headed back to Gallivan. The man in the passenger seat, Raymond, knew by first name only, the man he had met just ten days earlier at the town hall, released a wheezing sigh and died in the passenger seat.

Raymond again pounded on the steering wheel. He was a helpless help. Instead of stopping at the school in Gallivan, Raymond drove back to the farm. He rounded up Chris and moved the dead man from the passenger seat to the back seat. Then Chris and Raymond went to Lemuel's bunkhouse and piled the other two dead men on top of the first in the back seat. Shovels and a pickaxe were thrown in, and Raymond drove to Rockhaven Cemetery.

Some years back, Mr. Randall Willowby donated an acre plot to the community for a Rockhaven cemetery. Bordered by a small aspen grove, Raymond glanced at his father's gravestone, befitting Charles' standing in the community. Raymond picked out an area in the opposite corner of the cemetery. Using the pickaxe, he started tearing through the prairie grasses. When a swath seemed large enough, Chris followed with a shovel, digging a fitting grave for each man. Raymond finished with the pickaxe and helped dig the last burial place.

Raymond figured the bodies would be claimed later by relatives of the men, but he had no idea how to contact any survivors. If anyone came to claim a body, he could direct them to the cemetery.

Returning to the farm, he reported to Julia and Flossie Mae.

"Basically, the doctors at the hospital recommend isolating anyone who takes ill. Caretakers should breathe through a mask or cloth. Fresh air must be brought into the room where the patients are bedded. Try to keep the patient's temperature down with damp, cool cloths; the patient should drink lots of water. A small shot of brandy may be administered as well."

Julia: nodded, taking charge.

"I have been the least exposed even though I have often looked in on my grandson. You three should bathe in the hottest water and wash your clothes."

Raymond drew water for the boiler, and he and Flossie Mae bathed and dressed, refreshed. Flossie Mae gathered all the clothes for washing. Raymond went up in the loft to collect his son, wearing a bandana over his nose and mouth.

The boy opened his eyes, groggy. "Are you playing bad guy, Daddy?"

"Yes," said Raymond, "as a matter of fact, I am. You are the good guy, and you must stay as quiet as possible while I move you over to Granny Julia's house. You take it easy. Are you feeling a little better today?"

"I think so, Daddy; maybe I can go outside tomorrow."

Raymond did, in fact, think his son was better. The boy dropped off to sleep soon after shifting into Julia's extra bed near the window in the loft. Raymond left the caretaking to his mother, turning to the chores in Julia's barn. A moonless night deepened, yet Raymond had not finished milking. He still had duties to complete on his farm.

Walking back from his barn, Raymond felt the night chill, wondering about the temperature. The thermometer on the porch read forty-seven degrees, not that cold.

In the middle of the night, Raymond arose to visit the outhouse; coughing and chilled, he threw a blanket down on the sofa in the living room, trying to sleep without bothering Flossie Mae. After a sleepless hour, he found his cough lessened sitting in the easy chair. Flossie Mae found him in the morning, sweat beading on his forehead.

On October 26th, 1918, Paul received notice:

> Paul A. Martensen – Struck off strength to the Second Canadian Convalescent Depot and took on power to the Fifteenth Saskatchewan Reserve Battalion. Please report to Sergeant Miller, company unit eight.

Upon entering his old barracks, Carl saw Paul, a head taller than the other soldiers.

"Hey, look who's back, fellas. What's your name, private, I forget? Does anybody know this shirker? Oh, I remember now, Paul, right? Paul Martensen. We give this soldier a toothbrush and assign him the latrine for cleaning. What do you think?"

Someone shouted, "Hip, Hip!"

As one, the company shouted, "Hurray!"

The men huddled around Paul, asking about the easy life, the nurses, and any rumors he had heard.

"You are out of luck, fellas; the hospital is even more boring than the barracks. The nurses looked like Carl's sister, ugly."

The rumors ran unchecked throughout the battalion. Soon, very, very soon, they would be ordered over to France. Indeed, they would be needed to replace troops lost in the gains from the successful offensive the allied forces had been mounting since the Battle of Amiens in August.

On November 11[th,] the battalion bugler sounded muster, and Sergeant Miller scrambled his company to join the rest of the battalion at the parade grounds on a rare, sunny afternoon.

The Camp Commander addressed the troops standing at attention.

"At ease. It is my duty and privilege to announce that at the eleventh hour of the eleventh day of the eleventh month, the Germans signed an armistice. Essentially, they have admitted defeat, and this long, devastating war is over. The Germans have signed the Armistice of Compiègne, and a cease-fire is now in effect. We have won the war, soldiers; we've won the war. That is all. Attention. Dismissed."

A rumble and a roar arose over the parade grounds as the soldiers began to shout, hug each other, and even dance. The regimental band struck up "When Johnny Comes Marching Home." All the soldiers joined in singing the first verse over and over:

When Johnny comes marching home again

Hurrah! Hurrah!

We'll give him a hearty welcome, then

Hurrah! Hurrah!

The men will cheer, and the boys will shout
The ladies, they will all turn out

And we'll all feel gay

When Johnny comes marching home.

In the barracks after dinner, Paul had mixed emotions about the war's end. A palpable release of tension, a relaxing wash of worries left his thoughts because of the war's end, a great feeling. The fact that he had not proven himself under fire twisted his gut at times as well. Yet he had survived undamaged through it all.

The Sergeant spoke to the men in the barracks that night just before lights out.

"I don't want to start any more rumors, so maybe just keep what I will tell you under your hat."

Sarge waited a moment to ensure he had everyone's attention.

"I think you should know that the commander has outlined some scenarios for the battalion. We may be put on the first available ship back to Canada."

The company erupted in cheers, and the sergeant waited again for quiet.

"The more probable scenario would be that we get shipped over to France for mop-up as part of an occupying force, allowing the active regiments a chance to come off the line."

Paul thought of the possibility of seeing Paris and The Louvre at last.

Sarge continued, "A third possibility would be that we might stay in England working on repairing and rehabilitating structures damaged from German bombs.

"In other words, I know many of you will have your twelve months in service put in early next year, but I wouldn't count on being released for a while yet. Any questions? Now you know what I know, which is nothing, as usual."

Still, the men slept quieter that night.

On November twenty-third, Paul opened a letter from Julia.

November 3, 1918

Dear, dear Paul,

With an agonizing heart, most profound despair, and overwhelming sadness, I must tell you by letter that your brother Raymond succumbed to this dreaded Spanish Flu epidemic. Raymond fought bravely for eleven days, but the flu rapidly progressed to pneumonia, taking another one of my precious sons to be with our Lord on November 1, 1918.

My grandson took sick in mid-October, but he has survived. I have asked John to come help with the farm. He has agreed to return. On your return, all will not be lost between John and you. Flossie Mae and Dorothy are taking our loss awfully hard. The boy cannot comprehend that his father is gone. We have told him he is off to war with you.

I will write more on another day when my sadness eases. I have decided to volunteer at the makeshift hospital here in Cut Knife. The need is great. I'll stay busy.

I love you, son. It is so hard to lose a son.

Stay well and safe,

Your loving mother

Julia

News has a hard time spreading in rural Canada where the telephone lines are not all in place and radios, run off electricity, are scarce. Yet the Cut Knife community heard about the armistice on November 12, 1918, proving the adage that good news travels fast.

On the farm during another subdued family meal, Edith Cordelia, avoiding yet another discussion of the family's difficulty in arranging a funeral for Raymond, decided the news might bring some cheer.

"It's all over town. The war is over. That's a good thing. A ceasefire is in effect. Surely Paul will be coming home."

The boy became excited.

"What? Granny? Is the war over? Uncle Paul? Uncle Paul is coming home?"

"That's right, my boy," Julia answered.

"Paul should be home soon. No need to send him any more pictures. You can hand your next picture to him in person."

The boy ran over to Flossie Mae and sat in her lap. She cuddled him a lot lately. Flossie Mae put a hand on his cheek.

"You'll have to hug your uncle when he gets home. He may not even recognize you. You've grown so much."

"When do you think he'll be with us, Edith?" Julia asked.

"No one knows yet when it will be. The army's so big it may be a while before they let him go. But I do believe Brother will come home now."

The boy cocked his head.

"Mommy, If Paul comes home from the war, will Daddy come with him? What about Daddy, Granny? When will he be coming back?"

"No, son," Flossie Mae maintained a steady voice, "Daddy can't come back with Paul, but it will be wonderful to see

Uncle Paul again, won't it? You can show him how many of your ABCs you can write. He will read you stories and tell you all about his adventures."

The boy's mouth puckered, his eyes wetting.

"But you said Daddy's at war just like Paul. I want Daddy to come home. Please, can Daddy come home now? I want Daddy to read me a story."

Flossie Mae, tears streaming, rose from the table, gathered her wailing son in her arms, and carried him up to bed.

Julia worked beyond measure to ease the suffering in the hospital hastily thrown together in Cut Knife. To prepare, she learned all she could about the epidemic from the various newspapers she picked up. She found an interesting article in the Regina newspaper.

An Appeal for More Volunteer Workers

TO REGINA FELLOW CITIZENS:

Last night I appealed to twenty-five men and twenty-five women to help in the hospitals and private homes overnight. In response, eighteen persons reported. As a result, we were able to provide more adequate help in St. Joseph's hospital for the night shifts and for a few private homes. There were several houses where men and women were needed to care for the sick through the night, and WE COULD NOT HELP THEM BECAUSE WE LACKED HELPERS. Today we must have, to help the urgent cases, twenty-five men and twenty-five women to care for the sick, some during the daytime and some at night. Workers are also needed who will not encounter patients. There is a pressing need for automobiles at eight o'clock sharp every morning at the school board offices.

Some people hesitate because of danger, but do they realize the excessive danger others face of overwork and long unrelieved hours? If we turn back because of trouble, we will hardly want to look others in the face who have risked their lives. This is a most urgent plea to each reader to report for service. Surely it will not be in vain. We are working in cooperation with the hospitals and school nursing staff.

Yours sincerely,

Hugh Dobson

Julia nodded as she read the article. She had the same problem with Cut Knife. She would carry on for all her family sacrificed in their homestead quest.

John had moved the family back to the farm within ten days of Raymond's passing. He found Flossie Mae walking around the farm in a fog. He saw her head out into the fields more than once, losing sight of her. An hour later, she would return. John guessed she just wanted to get away from the reminders of Raymond that haunted her everywhere she turned in the house. A week after John returned to the farm, Flossie Mae asked John into the house, and they sat down at the kitchen table.

"John, I want to sell the farm. Of course, I'll need your help, but I hope to return to Chicago before Christmas."

John knew he must convince her otherwise.

"Why not stay, Flossie Mae. I can help you along the way. I know Raymond had a record harvest this year. You can probably hire two hands next year. The kids love this place. The boy's smile is something to behold whenever he steps outside, don't you think?"

"I do understand, John," Flossie Mae said, "but I've never been in tune with this place. As much as I loved Raymond, I never loved this life. My father, Chester, and his second wife have assured us we can stay with them if we need to until I get settled in Chicago. I hope you understand."

"Alright, Flossie Mae. Why don't you let me break the news to Mother? She'll be upset, of course. She will be losing grandchildren."

"We'll keep in touch, John. But this is the best thing for me. There is a hole in this place now that he is gone. Those cigars he would smoke on the porch, him fixing my bath; the strength of him."

"Father got Lemuel, and Raymond started on those cigars during those first nights up here on the prairie."

"I need to get away," Flossie Mae said with finality.

"I'll start checking around," John surrendered, "The price of wheat is at a record. I think the worth of this place will surprise you."

On December 15th, Flossie Mae purchased three train tickets to Chicago with a transfer to Winnipeg. One for herself, one for Dorothy Martensen, and one for her son, **Harry Buffington Martensen, Jr.**

Flossie Mae and her children began the one thousand four-hundred-mile trip back to Chicago.

Sitting at a café on the Avenue des Champs-Elysées, Paul read an article from the December 12th Times:

6,000,000 DEATHS FROM INFLUENZA

Estimate for the World for the Past 12 Weeks. "Flu"
Five Times Deadlier Than World War.

Having finished his croissant and peach jam, Paul folded the paper and left it on the table. He headed toward the Louvre, still startled at the numbers in the article. Numbers that did not even include the smaller towns in Saskatchewan, like Gallivan, Rockhaven, Cut Knife, or the Battlefords. He planned on returning to the farm to help John and Mother. For how long, he could not decide. He had added even more skills than soldiering since the Armistice. He had seen the foreign, and he enjoyed the strange. He had learned that he wanted to see more of the world beyond Cut Knife.

Paul spent seven months after the Armistice in France and England. His regiment helped repair bridges, poured concrete for roads and runways, and rebuilt plumbing runs in bombed villages. They cleared debris, searched for landmines, and filled in trenches.

Paul's discharge medical exam in England stated:

General health and condition: Good. May 5, 1919
(mole on the left breast.)

Paul shipped back to Canada to the Saskatoon dispersal area "P." The Deputy Director of Operations discharged Paul from Service due to demobilization on June 25, 1919.

On June 27, Paul walked up to the farm, having hitched a ride from New Battleford. He shook hands with John and hugged his mother. After lunch, he changed into his plaid shirt and overalls. They hung a little loose, but his shoulders were broader. He would visit Raymond's grave tomorrow. Today, under John's direction, he rode Spar to the oats field on Julia's farm, hitched up the cultivator, and began tilling Julia's back forty.

3

RADIOMAN

The ants go marching one by one; hurrah, hurrah!

1925

Florence glanced down at the folded, open Illinois highway map in her lap: Seneca, the next town. Their sedan had just passed through Marseilles on the way to Joliet, keeping to Highway Seven. This October morning's sun dried the soaked leaves raining down from the overhanging trees, covering the road ahead. The leaves left on the sugar maple branches glistened like gold nuggets. The scarlet maples seemed to be on fire in the wind. The paved road was slick from the leaves. John Neal still managed a steady thirty-two miles per hour. The family anticipated arrival at their apartment building near the north side of Chicago by the afternoon.

Looking over at John concentrating on the road, Florence felt pride and love in equal measure. She set aside thoughts of John's former family and Jennie, the wife he had divorced three years prior. Florence had met John when he came in to pay his bill at the gas company where she worked. John, recently divorced, had moved to his apartment and needed to switch billing addresses.

He had looked sad and apologetic as he explained his situation, but not too sad; he asked her out on the spot. When he asked, Florence reflected momentarily at the similarity of her introduction to John Neal to her introduction to Harry fifteen or sixteen years ago. She met John after turning thirty-six. Florence had been twenty-one when Harry sat down for coffee. She had smiled with measured interest in this man pushing fifty, fit as Harry had been standing over her desk.

She moved to an apartment at 2106 Wilson Ave. in Chicago when she secured her position at the Peoples Gas Building in the one hundred block of Michigan Avenue. Father, the building manager for the Gas company, saw the posting for the position of saleslady on the cork board in the administrative offices. Chester Buffington (father) had married Nels three years before Florence, Dorothy, and Harry Jr. moved back to Chicago from the farm in Saskatchewan.

Florence appreciated Chester's hospitality in sharing his home, yet there had been tension between Nelsena and Florence from the start. Florence's birth mother died in 1910 at the age of forty-five. Five years later, at fifty-two, Florence's father remarried Nels; at thirty-five.

Chester, perhaps rightfully so, focused all his attention on his new companion, Nelsena, only eight years older than Florence. There seemed to be little emotional commitment left over for Florence and her children, reminders of his dear first wife. Harry Jr, in particular, became even quieter around Nels and Chester, spending most of his time in the fenced backyard behind Chester's home, a far cry from the never-ending wheat fields on the homestead. He had been so young when they moved to Chicago that Harry lost most of the memories of his earliest years.

Florence could not have been happier to be back in the windy city. Electricity, telephones, cars, busses, trains, libraries; the diversity of people and intellect played to Florence's strengths. She insisted on being called Florence rather than Flossie Mae because it sounded more sophisticated. Harry became reticent at school as well. It took Harry nearly three years to pick up a Chicago accent. Jeered at school as he grew to be gangly, he remained solemn, although his teachers never singled him out unless they needed the correct answer during a lesson. His fellow students began to ask for his help with their schoolwork, and Harry started to fit in, gaining their respect.

Then Florence had moved to the apartment, and Harry loosened up even more, seeming to appreciate being out from under the thumb of Chester and the tension between Nels and his mother. At twelve, Harry took on the responsibilities of the man of the house. Florence humored the boy; they were as close as a boy without a father can be. When John Neal appeared on the doorstep, Harry Jr. returned to his shell of suspicion. Fiercely independent, Harry hung out with older boys after school. He equaled the height of boys two years older. Harry smoked Chesterfields out of the vending machine at the bus stop. He consciously avoided significant trouble while running with his friends because of his love for his mother. He also experienced a constant quandary over his place in the world among boys with fathers.

Purchased from the neighborhood grocer in 1925 for $1140.00 as a family wedding present, the 1923 Hupmobile Series R Sedan became the pride of John and Florence Neal. Today they were returning from the newlyweds' family-centered honeymoon; Florence had insisted on bringing her children, Dorothy, fifteen, and Harry Jr., nearly thirteen, along to The Starved Rock Lodge at the Illinois State Park and Recreation Area near Lasalle, Illinois. The newly formed family spent three days exploring the Illinois River's canyons, sandstone formations, caverns, and shores.

By the time of the wedding, five days ago, at the end of September 1925, Dorothy had accepted her mother's fiancé, John Neal. Harry, less sure, masked his distrust with politeness. He preferred to stay on his stepfather's good side. Six-foot-tall John Neal, broad through the chest with shoulders to match, had no flab overflowing his belt. Gramps was as tall as John but no way near as stocky. When they first met, John's hands engulfed Harry's in a solid handshake. The man smiled at Mum continuously and Dor, but John Neal meant business to the rest of the world.

Harry could not figure out how the man felt about him. Harry, very politely, turned away from the idea of changing his name to Harry Neal. He remained a Martensen. His name was the only thing that truly belonged to him, even though Harry had almost no association with others by that name. There were cousins in Chicago he had never met. Florence moved away from the homestead and the Martensen clan physically and mentally. She had survived the harsh Canadian life but had rarely enjoyed it. Dorothy became a Neal.

John Neal respected Harry's decision to retain his name. He treated Harry fairly from the start and never pushed. If something needed doing, like washing the car or shoveling snow, John had not yet ordered him in any way. He would place two sponges in a bucket of soapy water next to the Hupmobile, attacking the car with one of the soapy sponges. Last winter, before the wedding announcement, John stuck a second shovel in the snow next to the neighbor's car buried on the street in front of their apartment building in Chicago. John picked up the other shovel, throwing snow like a human windmill, uncovering the stranded vehicle. Harry felt almost embarrassed by the man's frenetic concentration and movements. Harry could not keep up with him, but he always tried. With the car washed or the snow shoveling completed, the two would walk into the apartment for coffee and a soda; nothing was said.

At least John Neal did not always appear to be mad like Papa. Harry thanked Mums profusely when she took the job at the Gas company as an inside saleslady and moved the three of them near Winnemac Park. He could not understand his happiness roaming the forty-acre park instead of Papa's fenced backyard. Mum told Harry the park did not compare to the one hundred sixty acres his father had worked up in Canada. The farm memories faded for Harry, but a sense of familiarity and comfort in wide open spaces remained.

Harry enjoyed climbing the Starved Rock with John, Dor, and Flo at the recreation area along the Illinois River. The canyon trails, cutting deeper and deeper into the sandstone walls, fascinated all of them. The waterfalls thundered down; spraying mist to the distress of Florence, who tried to maintain her hairdo until John roughed her up and laughed; something Harry would never have attempted with his mother. It turned out to be a strange and enjoyable vacation. Harry had never witnessed his mother so happy. For that alone, he appreciated John.

On the second day of the excursion, John asked Harry to drive into town for a few supplies, soda, toothpaste, etc... When they got to the car, John hopped into the passenger side, indicating the driver's side to Harry. Harry would be thirteen in December and had never driven a car before. To be trusted with the Hupmobile seemed unthinkable but exciting. Harry set aside his nerves and listened to John's instructions. Yes, he could reach the pedals and see the road ahead simultaneously. Harry spent half the trip to town getting used to the sliding gear transmission, but his oversteering calmed down in the first mile. They met a few oncoming cars. Overall a satisfying experience, despite the deep stains of sweat soaking Harry's shirt and the driver's seat from the tension of the lesson. John's body language never altered from a relaxed, nearly complacent manner as he concentrated on the road ahead, voicing instructions. Harry found a convenient space to park the car. They both entered the store, purchased their necessaries, and returned to the lodge at the park with John driving and no further words about the experience. Neither John nor Harry related the adventure to Florence or Dorothy, which suited them.

Rounding a bend on Highway Seven toward Chicago, John noted a woman waving frantically, running toward them from an old truck canted on the side of the road. As John Neal opened the driver's side door, the negro woman began to scream.

"My husband, you've got to help him. He's under the truck."

John yelled over his shoulder as he ran.

"Harry, come on. Flo, see if you can stop another car. Dorothy, see if anyone's home at that farm down the driveway and call the police."

"Please hurry," the stranger pleaded, "his leg."

When John and Harry approached the truck, they saw a man who looked dead or passed out, white as a sheet, his leg under the rear axle, a wheel and a tire lying at the bottom of the gully, the car jack lying broken in two next to the axle.

John circled to the truck's other side, noting the empty truck bed. Scrambling to his knees and then lying flat to examine the rear axle, he jumped up, came around to the rear side of the truck, put his back against the truck bed next to the axle, and grabbed the bottom of the bed with both hands at his side. He stomped his heels deep into the gravel beside the pavement and bent his knees.

"No springs on this old jalopy. I'll try to lift this corner. You take the fella by his wrist and pull him away as I lift. Don't stop pulling until he's free, no matter what. He may wake up and struggle. You've got to keep pulling. No car's coming yet."

John looked down at Harry, who had taken one wrist in both hands. Harry did not have time to contemplate trying to pull a man of at least one hundred forty or one hundred fifty pounds semi-buried in the gravel, the weight of the truck and the gravel offering resistance. The man's hand was cold and lifeless.

"Nothing for it," John said, "Ready."

Harry saw John take the weight of the truck into his arms and shoulders, the muscles so taut Harry thought they might snap. His neck muscles stretched, his face turning beet red. Incredibly, the truck bed rose. Harry pulled. The arm stretched to its limit, but the body did not move. John let out a "humph" and continued lifting. As the axle weight came off the leg, the man revived, thrashing in pain as Harry pulled and pulled, determined not to let go. In seconds, the limb came free from the axle. Harry tumbled backward onto his rump. John dropped the truck bed and scrambled down the gully to Harry, calming the man and examining his injuries.

Harry saw a massive dent in the leg, but luckily the broken bone had not pierced the skin. The negro woman and Florence hovered over the injured man, trying to administer water Dorothy had brought from the farm. An ambulance and a police car arrived in minutes, loaded the moaning man onto a stretcher, and into the ambulance.

Harry, in a daze, began to shake uncontrollably. He had thought the man dead at first, and then the thrashing and screams sent shivers down his neck. Harry had not let go. Over now, he could not stop his teeth from chattering. The policeman retrieved a blanket from the ambulance, and Florence wrapped it around him. John came over and rubbed Harry's back, shoulders, and arms. Harry, at first, could not even look at the person he had thought dead just minutes ago. When he did glance over at the man, his wife sitting in the ambulance beside him, the man's skin appeared as dark as his wife's; the color now returned to his features.

As John walked with one of the policemen over to the police car to help with the police report, Harry heard the policeman's partner talk to Mum.

"I never would have believed one man could lift that truck, ma'am. That boy and his father did an extraordinary thing here! The guy in the ambulance owes his leg to them."

Florence nodded in the direction of her new husband.

"I don't know how they did it either, officer, but they did. I saw it."

John returned from the police car, indicating things were wrapped up and they could continue home. The rest of the way home, Harry, cocooned in the blanket, kept shaking his head, watching the back of John's head as he drove. He could not believe it either.

Chicago downtown life in the mid-1920s concealed loud and exciting activities behind the quiet of closed doors. Florence reveled in the city's possibilities. She would occasionally talk John into an evening out at Bert Kelly's Stables, a speakeasy, sipping highballs containing purported Tennessee bourbon. Florence loved to dance. To stave off turning the dreaded forty, she learned the Charleston, showing the steps she'd mastered to John, Dor, and Harry Jr. Harry had not spent time on sports at school, being all arms and tripping legs, but it turned out he had a natural, easy rhythm for dancing. He liked the jazz music spewing from the apartments' open windows and the downtown clubs' open doors. Some said Chicago embodied jazz.

Political turmoil in the city raged along with the excitement. Vestiges of the Hertz Checker taxi wars were still common. Mayors were elected, corruption uncovered, and officials tossed out to be replaced by ineffectual reformers. Chicago may as well have been the wild west. Women had made gains in the workforce since the beginning of the century. Their dresses after the "Great War" reflected their independence, short, sleeveless, with hairstyles short and pulled into a bob. Flo, older than typical flappers, did not let that stop her. She could swear better and louder than John. Harry took after John, thinking Mum's language a little unfitting.

The day after Valentine's Day, 1929, the Mob killings suspected to have been carried out by Al Capone's men filled the front pages of Chicago's newspapers. This unsettled Florence. Perhaps Chicago had become too unruly.

Harry went to school on Monday, October 24th, 1929, concentrating on his upcoming math test in the fourth hour. He overheard three teachers outside of the lounge talking about stocks and bonds. Their discussion sounded grave, but Harry could not figure out why. The math test gave Harry no trouble. He thought he might have missed one of the problems, which would still mean an A or perhaps an A minus.

That night, the Sun-Times carried a story on the stock market's tumble the previous Thursday, followed by the rally on Friday due to heavy investors setting a positive tone. The paper had been printed before the close of the market Monday. The skid continued; margins were being called in. Would Tuesday see a continuation of the slide, or would there be another rally? The Sun-Times quoted economists who indicated they were confident the latter would occur.

The students were chatting about the stock market at school; as if they knew what they were discussing. Harry had little interest in margins, points, loans, buying, and selling. Florence reminded Harry and Dorothy weekly about their college fund, held in a separate bank from her checking account. She would tell them 'out of sight,' 'out of temptation,' and they had better keep up their studies. The down payment from the sale of the homestead in

Canada formed the basis of the fund. Once, temptation did overcome Florence. John and Florence purchased the Hupmobile as a result. The monthly land contract payment from the farm went into a separate account in a bank close by. No stocks.

Wednesday's Sun-Times used the largest headline font Harry could remember, "Black Tuesday."

Sometime in January 1930, Harry began to think it strange that the tenor of the neighborhood and town had turned so quickly from optimism to concern. Flo and John were suddenly more conscious of the budget, even though both were working and continuing to bring home the same amount of money. Harry heard at school that a tenth grader's father had committed suicide in November. The event seemed inconceivable to Harry, but another father committed suicide in December over the bankruptcy of his company.

The paper paraphrased Hoover on March eighth, 1930:

President Hoover predicted today that the worst effect of the crash on unemployment would pass within sixty days.

A story in the Sun-Times, on April fourteenth, 1930 issue reported that over six hundred banks had closed in 1929. Florence became alarmed. On the fifteenth of April, Florence took the morning off from work to check on her savings account at Meridian Bank, only to arrive and stand in a long line that stretched outside the bank's doors and around the street corner.

The teller told Florence she could not retrieve the funds from her account now. When Florence asked when she could see her cash, the teller could not rightly say. A week later, John went with Florence to the bank. The doors were locked, and a sign on the door indicated the closure of the bank.

When Harry heard about the extinction of the college fund, he was not as upset as Dorothy about the loss. After all, he had never seen the money, like a cloud in the sky that had blown away, nebulous. It did get him thinking about his future. John Neal had never attended college, yet the man worked hard and brought home money every week since Harry had known him. He had been a cement mixer and concrete worker on construction sites.

Currently, John is a sales manager of a vacuum cleaner sales force. He had been a smithy and a meat cutter. He worked, period. Nothing seemed to phase his stepfather in terms of work. John had worked since he turned thirteen, and he told Harry he figured on working till he died.

Florence still worked at the Gas company. Dorothy had a job as an employment application investigator for the telephone company. Harry informed Florence that he intended to spend a week looking for a job instead of attending classes. His grades could weather the interlude if nothing turned up.

But something did turn up. Harry took a position at the Metropolitan Motor Coach Co. in Chicago as an "Abstract Clerk." Any occupation connected to the automotive industry seemed a safe bet; everyone wanted a car. Most in Chicago need a vehicle to get to work. Harry was sixteen at the time. The job paid Harry much less per hour than what the other abstract clerks made working in the same office. With four incomes in the household, the Neal family remained secure. Harry dropped out with only one year of schooling left to receive a high school degree. He promised Florence that he would complete his degree studies soon. If possible, he would save money for college.

The Metropolitan Motor Coach Co. went out of business within three months, and few bought vacuum cleaners during the downturn. John drove to Cleveland to answer a want ad in the Cleveland Press for a meat cutter and got the job. The Neal family had gone from four members employed down to one. But one position is a lot better than the fate of several of Florence's friends living in the apartment in Chicago. John stayed in Cleveland until he located a 1770 E. 71st Street apartment that needed a maintenance man. Now he had two jobs and traveled back to Chicago to move the entire family.

Harry worked with John, maintaining the apartment building, while Florence and Dorothy kept the facility spotless. Florence prepared the apartment for the next renter when a family moved out. The Neals kept busy. The knocks on their door were constant. Toilets backed up or were discovered leaking through the ceiling.

Broken windowpanes to replace, stoves that quit working, radiators that hissed; John and Harry were rarely stumped. Harry worked with plumbing tools, electrical wiring, and sheet metal.

The family played bridge and cribbage in the evenings for amusement, cutting back on dining out in favor of an evening at the talkies. Alfred Hitchcock's "Blackmail" and Edgar G Robinson in "Little Caesar" were favorites, reminiscent of the gang brutality in Chicago. Luckily, the downtown Cleveland Public Library was only three miles away. Harry became an avid reader; books on loan from the library were devoured, week in and week out. Summers were spent on the beaches of Lake Erie. Thin as a toothpick and gaining height, Harry seemed to repel the girls on the beach. Shy and having to overcome his Chicago accent, he dated Betty Olquist, a recent high school graduate.

Betty did not impress Florence. Florence deemed Betty, as reticent as Harry, an undesirable match for her handsome boy. Harry, on his part, discovered that Betty had no ability on the dance floor and drifted away from the relationship at the end of summer in 1931.

In September of 1931, Harry landed a job as a Parts Clerk with the Nash Cleveland Company. He learned the stock quickly, taking manual after manual home to study. The state of the economy puts pressure on everyone's job. Harry, not yet eighteen, made a determined effort to rise in value in the hearts and minds of his supervisors. By 1933, salesmen consulted with Harry on the workings or use of a part. He had received permission to reorganize the stacks. He helped upgrade the labeling system for the shelves. The new system helped when space needed to be assigned for a new part. The shelved pieces would be shifted; the labels slipped from their holders and moved.

Harry, Florence, and John voted for Franklin Roosevelt in 1932. Dorothy voted for Hoover because she had married Verne, a man in his late twenties. She stuck by him, in and outside the voting booth. Harry and John Neal felt fortunate to be working. Skinny as he was, Harry never went hungry. He passed three street corners on his way to work, where groups of men huddled around garbage cans burning busted-up furniture for heat. Signs carried by women and even children pleading for work or food were far too common. Harry expected the "New Deal" Roosevelt promised to help the people standing in church charity lines. According to the Cleveland Press, the nation's unemployment rate approached twenty-five percent. The manufacturing-based Cleveland unemployment rate probably topped thirty or possibly thirty-five percent. Harry always arrived early for his shift and only missed two days from illness the entire year.

The repeal of prohibition occurred in 1933 when Harry turned twenty. Ohio held out as one of the last three states to ratify the Twenty-first Amendment. Drug stores in Cleveland sold off-site liquor in February of 1934, while the state-mandated liquor stores were established. Harry accompanied John downtown to the swanky Cleveland Club, which was allowed to serve alcohol beginning in June of 1934. By then, the club had Anheuser-Busch beer on tap. Harry found the beer an acquired taste he would have to work on.

In December of 1934, the Cleveland Nash Co. went out of business. Harry hunted for employment again. John Neal moved the family to an apartment at 3306 Bosworth Road, about nine miles west of the apartment on 71st Street, with downtown Cleveland halfway between. With the larger apartment complex, John's pay as Maintenance Manager increased. He was responsible for supervising two maintenance men, but his stepson still operated as his right-hand man. Harry helped John while continuing to look for work. Walking by a high-rise construction site in the icy wind coming off of Lake Erie in January 1935, Harry decided to check in at the site trailer, finding work as a blacksmith's helper. Harry stoked the fire for the next five months, lugged coal, and pounded steel into every shape imaginable for the McKee Construction company. His shoulders widened, and his arms strengthened, yet Florence still called him "a toothpick." In May, the high-rise finished, and Harry again looked for employment.

One of the maintenance men working for John moved back to Alabama. Harry took up the slack, thankful to be away from a blacksmith's furnace and glowing red steel. The apartment's real estate company contracted with John to handle more and more odd jobs associated with their property holdings. Harry helped remove trees, install garage doors, repair sidewalks, and refinish furniture. The tasks were varied, accomplished in John's off time from apartment management so Harry could continue to look for a more permanent position.

In late May of 1935, Harry was hired as Assistant Parts Manager for the United Motors Service Co., Located at 3705 Carnegle Ave. in Cleveland. The company stocked Delco-Remy parts for General Motors cars. Delco-Remy and its subsidiaries manufactured Klaxon Co. horns, Remy starters, and Delco electrical components, including car radios. The United Motors Service catalogs were comprehensive. With his prior experience at Nash Cleveland, Harry quickly grew accustomed to the thick directory, warehouse shelving, and part locations. Nevertheless, he carried one of the catalogs home each night to study and stay ahead of the other counter clerks.

Harry cashed out the register at the end of the workday and brought the charge slips up to the accounts receivable department. The office staff had been trimmed in the thirties. Only the most senior employees manned the accounting office, except for Carol Wittrom. Harry handed the charge slips to Carol at six o'clock each day before leaving for home. By the end of September, Carol saved her best end-of-day smile for Harry as he confidently whisked around the corner to her desk. Harry could not help but notice. She had the whitest teeth and widest smile Harry had come across. He casually checked with his boss about the policy on company associates dating. Mr. Simmelt gave Harry the green light.

"You must be referring to Miss Wittrom. Don't blame you a bit. She's turned down more than a few of us from the warehouse. Luck to you."

Carol saw the tall man as an up-and-comer. Harry, twenty-one years old, had walked into the General Motors Service Company, one of the prestigious General Motors affiliates, and landed the position of assistant manager out of seventy out-of-work applicants.

Harry asked Carol to dinner. Surprised when Carol accepted, given her reputation in the warehouse as the "ice angel." Harry picked Carol up in the 1934 Chevrolet Standard coupe he had purchased with some of his hard-earned savings. In the lounge of the Cleveland Club, while the couple waited for their table, the headlines on the newspaper lying on the side table caught Carol's eye: *Gruesome Murders Discovered in Kingsbury Run.* Carol spread the newspaper on the coffee table. They both hunched over to read the article.

The Kingsbury Run neighborhood, a couple of miles east of Neal's apartment complex, was the site of the victims of the so-called *"Torso Murderer."* The remains of two men were found yesterday, according to the newspaper, their heads severed from their bodies and genitalia.

Eliot Ness held the position of Public Safety Director of Cleveland in 1935, an appointment with authority over the police department and ancillary services, including the fire department. Just as he had in Chicago during the "Capone" era, Ness declared that the Torso Murderer would be apprehended.

Thankfully, the Cleveland Club hostess signaled Harry and led the couple to their table. Harry learned of her family over an entrée of thickly sliced chicken breast, mashed potatoes, and gravy, which Carol also ordered. Carol had a younger brother and sister. Her parents were divorced, and the two younger siblings spent weekends with her father. Carol's ten-story apartment building soared above the neighborhood five blocks from Harry's apartment complex.

Carol had taken the job at General Motor Service Co. after obtaining a one-year secretarial certificate from Davis Business College in Toledo, Ohio. Harry spoke of the differences between Chicago and Cleveland. He told a little about his mother's homestead in Saskatchewan. Carol found Harry's easy-going manner comforting and thought Harry tinged with a touch of shyness, perhaps due to his height. Carol's family had moved back to Ohio from Kansas just before the market crash. Carol's grandparents had just returned from western Kansas last December.

"As if the depression wasn't enough trouble for them, Big Bow, Kansas, has been experiencing a drought for the last five years. My grandparents experienced the brunt of those dust storms you probably heard about."

"The Dust Bowl!" Harry sympathized, "Were your grandparents a part of that?"

"The third storm left six inches of dust, sand, and dirt in their house. It came through even the smallest cracks. They could not keep it out. The storm and dust lasted for days. They just left and came back to Ohio. My mother's family took them in. How about your parents, Harry, are they still together?"

"Mother remarried in 1925. My birth father died just before I turned five. I can't really remember him. John Neal is my stepdad, and he and Florence seem happy. I think Mum misses Chicago."

Harry changed the subject.

"How about splitting a piece of Lemon Méringue pie."

On their second date in October, Harry took Carol to a jazz club with a dance floor. Carol danced a pretty good two-step.

Harry leaned close enough to whisper, "I like your perfume, fresh..."

"I like Elizabeth Arden products," Carol whispered back, "It's called Blue Grass."

Carol wore a bright red, ankle-length gown with thin straps across her shoulders. Harry kept thinking he should put his arm around her shoulders to keep her warm. Her black hair set the dress off.

Over the next several months, Harry and Carol went on four additional dates. Two dinner dates, an evening of dancing, and a movie date. Harry chanced to hold Carol's hand during the movie, "After the Thin Man," with William Powell, Myrna Loy, and a little wired hair terrier. He kissed her "Goodnight" at her door. Both strived to keep their relationship casual. Harry did not want to seem too familiar at work in deference to a professional work environment. Carol appeared ready for fun but not prepared, Harry believed, to settle down.

Florence stopped by Harry's counter at the United Motor Service Co. in August to drop off a paper bag containing a sandwich and an orange for his lunch.

"Harry, you should introduce me to Carol. You can take a minute for that, can't you? You've talked about her, but if I met her, I'd know what she was like."

"Alright," said Harry, "this way Mum."

Carol stood when Harry and Florence arrived at her desk, guessing the identity of the older woman with Harry might be his mother. Florence looked to Carol to be in her late forties but trim and well-dressed. Florence shook Carol's hand, pleased to meet her.

"You must come to dinner this weekend for a home-cooked meal. Are you available Saturday, August 11th? We usually sit down to dinner at around seven o'clock."

Carol accepted, "Thank you, Mrs. Neal. I'm available and can bring something to help with the dinner. How about a bowl of salad? Would that help?"

Florence, not one to relinquish her role as matriarch, said, "Oh, no, dear, not to bother. Harry will pick you up. Lovely meeting you."

Carol caught the undertone in Florence's voice.

"Nice meeting you as well, Mrs. Neal."

That Saturday, Carol met John, Dorothy, and her husband, Verne Constantine, in the living room of the Neal apartment. Carol knew Harry well enough by this time to relax and enjoy the evening. Florence had whispered to Harry as he set the table how she thought Carol pretty and friendly. Carol whispered to Harry just before dinner what a pleasant family he had. John fawned over Carol with an appropriate amount of attention.

After dinner, the group gathered around the radio console to hear the results of the day's Olympic events in Germany. The announcer summarized the achievements of America's Jesse Owens.

"Jesse Owens, taking the first-place position on top of the medal stand, offered an American salute during the presentation of his gold medal for the long jump. Owens defeated Nazi Germany's Lutz Long, who addressed his Führer with his hand and arm extended in the Nazi salute. Lutz, standing to the right on the block, one step down. Naoto Tajima of Japan, who placed third, stood on Owen's left, one step down on the platform."

The announcer was silent while the radio audience listened to the tremendous applause for the Nazi athlete and the muted applause for the American.

"Owens has triumphed in the track and field competition by winning four gold medals in the 100-meter and 200-meter dashes, long jump, and 400-meter relay. He is the first athlete to win four gold medals at a single Olympic Games."

The announcer paused again, allowing another moment for the radio audience to absorb the significance of Jesse Owens's medals.

"This is a day that will be long remembered by Americans and sports enthusiasts worldwide, to the chagrin of Adolf Hitler of Germany."

Harry circled around the coffee table in his excitement.

"Isn't that something! All the thousands of Nazis in the stands saluting Hitler, even though Jesse won. What do you think, John?"

"I think the world is a mess. But Owens is a bright spot."

Carol pulled Harry back down to her side.

"I'm afraid," she said, "I'm not much of a follower of sports, Harry."

"You've never heard of Jesse Owens? He's a Buckeye. Went to Ohio State University in Columbus. He's been setting all sorts of world records. What's more, he is a negro."

"Oh, that explains it, doesn't it?" Carol said, patting Harry's knee, "Negros may not be good at anything else, but they seem to be good at sports."

Harry did not want to believe what he had heard from his girlfriend. When he calmed down, he set the record straight.

"I read that he worked to pay for his education at the same time he trained and attended classes. He never received a scholarship. He had to stay at a different hotel than the track team whenever the team traveled. I would guess that Jesse Owens can do anything he wants. Maybe now he'll receive the respect he deserves."

"Respect may still be a long time coming from some people, Harry," said Florence, "I knew Sweetgrass Cree Indians up in Saskatchewan, skillful farm hands, that were looked down upon because of their color."

John Neal lit a cigarette, waving his hand at the smoke. "And look at the Jews being ridden hard by the Nazis in Poland."

The Constantines whispered to each other, Verne shaking his head.

Dorothy offered, "If the Jews in America converted and became protestants, they would blend in and not have any trouble."

"Dorothy," Harry said, exasperated, "sometimes you might just want to stay out of the conversation!"

Carol attempted to smooth the building tension between brother and sister.

"She has a point, Harry. That's all she is saying."

Harry knew Verne contributed modestly to the John Birch Society and supported his wife.

"A big point," Verne said, "Dorothy is right about the Jews."

Harry stood, turned toward the Kitchen, clenching his fist. Florence fetched the playing cards from the desk, took off the rubber band holding the deck, and flicked the cards with her thumb, altering the mood in the room.

"How about a game of Rummy?"

By September of 1936, four more victims of the Torso Murderer had been discovered. Carol kept track. Identifiable victims were generally indigent men or drug-addicted women from the deteriorating Kingsbury Run area. All the victims were beheaded, and many were dismembered above the hips. Opening a burlap sack in the back of an alley might reveal a leg, an arm, or a head of a long-dead victim, unidentifiable from rot.

Harry and Carol celebrated New Year's Eve at the Hotel Winton's Rainbow Room. Harry purchased tickets to the dinner/dance show featuring Artie Shaw on November 1st, the day the tickets went on sale. To Harry's delight, the band enlisted Billie Holiday as the featured singer for the evening. After the couple savored their dinner plates and dessert, the band rocked the huge Rainbow Room. Carol wore a thin-strapped, full-length blue silk gown that filtered to dark grey at her thighs. Harry had his new black tux with a white rose on the lapel. Tall enough to match Harry, Carol never wanted to sit down. During the band's break Harry, dying to loosen his shirt collar and tie, relaxed at their table, still in the glow of the last song.

"Blue Moon! What a great number. I hope she sings that again later."

"Yes," Carol agreed, "You held me pretty close, Harry. Wonderful. I can't quite tell from here. Is Billie Holiday a negro?"

"What difference does it make," Harry said, "She has a unique voice?"

"But she's singing with Artie Shaw's band. I wouldn't think the Rainbow room would allow that."

Harry tugged at his collar. Wondering if the dancing or Carol's implications steamed him more.

"Now you sound like Dorothy and Verne. We're here for the music. Let's enjoy the evening."

At two o'clock on the first day of 1937, Carol asked Harry into Carol's apartment for a nightcap. While Harry mixed a second cocktail for them, Carol changed out of her gown into casual pants and an Angora sweater. Harry's jacket lay across the back of a chair with his tie, his shirt collar finally unbuttoned.

Carol emerged from her bedroom, looking soft and proud of her figure. Taking steps to the couch, she sat thigh to thigh close to Harry, who encircled her, kissing her. He nuzzled her neck, the fluff of the sweater tickling his nose. His hand found the bottom edge of her pullover, and Harry slipped his hand up her back to

Carol's bra. Carol held Harry's face in both hands as she kissed him, his shadow beard now rough against her hands.

Harry broke off, standing, unsure, looking over at his jacket. Carol took his hand and began to gently pull Harry toward the bedroom. Harry glanced at the bedroom and then back to the chair and his tux jacket. He took Carol into his arms and kissed her with slow pressure, long and ardent. Then he took both her shoulders.

"I better get home; we must both be at work tomorrow."

Carol shook her head, unsure, and then stepped away, picking up and handing Harry his jacket and overcoat.

"You're right, Harry; I had a wonderful time. This was, this was, thank you."

Harry bounced down the steps outside Carol's brownstone, warm and flushed in the January wind.

In 1937 John Neal took over responsibility for maintaining a second apartment complex on the adjacent block. John's days and Harry's nights were again punctuated with emergencies. Harry, now twenty-three, became restless for a more challenging career than managing the General Motor Service Co. Parts counter. In his early sixties, John began looking forward to a time when he could slow down. John and Harry discussed various schemes and ideas over supper. Florence still wished for Harry to attend college.

"If you want more challenge, you'll have to study. John and I will make do if you want to go to college. The economy is picking up now as well."

Harry, always dedicated to his mother's security, thought that idea farfetched.

"I'm betting I can learn more technical skills on the job, Mum."

Still, a savings fund "nest egg" grew between John and Harry in a Federal Deposit Insurance Corporation (FDIC) bank account.

With the addition of the second apartment complex, Harry's time for dates with Carol evaporated. Harry also spent time before the workday began in the morning tinkering with the automobile radios returned to the United Motor Service Co. under warranty. The radios would invariably wind up on a desk against the rear wall of the warehouse. A Delco Rep would collect the radios monthly to transport them to the factory. A month later, the radios would return, either repaired or replaced for reinstallation into the automobiles.

Harry would examine the factory-returned radio and note what he suspected had been fixed. Burned-out radio tubes were obvious. Broken solder connections took longer to spot, but Harry loved the challenge. Harry would find a new resistor or condenser on some radios returning from the factory that had not been part of the original radio. Evidently, technological improvements were being incorporated into these warrantied radios.

When the radio in a car stopped working, the owner had two choices. He could pull the radio out of the car and bring it to Harry's counter for repair or pay for United Motor Service Co. to yank it out. By mid-1937, with more than a million radios installed in American automobiles, the radio became a more common automotive maintenance issue. Harry was responsible for dismantling and reinstalling the radio when the customer decided to pay United Motor Service Co. for the service.

The radios were housed in a tin box about nine inches tall by eight and one-half inches wide by nearly ten inches long. The tin shielded the radio from the engine and starter coil interference. Next to the housing, clamped to the chassis, sat the radio rechargeable battery pack, close in size to the radio housing. A radio tuning dial/volume control box connected the housing mounted on the car's floor to the console via a cable. Sometimes a clamp on the steering column held the control box. A wire ran from the radio housing to the antenna mounted on the roof outside the car. The eight-inch diameter firewall drum speaker might be mounted on the case or elsewhere in the automobile.

After a couple of months of scrutinizing the radios on the warehouse bench, Harry began replacing burned-out tubes himself. By comparing the part number on the vacuum tube with replacements from the spare parts kept in the warehouse, Harry saved the month-long turnaround time for the factory to do the same thing. He rigged up a test bench on a corner of the radio warranty bench. Harry carefully re-soldered broken connections. If his repair worked, he called the customer for reinstallation. If the radio still did not work, Harry sent it on to the factory. Soon, eighty percent of the radio repairs were accomplished in-house.

Harry became obsessed. An article in the October 1937 issue of Popular Science pointed out the spare time and full-time opportunities in Radio, offering a method of training men at home in their spare time to become Radio Experts.

By the end of 1937, Carol drifted out of Harry's life. He was so busy with work, his ad hoc maintenance work with John, and his fascination with the auto radios that he lost focus on his girlfriend. He concentrated on bettering his opportunities so he might someday think about progressing with his relationship with Carol. They were both having fun when they did date. Their discussions over dinner never strayed far from the enjoyable music or food.

Carol kept track of the Torso Murderer. Throughout 1938 and the beginning of 1939, the details of nine gruesome murder scenes in Kingsbury Run and the greater Cleveland area splashed across the front page of the Cleveland Press. Eliot Ness interrogated one of the prime suspects, Dr. Francis E. Sweeney, and ordered the demolition and burning of Kingsbury Run, from which the killer took his victims.

Two victims were discovered near the city hall where Eliot Ness worked. Still, no arrest, and no one was charged.

Harry approached Carol's desk on Thursday at six o'clock with the charge slips. Carol smiled widely at a man in a suit (an expensive, tailored suit) who paid off his charge account. Carol looked up at Harry, blushing red.

"Harry, this is Mr. Grodin, president of Imperial Chevrolet on Wilkes Street. Mr. Grodin, this is Harry Martensen, Assistant Manager of our Parts Department. Mr. Grodin has asked me out to dinner tomorrow night, and I have accepted. I hope you don't mind?"

Harry minded in the extreme but caught himself in time to smile at Carol and Mr. Grodin.

"Of course not, Carol."

"He wants to take me to the restaurant on the top floor of the Cleveland Hotel."

Harry thought M. Grodin looked shorter than Carol, probably of the country club set.

"Why that's a real opportunity, Carol," Harry said, wearing his best smile, "I've heard their Lemon Méringue pie is the best in the city. Have a great time. Mr. Grodin, nice meeting you."

Harry left work for home, acknowledging the end of fun with Carol.

Over the next three weeks, Harry dredged up every memory of his time with Carol. Now that it seemed over, he wondered whether he had missed something, expected too much or too little, or was Carol right for him. Florence somehow guessed the lack of dates with Carol signaled a change in the relationship.

"What's going on, Harry? You seem to be awfully quiet these days."

"Mums," Harry confessed, "Carol is dating the owner of the Chevrolet dealership. I guess I can't figure out what happened between us."

"If you can't figure it out, Harry, it's for the best. You know, time and time again, when you brought Carol over, I felt you two were not on the same page. You never did get to the important stuff, did you? Like religion, money, sex?"

Harry did not find Florence all that comforting but was correct in her logic. She continued, "I'd say Carol held a few prejudices that have been bred from you. What is to be will be. Harry, you may or may not get back together; I'm sorry."

Weeks later, Harry decided his time with Carol reminded him of the disastrous crashing and burning of the Hindenburg two years ago.

Harry broadened his study of radios and electronics. Britain and France declared war on Germany on the first of September 1939 in response to Germany invading Poland. Harry took notice, assuming Hitler would, at last, be stopped. At the time, Harry focused on passing his Amateur Radio License test. He could tap and read up to fifteen words of Morse code per minute. His goal of twenty words per minute seemed reachable. In addition, Harry now understood electrical values, such as volts, amperes, and ohms, in metric units. Harry would need to know radio and signal fundamentals to pass the test. He felt confident in his electricity, components, and circuits knowledge. Propagation, antennas, and feed lines were another story, but Harry kept learning. He enjoyed reading. Harry received catalogs in the mail about radio equipment and manufacturers and studied them cover to cover. Do-it-yourself amateurs often built their own gear, and Harry made lists of parts, boards, and tools he might need. He would need to know communication protocols with other amateurs for the test. Harry knew the test would include questions on licensing and operating regulations.

On September 3rd, 1939, John, Florence, Harry and Dorothy, and Verne Constantine gathered in the parlor around the console radio for President Roosevelt's address to the nation from the White House. "He would do his utmost," he said, "to keep Americans safe and avoid the war in Europe." Likewise, the U.S. Congress had passed several Neutrality Acts, pledging to stay out of the conflict.

Dorothy married Verne Constantine in 1930 at nineteen. Florence did not appreciate Verne more than she had liked Betty Olquist or Carol Wittrom, Harry's girlfriends. Verne alluded that Roosevelt, a communist, and his socialistic endeavors would destroy America. Florence told him, "Bosh and nonsense!" People needed jobs. Harry's sister seemed happy with Verne, but Harry, Florence, and John did not appreciate Verne's views. Harry's brother/sister relationship had always been formal, and with Dorothy's marriage to Verne, Harry felt even more distant.

John and Florence settled on building a "tourist court" in Chattanooga, Tennessee. The Tennessee Valley Authority promoted by Roosevelt had created an influx of people and jobs. The dams that came online in the late thirties provided electricity and modern conveniences for the homes and factories in the valley. The area attracted textile factories and manufacturers seeking cheap labor and utility costs. After three years of planning and saving, Florence and John thought to take advantage of the booming area. Harry also saw an opportunity in their dream, eager to join in.

The Neals took out a small mortgage loan to purchase a two-bedroom bungalow sited on two hundred by two hundred fifty-foot parcels of land at 5611 Ringgold Avenue in Chattanooga. Harry and John drew up plans for eight cabins and an addition to the house to provide a small store and diner. They purchased all the materials locally with money from the "nest egg." Harry and John provided all the labor. Harry and John began their day for eight months with breakfast at five-thirty in the morning. They were hammering and sawing by six o'clock, stopping only for lunch, supper, and loss of light to hit a nail.

On October 29, 1940, Harry Buffington Martensen received a Class A Amateur Radio License after passing the test at the Nashville Federal Communications Commission field office.

In February 1941, the two builders finished the diner addition: including a soda fountain counter, three small four-tops, and a kitchen. Six cabins were complete, and customers rented by day and week. Florence handled the short-order duties, with Harry filling in on the weekends.

Harry could whip up any egg dish. He grilled rare, medium rare, or well-done steaks to order, as well as sausage, hash, and grits. Harry could manage twenty pancakes on the griddle at once. He had added wood framing and concrete foundations to his skills as a plumber and electrician. In addition to the rush of cooking in the kitchen and serving in the diner, Harry enjoyed meeting customers and developing regular patrons. He became known for a ready smile. The location of *The Lightning Diner* on Route 41 seemed to assure a supply of customers. The well-stocked lake was within walking distance from the cabins, and a trout stream in the opposite direction catered to fishermen on vacation.

The slow winter season for tourists set in. Harry carefully surveyed the businesses in Chattanooga and applied and was offered a position as Assistant Parts Manager for Sharp Battery and Electric Company of Chattanooga. The company manufactured batteries and battery parts for the automotive industry and auto radio batteries. They had an area in the warehouse designated a radio repair shop and service counter. With his extensive parts management experience and radio studies, Harry took on more and more responsibilities in the radio department.

In June, newspaper accounts of the German invasion of the Soviet Union became the main topic of conversation at the *Lightning Diner.* For such a small country, Germany, perhaps the size of the state of Texas, seemed to be trying to take over England, the rest of Europe, and now the Soviet Union. How could they hope to take on such a vast territory? Hitler must be crazy. So many Germans believed in him. Harry remembered the 1936 Olympics, Jesse Owens, and the stadium full of saluting Germans. Surely the Soviet Union would crush the German pipsqueak. By October, an early bitter winter in Russia finally slowed the German advance to the relief of the Neals and the diner's patrons.

Harry helped Florence on grill duty at the diner on Sunday, December 7th. There were two customers at one of the four tops. They had stopped in on their way to Nashville for a late Sunday dinner. They ordered steaks, medium rare, mashed potatoes, and gravy; cherry pie to follow. The customers asked Harry to turn up the game on the radio between the New York Giants and the Brooklyn Dodgers. Harry, not a football fan, reluctantly upped the volume, a customer is a customer, and Harry obliged. At 2:30pm, after a twenty-five-yard run back from a fourth down punt, an announcer broke in with an emergency announcement from the United Press that Japan had attacked Pearl Harbor. The younger man at the two-top gripped the table, "Did I hear that right? Japan attacked Pearl Harbor. Where in hell is Pearl Harbor? Korea? What about the game?"

Harry shushed him.

"Listen, just listen, will you, fella?"

More announcements followed from Pearl Harbor, a strategic United States Naval port in Hawaii. Japan had bombed the airport, targeted battleships in the bay, and strafed army and navy barracks. Hundreds, if not thousands, of US servicemen and support personnel, were killed or injured.

Within a week, the United States declared war on Japan and Germany. No further talk of neutrality graced American dinner tables. Harry had been on his dream job at Sharp Battery and Electric Co. for ten months. Boys and men were enlisting in the army in more significant numbers in the months following the declarations of war, but Harry became interested when he heard of the need for radio men. Not a teenager reveling in the adventures of war, Harry, twenty-eight years old, had tracked Hitler's insidiousness since 1936 and felt Germany and Japan due for defeat. Harry did not hunt and had never fired a gun, yet he thought he could help the war effort with his radio skills. Harry tried to enlist after MacArthur's withdrawal from the Philippines and the accounts of the defeat at the battle of Bataan. On April 1st, 1942, Harry entered the army recruiting office in Nashville, Tennessee. Lieutenant Robert Sternaman rose from behind his desk and shook Harry's hand. Harry handed the Lieutenant the application he had filled out in the reception area, where fifteen other recruits awaited their interviews.

"Mr. Martensen, welcome to the war effort. Let me take a minute to review your application, and we'll have you enlisted in no time."

Lieutenant Sternaman sat down with Harry's application, scanning it as he had for hundreds of other recruits. He looked up, feigning interest, smiling.

"Your draft registration card shows a status of 1-A, but your number has not been called up yet. Let's see, you're in good shape with no gun experience. Amateur Radio License is interesting.

Twenty-eight years old. Barring any unforeseeable outcome from your physical, we could sign you in and have you training at Fort Bragg within a week."

The Lieutenant seemed more interested in the prospect of fifteen more soldiers than Harry personally, so Harry pressed his case.

"I understand you need radio operators and mechanics for the bases, bombers, and fighter aircraft. If I volunteered, might I have a shot at radio mechanic training?"

The recruiter's smile curled up on the right side of his face.

"Harry," he explained, "We need men ready to do anything and everything it takes to stop Germany and Japan. We need boots on the ground. We need support personnel. We need flyers, mechanics, and tank operators."

"So, what's the problem?" Harry thought.

Lieutenant Sternaman stated, "In short, we need you; but look, radio school is part of a specialized training program, and the requirements are a college degree. You have not received a high school degree. I cannot put you in that program."

Harry had made his way in the world since the train ride from Saskatchewan to Chicago. He tried to get through to the recruiter.

"I spent two years studying to pass my Amateur Radio License test. I know I could handle radio mechanics' school. That would be the best for you, the army, and me."

"That may well be, Harry," Sternaman looked again at the application in case he had misread Harry's qualifications, "I just cannot put you in that program based on the regulations and procedures I must follow."

"I understand," said Harry, "The Sharp Battery and Electric Co., where I work, provides learning opportunities in radio that benefit me and the war effort. I'll keep working for now. I appreciate the information, Mr. Sternaman. Thank you."

The situation Mr. Sternaman described did not make any sense to Harry, but of course, the workings of the United States Army were as foreign to Harry as going to college.

In June, newspaper articles about the Battle of Midway Island were the talk of the Chattanooga Lightning Diner and after-church socials. The Japanese Navy had been turned back, payback for Pearl Harbor.

On August 3rd, 1942, Harry received an **"Order to Report for Induction"** at the Reception Center at Ft. Bragg, Fayetteville, North Carolina. Harry passed his physical examination at Fort Bragg on August 15th. He stood 73 inches tall (six feet, 1 inch) and weighed 153 pounds. His Army Service Number (ASN) was 34364887. Harry sat down with Lieutenant Sanders for his personal interview and reiterated his desire to train as a radio operator/mechanic.

"A recruiter in Nashville told me in April that I am ineligible for training because I don't have a high school diploma. I would study day and night if allowed that training."

Lieutenant Sanders thumbed through the three-inch recruiting manual open at his elbow. He found the page he was looking for, reread the appropriate paragraph, and kept his finger on the page. Looking up at Harry sitting across his desk, the lieutenant smiled.

"We're a little more organized now, Mr. Martensen. Your Amateur Radio License qualifies you to take our aptitude test for specialized training. Take this test registration form to room 305 at 1:00pm and report back to me for the results at o 8 hundred hours tomorrow morning."

"Thank you, Lieutenant; I'll do my best."

Lieutenant Sanders reviewed the aptitude tests and his General Classification Test the next day. He issued Harry's classification card with a high recommendation to attend the Radio Operators and Mechanics School in Chicago, Illinois, upon completing his ten weeks of basic training.

The Quartermaster at Fort Bragg issued Harry the following:
Clothing
5 Undershirt, Cotton, Protective, Olive-Drab
5 Drawers, Cotton, Khaki, Protective, Olive-Drab
2 Shirt, Cotton, Khaki

1 Necktie, Cotton, Mohair, Khaki
2 Trousers, Cotton, Khaki, Protective
1 Belt, Web, Waist, EM
2 Cap, Garrison, Khaki
2 Shirt, Wool, Olive-Drab
1 Coat, Wool, Serge, Olive-Drab
2 Trousers, Wool, Serge, Olive-Drab
1 Cap, Garrison, Serge, Olive-Drab
5 Pair, Socks, Cotton, Tan
3 Pair, Socks, Light, Wool, Olive-Drab
2 Jacket, Herringbone Twill
2 Trousers, Herringbone Twill
1 Hat, Herringbone Twill
 2 Pair, Shoes, Service
1 Pair, Gloves, Wool, Olive-Drab
1 Pair of Leggins, Canvas
4 Handkerchiefs, Cotton, Olive-Drab
1 Jacket, Field, Olive-Drab
1 Raincoat, Rubberized, Dismounted
1 Overcoat, Wool, Melton, Roll Collar, Olive-Drab
1 Cap, Wool, Knit
 1 Manual, Basic, Field (FM 21-100)
1 Liner, Helmet, M1
1 Helmet, Steel, M1
Individual Equipment
1 Bag, Barrack
1 Can, Meat
1 Canteen
1 Cover Canteen Dismounted
1 Cup, Canteen
1 Fork, 1 Knife, 1 Spoon
1 Tape, Cotton, Tag, Identification
2 Tag, Identification
1 Brush, Tooth
1 Razor, with 5 Blades
1 Brush, Shaving

1 Towel, Bath
2 Towel, Huck
1 Comb

Harry stepped off the train at Grand Central Station in Chicago at the end of October and walked to the Congress Hotel. He reported for training with the duty sergeant at the reception desk, who assigned Harry a bunk in room 412 with Bob Sturgis, another trainee who had arrived a day earlier. The AAF-converted hotel would be his home and classroom while in Chicago.

Weeks ago, at the Reception Center of Fort Bragg in August, Harry had boarded a train headed to Miami for basic training in the United States Army. Harry would not allow rough treatment, rumored about in "Basic," to spoil his chances for radio training. John Neal, his stepfather, had provided Harry with the will to conquer basic training without complaint. Work day in and day out with sweat on his brow, nothing new to Harry.

Harry began school in allocated conference rooms in the Congress Hotel in Chicago. In the third week of November, classes and quarters were moved to the Stevens Hotel at 720 South Michigan Avenue. Bob and Harry continued as roommates on the 19th floor with a spectacular view of S. Lakeshore Drive and Lake Michigan.

Harry practiced Morse code in the Coliseum on Wabash Avenue, between 14th and 16th Streets. The Sevens Hotel housed the radio mechanics laboratory. Harry and Bob spent six hours daily in class, three on mechanics and three on code. They attended class six days a week. Both Bob and Harry were lucky to be part of the first shift. The second shift ended at twelve midnight. On Saturday nights, servicemen could enjoy bowling, dancing, entertainment, and drinks at the Servicemen's Center at the corner of S. Michigan Avenue and Congress in the converted old opera house. Bob patronized the Servicemen's Center regularly. Harry studied in his room seven nights a week for the first two months of classes. He felt he needed to work harder than the other servicemen who came to the course with more advanced college courses or, at the very least, a high school degree. He would be pushing thirty next year, older than most students. Harry had been out of the school routine for over twelve years at the beginning of the radio classes. He wanted to learn, relished the learning opportunity, and felt he had a lot to prove, but he worried he would be unable to keep up.

By the first part of December 1942, Harry's weekly test results and Instructor's grades indicated his dedication to his studies. The practice for his Amateur Radio License came in handy during the code portion of the studies. He could now read and send over twenty words per minute, top of the group he practiced in. The instructors were teaching a new method of learning code using a di-da-dit system for reading the dots and dashes representing the letters of the alphabet. The older way of vocalizing each dot and dash was much slower. Instruments, recordings, and earphones were installed in the code laboratories to simulate actual telegraph and radio sounds for the code. Friday's became challenge days. Each student challenged another student to a timed duel for sending and receiving a hitherto unknown paragraph of army information prepared by the instructor. Harry enjoyed these challenges and usually won. Since many students wanted to challenge Harry, he received even more practice.

Radio mechanics are responsible for maintaining, testing, and repairing radio transmitting and receiving equipment. Their functions include inspecting the signal strength of transmissions, replacing defective components, such as wiring, or performing equipment inspections. Harry's experience in warranty auto radio repairs gave him a short leg up on the practical side of radio repair. Soldering required manual dexterity to work within the confines of the radio chassis. Harry enjoyed the hunt for problem components the most. With detective skills and problem-solving, logically eliminating possibilities, Harry could get lost in the workings of the equipment in front of him on the test bench.

Typically, the chassis consisted of a sheet metal frame or pan, sometimes with a wooden bottom. Components were attached, over insulation, when connecting to the metal chassis. Their leads were attached directly or with soldered jumper wires or sometimes using crimp connectors or wire connector lugs on screw terminals. In the early classes, circuits were large, bulky, heavy, and relatively fragile (even discounting the breakable glass envelopes of the vacuum tubes often included in the layout.) Labor-intensive circuit board production made the products expensive. The army required manufacturers to produce smaller, lighter equipment to fit in a plane's console or overhead compartment. That meant that the solder connections were close, cramped, and challenging. Some students could never find the problems in the tight small areas of the equipment, let alone fix the tiny resistors soldered between two vacuum tubes.

Harry spent all his evenings trying to catch up on the theory of radio signals and the electrical considerations of the components that generated them. Ohm's Law relates voltage (E), current (I), and resistance (R). The equation for Ohm's Law is $E = IR$. Knowing two of the variables, Harry learned to calculate the third.

The Power formula is $P = E \times I$ where P is the power in Watts (W), E is the voltage in Volts (V), and I is the current in Amperes (A): more calculations. Advanced math, algebra, and calculus were covered.

Harry learned radio and signals fundamentals, electricity, components, and circuits. He studied propagation, antennas and feed lines, AC power circuits, antenna installation, and RF hazards.

The coursework proved to be enormously challenging. Each week at least one and sometimes up to three out of the four hundred and eighty students in the program were shipped out to less demanding specialization programs for failing progress tests in code, mechanics, or radio theory.

Bob found out from personnel that Harry's birthday fell on December 20th. This year he would be twenty-nine. On Saturday, the nineteenth, the code class surprised Harry with chocolate-frosted yellow cake and ice cream during the last fifteen minutes. When dismissed, Harry and Bob rode the elevator up to their floor, and Harry changed into his clean/pressed shirt, tie, and crisply pleated pants. Regulations mandated that servicemen be at their presentable best when venturing out in public. Shoes spit-shined, face shaved and washed. The duo met Eugene, and Tim down in the lobby and, along with Bob, literally dragged Harry over to the Servicemen's Center for three lines of bowling and beer. Harry took the "old man" derision with a good-natured, broad smile. He loosened his tie and relaxed for the first time since arriving in Chicago, where he had grown up. Chicago, his city. He knew the streets, the trains, the "EL" schedules, and the bus and taxi stops. He knew the accent, the jazz clubs, and the restaurants. After bowling, Eugene and Tim decided to bar hop, but Bob wanted to show Harry the ballroom.

"There's a girl named Gladys I met up with twice now, and she usually has a friend with her, Sarah. Maybe we could dance a little. You dance, Harry?"

Harry burped beer and responded.

"I do, Bob. Might as well."

The converted lobby of the 4300-seat auditorium in the old opera center housed the nightclub. It held hundreds of tables and three dance floors. Perhaps as many as five hundred servicemen hung on the walls or sat at tables this Saturday. Girls mingled with the servicemen, volunteering to dance and socialize. To get into the nightclub, the women, who were not armed forces members, presented a Recreation Center for Service Men - Girls' Identification Card. The women had to be sponsored by one of the women on the membership committee to receive a card.

Bob and Harry drifted to an empty table in the corner of the lobby just off the dance floor where Bob had spotted Gladys the previous two weeks. Bob went off to try and find Gladys. Harry sat down for a smoke. The band at the back of the elevated stage consisted of students from the University of Chicago jazz ensemble. The band had a piano, bass fiddle, trumpeter, two saxophone players, and a drummer with a complete Gene Krupa set. In front of the band, three girls huddled around a microphone stand alternating between solos, duets, and group harmonies as tight as the Andrew Sisters. All the student band members were exceptionally talented, especially the jazz pianist and drummer. The group played popular covers.

The red carpet in the lavish lobby had a subtle light grey fleur-de-lis pattern. Areas converted for dancing consisted of oak parquet flooring (sanded, varnished, and scattered with fine sawdust.) Thick, fluted stone columns soared to the high ceiling, with lantern lighting encircling them nine feet above the floor. Chandeliers hung, centered between the columns. The space is elegant, warm, and relaxing.

Harry noted the dancing couples in the open area near his table. His eyes roved back to one girl dancing rings around a navy man. A brunette, she never stopped smiling even though the navy man seemed to have three left feet. She looked strong, with Betty-Grable legs. Harry imagined she had been on dance recital stages since eight. Her light blue pleated skirt might have creased the middle of her knees if she had ever stopped moving. She never did! The skirt swirled out with her turns and boogie-woogie steps. Despite her strength, she seemed to float through her turn-stop-reverse movements. Her knees stayed slightly bent, and her feet moved fast or not, depending on her next planned dance step. Her face was round and soft of chin and cheekbone. Her permed hair cut to just above her shoulders. Harry thought the girl's eyes were captivating, reminiscent of Egyptian or perhaps Cherokee heritage. Exotic.

At the end of the dance, the girl thanked her partner and drifted off. Two minutes later, Bob approached the table with a girl with blond hair and a second girl in tow.

"This is Gladys and her friend Sarah. This tall drink of water is Harry Martensen. His birthday is tomorrow. What is it, Harry, twenty-nine, right?"

Harry, stunned, let Bob do the talking.

"Won't you sit down, girls? Shall we order drinks?"

Damn, the second girl, Sarah, was the girl Harry ogled on the dance floor.

Harry swallowed, putting out his cigarette, "Pleased to meet you, Gladys, Sarah. Say, Sarah, I've been sitting in a classroom all day. How about a dance?"

Sarah smiled, "This number is kind of fast. Do you want to wait for a two-step?"

"I'll be OK," Harry stammered, "I'm not over the hill yet."

On the dance floor, Harry took the initiative and started the jitterbug. Sarah's eyes widened momentarily, and then she grabbed Harry's hand and joined in. They moved in tandem or in opposition, grabbing a free hand for a reverse spin when it felt right. By the end of the dance, Harry held Sarah tight against his six-one frame from behind as they step-ball-changed left and right until the music ended.

Back at the table, Harry pulled out a chair for Sarah before sitting down. The drinks Bob had ordered arrived for the four of them in a moment. Highballs for Gladys and Sarah; beer for himself and Harry. Halfway through their drinks, the band began a favorite song of Sarah's, "I've Got a Gal in Kalamazoo." Harry and Sarah stood simultaneously and took off for the dance floor.

Harry stayed out of most of Sarah's dance moves, ready to lead if necessary, hold or balance her at arm's length, and admire or match her step by step when she cued him with a sideways glance and a wink. A subtle dancer, Harry displayed excellent rhythm without letting his six-foot-one-inch frame look awkward or overpowering. He kept his back straight and knees bent, moving on the balls of his feet during the two-step without stepping on Sarah's feet. Sarah appreciated Harry's ability to lead her through a slow dance. They floated together as if they had been partners for years.

Three times when they sat back down at the table with Bob and Gladys, servicemen approached and asked Sarah for a dance. She did not turn them down; she danced with the sailor and the privates with the same smile Sarh offered Harry, yet she always returned to Harry's table after the music ended. As a volunteer,

Sarah tried to help each serviceman feel at home away from home. Harry admired her stamina and politely stepped aside while she went off to dance with the others but beamed when she returned.

Bob hardly noticed Harry and Sarah. His eyes never left Gladys, and she did not seem to mind not dancing. The few times they approached the dance floor on a slow number, they barely moved, opting instead to continue their conversation as if no one else existed in the lobby.

Sarah and Gladys excused themselves to the powder room. Harry remained quiet, but Bob wanted to compare.

"Sarah is quite a dancer, isn't she, Harry. When I met them several weeks back, I knew she was too much for me. You seem to be holding your own."

"She is a wonderful dancer," Harry said, "We have not spent much time talking. She sure is kind to all the men here. I doubt she likes me in particular."

"Yep, she likes you," Bob laughed, "Gladys said she's never danced with anyone as often as she has with you. Makes it a rule. Two dances and on to the next."

Harry looked around to see if the girls were in sight.

"She's different, all right. Confident, proud, pleasant to everyone."

Gladys and Sarah returned to the table. Gladys gave Bob a wink and a nod. They must have discussed Harry on the way to the powder room. Harry, suddenly shy, did not know how to proceed. He wanted to see more of Sarah, wondering, *Is it against Recreation Center policy?* Ultimately, Harry decided to ignore a few rules at his birthday party. He stood up and gripped the back of Sarah's chair, ready to help her up.

"The band announced they had time for two more slow numbers. Care to dance, Sarah?"

"Yes, Harry," said Sarah, "I'd love to."

Harry held Sarah close on the dance floor, letting the music captivate his mood; her hair tickling his cheek. Sarah probably stood five feet five or six and wore dancing shoes with inch-and-a-half heels. She sure seemed to fit. She had what Harry thought of as a great figure.

"At the risk of being too forward, Miss Azlin, you have made my birthday a delightful evening. I've never danced with a partner like you. Is it against the rules for me to ask for your phone number? Just say 'no,' I'll understand, or if I'm out of line, I had to ask."

Sarah did not hesitate.

"I've had a great time tonight as well, Harry. Please call me Sarah, and my phone number is LAK-4285. I'm usually home from work by 6:30pm."

After the band retired. Bob and Harry accompanied Gladys and Sarah to the front vestibule. Harry volunteered to step out into the freezing Chicago winter and hail a cab for the girls. Bob stayed inside to keep Gladys and Sarah company. Once the girls ducked safely into a taxi and the driver drove away, Bob and Harry returned to their room at the Stevens.

The next day, Sunday, Harry started studying right after breakfast. Mired in the theory of radio waves and a comparison to light waves, last evening's dancing and Sarah popped to the top of his thoughts, *probably at church.*

At one o'clock, Harry's focus was torn between radio waves and the memory of Sarah's jitterbugging hips; he picked up the phone and asked the operator to call "Lakeside 4285."

He heard the phone ring, and someone answered.

"Hello, Sarah?"

"This is Gladys, Sarah's roommate."

"May I please speak to Sarah if she is available?"

"I'll see. Who may I say is calling?"

"This is Harry; we met last night, Gladys."

"Just a moment."

Thankful for the pause, Harry wiped his sweating hands on his pants.

"Hello?" Sarah answered.

"Hello, Sarah. This is Harry Martensen calling. I hope it's OK calling on a Sunday."

"Of course, Harry. Happy Birthday!"

"Yes, thank you. Now I am an old man. Twenty-nine."

"I'll be twenty-three in August," Sarah confessed.

Harry thought momentarily; Sarah had already thought about their age difference.

"Sarah, I had so much fun last night. I wondered if you were attending the Recreation Center celebration on Christmas day, this Friday."

"Will you be going, Harry?" she asked.

"Yes," Harry said, "we have just the 25th off."

"Gladys and I were planning on going about 8:00pm. She will call Bob a little later."

Harry's heartbeat ramped up even faster.

"Oh, well, that's swell! I'll start looking for you at the same table we sat at last night. See you then! Goodbye!"

"Bye, Harry," Harry heard her laugh, "see you soon."

Harry returned to his study of wavelength, his mind more at ease. Now he started to worry about whether he should get a present for Sarah. Of course, they had just met. *Inappropriate?*

Bob returned to the room in the afternoon and called Gladys to verify their date on Friday evening. Bob and Harry discussed a small gift for each girl, and the idea of a pretty pin seemed to be their best bet. On Wednesday, Harry went shopping at Marshal Fields and found a two-inch ballerina pin with sparkles at the hem of a purple glazed tutu and one more prominent sparkle at the dancer's shoulder.

Friday, Christmas day, Harry set aside his manuals and notes. He braved the wind and sleet, taking the "EL," transferring to a bus, and walking four blocks to his grandfather's house. Surprised to see Harry, Chester Buffington barely recognized him in his long olive-drab overcoat and wool cap. His grandfather invited him to warm up by the fireplace in the living room.

Papa inquired about the health and doings of Flossie and Dorothy. Harry talked about his schooling at the Stevens Hotel. Nelsena excused herself and went into the kitchen to prepare lunch. Papa asked about the tourist park John and Harry had built; he had never seen it, only photographs. Harry described the long hours and heavy work he and his stepfather had accomplished laying the foundations and roofing the cabins.

"The war has taken a toll on the tourist trade in Chattanooga. Hunting and fishing are way down. Men that frequented our tourist court are overseas in Europe or the Pacific. John's cough is worse; he can't seem to shake it. Mum is still going strong. Dorothy and Verne, the same."

The conversation turned to Harry's schooling.

"Tell me more about Morse Code. That is kind of like a foreign language, isn't it?"

Harry asked Chester to read a paragraph from the book next to him on the end table. As Chester read, Harry tapped the code on the coffee table, asking Chester to either slow down or speed up until Chester's reading matched Harry's ability to stream the code. Nels, returning to announce lunch, thought Harry's tapping sounded like a squirrel chewing nuts on the back porch.

Harry stopped at the Recreation Center on his way back to the Stevens. Finding friends in the bowling alley, he joined in for a couple of lines of bowling. The group retired to one of the small conference rooms for poker. Harry, distracted by thoughts of his upcoming date with Sarah, lost four dollars before realizing he wasted possible date money. He begged off the game and returned to the Stevens to shave and shower.

Harry had time to write a short note to Florence and John. He did not mention Sarah.

At eight o'clock, Bob returned to the room to get dressed as Harry finished ironing his dress uniform. The two nattily dressed servicemen walked to the Recreation Center, hunching along in their long overcoats. The temperature had dropped into the teens. They sat at an open table next to the table they had occupied the previous Saturday. Bob and Harry did not have long to wait. Sarah waved to Harry as she approached the table. Harry helped her out of her coat, brushed off droplets of melted snow, gathered Gladys's coat, and took them to the coat check room. Bob ordered drinks, and the two girls enjoyed a smoke. Harry sat down and extracted a cigarette from his pack, trying to steady his hand as he lit up.

He had a right to be nervous, he thought. Sarah wore a grey dress, hemmed at the knees, belted at the waist, with thin shoulder pads. A square cut in the dress dipped down in front. The look was professional but loose enough for dancing. In short, she looked swellegant.

Harry looked to Bob for clues about the presents they had brought for the girls. They had agreed to each wait for the right moment, alone with their date. As it turned out, when the drinks were just about empty, Gladys and Sarah eyed each other and pulled out small packages from their purse. Sarah placed her present near the Christmas-themed centerpiece on the table, a simple white pine bough and pinecone with four candy canes hooked together on top.

Sarah pushed Harry's present to him.

"We thought you boys needed a little Christmas present to cheer you up since you're so far from home. Now, don't be embarrassed; these are small gifts."

Gladys handed Bob his present.

He accepted, "That's sweet of you girls. Harry, I say now is the time."

Harry and Bob reached into their service dress coats, produced small, flat boxes wrapped in Christmas paper, and laid them on the table before the girls. Harry suggested they order a second round of drinks before they opened the presents. All agreed.

When the drinks arrived, the girls could wait no longer, opening the little boxes to discover the pins.

Bob and Harry opened their presents. The girls had picked out small buoy-shaped bottles of Old Spice aftershave. Harry opened his up and slapped some on each of his cheeks. He had never used aftershave before but found he liked the scent. Not like a woman's perfume and stung for a moment when applied to his cheeks. Amid laughter and smiles, the four finished their drinks and headed for the dance floor. Charlie Barnet fronted his twenty-piece band playing swing music to the liking of Sarah and Harry. Hits like

"Cherokee" and "Skyliner" were requested. The first dance, the presents, and the two drinks broke the ice. Harry settled down: enjoying dancing and the closeness of Sarah. He had not enjoyed the company of a woman for a long time. They danced all evening, just as they did the night they met. Near the end of the band's last set, Sarah again thanked Harry for the broach. Harry thanked Sarah for the Old Spice and then moved into new territory.

"Sarah, could I have the pleasure of your company on New Year's Eve? I want to take you out to dinner. I have a reservation at the Rush Street location of Isbell's Restaurant."

Sarah appeared wowed by the prospect.

"That is an excellent restaurant. Right around the corner from my apartment, too. How did you do it? It's quite a popular restaurant, particularly on New Year's Eve."

"The catch is that the reservation is for 10:15pm, the soonest I could make it. I could meet you at your apartment. We might walk to the restaurant and, after dinner, listen to Guy Lombardo and the Royal Canadians on the radio in the bar at midnight."

Sarah took a moment, reflecting on her knowledge of the restaurant.

"The bar doesn't have a dance floor, Harry."

Harry remained calm, "Wouldn't that be OK, for a change?" he asked.

Sarah smiles, "Just the two of us; that would be lovely, Harry. Thank you!"

"Should I pick you up at your apartment?"

"That would be fine, Harry," Sarah said, "I live at 106 E. Bellevue Place."

"I'll knock on your door at a quarter to ten next Thursday."

Sarah told Gladys of Harry's plan after they returned to their apartment that night. Gladys said that she, too, had accepted an invitation to dinner for New Year's Eve, but she did not know for which restaurant; Bob wanted to surprise her.

When Bob and Harry arrived back at their room on the 19th floor of the Stevens, they discussed their success at lining up New Year's Eve dates. They agreed that going their separate ways for the evening would be best. What to do after ringing in the new year? Would they be invited back to the girl's apartment? What might happen there?

Harry decided not to worry about it. Bob and Gladys were further along in their relationship. Harry just wanted the evening to get to know Sarah better.

On Thursday, three members of Harry's code group challenged Harry. He won all three matches, but the challengers were getting better. Harry beat the last challenger by only eight seconds. In Mechanics theory, the weekly content test had been switched from Friday to Thursday, cutting Harry's study time by a day. Harry had absorbed each new concept by this time in the course, confidently leaving the testing room.

He washed his clothes on Wednesday while he studied and spent Thursday afternoon ironing. Bob left to pick up Gladys at five-thirty; he had made a much earlier reservation for dinner. Harry went out for a snack at the soda fountain in the F. W. Woolworth's five-and-dime store three blocks from the Stevens at six o'clock. At nine-thirty, he returned to his room, splashing on Old Spice just before taking the elevator and hailing a cab to take him to Sarah's address.

Harry rang the buzzer for Sarah and Gladys' apartment in the vestibule of the three-story building at 106 Bellevue Place at nine forty-five precisely. He proceeded to the third floor and knocked on Sarah's door.

Sarah opened the door in an elegant winter suit of a black silk crepe material with a short apron peplum in front, decorated with jeweled buttons of gold, aquamarine, and topaz-colored stones. The dress came down two inches below her knees. Stockings and high heels finished the look, putting Sarah closer to eye level with Harry's tall frame. Harry resisted the temptation to stare at Sarah's legs and wolf whistle. Sarah held a copper-colored velvet dress hat for the walk to the restaurant. She opened the door wide and invited Harry in for a quick tour. Harry appreciated how Sarah strode through the apartment as comfortably in high heels as bedroom slippers. She walked like she danced, smooth and confident as if on a fashion runway.

The living room, big enough for two couches, also contained an easy chair, coffee table, and two end tables. The small kitchenette barely held the essential appliances and a two-seat banquette.

The hallway from the living room led to two cramped bedrooms. Sarah's room consisted of a double bed, a nightstand, and one dresser. Harry saw the stack of books on the nightstand, suggesting an avid reader. Harry complimented her on the décor and furniture in the apartment, picking up the top paperback on the nightstand, a Michael Shane detective novel.

"I may want to borrow this when you're done, Sarah."

Sarah said, "I finished that one last night, Harry. If it fits in your overcoat, you could take it with you tonight."

Harry stuffed the paperback in his overcoat front pocket.

Time to leave for the restaurant. Harry asked Sarah if she still wanted to walk. He would be happy to call or hail a taxi. Sarah said she would like the fresh air; the restaurant is two blocks away. Light snow pattered Harry's shoulders, but the sidewalks, mostly, had been shoveled clear by the apartment building residents. The quiet snowfall softened the streetlights and, through the haze, the nearly full moon. They both enjoyed a blanket of silence. Harry had hold of Sarah by the elbow in case she began to slip. He also concentrated on his steps, shortening his usual long, quick stride to match Sarah's. Sarah's round, wide-brimmed hat protected her face from the snow.

The customers that filled Isbell's restaurant had dressed to the nines, but Sarah and Harry turned their share of heads as they were led to the table. After ordering highballs, Sarah chose the Half Broiled Spring Chicken on Toast in Butter Sauce. Harry ordered the Breaded Pork Tenderloin, Country Gravy, and Fresh Apple Sauce. Potatoes, Rolls, and Butter were to be served with the entrées. Harry asked Sarah about her family while they waited for dinner.

"Born in Coleman, Texas. The family moved to Chicago about the time I turned five, after the birth of my younger sister, Fay."

"Whoa, pardner," Harry chuckled, "That explains a lot right there. The way you dance, I should have guessed you're a cousin of Pecos Bill."

"You may have something there," Sarah said, "They still call my older brother Ken 'Tex.' He can't seem to get rid of the drawl. The eldest in my family is Louise. She works in Social Service for the Illinois Emergency Relief. My father's name is Charles, and he was born in Mississippi. My mother's whole family is from Texas by way of Louisiana. Her name is Bertie."

Harry kept his own history short.

"I have an older sister, Dorothy. She married Verne Constantine at nineteen. My mother is healthy. Is your father still working?"

"Right now," Sarah continued, "he's a janitor for an apartment building. He used to own a grocery store when we moved up from Texas. The store died in the depression. He used to cut and wrap his own meat; friendly to everyone in the neighborhood; disappointed when the store went under."

"So, he went to work as a janitor," Harry sympathized, "My stepfather and I worked as maintenance men for a couple of apartment buildings in Cleveland."

"After the store closed," Sarah leaned in, "Father worked as a security guard for the railroad. He patrolled the yard on the night shift."

Sarah spoke even softer, apparently remembering a tough time.

"One night, he confronted two men stealing meat from a refrigerated car, and they shot him. Father quit eight days later after he left the hospital. An article and picture of Dad appeared in the Sun-Times.

"We got by. Louise got the job with Social Services, so our family did OK during the early thirties."

Harry admired Sarah's comfort in revealing her father's nearly fatal experience.

"So many people out of work back then, He said, "But I never really noticed it either in my family. We all worked and got by. Do your Mom and Dad still live in Chicago?"

"Yes," Sarah said, finishing highball, "our house is a block from Garfield Park. Do you know where that is?"

"Sure, I lived across from Winnemac Park, about ten miles north of Garfield Park," Harry said, noticing the waiter making his way toward their table, one arm loaded with plates. "Ah, dinner is about to be served. I'm starving."

The couple ate in relative silence, commenting only on the dinners before them. Harry cut a small portion of his breaded pork tenderloin and passed it onto Sarah's plate to try. Sarah reciprocated with a piece of her chicken. Both dinners were judged to be delicious. After the couple finished their cherry pie a-la-mode, Harry paid the bill. They moved to the last open table in the bar. Harry found out Sarah had taken dance lessons for many years. Sarah's heroes were Martha Graham in New York and Ruth Page in Chicago. Harry wanted to know why.

She explained.

"Take Ruth Page, for example, Harry. She says that the dance movements should reflect the social and political tone of the music, opera, or ballet being played. Dance should involve creative thinking and emotional expressiveness. It's not just a combination of traditional ballet moves and positions but art in its own sense if the choreographer and dancer dig deep enough."

Harry drew a comparison to his hero.

"That's the way I've thought of people like Jesse Owens. He wasn't just an incredible runner and jumper. He made his mark by believing in himself and pushing past barriers others put before him."

Harry, ready to educate Sarah on Owen's biography, saw that he need not bother. Sarah's nod suggested she knew of Jesse Owens and his accomplishments.

"Yes, he is amazing as well," she said, "With a bit of luck, we can rid the world of Hitler and his Nazi followers and get back on track."

"Yes, the war. The war is changing everything.

"To be honest, Sarah, I'm not much of a guns and bullets man," Harry admitted, "Basic training included rifle training. I'm trying to contribute by learning everything I can about radio equipment. With better technology, planes, and ships, instruments are just as important to the war effort."

"I get it, Harry," Sarah said, "I hope you never have to kill someone. I could not bear that either."

Harry leaned back, relaxed.

"You're quite a gal, Sarah. Let's listen to the Royal Canadians. It's close to midnight."

Just before 12:00am, the hostess in the bar encouraged everyone to stand for the countdown.

Ten, nine, eight,

Seven, six, five,

Four, three, two, one, Happy New Year!!!

Happy New Year!

Harry pulled Sarah around, embraced her tenderly, and lifted her chin so he could look into her eyes, kissing her long and slow. When he pulled away, Sarah reached up and kissed Harry again. The crepe material of Sarah's dress moved across her skin as Harry's hands slid across her back, tickling her to laughter.

Harry and Sarah stayed for another hour, talking while the bar thinned out. They walked back to the apartment. Harry accompanied Sarah up the stairs in her building to her door. The radiator near the building entry kept the halls and stairs warm. Sarah leaned against the wall next to the door, gazing up at the tall man with thinning hair, combed back.

"That is the best New Year's Eve ever, Harry. Thank you for everything."

Harry pulled her away from the wall, urged her head onto his shoulder, and whispered.

"Yes, I feel the same, Sarah."

Harry broke away and took Sarah's face in his hands.

"I'm going to kiss you now. I'll say goodnight too, but I hope to see you again, get to know you more, and kiss you more!"

Sarah went inside her apartment and closed the door. Harry left the building, walked to the corner, and hailed a cab to return to the Stevens, feeling content with anticipation for future moments.

Harry and Sarah went out dancing with Bob and Gladys every Saturday. Sarah invited Harry up to her apartment every Wednesday night. Gladys extended her shift at the Meat Institute on Wednesdays until nine o'clock, as required for her job, so Sarah had the apartment to herself. Harry and Sarah would make dinner together, talk and scrounge on the couch.

The last Wednesday in January, after a quick dinner, Sarah told Harry to remain seated on the couch while Sarah went into the bedroom and changed into what Sarah labeled her *'swoosh.'* To Harry's surprise, Sarah returned dressed in an off-white peignoir outfit, including a floor-length silk robe with a feather ruffle on the hem (swoosh.) Sarah paraded into the living room and began twirling around and around until the robe *"swooshed"* out around her as if she were Ginger Rodgers. Not about to remain seated, Harry rose to twirl Sarah around in a waltz hold until they were both dizzy. They kissed and flopped onto the couch. Harry accidentally caught the hem of the beautiful material, pulling on the fabric enough to rip the seam at the shoulder of Sarah's robe.

Red-faced, Harry apologized again and again for ruining Sarah's swoosh. Sarah just laughed, took off the robe, and threw it over onto the easy chair, returning on her knees to the couch next to Harry and kissing him, guiding his hand to her breast. Harry, flummoxed for only a moment, encouraged Sarah's advances. Within minutes, Harry rose, took Sarah by the hand, and led her into the bedroom.

"Hurry, darling, let me kiss you. Where is Gladys?" Harry wondered?

Sarah closed the door to the bedroom, just in case, stripping off her nightgown. She lay on the bed in her flare knickers, breasts jiggling as she moved. Harry stripped down to his skivvies and joined Sarah, beautiful Sarah, on the bed.

"I know this is forward and soon, Harry, but I need to know. This war makes a rush out of everything."

Harry's hands roamed the mounds and crevices of Sarah's figure. His touch was as delicate as a surgeon's. Patient in his excitement, Harry wanted Sarah to continue needing him. He carried a trojan in his wallet but, during his ardor, had the sense to decide not to go 'all the way' with this wild Texas dancer. Harry liked everything about Sarah. He was no teenager. He suspected their relationship might be worth a lifetime together.

Afterward, Sarah snuggled into Harry's neck and softly tapped the dimple on his chin. She dabbed at the countless freckles on his shoulders. Happy!

Harry telephoned Sarah a week before Valentine's Day.

"Valentine's Day falls on a Sunday this year, Sarah. Perhaps we could prepare a Valentine's Day bunch for some of your friends."

Sarah, touched by Harry's thoughtfulness, began to panic.

"I can barely turn on the oven, Harry; brunch sounds ambitious."

"Breakfast is my specialty," Harry said, "I would prepare all the food. You would be my runner."

"I don't know, Harry; We could fit another couple besides Gladys and Bob here."

Harry shook his head as if Sarah could see him smiling over the phone. Perhaps he had not yet mentioned his expertise as a short-order cook.

"I am thinking maybe ten couples. I have heard you mention Bernice, and maybe Fay has a boyfriend. I've checked on using one of the small commercial kitchens and a conference room at the

Stevens. All you need to do is line up the guests. I'll buy all the food and be ready at eleven o'clock on Sunday."

"Are you sure, Harry? Breakfast for so many people!"

"I really want to do this, Sarah. I want to meet as many of your friends as I can."

Sarah became excited. She wanted her friends to meet Harry. But she wondered what could become of her friends meeting a serviceman who might be here today, gone tomorrow overseas.

"Gladys says your course at the Radio Operators and Mechanics School ends on the 28th. Then what will happen."

"It's the Army, honey. Anything can happen," Harry cautioned, "More schooling, a base assignment stateside or overseas; I won't know until the orders come down. Whatever happens, I want to take as many memories as possible. I can do this, I know, and I want to."

Harry needed the distraction of the brunch to keep him from dwelling on the unanswerable question of where he would be going in March. The schooling wound down. Most of the material had been covered, and there were only two tests in Mechanics and one final code test. Harry had done well in the course, but now, knowing the ways of the army, he knew he could not predict what might come next.

Each evening Harry went out to the grocery store and bought food, slogging it back to the kitchen he had arranged at the Stevens. He kept Sarah busy as well. He gave her the menu to type up at her work. She oversaw the party favors, centerpieces, and music. Harry and Bob moved the Zenith stereo and record player from one of the lounges. They also rolled in an upright piano from another conference room.

Sarah and Harry readied the room at nine o'clock on Valentine's Day. They arranged two six-foot round tables with white linen tablecloths in the Stevens' conference room. Red and white crepe streamers looped down and crisscrossed from the room's four corners. Sarah prepared the plates, silverware, white linen napkins, and party favors for the sit-down brunch. Four couples would be at each table. Harry and Sarah would eat later.

Twenty minutes before the hour, Harry fired the griddle in the kitchen and put on a white apron. The couples streamed into the conference room at eleven; by ten after eleven, all the group occupied their seats at the designated tables. Gladys and Bob, of course, were joined by Bernice and Derek, Mary and Kathy, and Sue and Jim. At the second table, Fay and her boyfriend Charlie were seated by Sarah's older sister Louise who did not have a date. Sarah's brother Ken, his wife, and Emily and Walter, additional friends of Sarah's, were also seated and ready to order.

Harry introduced himself as the host of the brunch and proceeded to describe the elements on the menu card placed next to each guest's plate:

Eggs: over easy, sunny side up, or scrambled

Pancakes – quantity

Sausage, bacon, or fried Canadian ham

Grits or hash browns

Toast and strawberry jam

Fresh fruit bowl

Strawberry shortcake for dessert

Once Sarah collected the menu cards, Harry sorted them in the order most efficient for the grill. Scrambled egg orders were combined. He summed the total number of pancakes and sausage and bacon orders. No one ordered grits (a Chattanooga staple), so hash browns for everyone. Fresh fruit bowls were prepared with a small plate covering them in the refrigerator.

Harry got to work, spreading the necessary amount of potato cubes tossed in oil onto the upper left-hand corner of the griddle. Bacon and sausages, along with the ham, were started in the upper right. Harry directed Sarah to wait to bring out the fruit bowls until he began the pancakes. Instead, he suggested she pour everyone the chilled squeezed orange juice, change the record to the Glen Miller Orchestra, and have Bob uncork the champagne.

In ten minutes, the sausage and bacon were ready. Harry transferred them to a steamer pan with a cover to keep them warm. He poured out twenty-four pancakes, stunning Sarah by flipping them in the air one by one when they bubbled at just the right time and letting them land back on the grill.

The pancakes were cooking on the flip side. Harry started cracking eggs into a mixing bowl for the scramble, a crack with his left hand and a crack with his right. By the time he finished whipping and beating the eggs, the pancakes were done, so he scraped them off the griddle into another steamer pan. His hands blurred as he checked and flipped the ham, stirred, and turned the hash browns. The scrambled eggs looked close to done. The pan with the eggs needed turning, and Harry turned the eggs upside down with a jerk of his right hand. The first pieces of toast were brushed with butter.

Harry plated the necessary items by looking at two menu cards for table one. Sarah carried the two plates out with the menu cards and exchanged them for the empty plates on the table. When Sarah returned, setting down the empty dishes, Harry began plating two more orders while Sarah picked up the next two. Harry urged her to pick up the pace.

In this manner, Sarah served all the guests their plates within four minutes of the first two plates placed on the table.

Harry stood back from the table while Sarah asked if anyone wanted more eggs, bacon, or potatoes. There were three takers, all men, at table one. Harry obliged. While the second round of eggs was cooked, Sarah and Harry prepared small plates with the strawberry shortcake dessert. Harry had mixed and baked the shortcake early that morning. Sarah served the strawberry shortcake while Harry refilled empty orange juice and champagne glasses.

The brunch wound down. Bob stood and tinked his glass with a spoon to get everyone's attention, calling Harry and Sarah from the kitchen for a cook's parade. The guests all raised their glasses for a toast to the chef. The men commented on the delicious fixings. A couple of the women seemed amazed Harry had pulled everything together in such a short amount of time. Sarah beamed with pride at discovering another skill possessed by the tall man at her side. Harry pulled up two chairs to table two.

"Say, Jim," said Harry, "Sarah tells me you work for an army truck parts factory down in Gary."

"I do, that's right, said Jim, "We've already changed our bumper design twice. Our latest can knock down a path through a Malaysian jungle if necessary. Six months ago, our factory turned out fenders for Studebaker. Derek's factory over there builds box and drum magazines for Thompson submachine guns, right?"

Derek waited to swallow a bite of shortcake.

"Yes, parts for the SMG M1928A1."

Jim nodded at the two girls sitting next to him.

"Mary and Kathy work in a munitions factory down in Gary."

Harry drummed a knife on the table.

"It's amazing how fast we're catching up to Hitler's arsenal, he said, "Now we hear he's been building up his military for the last ten years or so. He has a head start."

Tom pounded the table, "In the end, he'll lose. Ninety thousand German troops surrendered to the Soviets in Stalingrad two weeks ago." Tom's defiance softened, "How about another shortcake, Harry; you're quite the cook."

"Strawberries?" Harry asked.

"Sure."

Gladys' brother worked on a battleship somewhere in the Pacific theater. She read every scrap of information on the war in that region and said, "Last week, our boys captured Guadalcanal from the Japanese."

"At a huge cost," Sarah said, "Two women on our floor at the office were notified by the war department last week that their husbands were gone. Guadalcanal. Ruth hasn't been back to work."

Jim summed up, "I guess we hold tight. Turn the tide. This brunch is an example. We keep going. Thank you, Harry and Sarah. Delicious!

"Time to go, Bernice."

The guests left. Harry began to clean up the kitchen and wash the dishes. Sarah dried. They worked in silence at Harry's typically furious pace. Sarah kept up with the drying for ten minutes, then broke down and began crying into her towel, running to the conference room. She had placed a plate down hard on the countertop. The noise startled Harry, and he noticed her leaving the room. He went to the conference room where Sarah, her back to Harry, seemed to be dabbing at her eyes. Encircling her from behind, Harry gave her a gentle squeeze.

"It's OK, Sarah. OK!"

Sarah, shaking, said, "I keep wondering what's next, Harry. We've had fun, haven't we, Harry, but where are you going? What's next?"

Harry turned Sarah to him, keeping her close, saying nothing until her sobbing and shaking eased.

"I still can't answer that, Sarah. There's nothing for it. But I will say this. At this point in my life, and with the war, I'm not looking for just fun. We have to see what each new day brings.

"If I do go away, I sure would appreciate a letter occasionally."

Sarah hugged her man tighter, "Oh Harry, I'm not much for writing letters, but I'll try. Promise."

The last two weeks in February went by in a whirlwind. Harry showed up late or early at Sarah's apartment, depending on when his class was let out. Sarah came home late from work more than once to find Harry asleep in the vestibule, waiting for her. Sarah invited Harry to her family's home for a short visit to meet her parents. After the introduction and a brief chat, Fay suggested a sing-along, and Sarah sat down at the piano, opened the Gershwin songbook, and Charles and Fay joined Harry and Sarah on "Someone to Watch Over Me."

Harry discovered his gal played the piano. Sarah found that Harry had no trouble carrying a tune in a strong baritone voice. Bertie and Charles, Sarah's parents, were polite but reticent to commit to Harry, a soldier and temporary resident of Chicago, about to be shipped elsewhere.

After the last Radio Mechanics class, Harry and Bob received duties for cleaning and organizing the classrooms, resident rooms, common areas, and libraries. Every inch of the hotel needed to pass inspection before starting the new sequence of courses. Bob and Harry stayed busier than when they attended class.

On the morning of March 7th, at the end of the morning drill, Sarge passed out envelopes containing orders to each serviceman. Bob would stay Stateside, assigned to Scott Airfield in St. Louis. Harry must report to Major James L. Caufield at the Valley Forge Military Academy, Wayne, Pennsylvania. The Stevens' duty sergeant had arranged train tickets for Bob to leave for St. Louis at oh eight hundred on March 8th. Harry's ticket, dated March 8th, indicated an eighteen-hundred-hour departure time. The two friends had no time to ponder their future destinations. They were assigned additional clean-up duty to mop and wax all the oak floors in all the ballrooms on the second floor of the Stevens. They readied for inspection at sixteen thirty.

Both men shared a cab to 106 Bellevue for a last rendezvous with Sarah and Gladys. As with many rushed goodbyes, the evening seemed awkward from the start. Harry had no real idea of his future other than heading to Valley Forge, the campsite of George Washington's army during the revolutionary war, somewhere in Pennsylvania. Harry could not add any more than that to Sarah's questions. He changed subjects.

"Why don't we dine at Isbell's Restaurant?"

Sarah agreed, "I'd like that. We should get away!"

Sarah held Harry's hand like a vice to the restaurant. Over dinner, Harry kept the conversation light and upbeat.

"It will take two days to get there with the transfer schedule. I'll be staying in Buffalo tomorrow night; on to Philadelphia on Tuesday."

"Will you stay at an Army Air Force Base in the area?"

"No idea, Sarah, but as soon as I know, I'll write and let you know."

Sarah put her fork down and put her hand over Harry's.

"What about us, Harry?"

"You said you'd try to write," said Harry, attempting to distract them both. His heart burned, not from anything he had eaten. "I'll probably have my hands full for a few days, but I'll write as soon as I get a minute. Lots of couples carry on this way. At school, half a dozen of the guys had sweethearts back home."

Now, Sarah seemed to gain strength, making light of the impossible situation.

"Oh, you'll forget about me in short order, Harry. I have had so much fun with you. I'll miss those freckles."

Harry wanted to know and remember as many details about Sarah as possible in their short remaining hours.

"Tell me more about your job. How did you land there?"

Sarah related stories of her job interviews after college. She spoke of her supervisor, Mrs. Grobman, and how much respect she had for her. Harry asked Sarah about Michigan State College in Lansing, Michigan, where she got her Bachelor of Science degree.

"My majors were Entomology and Journalism. I loved them both. Ask me anything about the sub-orders of Coleoptera."

"You'll have to break it down for me, Sarah, but it sounds interesting; insects, right?"

Sarah explained. Harry listened through the entire dinner. Over an after-dinner drink, the couple reminisced how often they had danced and scrounged together. Harry decided they should head back to the apartment. The restaurant was closing for the night.

Sarah could not tear herself away from Harry's arms at the apartment.

"Come in, Harry, scrounge, and cuddle with me tonight. I will miss you, so."

Harry, aroused, asked, "What about Bob and Gladys?"

Sarah turned, opened the apartment door, and said, "Let me go in and see."

Sarah went into the apartment but, in a minute, opened the door.

"They're in bed in Gladys' room with the door closed. Do you want to sleep over?"

"Yes," Harry said, "I most certainly do."

Harry and Sarah filled the night with closeness, the touches of soft skin, the bumps of hard nipples, the counting of freckles. They slept engulfed in subtle perfume and the contentment of Sarah's breath.

Early in the morning, they woke to the aroma of coffee and heard Bob and Gladys rustling in the kitchen. Sarah and Harry threw on their clothes and entered the kitchenette for coffee with Bob and Gladys. Sarah agreed to meet Harry at the train station at 5:30pm after work. Bob and Harry hurried away to hail a cab after one last kiss from both the girls.

At the Stevens, Bob grabbed his duffle, shook hands, hugged Harry, and hurried to catch his train.

Harry had time to write Florence and John with an update. After lunch, he left the Stevens and window-shopped on Rush Street. Harry spotted a bracelet for Sarah set with purple stones that Harry thought might match the purple sparkles in the broach in her Christmas present. He could afford it. He impulse-bought it.

Harry waited on the platform for the train to Buffalo, New York, leaving at sixteen hundred. He tried to look nonchalant, but as the impending departure time drew closer and the train pulled into the station, Harry became anxious that Sarah might not see him off. He tried to tell himself it would not matter; he must look to his future now in Pennsylvania.

Sarah came running toward him, the echo of her high heels clicking the brick pavers. Harry's shoulders relaxed, relieved. He greeted her with a huge smile and a sparkling wink. In ten minutes, Harry waved to Sarah out the train window. She waved back; pointed to the bracelet on her wrist, holding onto her smile.

Major James L. Caufield possessed slick black hair down to his ears, short and grey from there to his cropped sideburns. His round chin made him look more like a professor than a field battled soldier. He stood as Harry entered the room. Harry saluted.

"Private Harry Martensen reporting, sir."

"At ease, Private," the major said, "Your trip from Chicago go OK?"

"Everything went as planned, sir. No issues."

Major Caufield sat back down behind his desk, indicating the chair on the other side of the desk.

"That's great, have a seat. I have your service record and would like to review some items with you.

"Let's see, born in 1913, thirty years old."

"Not yet, sir," Harry corrected the major, "my birthday is in December. I'm twenty-nine."

Caufield nodded, jotting a note on the pad near his right elbow.

"Be that as it may, I have several of your immediate superior officer's reports going back to basic training that indicates a willingness to pitch in, takes responsibility, and cooperate with your fellow soldiers and superiors.

"I have three instructor's reports indicating your leadership potential. To quote, 'Martensen leads by example, encouraging his fellow servicemen to excel as he excels.' I have similar comments from the other two instructors.

"You have no blemishes on record.

"You're in great shape, six feet one hundred seventy-three pounds. Drill technique – excellent."

The major paused and looked up at Harry, allowing him to add anything that had not made the report. Harry did not know what to say, so he sat still, smiling.

Major Caufield smiled, looking back at Harry's service record folder.

"Now we get to the good part: First in your Code section, first in your Radio Mechanics section. In fact, out of four hundred and fifty students in the latest class at the Radio Operators and Mechanics School in Chicago, you achieved second place in test scores and instructor reviews. Congratulations!"

Harry beamed at this news. *Second out of so many trainees. Wow.*

"Thank you, sir," said Harry, "I am grateful for the opportunity to take that class. I studied. It had been a long time since I had been in a classroom."

"Our review committee thinks you have potential as a commissioned officer in the Army Air Corps. That is why you are here. The Cadet Communications Officer training course at the Valley Forge Military Academy is your next step. Show us that same work ethic applied to learning an officer's duties, responsibilities, and leadership skills.

By the way, the program is race integrated. Negro and white candidates will share officer's quarters, with bunkmates assigned alphabetically, regardless of their race, and all the candidates will train together. Any problem?"

"Absolutely none, sir," Harry replied and meant it.

The major was pleased with Harry's rapid acceptance of his outlined conditions. "Pass this next course, and you will be honorably discharged from the Army to allow you to join the Army Air Force as a Commissioned Officer.

"Again, if you do well at Valley Forge, you'll finish training at Yale in the Advanced Radio and Radar school, and then it will be back to Illinois for a one-month course at the AAF Cryptographic Course at Chanute Field.

"The next four months will be very intense."

"Yale University? Harry asked, flabbergasted."

"Ultimately, the war may preclude this path, so take it one step at a time. You will need to work at least six months stateside under a seasoned communications officer before you get a base of your own. The war means that your ultimate assignment will probably be overseas.

"So, what do you say?"

Harry reflected on that first recruitment interview in Nashville and how far he had come since that rejection. Sarah came to mind. He could not wait to tell her the news.

Harry stood, excited and jumpy, "Let me get started. Thank you, sir."

The two men stood and saluted each other. Major Caufield shook Harry's hand, but the major had one last thing on his mind.

"We need to get a picture of you for the Chattanooga Times Free Press. The war department likes good press. The war makes that difficult, of course. An army journalist waits in the next room to get your details; parents, address, etc..."

Harry walked from the journalist's interview to his assigned dorm room to stow his gear. His roommate had evidently arrived and unpacked earlier in the day. The scent in the room seemed different, somehow, almost foreign. The framed picture on the second desk highlighted a smiling, attractive negro woman.

Harry thought of Sarah and wished for a picture of her. He decided to write to her soon with a request for one. Classes would begin the day after tomorrow. Tomorrow he had to get the lay of the land, requisition his textbooks, and report for drill and duty assignments. Harry knew he might wash out immediately or after each bi-weekly test. He kept the thought of becoming a commissioned officer, the prestige and the considerable raise in pay that entailed, tamped down in the back of his mind. Harry resolved to prove himself yet again. He would study and study some more. If he became confident of his success, that might change his prospects with Sarah. A college graduate and a commissioned officer. They would make a good couple.

Jeffery Gardener (nicknamed Woody,) Harry's new roommate, returned to the room late. The two spent the next twenty minutes getting to know each other. Jeffrey had married his wife (in the picture on the desk) just before Pearl Harbor, where his two older brothers died. Harry mentioned Sarah as a gal from Chicago he really liked. Jeffery seemed just as confident and determined to succeed as Harry.

Jeffery did not mention anything about their color difference. Harry never brought it up, either. Too excited to sleep, Harry brought out his board, pegs, and a deck of cards, and the new roommates played cribbage for an hour before turning in.

3/14/1943

Harry, darling,

Right now, I don't know exactly where you are – I've tried all day to find Valley Forge, Pa., on a map and couldn't. I suppose you have already installed yourself somewhere, and darling, I wish it weren't so darn far away!

At about 7, Bob called Gladys long distance from St. Louis, and that set us off, and we took Vivian, the gal next door, and went out to the show. Oh, Harry, tomorrow is Saturday, and I don't look forward to it. No "Hi! Hon" as soon as I get settled at work, and no plans for meeting you as soon as you can escape from the Stevens. Already the emptiness of this damn city has made itself felt – and everywhere I turn, there is a memory and a sweet pang of happiness for our days together. You know, darlin, how much our times together were beginning to mean to me. You know that only since 1943 came around have I begun to examine our acquaintanceship with a query as to its possibilities – and now, to have you leave just when the sound of your voice over the phone could make me eager to see you. When the thought that I would see you within the next few hours – where these things were beginning to be and to take concrete form – where I realized that soon I could even put these emotions into words – then to have you leave me.

That's the unbearable part! You had to leave when things were beginning to shape up; I mean, from my standpoint, we didn't have a chance to see what cooked with us.

There are so many things I'd like to say to you tonight. Can you imagine the greyness of the city as I left work Thursday and walked down streets that you won't be walking down for so long now? Can you imagine the emptiness of an afternoon without a call from you – nobody giving me that same pickup daily? Can you feel in your fingertips the loneliness of no one important to look forward to seeing?

It's probably not at all this tumultuous for you. It won't be long before your feelings will be just "Auld lang syne" for the Chicago days.

Those are the things I am afraid of – and I know that is one reason our conversations had a nebulous quality – I don't think I want to be just a vague memory to you, Harry.

Tonight, of course, I am missing you with every fiber of my being – if you appeared in rags or in ashes or any horrifying garb, I'd be glad to see you – if you appeared coming my way.

You see, I can still feel the memory of Wednesday nights – and the warmth of you is still high in my consciousness – and the longing for you tonight is agonizing.

All day today, I have formulated ways and means of seeing you – and when you have your definite schedule for the subsequent sessions, I want to know – how long you will be at Valley Forge – then where? When known, I can start moving on a definite campaign to be where you are again.

You have the knowledge – even as I do – that the next few weeks will show whether this state of mind is acute or seems to be chronic. Right now, of course,

I am so choked up that Kleenex after Kleenex is landing in the fireplace.

That damn fireplace – and every time I hear "You'd Be So Nice to Come Home To," I want to fight the injustice of it all – that there you are and here I am – and we could be having such a wonderful time together.

And as soon as you can safely inquire – get the lowdown on furlough possibilities for yourself – of course, I would take the last half, after you've spent some time in Chattanooga – and be so damn glad to see you just for half a furlough.

Gladys sends sincere wishes for your continued good fortune – my mother is incredibly happy for you – Bernice "understands why I feel low now that you're gone" - oh, darlin.

Sometimes I think I'm such a damn fool – it's taken me an awfully long to get enthusiastic about something – I need to examine and analyze it so long.

That "Old Black Magic" is beating along my bloodstream tonight, my dearest Harry. Maybe this is a letter better left unsent, but you know me well now, Hon, and know what I mean and what I'm trying to say – which is that I wish you were here – Oh Harry, how I wish you were here! And that is right from the heart of

Sarah

3/15/1943

Dear Harry,

Here I go again; I can't get out of this mood.

Whatever I do, I wish I were doing with you – wherever I am – I wish you were there – I miss everything we used to do. I've no one even to talk to like I used to speak to you – How wonderful to listen to such confidence, value your opinions, and hear what you had to say on the subject.

I'm not hungry – the food won't go down these days – and the nights – darling, tonight would do justice to June – it's beautiful and would have been perfect if you had just been here.

I've smoked so much my throat aches but so does my heart, so that's a minor detail – I won't hear any songs on the radio until everything we heard together is gone. I don't know how long it would even take me to get enough of you, darling – because I saw no sign of getting enough of you – and as I told you one night – there were so many wild ideas I would have liked to try – if I had had the nerve – or if you wouldn't laugh at me – you were so sweet, my darling.

Today I began to wonder if maybe as long as you are so much older than I am – you must have heard all this so many times before – perhaps the words in my letters are the exact words you've heard before – but darling, maybe it's just because it's an old feeling.

Tonight (Monday) when I got home, I opened your first letter and oh, my dearest, if it could have been you!

I'd give anything right now to walk down our two flights of stairs and find you at the door. Remember that night I came home and found you curled up in front of our door – Harry, hon, I am always so glad to see you – every time you come over.

I do not like to think of you being within easy distance of Philadelphia. I am already jealous of any girl you may meet there. I want it to be me with you – and I know just how empty a bunk feels – I feel that emptiness every night now, my dearest.

I wish you could give me your address, Harry, dearest; I want to stay in your memory – I want you to come back someday, Harry, to Chicago. That's all I can ask or hope for, right?

Tonight, I'm going downtown with Bernice to hear an all-girl orchestra (symphony) and a 12-song piano feature play what seems to be some very intriguing numbers – including Ferde Grofé's " Grand Canyon Suite," the "Blue Danube," and Gershwin's "Rhapsody in Blue." I got some free press tickets and box seats at the Orchestra Hall, and I asked Bernice instead of Gladys because Gladys doesn't like anything but jazz – and while I love it all – I know Bernice will appreciate going too.

Wish to hell you were here. I never did get to take you to the Panther room. Cab Calloway is coming on March 26.

Now, dearest, I must run! If the music is fine, I shall be inspired to write again later tonight – wish I could tell you everything, darling – miss you – want you here – oh, you'll be sick of those words – but hon, I mean it all.

Yours,

Sarah

3/16/1943

My darling Harry,

Now I am over at my mother's, and I miss you as much here as I do at home. Every time I walk by the "music room," I could cry because you are not snoozing on the lounge, so we can go home and scrounge.

The ride over here this morning was long and lonely – no gaiety, no laughter – no you! Every place I go is so steeped in memories of you and the fun we had. I can go nowhere without this longing being awakened in me.

Sunday has been my loveliest day of the week for a long time – and now it's the loneliest. All these beautiful sunlit hours – and you are not here to spend them with. I think of our little place at 106 – which neither Gladys nor I could bear to stay in today – all empty and sunshiny – just waiting for you and me to walk in, zip into swoosh, and you warm up the room. This afternoon my mother and I went to the basement to get my summer clothes out of storage. Oh, Harry, dearest, why won't you be here for spring and summer? I know you were getting sick of looking at me in the same damn clothes all winter, and now just when I can go into a new set – where are you?

I am so glad when I think of our beautiful hours together. While you were here, I spent every free moment with you – glad we never spent minutes "not speaking to each other" - thankful the only times you ever saw me crying were when I thought about you leaving me.

Oh Harry, darling, if sincerity could have pulled you through the ether from Valley Forge to Chicago, I would have drawn you here last night by sheer force of will. Gladys and I would have given anything to see you and Bob come walking in – loud, gay – eager – all of us harmonious – cares gone for the time we were together.

Harry, I hope you are not getting letters like this from Chattanooga – I can't help but think there must be many girls who would have given anything to be in my golden slippers over the last four months! And I suppose Valley Forge will add another to the list.

The trouble is, I knew all along what a rare genuine article you were. I marvel at your sweet consideration and kindness and how tender and understanding you are.

This city is so crowded, and there are always people everywhere, and yet right now, it is the loneliest place in the world, and I cannot recapture our undying zest! Oh, we did have fun.

Darling, thank goodness I get my check tomorrow - I am always delighted when I make it up to another payday.

Tomorrow night I will get my hair done – wishing that darling-looking thing were coming to pick me up. Oh my God, Harry, every minute I think of the millions of things we never talked about – how many things I don't know about you – all our chances for really knowing each other as I wish we did – pushed so far in the future.

Dearest, please write to me as often as possible.

I think you're the swellest guy I've ever known – and I miss your dimple, laughter, and freckles, and, darling, I'd rather have you come back than for me to find something or someone to take my mind off missing you. That's why letters are important, darling.

I guess you know what I'm trying to say. You usually did, and I always liked talking things over with you.

I'm so glad you helped me select my green dress and coat – those were lovely afternoons.

You may see further into me from these written words than you could while here. I never could talk as effortlessly as I could write.

Darling, Harry, there goes that damn useless pounding in my ears again, "Hurry Harry, Hurry Harry, Hurry Harry" - and to know you cannot come is hell, my darling.

Sarah

Only four days passed before Harry's resolve to study day and night so as not to think about Sarah began falling apart. He reread the last letter he had received from Sarah again. At twenty-two hundred hours, Harry placed a long-distance call to Sarah.

"Hello?" Harry recognized Sarah's voice, melting.

"Miss Sarah Azlin, please," the long-distance operator said.

"This is Sarah Azlin."

"You have a person-to-person call from Harry Martensen; go ahead, please."

"Harry, is that really you?"

"It's really me, darling. We have three minutes. The rates are better late at night; I hope you don't mind a late call."

"Of course not, Harry. It's great to hear your voice."

"Yes, yours as well."

"I have missed you so much."

"I missed you too," Harry said, "that's why I had to call. I need to study day and night here, and the class is run at an accelerated pace. They are piling on an incredible amount of stuff. I need to run to stay three steps behind.

"Thank you for writing to me. I did not expect to receive a letter so soon." Harry swallowed to keep from choking. Sarah wanted not to waste even a tiny pause.

"Believe it or not," she said, "I've been writing to you nearly daily."

"With all the studying, papers I have to write, drill, and duty assignments to complete, maybe I'll call instead of writing till they ease off.

"Then again, maybe they won't ease off; it does not look like they will."

"That's OK, Harry, Sarah encouraged, "You can do it. I know you can."

Harry looked at the clock on the wall of his room. He pressed on, not wanting to seem too anxious with his news. "That's what I wanted to tell you. If I can make it through this course, I'm on a path to becoming a Commissioned Officer, Lieutenant."

Sarah stopped short and only managed after a moment to say, "Wow!"

Harry filled the silence, "I'm trying not to get too excited. One person is already gone from our class. It is much tougher than Chicago."

"Do your best, Harry. I know you will."

"I'll make it through," continued Harry, pretending confidence, "That's not all. If I pass rigor here, I'll head to Yale University for an Advanced Radio and RADAR course."

"RADAR," Sarah shook her head at the phone, "I have no idea what that is."

"Neither does the army. It's some new weapon or defense system."

Silence again.

"Wow!" said Sarah.

"My time is almost up. I have so much to tell you. I have a negro roommate, Jeffery Gardener; we call him Woody; he is smart and will probably command a negro squad someday.

"Oh gosh, I've got to go; time's up. I will try to find time to write you the details." Harry saw the secondhand march around the wall clock. Sarah suddenly feared their time would expire.

"What about a furlough?" she asked.

"Way too soon, darling. I'll let you know. Goodbye, Hon."

"Goodbye, Harry, thanks for calling. Miss you!"

3/18/1943

Dearest Harry,

Well, are you going to Philadelphia this weekend to have your picture made? That is about what I want the mostest of the most now - as long as I can't have you in person.

Bob has asked Gladys to marry him - and she is considering it, but there is so much stacked against them simply from a religious standpoint. And from our brief conversation on that subject on the corner of Montrose and Lincoln one morning, I know that you and I have both been burned at that incendiary bomb's going off. And for me, that marked the end of all associations that could grow into anything!

As far as religion is concerned, I think one Protestant church is as good as another. I think it is well for parents to put in a certain amount of Sunday mornings to locate a church where they can go, find agreeable friends, and hear worthwhile things.

I have been active in church work.

All of that ended when I went to Michigan State in 1939 - and after 2 years - when I got back – I could not fit back in. I think most of the kids resented the diploma I had when I got home (there were only 3 out of our crowd that went on to college), and also - most of the old couples had married, and I tried in vain to fit back into the scheme of things.

I guess full realization of the futility of my efforts struck home when the girl I had considered one of my best friends married a guy I knew to be one of my best friends because I had helped his romance with Betty along, and they didn't invite me.

But then life had gone on so well for two years without me - I had lost interest in most of their personal problems - which had mainly resolved themselves down to "What are we going to do with a kid on the way - and only $35 a week income between us?"

So, what the hell? I was in their hair. I got the hell out regarding church activity, although last spring, they called me in to play a Russian actress in the Spring play. I had fun doing it as usual.

Darling, the happiest times from 13 to about 18 were tied in with Sunday school and those kids. We met or had a party every Friday night - we spent all Sunday morning in church, rushed home to get something to eat, and returned to play badminton or practice a play.

The moral or spiritual values I may have were derived in fellowship - right?

Gee, Harry, look what this consultation with Gladys about Bob brought on. I hope I haven't bored you with all my philosophical rambling.

Miss G sent me to lunch at the Flamingo Room at the Bismarck today - a blessing because I could not decide whether to eat lunch or dinner.

Anyhow, this religion business is vital when you look at it from the "head of the family" viewpoint, don't you agree?

Because I'm very family minded, I have given more thought to this, probably, than Gladys as she is sure she wouldn't want to raise kids as Catholic, but I believe you have to raise them as something, don't you darling, at least in coordination with your own ideals.

Harry, write – write often - oh darling when I think of the anticipation with which I dream about seeing you again – and the excitement with which I'll address my first letter to Lieutenant Harry B. Martensen - believe me, darling - lookout for my cloud again!

Your Sarah

3/19/1943

Hi darling,

My primary thought now concerns you and how soon I can be with you again.

Darling, I had no idea this would result from your sojourn in Chicago. Last month I began to care a lot more about seeing you. In the last few weeks, I would have moved mountains to prolong your stay in Chicago – but now I spend time devising ways and means of getting to where you are. And Harry, don't think it's because no one isn't anyone else around or I am lonely for just "a man." On the contrary - the week you left, I met and impressed the photographer editor for Life Magazine here in Chi. Oh, my dearest, how you would like his job – all he does is get a wire from New York, take a couple of photographers, and go out and tell them what pictures to take. Between him and three other soldiers stationed here at the Headquarters Corps, I have been well supplied with manpower. In fact, Gene (the Life guy) calls about 4 times a day when he's in Chicago. If you would not want me to meet you in Chattanooga - whatever you say - that's what I'm willing, will be ready, and even more eager to do; about spending my vacation with you. That lovely little stream you spoke of in the hills near

Chattanooga where we could go swimming near a waterfall sounds like a place out of paradise.

I only want you to know that if you get interested in one of the Pennsylvania girls – or if there's a gal from Chattanooga you'd rather see on furlough – please be truthful with me, Harry. You know I would be with you – and while you may not have had time to look the gals around there over yet, you will, and if that diminishes your interest in me – please tell me, Harry.

You told me you were past the "keeping girls on pins and needles" stage on New Year's Eve. Remember that Harry, if anything (female) comes up.

When you cross the line and get that single gold bar, you'll be in the officer's world - and I know what that means – from the standpoint of girls.

I do not know, darling, anything more rotten than war. A depression is degrading, but wars are more so.

I am so sleepy right now; I would give anything if I could see you lift your chin, and I'd crawl in there and curl up – my dearest. Sometimes I think I'll never know as much happiness as I had in your arms again.

You have so many fine character traits, superior to so many guys I have known – and in many ways, far ahead of all I have been acquainted with – Oh, gee, Harry, I miss you all day and night.

My resolve is good, dear; this is the first siege of tears since last Sunday - they do not do any good - I miss you just as much after as before - but somehow, they do appear.

I'm tired of the tears and hungry for the taste of you. Harry, will you come back as soon as you can –

To Sarah

On March 21st, 1943, six days after his first call from Valley Forge to Chicago, Harry jotted down the points he wanted to cover if Sarah answered the phone. He had read all of Sarah's letters at least three times. She seemed to be really missing him. She seemed nervous that the distance between them might cause Harry to look to women who were closer and perhaps forget about her. She wrote every day, which she had said was not her nature.

Everything in her letters pointed to deep feelings for him. On his own part, Harry could not stop thinking of Sarah, no matter how hard he tried to study. Her legs, her laughter. Sarah, twirling in her swoosh. Sarah nuzzling.

"Hello?" Harry heard Sarah's voice on the line.

"Miss Sarah Azlin, please," the long-distance operator said.

"This is Sarah Azlin."

"You have a person-to-person call from Harry Martensen; go ahead, please."

"Harry, how wonderful that you called."

Harry tried to sound nonchalant, "I know it's only been a week, but,,," Harry looked at his notes to settle down.

"I wanted you to know I did well on my last test. I'm getting into the swing of things here. I believe I am doing OK."

"That's great news," said Sarah, "Of course, I knew you'd be OK."

Harry checked off point one on his list and moved on to point two.

"I also wanted to say that I have been thinking of you all the time."

Sarah interrupted, "I think of you all the time too, Harry."

Point three.

"There is no other girl in Chattanooga, Sarah. I guess I never made sure you knew that."

"So, it's only me you're thinking of. Is that what you're saying?"

"Yes, and there is no one in Philadelphia I'll be looking at either, darling."

"Oh, Harry. I'm so glad," Sarah soothed, "I think only of you as well."

Harry held his thumb next to his next point.

"I remember telling you in Chicago that at this point in my life, I wouldn't keep a girl on pins and needles about my feelings for her."

Harry had underlined and starred his next point.

"I think now is the time for me to tell you. I have passionate feelings for you, Sarah. I want us to get married."

"Married!!!"

Harry rushed to fill the silence from Chicago.

"Of course, we will have to discuss a lot of angles, but what do you think? Maybe you could write to me and discuss more details."

Alright, Harry," Sarah had found her voice, "I'll try to think logically, as you have, and write down my thoughts. You cannot know how happy I am now and for the coming moments."

In his room, Harry's shoulders relaxed, tension slipping away.

"Our time is almost up. I think I've covered everything. Goodbye, darling. I'll be waiting for your letters as always."

"Goodbye, Harry, darling."

3/22/1943

Harry, my darling –

Long after the war is only a sad memory; I will remember that on March 21, 1943, there came from Wayne, Pennsylvania, one of the most important telephone calls of a lifetime.

Don't you know you've never said, "I love you?" And darling, I have never said it to you! And yet there we were in the advanced proposal stage with no preliminaries.

I know I've been thinking of nothing else since you left - if we pull through this long separation and find that each of us has made a permanent place in the heart of the other, then we must work out a way to harmoniously live together.

This brings up so many questions - and I know you were thinking logically from your remark, "There are a lot of angles we'll have to discuss." And you must have your commission, darling - so don't lie awake worrying about us - and don't neglect any military obligations to take time out to write to me – or to think about me - (I'm taking care of the dreaming here at the Chicago branch.) The following two months will help us test the case – and when your furlough comes through, Lieutenant Martensen, I think I should meet you in Chattanooga to be introduced to your mother and stepdad. Whatever is in store for us, my darling will be - if it's in the cards at all - and you know that I am inclined to go slowly in crucial decisions – as you are too, I believe. After all, it took me a long time to find just a fur coat and a long time to actually decide on it, and you know it, so you'll understand that we'll have to get together and have some significant discussions. All of this means, Harry, that I love you, and I am willing to try to go on from there if it seems that the greatest happiness lies in that direction. Isn't that exactly how you feel about it, Harry? Whatever we do must be for the best - and we must expect to find all that life holds – together.

My dearest, I am so sweetly content tonight - even though you've not said, "I love you, Sarah," I know you must, or you wouldn't have asked me to marry you. I can feel that strength across the miles - and I hope you can, just for a moment tonight, feel the magnetism in my heart for you.

My family did not get to know you as well as they would have liked to know you if they could have known we would come to contemplate marriage. I have talked to them about you, and my mother knows that I care for you - they leave the rest to me and us to work out as we may hope for.

I suppose your mother feels the same way about me - and I look forward to meeting her and, I hope too, convincing her that if that's what we both want - "I'm the one for you."

Afterward, I telephoned Dorothy - but then suddenly became shy about telling her - and though we talked for some time, I did not even mention that you had called.

Harry, know I love you - but never lose sight of the ifs involved. I think of you with passion, tenderness, pride, faith, logic, and unreasoning desire!

Yours,
Sarah

3/23/1943

My darling Harry,

What an excellent letter I received yesterday. Do not worry about not writing to me often if you can find time over a weekend to "catch me up" on your past week's activities.

First, I am proud of your continued good grades - 98 and 94 sound as sweet as "You'd Be So Nice to Come

Home To" does to my ears. I want you to be the best, and it seems you have the powers of concentration. Darling, I know your work will continue at the same high level and therefore take Yale for granted. This does not mean I won't be 100% thrilled when you finally get there.

Of course, I'm hoping you'll end up as a permanent party at the Stevens - I know you're needed there and certainly are required at 106 E. Bellevue Place. Your letter sent me into a mood that only you could satisfy, my dearest.

Darling, don't think because I like your high grades, I don't want to know about the few lower ones you might possibly get. I'm no wizard at knocking down all A's myself!

I wish you were around, so we could do your extracurricular studying together!

I wish I could help you while you're there in school - I must admit I love to think of your getting along so damn well – but if only I could contribute somehow to your progress. Oh, Harry, you are a wise lad. And I'm glad!

Tomorrow morning at 9 o'clock, I have to give a pint of blood - I am scared - wish you were here to hold my hand - although I know it's only a pinprick.

"Pure Milk" may come over from the printer today – we're so damn late because it's a 24-page paper this time instead of the usual 16 pages. Of course, I will send you one, with everything I wrote marked in red, so you can see what your baby is up to by day.

Bob gave Gladys a green jersey robe - I'll bet she gets into that in nothing flat this p.m. As I would tip into swoosh. This reminds me that you have been gone long enough that my mother won't ask, "How did this happen?" I'll take my swoosh nightgown to Mother and have her put in a new zipper.

As soon as I have some cash on hand, darling, I'll have a picture made for you. But I want a very flattering one that will look swellegant in your room even if it doesn't look like me. Until all that works out, you'll have to sit tight.

Now, dear, I must get to work - some things must be done - even though Miss G. isn't around. And she said I should take a crack at laying out the "Fighting Farmer" page for April. We will have a purple cover in honor of Easter, and the shot on the front of a cross against the sky is superb - I hope you'll like it, darling.

My darling, how true and sweet your words sounded - we must have an opportunity "to further understand, appreciate, and love one another." Those are good words - adult words -- made me want to take up permanent party duties in your heart.

Darling, if we take it cool, we may end up way out in front of the eight ball as far as the war, worry, and the whole damn world is concerned.

But sometimes I think of the warm nights coming, and taking it cool is difficult. My dearest, I'll take my vacation when you have your furlough. Then we can renew Auld Lang Syne and old lang scrounge - and try to investigate the future a little!

Yours,
Sarah

3/25/1943

Harry darling,

Bob and Gladys just turned in for the night - I wish you were here – darling, do you suppose the longing to be with you would ever diminish so that I wouldn't be eager to go into your arms at night?

Right now, that is all I can think about - but is it because I never satisfied my desire? And yet, I think of all the many things we did together, and I believe we have more in common that makes us want to be together besides the all-important sexual attraction.

I will admit, darling, that you abruptly phrased your proposal - but I know the phraseology came after due consideration on your part of many aspects - and, therefore, to be valued.

Dear, giving you a definite answer can only come after we have spent more time together and have told each other many things. I'm sure we are not caught in the war hysteria, but we may be stuck in the web of an enforced separation which enhances the appeal each may have for the other.

And yet, I am somewhat secure in your love - I can be here in Chicago and feel as I do tonight. Our passion is growing, is having a chance to develop – and may yet become completely overpowering over the obstacles of war, etc.

Darling, if I decide to answer, *"I do,"* - I might feel that we'd have to wait until after the war (unless you were so stationed that we could live together), and yet, by the time June rolls around, I may even feel that if we're going to be married, it must be at once. I cannot say, and I wish we were together to talk this all out.

Darling, the truth is - I wouldn't leave my job because whatever lies ahead after the war - I want to have an assurance of adequate income - and I'm just too active to be willing to "hole in" in some town near wherever you might be stationed. I want to keep the stable element of an on-the-line check in my life because who knows what will occur after the war?

And if we were married during the war - I would have to keep working - not only from an economic viewpoint but also from that same mental aspect.

In fact, darling, I know that until there is a child to be taken care of – I am sure I would sooner work than manage a household - from the smallest apartment to a fifteen-room penthouse - I would still like to go to work than lounge around all day.

And so now you have one of the facts before you, which worries me. I don't know what decision we could make - on this matter and many others - all of which will give us plenty to talk about when I can see you again.

I guess it's a pretty damn good thing I will give a pint of blood to the Red Cross Wednesday morning. Maybe a little bloodletting is what this high geared gal needs right now. I'll keep it up every eight weeks until you're on my horizon again. Darling, there's so much emotion in me right now I ought to be wearing one of those 'Dangers 2000 Volts' signs. Actually, I'll have to stop typing because I'm charging this typewriter through my fingertips as if it were full of electrons..... wish my darling electron was in town from Wayne, Pa!

And now, dear Harry, to bed and to dream of you - "the lover I've been waiting for -"

Sarah

3/26/1943

Dearest Harry,

I could not mail the enclosed letter at 10 because the "Blood Donating" got the best of me. I felt so foolish because I'm such a sturdy–looking individual – and there I blacked out every time I stood up. Finally, I decided to be firm and go on to work – and what do you suppose happened – when the elevator went down, I went down too – so they returned me to the Red Cross lounge, where, if you had been there, we could have scrounged for an hour and a half. I pulled into the office at 11:30, and even now, I feel woozy.

Miss G has gone to a luncheon – and I want to go too, Harry. I am sleepy and feel nothing would be as rejuvenating as seeing you. I nearly told them to hold my blood on file in case one Harry Martensen ever needed it anywhere during this war – but I believe you will not need it, so I didn't.

Darling, when you say you love me, do you mean you think whatever feeling you have for me will last a long lifetime? Oh, Harry, being far from you is so hard. I do so want to see you and talk to you. My darling, tonight I'm going to get my hair done, and then my sister and I are going to the Ice Capades. This production is rumored to be one of the best staged on ice. So, I'm instead looking forward to seeing it and wish, oh so sincerely, that you were here to go along.

I just drew a diagram of the Lincoln – Paterson Streetcar route for one of the girls in the office. She looked at it and said, "All that for eight cents!" I should have told her, "Yes. All that and heaven too," if Harry were going with you as he used to go with me.

I could not mail #00W22 at 10; note when you receive this – sent about 1:30 in the afternoon.

I wonder so many things about you that the army hasn't allowed me to learn. I wonder how you look in civilian clothes. Hon, if we go to Chattanooga on vacation and leave, I'd love to see how you look and if you can still fit (Mr. 6 x 1) into a suit. You know how I look in every kind of suit – but my horizon, you must admit, seemed much more limited than yours!

Last night I saw a beautiful brown gabardine suit, and I tried to visualize you in that. Then there is a blue worsted about the shade of my blue suit, which I thought would look elegant too. However, I think brown gabardine has more oomph. You told me you preferred only white shirts – honey, that's wonderful – but maybe for lounging and scrounging some noisy ones? I have a weakness for white-on-white shirts myself.

Darling isn't this weird – but I think of all these angles and the religion and family angles you have mentioned – and the romantic aspects would take care of themselves if we were together.

Today is a balmy spring day – just teasing us all with a hint of better things to come – much as our four-month session seems to have done to you and me.

Harry, don't you think you'd get fed up with me in a short time if we were married – or would you want to really "settle" and make it "for keeps" and forever – with always a spark of the original flame left?

These are the things that bubble in my brain – and the next two months can't pass fast enough so that I can be with you, my love,

Sarah

3/30/43

Tuesday 9:45pm

My Dearest Sarah,

Have only a few minutes left in the day, Darlin, but I have had you on my mind today, yesterday, and always that I could not go long without talking to you a little thru a letter.

Are you fully recovered from your blood donation? Gee, Hon, take it easy on that stuff. It would be best if you didn't get run down or catch a cold now that spring and summer are so close, tho I think it is swell of you to do it and know that it takes a lot of courage to give it, even tho it is for a good cause. But then I also know what a swell sort of person you are.

Regarding your thoughts about marriage raised in your letters of the 25th and 26th, I think you have thought out some rather good aspects. I'll be transferring to Yale on the 1st, but the big news is that I will receive a month of training at the AAF Cryptographic Course at Chanute Field in Illinois in May. If you have me, we can be together every weekend in May. We'll talk through the marriage idea then. There is nothing in your letters that causes me concern. You will be my partner. We will work things out together in wartime or when peacetime returns.

Harry

In the mail on April 22nd, 1943, Sarah received a letter from Harry with a newspaper clipping and a photograph from the Chattanooga Times Free Press commending his second-place finish out of four hundred and fifty students at the Radio Operators and Mechanics School in Chicago.

Honor Graduate – Harry B. Martensen, son of Mrs. John F. Neal, 5611 Ringgold Road, recently graduated from the Army Air Corps Radio School, Chicago, Ill., with the second highest honors in 450 competitors. Martensen, a former radioman at Sharp Battery Company here, will receive final training at Cadet Communication School, Valley Forge, Pa., where he will be commissioned a second lieutenant.

Harry stepped off the train in Chicago on Sunday, May 2nd, 1943. Two minutes later, he spotted Sarah standing amid the departing crowd heading for the vestibules. They stayed in each other's arms until they were the only ones left on the platform, the tension leaving Harry's lower back. Finally, a shaking, quivering Sarah settled down.

They left Union Station, walking hand in hand eight blocks east to Grant Park on Lake Shore Drive. The sun winked at them through the openings between skyscrapers, and the wind was slight and warm. Harry had three hours until his bus would depart on the three-hour trip south to Chanute Airfield. His class would begin at oh eight hundred hours on Monday.

As they walked, they planned the upcoming two weekends. Harry would travel back to Chicago by bus to spend Saturday afternoon, Saturday night, and Sunday morning with Sarah. Having spent the last two months apart, communicating through letters and long-distance phone calls, they tried to squeeze in the details of their missing time together. Harry, happy to hear Sarah's voice. Sarah kept choking Harry's arm close to her as they walked.

Sitting on a bench near the Art Institute, the couple wound down, enjoying the silence of being together, close, warm. Harry stroked Sarah's hand, occasionally reaching over and tucking a wisp of her hair behind her ear, memorizing her profile again.

Sarah jumped up, pulling Harry toward the Art Institute. They spent their last forty-five minutes together wandering the halls and quietly admiring the paintings. In time, they walked to the Greyhound Terminal for yet another goodbye.

The cryptographic course turned out to be the least challenging of all the classes that Harry conquered. Morse code, after all, is like a foreign language, and so the theory of coded messages seemed relatable. Standard codes were almost fun to decipher. The students were also given examples of code that no one had yet cracked. The trick, of course, is to use an obscure key for the translation so that only the parties with the keys can translate the message. Still, codes could be cracked by examining repeating letters or symbols and trying different combinations of translated vowels and/or consonants. Harry, at times, became lost in the focus of the attempt, and the week passed by in a flash before he stepped back on the bus heading north to Chicago.

Together, Harry and Sarah planned their future. The trend in the war on all fronts seemed cautiously optimistic. Two hundred fifty thousand German and Italian soldiers surrendered to Allied forces in North Africa. The news that thousands of Jews had died in the Warsaw uprising in Poland sobered them. The war continued.

Sarah wanted to ensure they reserved a time for Harry to visit with her parents. Harry suggested they all go out to dinner on Saturday night. Harry wondered if it would be OK to ask Charles about the railroad yard shooting during the depression that put her father in the hospital. Sarah suggested Harry play it by ear.

"You know, Harry, I have yet to meet your parents. We'll have to meet in Chattanooga during one of your furloughs. You've told me some wonderful things about them. I want to get to know your mother, Florence."

Harry had news on that front.

"They're trying to sell the tourist court. The place is another victim of the war. Hunting and fishing are way down. All the men in the army spend their furlough time to be with their families or sweethearts."

"Oh, Harry," said Sarah, "I'm so sorry. You worked so hard with them to make it go."

Harry shrugged; he had learned invaluable skills from John.

"They're probably going to move to Missouri. John has a son there. It's amazing how fragile he's become in just this last year. He has a bad cough. He's sixty-seven."

"We'll just have to travel to Missouri at some point," Sarah said, adamant, "I think it's important."

On the positive side, Harry would receive his commission. The boost in Army pay for an officer and becoming a married couple seemed significant. The allowances made for living quarters and other benefits meant that financially the couple could cover living expenses with a modest cushion.

Waiting until the end of the war felt counterintuitive. Waiting to live until ideal conditions aligned seemed like chasing and holding onto a cloud. Would the war ever be over? If it did end, would it be months from now, years? If Harry were sent overseas, would he survive? As a ground crew officer, his chances for survival were good but never assured.

On the second and last weekend together, sitting across from each other over coffee at the Bluebird Café, Harry explained his feelings.

"We've looked at this thing from every angle we can imagine. Perhaps I do have stars in my eyes. We met almost six months ago and are discussing getting married."

"Yes, crazy," Sarah admitted, "but we could make it work."

Harry gripped his chin, deep in thought for a moment.

"My point is that I feel I am already married to you, have been since New Year's Eve, maybe from the first time I saw you dance. You are the one for me, Sarah; I have no doubts about that. War, or no war, I want everyone to know that."

Sarah took Harry's hands, covering them in the middle of the table.

"Harry, I know I said at first that we would have to wait until the war is over, but I think I miss you more and want to be with you more every day.

"I can't believe I have been so lucky to find a gentleman, a hardworking man who respects my job and independence."

Harry agreed, "I'll know where I will be assigned within two weeks. We'll make final plans then if it's stateside. If not, we'll adjust the plan a little. OK, my love?"

"Yes, darling, yes. I can't wait."

During the last week of Cryptographic class, orders came down for Harry to report to Florence Army Airfield in South Carolina on Monday, May 17th, at oh nine hundred hours.

5/20/1943

Dearest Darling, Sarah

Right about now, you're opening those pretty eyes and getting ready for work, and right now, I'd love to be there to love and be loved by you. To start each day with you and be happier than we've ever been all day. To have each day last until the following day is my ambition. Making each day count toward a whole, happy, contented life and loving each moment we spend together is my formula for "living," Darling; only you could do this for me. My only hope is that I have a chance to show you that I can do the same for you. I get "panicky" when I think of the possibility of being unable to stay in the States long enough to show how much I love you and prove to you that we could be happy together. B.C. 1942 (Before Chicago,) the army term had no terror for me. Sure, I had a business, folks, and friends I hated to leave (and by company, I don't mean the tourist camp, particularly, but business as a whole,) but the future and after the war period was vague and unplanned. I had nothing in mind as to what I wanted to do. Now there is only one thing that interests me: getting the damn war won as quickly as possible, so I can come home to Sarah. The one consoling factor about this war is that it allowed me to find the girl I can be happy with in the years to come, and if the price of that meeting is a year apart from one another, I guess the cost is not too high; only please "Dear Fates" let me see her long enough to convince her of these things.

Darling, the bag is "PERFECT." I got it on Tuesday, and some green-eyed boys were around here when they saw it. I can't begin to tell you how much I loved your picking it out for me and how much special significance the bag takes because you saw and liked it and knew I would like it too.

For every other word this morning, I want to write Sweet, Darling, Sweetheart, Dear, or Hon cause that is just what you are to me – do you mind, Sweet? This morn I have time to be "with you" for a change. I've been going like a house afire for the past two weeks, and it is beginning to get me down, as my letters have no doubt indicated. The squadron reorganization, new classes coming in and old ones going out, details, school, and what have you have kept me on the go. However, I went to bed at about 8:30 after a shower and a shave last night, so I had a good rest and felt like a million this morning. A couple of weeks ago, while on guard duty, the office sought me to sign an insurance paper. They could not find me, so I got gigged – 5 gigs, which meant a loss of open posts this week. I didn't really care cause I had no place to go and had all my shopping done, so I had planned to stay in and get the needed rest. Besides, we now have an "Honor System" in effect here that allows us to go shopping and what have you for 2 hours a day, so I will take advantage of those hours next week to do my personal jobs.

This morning I went on a mental trip to places you had clipped out of mags and sent to me. How soon after the war shall we visit them? As soon as I return, shall we wait six months before taking off? I've always wanted to see the world, and while I might visit many places in the army, what I really want to do is tour them with you. That is a definite plan of mine. It's been on my mind for several years, but never before have I had the urge to make concrete plans for such a trip. It's because I think you and I would do the things we want to do that we would get along. Would you like to go touring for a few months? Naturally, I'm primarily interested in a home with you and children as a central point around my life, but you once mentioned that you'd like to see some places; I see no reason not to see them. All we'd have to do is decide to do something and then go ahead and do them.

Hon, remind me to spank you when I get you off in a corner sometimes for that note on the back of the pic "out a walking." I didn't even see the other three girls in the pic for two days, and when I did get around to looking at them – well, they don't even hold a candle to you. Believe me, Hon, you're a damn swell-looking girl - wait till I get a hold of you and give you that spanking.

By the way, are you buying the Trib, or is that your Dad's paper? I enjoyed the pics on the back of the editorial page and read the article on Truax Field with interest. I have much to say about the course that is not for letter and will explain further when I see you. So far as it is an article on Radar, they gave out little info that is not public, and that's as it should be. If there ever was a time that we should keep some secrets in this country, it's now cause this old war is not won yet by a long shot, and I'm inclined to believe our job is in the East rather than Europe. At any rate, I hope to go to that theater of the war if I must go to any, although I know conditions will be worse there than in Europe or Africa.

Now, Sweet, I'm going to end this letter, air mail it, and then start another one after dinner cause I'm wound up and have lots more to say, but I want this one to get into the mail to you, OK?

All my love,

Harry

Upon arrival in South Carolina, Harry waited for the return of the Air Base Wing Commander, Colonel Jensen, from a conference in Miami. On May 23rd, he reported to Colonel Jensen's office. There he met the Base Communications Officer, Tyler Forrester.

Captain Forrester looked forward to leaving the Army Air Force. Harry would shadow the captain for six months until early 1944, when Major Forrester retires. At that point, Harry would take over as Base Communications Officer. When the AAF discussed future plans, the officers said the War might preclude the scheme.

Harry interpreted the plan as the Army Air Force seeking to ensure that only seasoned officers with experience were sent into combat zones. For the next week, Harry stuck to Captain Forrester like tree sap, finding the captain likable yet a little forgetful. Harry felt sure he knew more about radio mechanics than the captain. Getting along in the military meant keeping one's mouth shut regarding one's superior officer. They got along.

On June 2nd, 1943, Harry received an honorable discharge from the Army early in the morning. At thirteen hundred hours, Harry joined the Army Air Force as a Commissioned Officer by the authority of AAFTTC. His AUS (Army of the United States), ORC (Officer Reserve Corps), and/or RA ASN number (Army Service Number) turned out to be Officer 862474. His pay grade converted to O-3 Captain.

He formally became a 1st Lieutenant in the Army Air Force.

Sarah and Harry selected August 3rd, 1943, for their wedding date. That week Harry would again be eligible for a three-day furlough. Coincidentally Bob and Gladys, as best man and maid of honor, would be able to attend, traveling the eight hundred miles from St. Louis. Two other couples from the bridge club Harry had joined were also invited. The Florence Air Base Chapel was chosen as the wedding venue. Sarah chose a light beige, knee-length suit and a shoulder-length white tulle veil. The men from the base would all wear dress uniforms.

Sarah garnered a six-month leave of absence from "Pure Milk." As she had discussed with Harry, she would not give up her job entirely. As much as Harry wanted Sarah by his side, he respected Sarah's wish to continue to work. He had lived in a home with multiple incomes for most of his adult life. The economics of two salaries, the possibility of saving for a house, and the smile Sarah displayed whenever she spoke of her job; were irrefutable.

The Base chaplain married Harry and Sarah. The couple exchanged simple wedding bands, and within an hour, they waved goodbye to Gladys, Bob, and the rest of their guests. They planned to spend three days at the newly renovated Chesterfield Inn in Myrtle Beach, South Carolina. The Inn looked quaint, the room clean and the queen-sized bed luxurious. The ocean breeze cooled the honeymoon suite. The couple walked hand in hand for miles up and down the beach.

Over dinner the first night, Sarah asked the teenage waitress where the best place for dancing could be in Myrtle Beach. The waitress pierced her lips and squinted, *"What kind of dancing is your style?"*

"We're open," Sarah said, "Jitterbug, lindy..."

'We're into the Rhythm and Blues down here," the girl replied, "Especially on hot nights like this one."

"We'll try just about anything. I've seen Cab Calloway at the Panther Room in Chicago," Sarah offered.

The waitress sized up the couple sitting at her two-top, "You can't get into the black nightclubs down here, but the music they dance to plays on the jukeboxes in the white club down the beach."

"Where? How do we find the place?" Harry asked.

"That's easy," the waitress said, clearing plates, "Walk up the north strand and listen for the music. If you follow the lifeguards at dusk, you'll also get there. The upper floor of 'The Pad' holds the lifeguards' bunks, but the downstairs has a dirt floor, and it's always crowded wall to wall with us young'uns. Not much to look at, but the beer is ice cold.

"Sounds like fun," Harry said, "We'll see if we can find it."

[280]

The waitress smiled, "We call it 'Shagging,' a slower, smoother version of the jitterbug. Cool man."

Harry left the waitress a generous tip.

At dusk, the newlyweds waited for one of the lifeguards to descend from his stand and followed him north. "The Pad" appeared to be several connected barns, but inside, the place hopped as advertised by the waitress. The dancers packed down the dirt floor so hard there wasn't much dust, and the footwork from "The Shag" sliding along the floor made it as slick as a waxed and buffed oak ballroom floor.

Sarah picked a couple and studied the footwork for a couple of records. Harry loved the smooth rhythm of the music and would have been content to listen the evening away. He stood out as one of the oldest in the room. His uniform and his height attracted some looks. When he finished downing his beer, Sarah appeared ready to *give it a whirl*.

The music played at half the speed of a jitterbug number, yet the basic steps were not that hard. After two records, they danced as well as most in the room: better than some. In an hour, the newlyweds turned heads as the "old timers" for their dancing. This new dance felt like floating across the dance floor; so smooth and the rhythm so easy Sarah thought she could dance all night without tiring, never relinquishing their spot on the floor.

Harry beamed at his wife in her element on the dance floor and reveled in keeping up with her. They exemplified a partnership, dancing just one aspect of that commitment. Late into the night, Harry hoisted a beer high over his head in the middle of the dance floor.

"This is Sarah," he shouted, "As of today, she is my wife. The best dance partner in the world."

Applause broke out from the couples surrounding Harry and Sarah. Sarah took one step right and, holding her skirt out in her right hand, curtsied, and rose, laughing.

Harry and Sarah toured the east coast attractions for two days, but at night they returned to "The Pad" for dancing and cold beer.

The beer joint was an easy seventy-mile drive from Florence Air Base. They vowed to return often.

The five months the married couple lived at the Base cemented their partnership. By Christmas, when they had to part again, Harry felt Sarah's need to return to her publishing company. He realized Sarah would always be her own person, and he loved her for it. As strong and independent as his mother, Sarah loved him emotionally and intellectually with all her senses. He knew that as well.

The war backdropped everything. US General Dwight D. Eisenhower, named the Supreme Allied Commander in Europe, provided a new round of scuttlebutt on base. The respected General's promotion appeared to foreshadow a US invasion of Europe.

Near the end of January, Harry called Sarah late on Wednesday. Sarah bubbled, *"I'm pregnant, darling."*

Harry lost his voice, shaking his head, eyes wide as if Sarah could see him.

"What? When?" he stammered.

"The doctor says August!"

"That's amazing, Sarah. Can't stand not squeezing you for a kiss right now."

"The way I see it," Sarah said, "I'll be back to South Carolina by June to find a good obstetrician."

Harry began considering the aspects and the angles.

"What about your job, honey?"

Sarah laughed, "Hon, I'm having a baby. That's my job."

That satisfied Harry, *Angles be damned.*

His excitement was impossible to contain, "I love you, Sarah. A baby, I'm going to be a father. I didn't have much father experience from my real dad. But John Neal was a good example. I'll do my best, darling."

"Of course, you will, darling," she assured, "I love you too. It won't be long now, and we'll be together again."

Harry thought Sarah sounded calm, collected, and adult.

"Oh, what if it's a girl!" said Harry.

"We'll cross that bridge when the time comes."

Harry wanted to run down the hall, find Woody, and tell him the surprising news.

"Must hang up and tell the boys, maybe buy cigars."

"Plenty of time for that as well," Sarah said in a calming tone.

"Alright," Harry said, settling down as well, "Goodnight, my love."

"Goodnight, Harry; I love you more than anything," Sarah sighed, "A baby!"

"A baby! Goodbye, love."

"Goodbye!"

In March, Captain Forrester, Florence Army Airfield Communications Officer, retired with a rousing sendoff thrown by the other officers on base and his crew of enlisted and drafted servicemen. Harry took over as Communications Officer. His new crew of six communications personnel responded favorably, especially when Harry demonstrated his radio mechanics and repair abilities.

On June 1st of '44, Sarah, eight months pregnant, reunited with Harry again. Harry, well prepared for her arrival, had a typewritten list of obstetricians with recommendations from some of the wives in the bridge group recorded under each name. He had moved back from the Officer's quarters to one of the base bungalows similar to the one they had lived in for the few months after their honeymoon.

The base buzzed over the news of the Allied troop invasion in Normandy the second week in June. Then, the agony of the losses swept the compound, fearful for the soldiers and officers they knew were leading the way. By the third week in June, the Allies were making progress inland. The newspaper quoted Eisenhower's broadcast to the people of Europe:

"Although the initial assault may not have been made in your own country, the hour of your liberation is approaching."

160,000 allied troops, half of them Americans, had landed on the beaches of Normandy and fought their way up the embankments against a solid German defense. Estimates were that as many as 6000 Americans had perished in the assault.

Army and Air Force base soldiers were worried about friends and relatives that may have perished.

Adjusting to life as a serviceman's wife, Sarah became reacquainted with friends and couples she met months ago. News from Europe in the newspapers and radio intensified the tension on the base as the Allies continued to progress. On June 19th, the U.S. defeated the Japanese in a massive air battle in the Philippine Sea. The Japanese lost more than 400 planes and three carriers.

In July, the USSR retook Minsk. In the Pacific, Japanese troops surrendered on Saipan. Later in the month, the U.S. Navy began an amphibious assault on Guam.

The Allies landed in the south of France On August 15th.

On August 27th, at Mcleod Health Hospital in Florence, a son was born to Lieutenant and Mrs. Martensen: Robert Buffington Martensen, eight pounds, two ounces.

In the spring of 1945, Harry, well-established as the Senior Communications Officer at the Florence Army Airfield, became privy to his upcoming deployment to the Pacific Theater. He now knew the general "where" but still had no idea "when," anyone's guess.

The Allies marched ever forward. Harry and Sarah's "Bug" crawled forward as well.

The Asia-Pacific war continued, however. Harry and Sarah discussed alternatives and decided Sarah would move back to Chicago with Robert while Harry shipped out overseas. That way, Sarah's family could assist with baby raising.

Harry and three other officers were rumored to be on the brink of transfer at the beginning of April. On April 18th, Harry helped Sarah and Robert board the train for Chicago. There were hugs and kisses but not many tears. Like many war families and service personnel, they resigned to separation. As Harry said, "Nothing for it."

The December/January German offensive, known to Americans as the "Battle of the Bulge," and the ensuing nine thousand American casualties affected wives, sisters, and parents in the churches and offices in Chicago and throughout the states. The Allies were not defeated, and the Germans ran out of reserve forces.

The Japanese were becoming increasingly desperate as the U.S. forces continued to destroy Japan's planes and ships. U.S. Marines were taking islands, and airstrips were lengthened to allow the new bombers to fuel and reach Okinawa and other targets in Japan. The Florence Army Airfield received stories of "kamikaze" aircraft loaded with explosives crashing into U.S. aircraft carriers. New procedures to combat these new suicidal warfare strategies were added to the training exercises. What defense could there be for such desperation? Even ground services such as communications towers and barracks could not be safeguarded from kamikazes.

Harry's letters to Sarah avoided the war story atrocities and body counts and focused on the technology that he thought may help win the war. Harry would keep the early warning RADAR systems in the fighter aircraft and bombers in optimum working operation. If the aircraft carriers could "see" the kamikazes coming, the fighter aircraft had a better chance of intercepting them before they could complete their suicide missions.

Weeks went by without formal orders. Same old Army.

3 May 1945

How about coming to the couch with me for a little chat – OK, Sweet? How has the Bug been today? I'll bet his poor little head is taking a beating these days with no place to sleep. - Hope the bed arrives pretty soon, if not by now. Hon, if you haven't done so yet –

I wonder if you would call Papa and Aunt Nell to say hello. Papa is pretty old and doesn't have much to do, and a little diversion means quite a bit to him

Yes, Darling, I miss you terribly – each minute of the day and all night. I frequently awaken at night now, and I know it's because I can't feel you in bed with me. I also miss that little Bug – not in the same way, but I miss his cute little face and ways.

The show is our one and only source of amusement. Buck and I saw Fred Allen in *It's in The Bag*. Corn, but not too bad.

One of the fellas in my section stayed two days overtime on an emergency furlough, and they will give him a Special Court Marshal. It wouldn't have been so bad, but he wired for an extension, and they refused it, and he stayed anyway. I tried to get him off as light as possible, but I don't know. Talked with him for about two hours this afternoon to make him see it the army way and take what's coming without feeling too bitter about it. Do you think he'll get only a thirty-day restriction if he acts OK at the trial?

Got a couple of promotions through yesterday, so the fellas feel surprisingly good. Even though each of them doesn't make a raise, it helps to know a few are given out now and then.

It's getting late now, Sarah darling, so I better return to the little cot in the B.O.Q. I loved our little talk tonight. Goodnight Sweetheart, Harry

On May 9th, all base personnel reported for a parade at o eight hundred hours. Colonel Jensen addressed the servicemen via a microphone and loudspeakers on the parade platform.

"Many of you have probably heard, but I thought I should make an official announcement. Men, victory in Europe has been achieved. Germany has unconditionally surrendered.

"Chaplain?"

The Florence Army Airfield Chaplain standing next to the colonel raised and spread his arms wide:

"Please bow your heads in prayer as we remember our fellow servicemen who will not come home from the front. Let us rejoice that many more will be coming home. Let us pray for those who will continue the fight to victory in the Pacific, and let us pray for the strength to carry on here at Florence Army Airfield.

"Amen."

"Thank you, Chaplain Thomas," said Colonel Jensen, "Sergeant."

"Parade Attention! Dismissed."

16 May 1945

Darling,

You should see me tonight. I got a nice short haircut, and it is also uneven as H____. The barber on the field should be a butcher. Oh well, it's clean, out of the way, and I've no one to be beautiful for.

By way of training, we are now wearing helmets, belts, carbines, first aid packs, ponchos, and canteens. I guess it's a good idea to get used to them. Our mail will continue to go out until we board the train, so you will get a few more letters. I'm happy it will too, for to write to you, knowing that you will be reading it in just a couple of days makes you seem so much nearer to me, much more like sitting down for a chat after a delicious meal fixed by my darling. My name in the lower left-hand corner means they are censored. We must censor the E.M. mail starting today, so we will have a job each morning from now on. All the ground officers will act as such. It is sad when someone else must read your innermost thoughts, but it has to be done. I guess we'll have to learn to forget anything we might read.

The $13.00 went to poker, not bridge. The fellas in the squad play a lot of bridge but all for fun. Glad about it, too, because I think that bridge for many is too argumentative - poker, on the other hand, is strictly individual with no complaints except toward the cards and one's own stupidity.

When spring and summer come to Chi, many of your and Robert's problems will be over. I think that a future trip to Letha's would be a possibility. To get away for a week or two would do you and Robert both good.

There is one thing that I wonder if you have thought of. I offer it only as a thought and in no way advise or expect it, and that is the possibility of living with Mum in a small apt if John should go.

I have no idea what your reaction would be to an arrangement such as this and have no feeling one way or the other, but chances are Mum would come to Chi, and Dor's place is too crowded now, so Mum would no doubt live somewhere by herself. She plans to work, and if she is able and can find a job, this kind of angle would have some desirable aspects and some undesirable ones, one of which would be a precedent of future living together which I would like to avoid if possible. One cannot say what they will or will not do, but I prefer to live with you and our own little family without the entanglements of either of our parents. All of this adds up to a situation that might arise, giving you a chance to be more by yourself than you are now. Mum would not be easy to live with, but it might be easier than constant contact with even your own folks if she worked. Above all, Honey, don't worry about the situation too much. I love your concern but would hate if I thought you were too unhappy there. I know we both believe in goodness and retribution, and I'm sure that with an "E" for effort, everything will work out for the best. Does any of that make sense? Guess I'll have to depend on your understanding of me to get my thoughts straight. If only we could talk for a few minutes with our arms around each other.

Didn't I tell you about receiving the chess set? - I meant to hon – the stationery is quite cute, but you should know by now there is only one pinup girl in my life, and that's my wonderful wife. Darling, I tried to show my love for you each day we were together. Sometimes not very well, I guess, but you know. If I didn't feel that you know that I love you with all my heart and that you love me in the same fantastic way, these words written on paper would be empty and without feeling. But with the knowledge of the old solidness of our understanding, love, and companionship, I like to believe the lines take on a new and wonderful meaning each time they are written.

I got a letter from Sgt. Brady, who shipped out a few days after I did, is in an O.R.D. in Salt Lake City, Utah. Haven't heard from anyone else in Florence but expect to any day now.

Now, my Darling, hug my little smidge and tell him I miss his gooey kisses, nightly climbs, and cute bedtime poses.

Goodnight Sarah darling,

Harry

On May 22nd, Harry reported to Colonel Jensen. After saluting, Colonel Jensen asked Harry to sit in the chair across from his desk.

"Your orders came through, Harry. You will ship out from San Francisco via the USS General A. E. Anderson transport ship on June 10th. Your stop will be Iwo Jima, and you'll take over the island's senior communications officer duties. You'll have a crew of twelve men and be responsible for keeping all radio and RADAR equipment operational."

"Yes, sir," Harry said.

"I'm sure you've heard the stories about the difficulties we had taking that island. Meatgrinder Hill, and so on. Twenty-five thousand troops dead or were wounded in the effort. We won't relinquish that island."

Harry shook his head in agreement. The Colonel continued, "You'll help see to that; we've held that little island since the last Japanese soldier surrendered there in March. The bombers flying out and returning to Iwo Jima are critical to the Pacific war effort, a stop-off point between Japan and our airstrips in the Marianas."

"When do I leave, Colonel?" Harry asked.

"You're due for another two-week furlough, Lieutenant. See the quartermaster for ticket vouchers. Just be on that San Francisco dock on June 9th, ready to depart. You did excellent work here, Harry; you gained a lot of respect from your crew and me. Sorry to see you go. Good luck out there."

"Thank you, sir."

Harry arranged train tickets to San Francisco via a ten-day layover in Chicago. He called Sarah with the news, squared away the next day, and boarded the train with a tightly packed duffle the day after.

Nine-and-a-half-month-old Robert, in the arms of Sarah, met Harry at Union Station. Harry's scratchy five o'clock shadow put off kisses from a struggling Robert, but Sarah sure did not mind.

Sarah's apartment looked spic, and span when Harry arrived, with a yellow cake and chocolate frosting on the kitchen table.

Harry could not keep his hands off of either Sarah or Robert. When Sarah put Robert to bed, Harry coaxed Sarah into the bedroom for a "real" reunite.

Harry spent just about every one of Robert's waking moments holding, playing with, or walking Robert in his baby carriage. In the evening, Harry and Sarah scrounged like they used to in the winter of '43. Two nights before Harry's train departure for San Francisco, Sarah's sister Louise arrived at the apartment to babysit. Harry and Sarah went out on the town for dinner and dancing.

Even with Harry's reassurances, Sarah could not hold back tears as he prepared to board the train for San Francisco. Harry was heading to war. Would he return? Would he be injured? Sarah, sick to her stomach as if morning sickness had returned, was sick of the war, sick of saying goodbye to the father of her son. She wanted it over.

Harry went through all the motions of being a soldier going to war as he traveled across the country and arrived at the point of embarkation on the dock in San Francisco to await the departure of the USS General A. E. Anderson transport ship. He checked in but kept to himself. He figured there would be a new set of servicemen to meet once he arrived on the island.

"Lieutenant Harry Martensen," the public address system announced, "Please report to the Master Sergeant desk in the north terminal."

Harry looked at the wall clock. He still had two hours before boarding time. In five minutes, he approached the information desk in the north terminal. Another soldier was scanning the crowd.

"Sergeant, you called my name. I'm Harry Martensen."

"Harry Buffington Martensen," the desk sergeant said.

"That's right," Harry said, producing his service identification card.

The desk sergeant nodded and gave the card to the serviceman leaning on the counter.

The soldier in a navy dress uniform and white sailor's hat examined the card and handed it to Harry, looking him up and down, squinting at his face.

"Lieutenant, sir," said the sailor, "Harry, I'm your uncle, Paul Martensen. I couldn't believe it when I saw your name on the roster before mine."

Harry blinked at the man. He was short, five foot five or six inches tall, a bit stockier than the lanky lieutenant. Harry recovered his manners, still a bit in shock.

"Uncle," Harry stammered, "From Canada?"

"Yes, your father's brother. Geez, you have grown. Have you time to talk? I just arrived stateside."

"I have a good hour before I ship out for Iwo Jima," Harry said.

"Do you mind if we get a beer? Been dreaming about a Stroh's for a month."

"Yes, OK," Harry said, "My memories are shaky about Canada, but it is great to meet you."

While waiting for their beer, Harry began to formulate several questions. A chance to learn about his family and possibly his birth father, wow, what an opportunity.

"So, you're a Navy man," Harry began.

"Not exactly," the short man replied, "I'm a Seabee. I'm with the Fifty-Fourth United States Naval Construction Battalion. At my age, I thought being a Seabee would be a reasonably good fit.

"I'm forty-six, and just finished a twenty-month tour of duty in Bizerte, Tunisia, clearing and rebuilding bombed-out buildings, homes, and bridges.

"I had a friend in England as tall as you. I heard through the Flossie Mae grapevine that you married a Chicago girl."

"Yes, Sarah Azlin. We have a baby boy now, Robert. They stay in Chicago while I head to Iwo Jima as the communications officer. I don't expect to see any enemy fire, but you never know."

"That is so true, I can tell you. I was stationed on the tip of North Africa, an easy trip for German and Italian fighter planes. I can dive into a foxhole faster than tying my boots. Half the time, I had no time to put them on.”

“It must be better in Africa now that Hitler’s gone,” said Harry.

“Yes, boring now, but the work is always there. The Seabees do incredible work. Rumor is that I will be heading to Guam next.”

“Gee, I just can’t get over meeting you like this.”

“Will you be heading back to Saskatchewan?”

“Hell no, I sold out to my sister’s relatives over twenty years ago.”

“Oh, so where do you live now?”

“I joined the merchant marines after I sold the farm. Seen the world. Japan, China, most of Europe, and the museums in Paris. All before the war, of course.”

Harry hailed the waiter for a second round. Checking the clock. He figured he could spend another twenty minutes with the only member of his family other than Mums he had ever met.

“Can you tell me a little about my father?” Harry asked.

“That seems so long ago, doesn’t it?” Paul said.

“I can tell he anchored, encouraged, and supported me. He was strong but the fairest man I have ever known. You know I had that lousy Spanish Flu and pneumonia as well. You did too. Raymond worried you wouldn’t make it.”

“Mum said I loved the farm up there. I don’t remember much,” said Harry.

“You used to run all over the place. The fields, the barns. Don’t you remember the big hailstorm?

“A little, I guess. So, what’s next for you?” Harry asked.

“I am due at the Waldorf Astoria to get my picture taken.”

“Wait, you’re getting married?” Harry asked, “A fancy engagement picture?”

Paul Martensen laughed and gulped another slug of beer. Wiping his mouth with his hand, he chuckled, “Naw, nothing like that, but it does involve a picture with a pretty girl.”

“Sorry to seem like I’m prying. I guess I'm just trying to get to know my uncle, " Harry said.

"That's OK. It is just a bit embarrassing. Perhaps you know about the John Wayne and Susan Haywood movie about the Seabees. Nationwide premiers are happening next week."

"No, I've been busy catching up with Sarah and my son."

"The name of the movie is *The Fighting Seabees*. Jinx Falkenburg and I will be photographed as a promotional gimmick."

"I've seen Jinx Falkenburg; she starred in *Lucky Legs*. I saw it last year on base in South Carolina. She does USO tours."

"That's the gal. I'm looking for a big kiss out of this."

"If you don't mind my asking, did you win the battalion lottery or something?"

"I guess you could say that. The Navy said they picked me because I am single and my record in both World War I and World War II. That is pretty unusual, especially for an enlisted private."

"That makes a lot of sense to me. It should be fun."

"Fun, I suspect, is the real reason. The joke may be my height. Jinx looks to be at least three inches taller than me. In heels, she is six inches taller than me. It is a publicity stunt. They filmed background scenes at Camp Parks, the Seabees training base thirty-five miles east of San Francisco.

"Hey, I can go along with it. I will briefly describe my work and what the Seabees are all about. The movie is excellent. Don't forget to catch it."

Paul checked his watch. Looking up, Paul said, "I better think about getting to the hotel. I don't want to miss my Hollywood Debut."

"I should let you go," Harry said, "Is there anything else you can think of about my father?"

"Only a hundred things, Harry, if I had the time."

"Perhaps another time, I should think about boarding the ship."

"Listen, Harry," said Paul, his voice lowered to a whisper, "Your father was a stand-up guy. Everyone looked up to him. He drove us as a family to make a success of the homesteads up there after our father died. He loved us all, helped us all, and encouraged me and my art studies. When I told the family I wanted to enlist when I was eighteen, he backed me all the way, even though I created extra work for everyone who stayed on the farm.

"He loved you and Dorothy, and Fannie Mae, that is for sure. Do not even think about forgetting that part of the homestead.

"Raymond did some pretty incredible deeds quickly and died young, at thirty-one. You are thirty-two, and look at you, a Lieutenant in the air force.

"I guess there is one more thing I should say. There are many stories about our family. You should know that your ancestors have contributed, just as you are.

"Good luck, Harry; I am delighted we finally met. See ya, Lieutenant." Paul saluted Harry, who returned the salute and shook his uncle's hand. Paul's grip felt somehow familiar. The strength, and at the same time, the gentleness. A Martensen characteristic?

When Harry stepped off the boat at the dock on Iwo Jima with a group of twenty-five other soldiers, the temperature was eighty-five degrees. Mount Suribachi, an inactive volcano visible to the south, Harry could not see a single cloud in his three hundred sixty degrees turn of the horizon.

There were three airfields on the island, and soon after his arrival, bombers came thundering in, passing low over his head, landing safely on Central Field. The group at the dock jumped into transport trucks and headed off on the nearly flat, featureless terrain to the barracks near the airfield. Harry picked an empty cot, unpacked his shaving kit, and met Timothy Masters, a munitions officer, who secured the cot next to the one Harry had chosen.

Harry spent the rest of June and July in meetings with the other officers learning the commander's preferred procedures and routines. In addition, USAAF P-51 Mustang fighters and B-29 bombers took off and landed daily. The fighter aircraft either accompanied the B-29 incendiary (napalm) bombardment of the Japanese mainland or attempted to destroy Japanese aircraft held in reserve at Japanese airfields. P-51s had damaged thousands of Japanese aircraft on these missions through July.

The island covered at most eight or ten square miles, so it took no time to acquire the lay of the land. The Central Airfield took up a significant portion of the island. The B-29 flying fortress bombers needed every inch of the island to land safely.

A severe lack of vegetation or trees on Iwo Jima affected the unremarkable landscape. The island's geology consisted predominantly of rock except for a small portion at the north end of the island. No native species of animals existed on the rock. The Japanese had unwittingly brought ship rats to the island. They could be seen skittering around the garbage dumps.

B-29 bombing raids were sent out every other day. Harry demanded his crew check the radio equipment and RADAR before each squad left which meant an o four hundred rise and shine. When the bombers returned, Harry retrieved an equipment report from each copilot listing any problems or malfunctions. Harry ensured his crew fixed any items noted before his staff could retire. He split his team into three squads so that someone stayed on duty throughout a twenty-four-hour day. Emergency landings could occur at any hour, and they did.

In mid-July, Harry received a radiogram that his stepfather, John Neal, seventy years old, had succumbed to lung cancer. Harry had arranged for Florence to remain in Kansas City with John's son. Harry wished to be by his mother's side. He did not eat more than a bowl of soup that day. Harry drifted through work for two days, heavy with the loss. John had taught him well; what it meant to work for a living and how to respect the women in his life. He owed just about everything to the man.

Doyle Colter, Harry's third shift supervisor, shook Harry awake at o five hundred hours on July 20th. Doyle explained, "The "Betty Davis" B-29 needs to get in the air, and the radio is on the fritz. Captain Menster and the co-pilot are swearing a blue streak at the boys. Our crew tried to fix it but had no luck. You better look, sir."

Harry, more or less dressed, said, "No problem, Doyle, I'm ready. Let's go."

The jeep Doyle had commandeered at the airstrip sped to the "Betty Davis," arriving three minutes from when Harry first opened his eyes.

Upon reaching the cockpit, Harry found Captain Menster fuming in the pilot's seat and Private Sanchez scratching his head and fiddling with the radio he had pulled out of the console. He gave Harry a pathetic look. Captain Menster ranted at Harry.

"Get this radio fixed, Martensen. We should have taken off twenty minutes ago. We must take off within the next ten minutes, or we won't be able to catch up and coordinate with the squad. There's no excuse for this. Heads will roll if you bastards can't fix it in time."

Harry tapped his subordinate on the shoulder.

"Move out of there, Sanchez; let me take a look. Captain, you didn't report any radio difficulty after your run yesterday, right?"

"No, I didn't, said Captain Menster, "Doesn't mean a thing. The damn thing isn't working now. That's all there is to it."

"Of course, Captain," Harry said, turning to the repairman, "Sanchez, did you swap the radio out according to the emergency procedure?"

"Yes, sir," Sanchez said, "I did, but when I plugged the replacement into the console, I saw a brief flash. This radio's dead as well."

"Sanchez," Harry ordered, "Go to the maintenance hangar where that P-51 is waiting for a carburetor and bring the radio from that plane. You've got five minutes."

"That would be a different model radio, sir."

"Just do it, damn it," Harry reinforced with a tight, even voice, "Don't come back without it. It will work in this plane in a pinch. Go.

"Doyle, I see the burned-out tube in this one and a short to the fuselage. Please bring me a BA76845V50 tube, an L365B resistor, and a soldering iron. You should be able to get back here within another three minutes."

"Yes sir," Doyle said and left the plane at a run.

Doyle beat Sanchez back to the Betty Davis, and Harry plugged the soldering iron into the extension cord, running back to the hangar. He replaced the vacuum tube. Harry soldered the L365B resistor between the two connectors just beyond where the vacuum tube passed the current back to the circuit. As he reinstalled the radio, he grabbed a playing card from the deck of cards the pilot and co-pilot used to pass the time on the 900 nautical mile trip from Iwo Jima to Japan. Before tightening the bolt, Harry slipped the nine-of-diamonds between the radio chassis and fuselage. After the reassembly, the radio worked flawlessly.

"That will get you there, Captain," Harry said, "Go get 'em."

"Alright," said Menster, "Get out of here, you guys. Let's go! Oh, and thanks, Harry."

Fighting 437th
Iwo Jima
3 August 1945

Dearest Sarah,

It's a heck of a way to celebrate our anniversary, but if we're apart, I guess it is as good as any. Worked like a little horse all day putting up the rest of the wiring in the officer's area wiring. Since more fellas have come in, our tent city has grown considerably. The job is done now, so we don't have to mess with it until we move. Hope that the "move" will be home! Out here, the only way to exist is to keep busy tho. The ground officers, who now are active, seem to be better satisfied than some of the fellas who lay around and have time to think how awful this separation is. Late when I got thru, but after a shower and shave, I felt damn good, so I took in a show. "The Southerners" -

liked it and saw much of South Carolina in the scenes. Hope you get to see it. I don't know if it is new or old. Most of the pics we see are old, but I don't recall hearing of this before. Story of poor white trash – only trouble – they acted much too ambitious and too concerned over things that (after being with them) you know, they ignore. The home and farm, tools, and living conditions were very accurately pictured, so it put an element of reality into the story.

Now, darling, I will give out with some snores and hope for dreams of the best wife in the world. Whenever I think of how happy I've been since our 1943 Aug 3rd chapel date, I can hardly believe my good fortune. You're the one for me.

All my love, hon,

Harry

On August 7th, 1945, a radiogram from Central Pacific command to the communications center on Iwo Jima announced the dropping of a massive new bomb on Japan the day before. This new bomb is one thousand times more potent than the "Grand Slam" (a twenty-two-thousand-pound explosive bomb), the biggest used to date in the war. The "atom" bomb leveled five square miles of Hiroshima and killed perhaps fifty thousand Japanese. Luckily for Harry, Iwo Jima was over 900 miles as the crow flies from Hiroshima.

Another radiogram on August 9th announced that a second atom bomb had been dropped on Nagasaki, Japan.

Then, on August 15th, news of Japan's unconditional surrender reached Iwo Jima. Harry could hardly believe it. After so many months and years, Japan had been defeated.

On September 2nd, Japan signed a formal surrender agreement on board the U.S.S. Missouri in Tokyo Bay.

The war's end created an instant staleness in an Army Air Force serviceman's life and routine. The planes only went up for practice runs, conserving fuel. Harry's three-shift communications crew procedures were unnecessary and consolidated into one eight-hour shift for his entire squad. Discipline had to be maintained with the use of parade drills. Within a couple of weeks, war seemed as remote as home. Of course, going home became the obsession of all the residents of the bleak island. The North Pacific command offered the servicemen on the island no clues yet on that topic.

On September 5th, a letter arrived from Sarah. Harry opened it, surprised to find only a small note.

> August 3, 1945,
>
> Harry, my extraordinary husband,
>
> Harry, Happy anniversary, darling. I am pregnant. We will expect another baby to arrive in the first week of March. Congratulations to the father, my dear, dear husband.
>
> Stay safe, darling,
>
> Sarah
>
> P.S. Robert sends kisses as well.

> Fighting 437th
> Iwo Jima
> 12 Sept. 1945
>
> Dearest,
>
> Not much to do today. This morn, I fixed another radio, and this aft, I played around with some little light bulbs working out a means of fixing radios that go bad in the future. Now I'm anxious for another radio to go bad so I can try out my idea. You see, most radios

we have around here use a specific tube that is particularly hard to obtain, so you have to replace that tube with one that is easy to get. The only trouble is using the "easy to get" vacuum tube; you need a hard-to-get resistor. (Complicated, isn't it?) So that's what the experiment with the bulbs is for, to eliminate the "hard to get" resistor. Maybe I won't wait for one of the radios to break down – might dream up a circuit and try it out. What have I got to lose?

Well, hon, I did get to bed early last night – I slept like a log and woke up feeling tip-top this morning. I even slept an hour before supper tonight – what a life! This eve we to the movies did go. I saw D. Powell and Clair Trevor in "Murder My Sweet." Reasonably good but not as good as the book. Remember the book?

Rumors fly thick and fast in the outfit, but I'm afraid they're just that. Some sound good, some bad, but I think it best to ignore them all and wait to see what happens.

One rumor that has been partially confirmed is a battle star for the outfit. We will get one, but not until orders are cut, and that might be a week or 2 months. That will give me 56 points as of Sept. 1st - which means nothing. The system of discharge we first heard of (58 points for 1st Lts) is figured as of May 12th, and it's believed that that plan has now been discarded, and the army plan of 85 points for field grade officers is in effect. All is confusion as per usual. I still think the only thing that will get the army moving is for Congress to raise the level and pass legislation forcing them to move fast. All of which is pretty farfetched.

About all that I am sure of these days is my desire to get out and come home to my darlings. The fellas here call the island "The Rock," and its likeness to that confining government institution is quite noticeable.

Enough of my griping – at least the war is over, and while I have to be somewhere away from you, I'm where some money can be saved so we can have some things to start our home with. I really am lucky. I've got so many happy moments with you to relive and many more beautiful times to dream of.

I love you, darling. Your one-gal man,

Harry

Fighting 437th
Iwo Jima
13 Sept. 1945

Dearest Sarah,

Another day on Iwo has passed, and I am writing to my darling again. Spent the morning at a meeting and on the line. I played radio repairman this afternoon and found the trouble after a long search, but I will have to wait till tomorrow to fix it. This evening I pitched horseshoes for relief from going to the show. That, sweet, is my day. No, it isn't either – I left out the best part of it. I received two letters from you and one from Mum.

I'm so glad some of my letters came through for you. I could tell from your last letter that very few had gotten thru and feared you thought I hadn't written. Not so darling, though I missed a few days, and I must admit that quite a few were short.

Just think – 6 teeth for the little smidge. Surely now Robert can eat a beefsteak. The bank balance sounds terrific. Really, hon, I had no idea that it could grow to that size in so short a time. You've done marvelous and must be watching every farthing but honey – be sure to get what you need and don't stint yourself to save money. It's there for you to spend if you need it, and that's what I want you to do. It makes me feel good to know you're pitching for our civilian conversion project, and I'll pitch in from this side too.

I don't like to think of you at home alone cause it will be hard to get around with Robert and all, but I feel it is as good a place as any, and I am glad you're keeping the apartment. If Dor has not found a spot by Oct. 1st and your folks are still at the farm and planning on staying until Nov., maybe Mum could stay with you for a month. You may or may not have thought of this, and whatever you decide is OK.

Can I do the dusting when we break open the box of Tigress? I dust real good, sweet – all over.

I must go shut off the generator now and turn these lights out. All the other fellows are in bed and trying to sleep. Good night sweet wife.

I love you, love you, love you.

Your Harry

P.S. Have been trying to get copies of our orders from Bluethenthal to the coast so I can collect your family home, but the group doesn't have them. I am writing to Bluethenthal for them, so I may get them someday.

Love,

Harry, your hubby.

Fighting 437th
Iwo Jima
25 Sept. 1945

My own darling,

Just got back from our nightly movie - "Blood on the Sun" with Jimmy Cagney; not too bad, if a little outdated now. Other than that, a pretty slow day. This morning at the line and this afternoon, I goofed off and read "Klondike Mike" in our tent. Also finished reading the play Cyrano De Bergerac which I enjoyed in spots.

Your long letter on Sunday came thru today and cheered me considerably, and I also got one from Dor. An excellent letter from the new management of the Sharp Battery and Electric Co. You remember that when we last passed thru Chattanooga, the place had changed hands, and from what I thought, the obligation of rehiring me (G.I. Bill of Rights) would be null and void. They wrote in this letter that my job awaited me regardless of the change in owner and management and wondered if I wanted my old job back, and hoped they would have a better position for me – when I thought I would get out, and in all, a genuinely pleasant letter. They said I did not have to commit myself at this time if I did not want to but could decide after I returned and that they would make room for me at any time after my discharge. I intend to write to them advising them of my unpredictable position and try to find what they would offer regarding employment. I don't want to commit myself at this time, but at the same time, I wish to maintain friendly relations with them cause I still do not know how tough things will be upon discharge, and Chattanooga might be a safe haven for us for a while.

Your letter deploring winter weather indicates a possible acceptance of a "midway" climate, and Chattanooga does have that. There is a better possibility of owning a Chattanooga home and/or business than in Chicago due to the necessary smaller capital investment. There are also disadvantages - first – the "South," - second, your family and friends – my family. These do not concern me except where they would reflect on your happiness. If when I return, you are convinced our home should be around Chi as we have often talked of – then we will give the windy city or nearby parts a whirl. If, on the other hand, prospects look better in Chattanooga, and you think you might be contented and happy there – why then maybe that's where we will wind up. What does all this sound like to you, darling.

Your shopping for Robert and yourself sound exciting and quite economical. How about the little squirmer you're carrying? Are you doing any buying on that score?

Oh honey, every time I sit and plan, and dream of our future together, the excitement of it thrills me, and I go off on that well-known cloud of ours.

I love you so,

Harry

The Thursday night bridge game in the officer's lounge included Harry and Tim Masters, partners most of the time now, at least for the last three months. They were being challenged by a drill sergeant, James Caraway, and his buddy Cory Cochran. The game of bridge entailed coded communications during the bidding process and was Harry's favorite card game. Cryptographic if you could get on the same wavelength as your partner. The benefit of finding a partner with equal intensity, such as his best friend on the island, Tim, meant winning a lot as long as the cards favored them.

Harry played out a three-notrump bid. A finesse to the board and the jack of diamonds sealed the round, and James sat helpless as his hand of high cards in other suits had to be discarded, play after play.

Tim collected the cards for his shuffle and deal, and Harry added to the scorepad. Cory leaned back in his chair, "At least we didn't double, Jim."

"We would have redoubled," Harry said, "This way, you've got a last chance."

Tim looked at each friend at the table. "Anyone up for a swim on the north beach tomorrow?"

Cory shook his head. "Not me, duty call in the afternoon."

"Count me out as well," said James.

Harry responded, "I'm up for it. Take the jeep?"

"We've got the afternoon. I'd just as soon walk," Tim suggested.

"Meet you outside the mess hall after lunch. I've got a meeting with the crew at eleven hundred."

The temperature at thirteen hundred hours had reached eighty-three degrees, with a stiff breeze occasionally gusting up off the road. Harry and Tim sometimes turned their backs to the wind to avoid the dust and gravel lofting up from the two-track heading north. After an hour and a half of walking, they figured they were three-quarters of the way to the beach, but the wind picked up. Still, not a cloud in the sky, and they sought a cove protected by cliffs and out of the wind. The waves around the east point would make for great body surfing, while the water at the cove would be smooth and warm. They decided to push on.

Both men wore bathing trunks and t-shirts, towels hanging around their necks.

Tim pulled out a handkerchief on the next gust, turned his back to the wind, and thought to blow his nose. The white linen escaped his grasp and danced away back south with the wind.

"Hang on a minute Harry," said Tim.

Harry watched Tim jog back along the road, sometimes bending down to snatch the handkerchief that would again blow away. Then Tim tried to run up and step on the hanky, but each time the wind and the cloth seemed to have minds of their own and billowed further down the road.

"Come on, Tim," Harry yelled, "Catch the damn thing!"

At least one hundred feet away, Tim finally stomped his foot down on the handkerchief and retrieved it. He turned to Harry, waving the white flag high over his head. "I surrender!"

Tim started walking back to Harry, then stopped.

"Harry, look there. What the hell is that!"

Harry squinted in the direction Tim pointed. The most gigantic rat they had ever seen sat on its haunches on the east side of the two-track.

"Stay away for a minute," Harry said, "That thing could gnaw your leg off.

Both men watched in wonder as the rat nibbled on his paws for half a minute, looking first at Tim and then at Harry. Both remained still to avoid attracting the rat's attention and an implausible possible attack. After a minute, the rat began sniffing the road, crossing to the west and into the scrub brush. Both the men relaxed; Tim started out to join Harry. Harry turned to continue to the beach.

BLAM!

Harry, knocked forward from the compressive force of an anti-personnel fragment landmine, heard the whine of shrapnel whizzing near his ear. The world became church mouse quiet, his ears shutting down from the blast. Harry rose to a kneeling position, dizzy. He turned to see Tim on his back in the road, not moving.

Harry staggered toward Tim, his balance in question. Tim shook his head from side to side, alive. His chest bled in three places, and he had a small cut on his forehead above his left eye.

Tim's khaki shorts, flack ripped and flapping in the wind, revealed a wound in Tim's right thigh that bubbled blood, covering his leg and beginning to soak the road. Grabbing his towel from his duffle, Harry folded it and placed it on the bright red wound, applying medium pressure.

Kneeling over Tim, Harry pulled at the holes in Tim's t-shirt, examining the tiny blood trickles at each location.

"You're OK, buddy," Harry shouted, "Got to see to your leg. We were lucky to be far enough away."

Tim cupped his ear. "What?"

Neither man could make out what the other said yet. Harry scanned the horizon in all directions, flat and empty. A tourniquet, let alone a travois or crutch, would be tricky.

Crazy to think of it at a time like this, but Harry recalled the time he helped his stepdad pull a man out from under an old truck outside of Chicago. He had been twelve at the time and almost fainted. John Neal remained calm throughout the emergency, giving the family directions and soothing the injured man's wife.

Officer's training includes a whole week of first aid. Harry had paid attention. He took both of Tim's hands, placed them on the towel, and told and showed Tim to keep pressing down to contain the bleeding. He took off his short-sleeved shirt and his tee shirt, threading the top through the sleeveless undershirt, tying it off, and then slipping the makeshift bandage under Tim's leg, ready to be tied off.

Harry yanked Tim's belt out of the belt loops around Tim's waist, planning on using it for a tourniquet. Then he had another idea. He looked down at his friend. "I need to use your shorts," he said, "No need for modesty out here."

Harry tugged Tim's shorts off and rethreaded the belt in the belt loops. Then he slipped the shorts back over the injured leg, positioning the shorts and belt on Tim's thigh, two inches above the wound. He threaded the tongue through the buckle and cinched the belt. Harry thought, *thank goodness for regulation belts: cinch and press on the clasp.*

Harry peeked under the towel with the tee-shirt/shirt bandage tied off tight over the towel layer and watched a small amount of blood dripping through his makeshift bandage. *Good enough.*

"That should fix you up until we reach base," he told Tim, "Now, do I leave you here and double time back to base, or do we both go?"

Tim nodded, his hearing apparently improving a bit, although when Harry spoke, the muffled conversation sounded like when he had his radio headset on.

Harry calculated they were five to six miles out from the base. At double-time, on his own, he could probably make it to the med station in less than an hour. Tim seemed to read his thoughts. "I think I can walk the way you have me trussed up," Tim said, and Harry understood him.

"I don't know. If we can make any headway with you walking, we're talking an hour fifteen to an hour and a half," said Harry.

"Conversely, I could adjust the tourniquet every fifteen minutes if we stayed together. Alright, I have another idea for a crutch."

The radioman helped Tim stand, but it was immediately apparent that if Tim put any weight on the injured leg, he would jackknife on the road in pain, opening the wound.

Tim swiveled around on his good leg until he faced the direction of the base. Harry stripped off his shorts, standing with his left leg adjacent to Tim's bandaged right leg. He told Tim to hold his leg up an inch above Harry's foot while Harry bent down and strapped their legs together with Harry's belt. He wound the belt around their legs several times and cinched the buckle so tight the pinch of Harry's leg almost cut off his circulation. With his left arm around Tim's waist and Tim's right arm at Harry's armpit, Harry counted to three, and they took some tentative steps. Harry's makeshift body crutch worked, if painfully.

Without a word, the couple began a three-legged walk to the airstrip.

Harry knew he needed to release the tourniquet every fifteen minutes, but he pushed a tiring Tim for twenty-five minutes before stopping. Both of their bodies were slippery with sweat. Harry undid the crutch belt, helped Tim lay down on the road, and checked Tim's bandage for blood flow before loosening the tourniquet belt. Tim swooned.

Harry cinched the tourniquet in half a minute and gently slapped Tim awake. Helping him back in position, Harry reattached the crutch belt, and the couple continued as before, albeit slower from Tim's near exhaustion.

Through the pain of carrying his friend, Harry kept stepping with his good free foot, dragging his friend's foot along on the next step. He labored for breath after five minutes, sweat pouring down his back, chest, and between his legs. Tim became more useless, his head drooping on his chest as he passed in and out of awareness. When awake, Tim tried to concentrate on helping Harry move forward. Harry's headache worsened, and he began to worry about dehydration. He thought he wanted to rest again; perhaps the tourniquet must be tended to again. *No, keep going, cannot stop yet.*

Fifteen minutes later, Harry did halt. The involuntary medic uncinched the crutch, laid Tim down on the side of the road, uncinched the tourniquet, waited thirty seconds, then cinched the belt again. He lay down next to Tim to rest for a couple of minutes.

Five minutes later, a cawing crow flying overhead startled Harry awake.

Harry forced himself to continue, reconstructing his walking partner's crutch. He drank half of what was left of their water and handed the canteen to Tim. Tim nodded off before he drank the water. Harry took the canteen back, slapped Tim hard, and forced a drink of water on his friend. Awake at the moment, the duo trudged off.

Harry's leg bled in two places from the chafing of the makeshift cripple's crutch. He ignored that pain and concentrated on his back pain. Harry's blood dripped on the road behind him when they rose from resting. Evidently, his back had sustained a scratch from a fragment. Tim found a ten-inch rip in Harry's t-shirt. An iron piece had ridden along his back as he had fallen forward.

Ten minutes of march later, Harry stopped again, bent over, and attempted to catch his breath while still holding up Tim. *If we stop now to rest, we will never get up.* Raising his head, he scanned the horizon ahead. Flat, no building outlines yet.

"Tim, wake up," Harry said as Tim's head slumped back. "We have to keep going."

"Sorry, Harry," said Tim, "I guess you should leave me here and go for help."

Harry shook his head, "We've made it this far. Got to be close now."

"I cannot take another step," Tim whispered.

Harry had had enough. He unclasped the crutch cinch, swung Tim around to face him, and slapped him twice, shouting, "You will walk with me, God damn it."

Tim shook his head awake, nodded agreement, and promptly crumpled to the road.

"Tim, Tim, get the fuck up."

No use, and nothing for it. With adrenaline pumping, Harry swung his friend onto his back, crossed Tim's arms at his chest, and cuffed them with the crutch belt. He reached behind, grabbing Tim's legs. With a "humph," Harry got to one knee and, with a second "humph," slowly straightened, moving forward with his one-hundred-forty-five-pound pack.

Harry took slow, steady strides. The rhythm of small steps and the balance of the weight on his back reminded the soldier of the forced marches of basic training.

The lieutenant became his own drill sergeant. He tallied his steps, "Left, right, left, right, I left my wife and forty-eight children in starving condition with nothing but gingerbread left, right, left, right." Minutes later, Tim woke up and joined the cadence.

Five minutes march; stand and rest, do not sit down; five more minutes march; repeat.

After fifteen minutes, Harry looked up, and the base loomed closer than he could have hoped. Two men spotted the couple approaching and jumped into a jeep, gunning it with a jerk to meet them. They disentangled Tim from Harry's back, carrying him to the jeep. Harry sat on the back bumper while the two crewmen drove to the base hospital.

At the bridge game two weeks later, Tim and Harry recounted their story to the other two players at the table, both men reminiscing about their good fortune at not being blown to bits. Their ears no long felt stuffed with cotton.

Harry mused that he had escaped the entire war without experiencing battlefield action, "Only to be bombed by an enemy rat!"

That night, after the game, Harry decided he would not share the adventure in a letter to Sarah. Her present delicate state must be protected. But thank God, he would be returning to her soon.

Fighting 437th
Iwo Jima
24 Oct. 1945

Dearest Sarah,

I'm that character they call O.D. tonight, so I have lots of time to type a letter to my sweet, but the heck of it is, there is still nothing to write about except what little I did today, and indeed by this time you are tired of hearing that same old stuff. Oh well, here is what I did anyhow.

This morning, we got up and about early and, after breakfast, on to the drill field for our weekly bout with the Infantry Drill Regulations. After beating our bunions around for an hour or two, we retired to a quiet corner to discuss the care and salvage of quartermaster equipment. Subjects such as these are of "such interest" to us, so we woke up a half hour later to truck on down to the EM's area and proceeded to salvage some clothes. At lunchtime, we put on the feed bag, having not-so-bad meat and the inevitable beans. This afternoon we were all scheduled for PT and games (not the kind I like to play,) so I instead worked on our power plant, cleaning and giving it a monthly inspection. By then, I needed to clean up and report for my OD job, so the day was shot!!!

As always, the best part of any day is the mail call, and today shined up because of a letter from you, darling, and one from Sharp Battery and Electric. He (Mr. Cagle, Mgr.) said they have found living expenses higher since I worked for them and, as a result, have raised their pay rate. He went on to say that many changes have been made in the company but that for men returning to the company, they have given better jobs to them ---- that they have a good organization and the company needed capable men who want to get ahead. They do not wish to make a definite promise of salary or position but wish to assure me that they are anxious to "do the right thing." All told, a genuinely nice letter, and I think the place sounds well worth looking into after I got home and straightened around. ---- Something to mull over in the future. ------

There is no question I will be rested enough to do some work when I get home; in fact, what worries me is that I'll be so darned rested I'll be too darn lazy to work. We'll put a first priority on the rocking horse, tho, and fix it so our bug doesn't bash his head so often. ----- No, let's wait until I get home before we prioritize things. Other things may be first on the list.

OK, on the check and the Christmas shopping, Hon. It's yours to do as you see fit, and whatever you get will be all right with me. ---- I liked Robert's pic; he's becoming a little boy. I don't think it is worth getting additional prints of, so I am glad you only had the one done. Don't worry too much about the rash. From all I can remember about other babies I've seen, they have all had rashes of some sort and seem to get over them in time. I'm glad you did go to the Doc, tho, for it never hurts to check up on them before they get too bad, just in case it might be significant. Tell Mama that I'll hurry just as fast as I can cause I have not only Robert's but Sarah's sugar to collect.

Last night we went to the other side of the island to see a USO show, "HI YA ROY." The actors were talented for a change, and the show was fast enough moving to be very enjoyable. The patter of the emcee was clever, the dancers danced, and the singers sang. More unusual than it sounds. Of course, it rained during the middle of it, but the show went on, and we sat in the rain. We know better, but there is nothing else to do anyhow.

Time for me to check the guard now ------ Well, the guard is OK, so I have nothing else to do for four hours. This is a very trying job.

Want some more delightful army routine? OK, here goes. The army sent over men from Saipan screened from a group being returned to the States. Many came in today, and about 80% had over 50 points. That means they will be here for about one month and then back to Saipan for shipment to the separation centers. What a life. The army claims there is no space available for shipping men home, but still, they can fool around sending them back and forth between these darned islands. BAH!

Darlin, I've run down. I think I'll sneak over to see the movie.

I love love, love you, Harry.

Fighting 437th
Iwo Jima
13 Nov. 1945

Dearest Sarah,

Wish I were there to help you with all the Christmas shopping, hon – we will have such fun doing it together, but I do know what a chore it must be to do it alone. Next one we'll do together, sweet!

I'm sending Robert's pic back – I'd rather not, but if it's Mama's, I'll return it.

Today, at long last, the package you mailed so long ago came thru, so I now have delish choc syrup to put on our ice cream and a dictionary to look up all of my spelling mistakes.

Well, we're getting everything packed up for moving. No orders as yet, nor do we expect to receive any definite ones for the next few weeks, but we're going ahead with the bulk of the work cause it's almost sure that the outfit will move to the Philippines. There's a bare chance that the "high pointers" (60 or more) will be transferred to companies headed stateside as units before the move. I'm sure pulling for that rumor to come true, for I have no desire to see any more Pacific scenery except that water between here and the west coast.

Hon, maybe I'm an optimist, but I still feel that by December, I'll get to my new home and should, on that basis, be there sometime in February when I want to get there.

Tomorrow is Wednesday, and you know what that means – drills and lectures. Yup, same old army!

All my love, darling Harry

In December of 1945, Harry learned he would be transferred to the Philippines instead of being shipped home. Since he had been packed and ready for the trip home for weeks and his squad and communications building had also passed inspection, Harry took the next transport plane to the Philippines.

Harry sulked, concerned about traveling in the wrong direction. Instead of heading east, back to San Francisco on the way to Chicago, Sarah, and baby Robert, Harry headed 1500 miles west to Manila. Worse, he had no clue; no one mentioned the duration of the duty in Manila. He had estimated he would be home in the States with Sarah by February. That would not be happening.

The lush flora and varied wildlife of the Philippines contrasted with the stark monotony of Iwo Jima. Of course, in this rainy season, inches of rain fell every day. Harry's duty as the only communications officer proved lightweight, except for drill days. He wrote letters and looked forward to receiving letters from Sarah. After a week, Harry put his homesickness aside and formed friendships with the other officers and enlisted men in the same boat. He became even more adept at bridge, double pinochle, hearts, poker, and blackjack. Life in the service crawled like a snail.

414th Fighter Group
Philippines
28 Dec. 1945

Dearest Sarah,

Today I received two lovely letters from my sweet, and so glad to hear from you, honey. It had been 18 days since our last mail call and an awfully long 18 days too. Enjoyed Alycia's letter and your comments. Peter sounds like an enlarged version of the little devil he displayed in Florence, SC, and about as bright. I hope the plastics business does not prove a flash in the pan as it might since the need to substitute materials is ending. From engineering reports, the field is not going to be as significant as first thought due to the inability of plastics to hold up under various kinds of weather and wear. The business will only be as good as P & A can make it, and that remains to be seen. As a civilian, he may get along much better than in the political army.

No darling, I don't worry about Mum – I will know her energy and continuous motion. Really, honey, my only concern is you. I know that during these next two months, you could use a guy like me around, and I'd love to be there to help and love you. Don't you think a taxi is best for getting to the hospital? I believe the cab companies have a "rush" service for emergencies and will guarantee a cab in only a few minutes. That would be better than having Papa drive you to the hospital due to your uneasiness while riding with him. Either that or have Brother spend a few nights with you around the 25th. In any case, hon, be sure and let me know what arrangements have been made so that I know you'll be well taken care of. If by any chance I am on my way home at that time, I'll let you know by radiogram what boat I'll be on so that you can reach me by radiogram. I understand that the service will be opened on June 1st. Darling –take care of yourself, and everything will be fine, I'm sure. While I, like you, would prefer a little bug named Laura, a smidge of powder and a diaper named Edward would be just as wonderful. Honestly, I can hardly wait to get home to my wonderful family.

Today I went to the barbershop and got the "works" - haircut and shave. The PX employs Filipino barbers, who go through the darnedest rigmarole. First, they shave, then apply towels. They massage your scalp, face, shoulders, arms, neck, back, and chest – then shave some more – repeat on massage – more towels – hair oil. I had to shower quickly to get everything off, but I got quite a kick out of the procedure.

Our foot lockers came thru, so I've got the radio hooked up and the rest of the things unpacked, so we're comfortable. We also had a house boy assigned to us – Denny is his name, a Filipino boy who looks 15 but claims to be 20. He makes our beds, sweeps the floor, and shines our shoes. What a life!

We're off to the show now, darling – you've all my love today, tomorrow, and always.

Your Harry

4 14th Fighter Group
Philippines
1/6/1946

Dearest Sarah,

Two things I've been meaning to tell you in the past few letters and have forgotten, and I am going to put them in the front of this one. We're in the 13th A.F. now (so what)? So here's a patch for our scrapbook. Let's see that makes: A.A.F. - 3rd A.F. - 1st A.F. - 7th A.F. - 20th A.F. and now 13th A.F. - quite a bunch, what?

Also, we're now on Atabrine! What a lovely yellow hue I'll be. They claim there is a dangerous type of malaria around these parts and against which atabrine is most effective, so we must all take our little yellow pill daily. So far, it has not affected me, and I'm hoping it will continue not to. It's been known to react on some systems, but I've had no ill effects.

We planned to go to Manila today but could not secure transportation, so we had to call the trip off. We hoped to watch an "all-star" ball team play. There was nothing to do here on the field. We loafed and listened to the radio for a possible point score reduction but heard nothing except that the army had decided to slow up its painfully sluggish demobilization.

Nice of Ken to give, I mean, lend us the crib, and yes, hon, I know what you mean on the pad. Good idea, too, for we both remember how Robert used to bash his head on the sides.

Yes, hon, Dor and her family sure seem to have their share of colds and bedtime days – I hope we can keep our family in better shape. Still, they haven't had anything too severe and, for the most part, are healthy youngsters. I don't worry about Dor or Mum, though I sometimes think about the situation. That's as it should be.

Darling, you can't imagine the thrill I got from reading your letters about Robert looking at the tree and your Christmas day. I'd sure give a lot to have seen it all. The presents sound grand, and of course, I'll reopen all the packages and have my Christmas one of these days, including those mysterious packages of mine.

Here are some more shots for our scrapbook. The church is built of "sawale" - a woven bamboo matting. They use a lot of it in or on buildings around here. Just put up a 2 x 4 skeleton and cover it with sawale and a thatched roof. No windows, but most places have shutters.

Honey, I worry about your cold, take care of it, and don't go out and get chilled. So much of that stuff seems to be floating around the States this season. It's the devil to think that it's been 2 weeks since you caught the damned thing, and I'm just now hearing about it. I hope that by now, it's abated, and you're back to a healthy stage.

Thanks for the T. & P. There's one week's chapter in the mail, and we're not sure what happened before the shooting started. All will be OK, tho, when our mail straightens out.

I'm off to bed now, darling – I know you love me, hon, and I love you for that and a million other reasons.

Always yours,

Harry

As Sarah's due date approached at the end of February, Harry decided to try speaking to Command about a family-leave furlough due to a birth. The commanding officer politely informed Harry that he could request leave once his wife gave birth, but not until then.

Mid-morning on March 2nd, Harry received a radiogram from Chicago on a rare sunny day. Harry suspected the radiogram would be a birth announcement and anxiously tore open the envelope.

Harry Martensen
Communications Officer
Clark Air Base, Luzon, Philippines
Father died January 29 -(STOP) Cancer -(STOP)
Edward was born March 1 at 1:34pm -(STOP)
Born with Cleft Palate -(STOP) Cleft Lip -(STOP) Surgery needed to correct -(STOP)
Come home please -(STOP)
Love You –(STOP)- Sarah –(STOP)-

Harry sat down and reread the radiogram, hands beginning to shake; forehead turning cold, feeling helpless. Minutes later, Harry shook his head, breathing deeply. He had a son. He now had two sons. His wife's father had died (the lung cancer had been much more aggressive than John Neal's.) Sarah must feel so alone. Harry's head began to turn cold momentarily, but he shook that off. Harry's family needed him.

He went first to the base hospital, one of the bungalows assigned to that purpose near the airstrip. The medical doctor on duty, the medical professional, turned to the library wall in the exam room, pulling a medical textbook from a high shelf. He thumbed through, found the page he wanted, and moved closer so Harry could look over his shoulder at the close-up picture of a baby with a cleft palate. Turning the page, the doctor found another picture of a cleft lip.

"This condition is one of the more common developmental problems in children. Something like one in a thousand or one in two thousand births, something like that."

Harry had no use for the odds now. In answer to Harry's expectant look, the doctor continued, "Yes, the condition can be corrected with multiple reconstructive surgeries.

"Your wife could use your support. I'll write a recommendation that might get you family leave time."

Harry felt marginal relief, knowing the incredible distance and red tape he needed to traverse. "Thanks, Doctor. When do you think I might pick up that recommendation?"

"About thirteen hundred hours after lunch," the doctor answered.

"I'll be back then, Doctor; thanks again."

At thirteen thirty, with the recommendation in hand, Harry asked Major Dillard, his immediate supervisor, to meet with the base commander and present his case for returning to Chicago immediately. Major Dillard and Harry together went to Colonel Petersen's office. Along with the recommendation from the base medical doctor, Harry brought the radiogram from Sarah. The

Colonel seemed sympathetic and ordered his secretary to type up the orders for his signature while Harry waited.

Armed with the Colonel's order, Harry went next to the flight travel clerk, who read over the order and checked his schedule of flights.

"The first transport out of here departs at nine hundred hours the day after tomorrow."

Harry asked, "Is there room on that flight?"

"Yes, that will take you to Northwest Field on Guam, about a five-hour flight. Good luck, Lieutenant."

Harry called his squad together, handed his duties off to his second, and informed them of the emergency that drew him back to the States. They wished him luck. The next day, he packed and cleaned his bungalow with Denny, his assigned Filipino boy. He offered Denny a large tip. The boy seemed offended and pushed it back at Harry. It took a lot of convincing from Harry, but Denny finally accepted the money. Harry knew it would help Denny's family.

The flight to Guam was turbulent but fast due to a strong tailwind. Upon landing, he showed his orders to the duty sergeant, who directed him to the Guam travel clerk's office. Checking his flight schedules, the clerk informed Harry that the next flight heading anywhere east would lift off in three days, leaving at eighteen hundred hours: a night flight to Kickham Airfield at Pearl Harbor on Oahu. The clerk directed Harry to the pilot's bunkhouse beside the airstrip.

Harry spent the days until the flight walking around the base and island, asking questions about the battles fought there. Three thousand U.S. soldiers died, and another ten thousand were wounded. The island, four times the size of Iwo Jima, stretched approximately thirty miles in length; five miles wide. Harry requisitioned a jeep and drove to the northern beach and passed the time reading a "Perry Mason" book while he lay in the sand.

On the morning of the flight, Harry sat fidgeting as weather conditions pushed the ten-hour flight to Hawaii back a couple of hours, but otherwise, he rested on an uneventful and smooth ride.

At the travel clerk's desk on Oahu, Harry caught a break. A flight to San Francisco had been delayed, due now to leave within twenty minutes. Harry took off for the transport plane on the run and made it. The flight took thirteen hours and forty-five minutes to reach San Francisco. Ten soldiers on the flight deplaned, kneeling to kiss the ground. Harry shook his head at the spectacle, then, overcome, followed suit.

Harry arranged a red-eye flight to Chicago, leaving at twenty-one hundred hours. He found a telephone booth and placed a person-to-person call to Sarah. She answered on the second ring, hoping not to wake the babies, "Hello?"

Harry relished that moment, hearing her voice.

"Hi, darlin; I'm on my way to Chicago."

"Harry?" Sarah exclaimed, shouting his name in excitement.

"Your long lost husband, yep. I'm in San Francisco. My flight to Chicago leaves in two hours. I'll take a taxi to get to your place; probably see you mid-morning."

"Oh, Harry!" Sarah choked, "I, I,,,"

"Let's not talk now, honey," Harry said, "Soon, I will be there. Soon we'll catch up. Can't wait to see the kiddos."

"Harry," Sarah began, "Edward,,,"

"Nothing to worry about, darling," Harry assured, "I know all about it. I love you; it won't be long now! Goodbye, Sarah."

"Goodbye, my love."

Harry, tired from the flight, still skipped up the stairs to the brownstone in Chicago. Sarah opened the apartment door before Harry knocked, drawing him inside. Harry dropped his duffle and crushed his wife to him, kissing her repeatedly. Robert came shuffling around the corner from the kitchen. Harry slowly, carefully scooped him up, carrying him around the room, speaking softly to Robert to help reacquaint himself. They played with blocks on the living room floor until Robert became bored and found a truck to push around.

Harry opened the door, where Edward napped and peered into his crib. Baby Edward snored, quiet but perhaps a bit labored.

Except for the area around his nose and mouth, the baby looked fine and now content. Harry closed the door and turned to Sarah.

"How is he doing? How are you doing?"

"I'm getting used to it. Edward seems to think everything is fine, although it is difficult for him to breathe sometimes, and breastfeeding did not work. Even the bottle is challenging."

"I understand there is corrective surgery," Harry said.

"Yes, but that is a few months away. Oh, the baby's awake. Would you like to hold him?"

"Yes, I would like that."

Sarah picked up the baby and handed him to Harry.

"Hello, Edward, I'm your Daddy. How are you this afternoon?"

As Harry picked up Edward, the baby stretched his little legs and arms above his little head, not fully awake yet. Harry saw the division of his lip, and when the Baby yawned, Harry could easily see the problem in the baby's mouth. Harry carried Edward about the room, getting used to his weight and fidgeting. He seemed about like Robert in size and weight at this age, at least as he remembered.

During the flights from Manila, Harry had wondered how he would react to his new baby boy. As soon as he picked up Edward and held him in his arms, staring hard at his nose and mouth, he looked at Sarah, shaking his head slightly, smiling at her. His son. Harry would love and cherish this boy no matter what life held for him. His mindset; he rocked Edward and did not let go until Sarah readied a bottle a half hour later.

Harry reported at the Stevens Command Center in Chicago, working his way up the chain of command, trying to explain his family-leave status. He attempted to suggest he be reassigned stateside until permanent demobilization with the rest of the fifty-points-earned soldiers in June of 1946. As usual, he would need to be Army patient. Two million soldiers awaited demobilization. He did manage to schedule an appointment with the recruiting and demobilization office in Chicago for the sixth of May. Harry must always carry the order to report and his family's furlough order.

Harry accompanied Sarah to her next doctor's appointment at downtown Chicago's Lurie Children's Hospital. Doctor Wilkers scheduled the corrective surgery for the cleft lip for the second week in June. The second surgery for the palate would need to wait until the baby was twelve months old.

Harry and Sarah discussed options while the doctor left the room to arrange the first surgery. Harry would be out of the Army Air Force and working, but where?

"I haven't contacted Chattanooga's Sharp Battery and Electrical Company lately. They have as much as promised me a job there when I get out of the service."

Sarah liked, appreciated, and felt comfortable with her current doctor. Said Sarah, "I guess I could come back to Chicago with Edward for the second surgery next March and stay at Louise's or Mom's place."

"Yes," agreed Harry, "It would be wise to follow through with the same doctor. I could try to find work here or perhaps in Kansas City, where Mum lives.

The doctor re-entered. Harry suggested the three possibilities they were contemplating. Dr. Wilkers took Sarah's hand, "I am not familiar with the hospitals in Chattanooga," he said, "I will say the Children's Mercy Hospital in Kansas City is an excellent institution. Many of our doctors trained there."

"Dr. Wilkers," Sarah nodded in agreement, "I've been comfortable with your advice since my obstetrician brought you in when Edward was born. I want to continue with the operations here in Chicago."

"That's fine," the doctor replied, "The initial two surgeries are critical, and I am accomplished in lip and palate reconstruction. Additional surgeries may be needed over the next two years, but they would be minor and could be handled by a plastic surgeon from Children's Mercy Hospital. I would highly recommend Doctor Oliver Barnes."

Harry spent his free time waiting for the date of the cleft lip surgery, getting reacquainted with his family as well as also studying material for his General Education Development (GED) high school graduation test. In June, the same week as the surgery, Harry received his high school diploma from Lakeview High School in Chicago.

The first surgery in June went well, according to Doctor Wilkers. The baby endured being anesthetized. Sarah and Harry were both pleased with the result of the operation. They survived Edward's fussiness while his lip healed, taking turns trying to soothe the baby. In two weeks, Edward perked up.

Harry, Sarah, Robert, and Edward, moved to Kansas City in late June after being discharged from the Army Air Force. Harry landed a job with Myers Motor Equipment Co. in Kansas City, Missouri as a salesman for automotive equipment. They found a small house to rent in Hickman Mills, just outside Kansas City.

All the savings Harry and Sarah had banked during the war paid for most of the first surgery. Harry's pension from the service would be set aside for the second surgery. Harry joined the Air Force Reserves and began to attend drills at Fort Leavenworth, Kansas, two days per month. The extra reserve duty money would help build a house fund.

Sarah went to Doctor Barnes at Children's Mercy Hospital in Kansas City for Edward's checkups. In March of 1947, she stayed with her mother in Chicago while Edward recuperated from the more extensive palate surgery. Baby Edward, now a twelve-month-old and crawling anywhere and everywhere, had to be placed in arm restraints for three weeks after the surgery to prevent his little hands from touching the stitches in his mouth, possibly causing infection. It was an agonizing time for Sarah and, of course, a crying time for Edward. While in Chicago, Sarah's mother, Bertie Azlin, proposed selling the family farm between Gobles and Bloomingdale, Michigan, to Harry and Sarah on a land contract at an attractive price. Bertie would live on the farm with them.

Florence, sixty years old and ever independent, decided to move back to Chicago, where she met Edward Sakreson, her future third husband, a retired shop foreman at a drop hammer shop.

Harry looked for work in Michigan. The family moved to the farmhouse in the summer of 1950. Instead of roaming the one hundred twenty-acre homestead in Saskatchewan, Harry pioneered on a forty-acre gentleman's farm in Michigan.

He would learn to milk a cow.

Turn the page for an excerpt from:
FILTRATOR

In Book III of the Martensen chronicles, Harry's son, the Architect, designs houses and software systems. The Vietnam War, AIDS Epidemic, the Great Recession, a Worldwide Pandemic, and climate change provide the backdrop to life in the era of political polarization.

The Architect raises his son, the Playmaker, and the Playmaker's son, the Analyst. Book III concludes the Martensen Chronicles as the Analyst's son, the Filtrator, navigates the challenges of the city-states' rise.

EXPLORER

Martins Army ants of the subfamily Dorylinae are nomadic and notorious for destroying plant and animal life in their path.

1950

The pacing man smacked another pack of smokes against his left palm before tugging the red band, tossing cellophane in the waste basket, popping a cigarette into a corner of his lip, and matching it, adding more smoke to the haze floating in the room. The aura surrounded the two-foot diameter, white, upside-down saucer-shaped globes of light suspended from long electrical poles hanging from the twelve-foot ceiling. The two-tone beige checkerboard linoleum flooring helped echo the footsteps of the pacing man.

The waiting room at Allegan General Hospital in June 1950 contained three leather couches in a horseshoe arrangement. A door in the southwest corner led to a hallway connecting four delivery rooms and a surgical operating room. Behind the center couch, a wall of bookshelves well stocked with Popular Science, Popular Mechanic, Outdoor Life, and other magazines awaited expectant fathers. Life, Good Housekeeping, and Better Homes and Gardens magazines in a separate section enticed occasional expectant grandparents. Used hardcover books packed on several shelves and dog-eared mystery and sci-fi paperbacks lined two shelves.

A second expectant father sat reading the fifth chapter of *The Case of the Baited Hook*, a Perry Mason mystery. He did not pace, this being his third birth, although the first in Michigan. The first child had been born in '44 near the base in South Carolina. The second was in Chicago four years ago. This man appeared to conspicuously regard the page, eyes moving across and down, focusing and maintaining steady breathing, as relaxed as possible to not let the Chicago birth creep inside his head. The smoke in the room was somewhat annoying. He had quit his pack-a-day habit when his wife had stopped smoking in '49. The lung cancer death of his stepfather in '45 and his wife's father in '46 and the Popular Science cancer warnings had made a lasting impression.

The corner door creaked open, and both men turned as Nurse entered.

"Harry Martensen," Nurse queried, "You are welcome to come with me now.

The reading man stood tall and thin in face and hair. Bending, he collected his coat and replaced the paperback on the shelf before following Nurse through the door and into the third delivery room.

His wife smiled, sweat and red blotches bordering her forehead and neck, her right arm surrounding a baby in a blanket.

Harry stared first at the baby for a time and then into his wife's eyes, attempting to read the emotions behind her smile.

Healthy?

The nurse picked up the baby and handed it to the man. He hefted the bundle, parted the blanket, pinched hands and feet, and scratched under the chin, the baby active but gentle and soft in his arms.

Boy! His third son. He again turned to his wife to read her smile, breathing the release of suspense that Chicago had not repeated. This child might forever be distinct due to that sigh and immediate bond.

Healthy!

The wife swallowed, looking back at the grinning, affable, six-foot-one-inch man holding the baby boy. Not a baby girl.

Four years later…

Today is the day. The sun, high and road warming. Waves rose off the asphalt at eye level to the boy standing in the east gully, fifteen feet from the occasional flash of a car along M43. The boy turned to check the farmhouse behind him, far to his left. All quiet. Mommy stretched out, napping on the couch; baby crib silent, and little brother in Granny's bedroom sleeping. The boy had bare-footed down the stairs, studying Mommy's pudgy arm hanging off the edge of the cushion, still; the back of her hand brushing the floor. He had cautiously swung open the pump house screen door, so the spring would not give him away and escaped into the July 1954 warm summer day: again. The boy focused on the road and the concrete drainpipe that ran underneath. The decision had been made; he just wanted to enjoy the moment. Mommy's invisible wall stretched left of the boy to the corner of the 40-acre farm. It turned ninety degrees, running the requisite 1,320 feet to the southeastern corner before turning again, paralleling the border in front of him, and then turning to meet the property's northwest corner to the boy's right. The wall, rising in front of the boy to the infinite, might as well have been electrified. The rule of not crossing beyond was etched in his mind by Mommy's repeated admonitions.

"You must never cross…." But down the slope, he saw the shadowed concrete tunnel he knew he could navigate and the bright summer on the other side. He stepped forward, cooled within the confines of the pipe, crouching, barefooting around pebbles left over from the last storm. The rough texture of the tube registers a new memory, but not much on the other side. Cattails stretched before him, nothing he had not seen on his side of the invisible wall. To the left and right were just tall weeds, but it did not matter. He crouched in the bit of sand at the pipe's exit and relaxed, breathing and listening. Red-wing blackbirds whistled amidst the cattails clicking in the breeze.

No need to go further, the boy scrambled up the gully and stood on the edge of the road, studying the farm before him from this new angle. Forty-foot-tall box elder trees stretched over the house in the backyard, lilac bushes blooming blue on the side of the living room window. He could see the alfalfa field stretching acres to the north from the road. The barns are visible through the trees up the long dirt driveway.

The boy stood tall along that road and made up his mind again. The street was quiet, with no cars. He walked back across the road and down the gully to safe territory.

What stirs a baby to start to crawl or take the first steps? A small adventure, but the boy believed in its importance. He would certainly not tell Mommy or Daddy. He did not care to tell his nine-year-old or eleven-year-old brothers. No, this first adventure would forever be his and his alone. But the boy's eyes brightened, and his smile touched his soul as he reached the backyard and began climbing his favorite tree, lost in thought. *What to do next?*

Author Request:

Please rate and review *RADIOMAN* on Amazon USA.

https://www.amazon.com/dp/B094G32RSG

or on Amazon UK

https://www.amazon.co.uk/dp/1732603448

Please participate in the author's quick, eight-question survey at:

https://www.surveymonkey.com/r/CTZHMDJ

Author's Blog and Website: https://johngerts.weebly.com

9 781732 603448